Ruby's Heart

Nikki Crawford

authorHOUSE

AuthorHouse™
1663 Liberty Drive
Bloomington, IN 47403
www.authorhouse.com
Phone: 1 (800) 839-8640

Published by AuthorHouse 11/07/2019

ISBN: 978-1-7283-3469-1 (sc)
ISBN: 978-1-7283-3470-7 (e)

Library of Congress Control Number: 2019917789

Print information available on the last page.

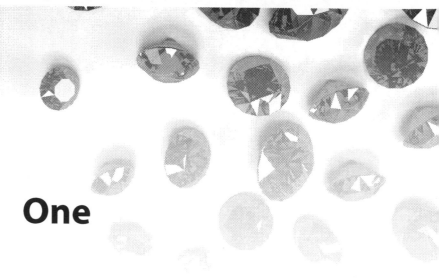

One

Ruby slipped outside into the cold night air. She was hoping it would help relieve her tension, but it only seemed to make things worse. She wasn't sure what it was that was bothering her, but she knew something was wrong, very wrong. Ruby could feel it in the air, and it shook her to the core, which was unusual. It didn't normally feel this strong when something went wrong. Ruby headed for her motorcycle knowing she had to do something. She didn't know what it was but if she woke up tomorrow to a horrific headline, she knew she would never forgive herself.

Circling the block, Ruby reached out with her senses to find the direction she wanted and quickly took off towards the source when she found it. She zigzagged between cars going as fast as she could, time was always of the essence when she got these feelings. She was already dismounting her bike and pulling out the keys before she had come to a complete stop. She knew she had found the source and quickly dismissed the feelings that had alerted her, so that she could focus. Feeling for her knife, Ruby pushed the doors open with barely any effort, but nonetheless they slammed into the walls behind them.

* * * * * * * *

She came sauntering in the door from out of nowhere. For the most part, she looked like she belonged with them. She was clad in leather and silver same as them, her skin was very fair and they were also very fair, but they almost seemed more pale than fair. The one real difference between them, and it was a big one, was her hair. Her hair was brilliant. Where all theirs seemed to be a very dark black, hers was red, a deep auburn red.

"Ruby," one of them drew out in a long, thick accent. "Haven't seen you in a while."

"What's it been, nearly a century Lucien?" she asked walking in with a slight sway to her hips as she headed over to this Lucien fellow. She stopped about halfway between him and Lucien. She stood there with her hands on her hips and her back to him as she looked at Lucien. This Ruby wore tight, low rise black leather pants with a silver chain hanging off her hips. Her top was a black leather halter that showed off her entire midriff and from his view the majority of her back. He wasn't sure why, but he couldn't help but notice her shoes, they too were black. They were easily 3-inch-high pumps, but they had a large surface area and she seemed to walk quite easily in them. And her red hair, her hair fell down her back in a long, thick red braid that was tied at the end with a strip of black leather.

Being ex-military, what he couldn't help noticing more than anything was the stance she had taken in front of him. She stood with her feet about shoulder width apart. She looked entirely relaxed while at the same time entirely tensed, ready to spring. He didn't know why, she seemed just as dangerous as the others, but he felt a need to try and protect her from whoever this Lucien was.

"That sounds about right," Lucien replied tapping his finger thoughtfully against his chin. He thought she had been exaggerating, but this guy seemed to have taken her comment seriously. Either they were nuts, or they took their role playing very seriously, but he was leaning away from the latter.

"I told you I would catch up to you some day," she said letting her hand slip behind her back. He could see her reaching for something hidden up under her halter, but he wasn't sure what.

"That you did," he said taking a step towards her. In a blink of an eye Lucien moved, and next thing he knew Ruby was hanging in the air with Lucien's hand at her throat.

He pulled out his gun and quickly stepped around to the side so that he would have a clean shot at this Lucien fellow. "Put her down," he demanded as he came closer to them. As he got a better look at Lucien, he could see that his face had twisted to look like something sinister and if he wasn't hallucinating, which he wasn't sure he wasn't, he would swear he saw fangs.

Ruby found what she was reaching for behind her back and pulled out her knife as she shoved the guy with the gun away from them as if he weighed nothing more than a feather. He landed hard against the wall, but he landed on his feet and seemed to shake it off just fine. Ruby brought her knife around and stabbed Lucien in the neck. She pulled the knife out practically severing his head as he released his hold on her and she fell to the ground. She landed gracefully on the ground in a crouch, ready to take out the other three vampires who were no longer looking on with amusement as to the situation but beginning to circle her and finding knives of their own.

"Bring it on," she said lightly with a hint of a smile touching her face. One dove at her, and she ducked as he sailed over her head. She quickly kicked the feet out from under one and reached up to stab the other in the heart as he came flying at her. She made easy work of the three. She quickly cut off the heads to make sure they were dead and turned her attention to the human who had brought a gun to a knife fight.

Ruby shoved him against the wall, pinning him so he couldn't get away. He struggled to get away from her but with little results. "What the hell are you doing in this part of town, with a gun no less?" she asked staring up at him.

"I always bring a gun when I come to this part of town, besides I'm a cop, I'm supposed to carry a gun with me."

"You would be better off with a stake in this part of town."

"Excuse me," he said raising an eyebrow at her.

"Guns just make them angry," she informed him.

"Them? You really are nuts. I suggest you let me go. I am a cop and you can be arrested for assaulting an officer," he warned.

"Do I look worried to you?" she asked looking over her shoulder at the bodies as if she wasn't worried about the man easily twice her size getting away. "Who the hell are you?" she asked turning her gaze back on him. It didn't make sense, she didn't usually have this strong a reaction to one man in danger. There had to be more to it.

"My name is Gabriel. You just killed those men like it was no big deal, and you practically threw me across the room."

"Those aren't men. They're vampires and if I hadn't come along when I did you would be dead now, consider yourself lucky. What I don't get is why they wanted you?" she asked to herself.

"What do you mean?" he asked confused. Oh my god, what was he doing playing into her delusions. They weren't vampires and they didn't seem to be after him, they had really seemed interested in her more than anything, but then she had killed the head guy.

"I could sense it the second you stepped in here, but why, you are but one man," she said letting go of him and pacing across the room. "Why you?" she asked more to herself than to him as she continued pacing. "What were you doing in here?" she asked slamming him into the wall again suddenly and holding him there.

"Well, I had gone for a walk to clear my head, and I thought I would stop and get a drink before heading back home. I saw a light on, and it looked like a bar from the outside, so I came in."

"That still doesn't make any sense," she said narrowing her eyes at him.

"I don't know what to tell you, it's the truth. You are the one with the knife that just killed four people and you seem quite strong, I wouldn't lie to you," he said looking down at her hand fisted in his shirt pinning him to the wall.

Ruby let go of him but didn't move far. "Were there any others here before I showed up?" she asked twirling the blade in her hand.

"A couple, a male and female. She was tall and blond, which was unusual considering the rest of them now that I think about it and he looked a lot like the others."

"Great," she said turning and walking a small distance away from him. Ruby turned back around and looked at him. He was tall, and well built. His muscles bulged under his shirt, but his strength was still nothing compared to hers. He seemed calm enough, but she was sure he was unsettled by all this. He wore a tight black t-shirt and a pair

5

of jeans. His face had a hard edge to it but still looked quite handsome. His hair was dark black and a little on the long side, not as long as some people wore it these days, but not short by any means. Long enough to tangle one's fingers in.

"What are you going to do?" he asked watching her just as intently.

"I don't know. You are not exactly dangerous, at least not like them," she added as his eyebrow shot up apparently insulted, "but I'm betting the other two will try and come after you considering their dead friends."

"But I didn't kill them," he said trying to point that out as if it mattered.

"No, but they are going to be able to find you a lot easier than they will me, and if they aren't completely stupid, they won't want to come after me. Besides there is something strange about all this, I get the feeling they would have tried again anyways but I'm not sure why. Come on," she said heading for the door.

"Why? Where are we going?" he asked suspicious.

"I was going to take you home, and then I was going to lurk around outside and see if they show up," she answered him.

"I think I can take care of myself just fine," he said.

Ruby turned slightly as if she was ready to head back towards him to give him another demonstration of throwing him against the wall. "They may not be as strong as me, but I can assure you they are stronger than you."

"Why are you helping me?" he asked suddenly realizing that was what she was doing or at least what she thought she was doing.

"Because I have nothing better to live for," she said softly as she turned to head out the door again. This time he followed her.

"What are you, and who were those guys?" he asked following her. He knew it sounded ridiculous, but she was incredibly strong, and it didn't seem to make any sense.

"I already told you they are vampires. You saw their faces didn't you, and you saw their fangs didn't you?" she asked as she swung her beautiful slender leg over a motorcycle.

"Yeah, but vampires. Isn't that a little ridiculous?" he asked looking down at her.

"I don't know about ridiculous, but they are definitely annoying. Get on," she said starting up the engine. "Where do you live?" she asked as he got on reluctantly. He told her and she took off down the street.

He placed his hands lightly on her hips to hold on. She was incredibly small. He had no earthly idea how she had just killed those four men. What was even weirder was that feeling to try and protect her was still there even after he had watched her kill those men. On one hand the idea of vampires seemed ridiculous and on the other he had seen their faces and the way they attacked her. Somehow, he found himself beginning to believe her.

Ruby began to swerve slightly. Gabriel suddenly realized his fingers around her hips were sticky and wet. He pulled one of his hands back and realized she was bleeding, a lot, and she was beginning to lose control of the bike. He reached around her to take the handles out of her hands. Ruby began to fight him to maintain her hold on the handles. "You are bleeding, let me drive," he whispered in her ear trying to get her to let go.

"I'll be fine," she said pushing his hand away.

"You are swerving, just let me drive. I won't hurt your bike. Ruby," he demanded trying to get her attention.

"Alright," she said loosening her hold on the handles so he could take them. She hadn't realized she was swerving, but then she hadn't really noticed she was losing blood. That didn't bother her, but she didn't usually lose enough to cause her to start swerving.

Ruby wrapped her hand around his forearm. She had a strong grip, but he could tell she was getting weaker. She was beginning to relax back into him from the blood loss.

Gabriel took the next right heading away from his place and towards the closest ER. "What are you doing?" she asked tightening her grip on his arm.

"You are losing a lot of blood. You need to go to the hospital," he said not letting her break his hold on the handles.

"No, you can't," she said turning her head to look up at him. "I'll be fine, but you can't take me to the hospital. It will end badly," she said the last almost in a whisper.

"Then what am I supposed to do?" he asked glancing down at her. The idea seemed ridiculous not to go to the hospital, but the sound of pure fear in her voice and the look in her eyes shook him.

"Just go to your place. I will be fine, please just trust me," she said staring up at him with desperation. He didn't know why, but he did as she had asked and turned back towards his place. This was madness, what on earth was he going to do when he got to his place and she was dead.

Ruby began to relax after he had turned back towards his place. He could feel her hold on his arm gradually loosening more and more as they got closer to his place. Ruby's head began to roll to the side until it came to rest in the nook of his shoulder. They were only a little more than a block away when he felt her hand finally slip away from his arm. Gabriel quickly wrapped one of his arms around her waist to keep her from falling.

He came to a stop in front of his building. Pulling out the keys, Gabriel quickly climbed off the bike while being careful to hold her up. He gently lifted her off the bike and into his arms. Ruby rested her head on his shoulder and brought her arms up around his neck. Well at least she was still alive he thought as he headed for the door.

"Where are we?" she asked drowsily not even bothering to open her eyes.

"We are entering my building," he said as he backed into the door to push it open. He finally came to a stop in front of one of the doors and began to try and fumble for his keys while still holding her. Ruby began to reach over towards the door. "Don't," he said sharply.

"What?" she asked softly looking up at him.

"I like my door on its hinges, I would prefer you not just pushing it open."

Ruby continued reaching for the door anyways, but as opposed to pushing the door open, she gently rested her hand on the door. He watched as she closed her eyes and then heard a soft click as the door unlocked. She began to pull her hand away as the door began to swing open.

Gabriel carried her on inside and headed towards the couch to set her down. "You may want to lay something down on your couch or at least check my back for blood before setting me down on it, so that I don't ruin it."

He couldn't believe it, she was injured and bleeding, and yet worried about his couch more than her own self. "Can you sit up on your own while I get some towels?" he asked looking at her doubtfully.

"Maybe," she said. Gabriel sat her down on his coffee table while he continued to hold her up. He quickly cleared the few things on the table and gently laid her down. At least his table could be cleaned later she thought.

He disappeared and quickly returned with a couple of large plush towels and began spreading them out on the couch. He had also grabbed a couple of wash cloths. "I'll be right back," he said heading towards his kitchen to grab a bowl of water. Gabriel set the bowl down on the corner of the table and moved to pick her up again. Setting her gently on the couch, he continued to hold her up so that he could check out her back and clean off any blood that happened to be there.

While she was sure he was quite strong, this Gabriel also seemed very gently. He held her delicately in his arm while he softly wiped away the blood that was flowing away from her wound and around her waist. Once he had that under control, he laid her back on the towels and continued wiping away the blood from her abdomen as he worked his way closer to her wound.

Ruby watched his face as he began to wipe away the blood over the cut. "This amount of blood doesn't make sense. It's actually not that deep," he said glancing up at her.

"It must have been deeper," she said softly.

"What is that supposed to mean?" he asked looking up at her confused.

"It must have healed quite a bit on the way here. If it had only been this deep to begin with, it would have been healed by the time we got here."

"Um sure," he said doubtfully.

"You don't believe me, but you'll see. It will be healed in an hour or two. Do you have any alcohol? Rubbing alcohol," she added at his funny look, "Not that I'd mind alcohol about now, but it probably wouldn't mix well with the blood loss. Though, I'm not sure how much good rubbing alcohol will do considering the worst has already pretty much healed, but I guess it couldn't hurt. I don't want to be fighting an infection tomorrow morning after all the blood loss tonight."

"Well it seems to have stopped bleeding for the most part. I'll go get the alcohol," he said getting up. He returned with the bottle of alcohol and a clean towel. "Do you think you can sit up at all or at least hold on to me to stay sitting up?"

"I can try," she said unconvincingly.

Gabriel reached behind her, and gently raised her back up into a sitting position. Ruby reached up to hold on to his shoulder with her hand. "Here, hold the towel here, so it will catch the alcohol," he said placing the towel against her skin a little below the cut. Ruby took the towel from him, holding it in place.

Gabriel began to pour the contents of the bottle against her skin just above the wound so that it would flow down over it as opposed to hitting it. "Are you alright?" he asked hesitating. He could feel her hand tightening considerably on his shoulder from the alcohol flowing over the cut.

"Yes, it's alright. You can continue," she said softly.

"Are you sure?" he asked glancing over at her hand on his shoulder.

"Oh, sorry," she said realizing how tightly she was holding on to him. She relaxed her hand and let it sit there but ended up fisting it into a ball and resting it on his shoulder ultimately. He had only just started, and she had nearly cut off the circulation from his arm.

Gabriel resumed pouring the alcohol over her wound. He could see the muscles in her abdomen tightening from the sting of the alcohol. Ruby turned into him slightly and rested her forehead against his shoulder while he finished. "You know it's funny," she said still leaning into him. "I didn't really even feel getting the cut, and it didn't hurt on the ride over here, but cleaning it up sure as hell is a bitch."

"I'm done," he said setting the bottle on the table. "It looks like that is going to end up scarring pretty bad."

"It will be a thin line down the length of it at the most. If I scarred from every cut I got, I would be covered in them," she said matter of fact. "Thank you for not taking me to the hospital," she said looking up at him.

"I don't know why I didn't, I should have. You are really lucky," he said looking down at her.

That was weird, why hadn't he taken her? Even he didn't know why. Normally people were like that when she pushed at their mind to get them to do something, but she had been way too weak to even attempt that.

"Sorry about slamming you into the wall," she said as he helped lay her back down.

"Which time?" he asked jokingly.

"All but the first time," she replied seriously.

"You stand by that one, do you?" he asked surprised.

"Yes," she said closing her eyes. "I had to get you out of danger besides he either would have turned on you and come back for me or you would have just made him angry."

"Get some rest we can talk later. I was going to go take a shower, will you be alright?" he asked standing up. Either she had passed out from the pain or fallen asleep because she didn't respond. He figured it must have been the pain.

Gabriel didn't like the idea of leaving her alone, but she had at least stopped bleeding and he was covered in a good amount of her blood now. He began pulling off his shirt as he headed for his room. After turning on the shower, he began to pull off his jeans and then climb into the shower.

He was beginning to think he had lost his mind. She was incredibly lucky, but he still should have taken her to the hospital, and he might yet. What he couldn't get over though is why he hadn't taken her to the hospital in the first place.

Sure, she was pretty. No, more than pretty, she was gorgeous, but that shouldn't have stopped him from taking her to the hospital. If anything, it should have motivated him more to want to get her to the hospital to keep her alive.

Maybe it had been the desperation in her eyes when she had looked at him. She had sounded terrified of the idea of going to the hospital. That should have worried him that she had something to hide, especially after killing four people, but it didn't, after all she had saved his life by killing them. More than anything he was concerned for her. She had been lucky the cut wasn't that deep, but she had lost a lot of blood and it seemed to have left her quite weak.

Gabriel turned off the water and climbed out while he dried himself off. Tossing the towel on his bed, he pulled out a pair of cotton pajama pants and pulled them on. Picking up the towel to dry his hair, he headed back into the living room where Ruby was resting.

Tossing the towel on the table, Gabriel sat down beside her on the edge of the couch. Picking up her wrist in his hand, he began to feel for her pulse. "Stop worrying," she said turning her head towards him.

Opening her eyes, she looked up at him. He must have showered while she was out. His hair was still wet, and he had changed, well sort of, he hadn't put on a shirt. She couldn't help but look. He was very well defined with large muscles. He was probably extremely strong for a human. He couldn't have been thrilled by how easily she had thrown him across the room.

"I can get you one of my shirts if you would like to take that one off. I bet some of your blood seeped into it and it can't be too comfortable."

"That would be nice if you don't mind," she said softly.

"Sure," he said disappearing and returning quickly with a clean shirt. "I would offer you pants too, but I don't have any that would fit you in the least," he said apologetically.

"I hate to ask, but could you help me put it on," she said lowering her eyes from his face. Gabriel helped move her up into a sitting position and pulled the shirt over her head. Holding her up, he reached behind her to unbutton the snap at her neck. After helping her get her arms in the sleeves, he made sure the shirt came down enough to cover her breasts, but not enough to touch her wound and then reached under the shirt to unzip the front of her halter and remove it.

Ruby could feel the brush of his strong fingers against her breasts as he unzipped her halter. Setting her top down on the table, he reached behind him for a damp washcloth. He intended to clean only her lower abdomen that had been covered by the halter, but he found himself wanting to make sure her breasts were clean and free of blood too. He watched her face while he cleaned her to make sure he wasn't making her uncomfortable.

Ruby kept her eyes focused on him while she reached up under the shirt and moved his hand up to clean off her breast. Gabriel rinsed out the washcloth and returned to cleaning her. When he was done, he dropped the cloth back in the bowl and brought his hand back up to rest just under the edge of the shirt.

He gave her plenty of time to object as he slowly moved his hand up to cup her generous breast in his hand. They weren't extremely large, but they fit very nicely in his large hand. He flicked his thumb over her nipple and began to lower his head towards hers. Ruby brought her hand up and brushed her fingers over his strong masculine jaw that was lightly covered in gruff from not shaving. She wrapped her hand around his neck as his lips touched hers. His kiss was light at first, but he quickly began to deepen his kiss. His tongue slid along the seam of her lips. She opened her mouth to him, and his tongue quickly slipped inside.

His hand slid around her back to pull her closer to him. She tried to hide it, but he felt her wince from moving her. He quickly pulled his head back from her and moved away the hand he had used to pull her closer while he continued to hold her up in a sitting position.

"I should go," she said trying to move to stand up.

Gabriel was there immediately trying to stop her while holding her up. "And where are you going to go, you can barely sit up let alone drive. Just stay here for now and regain your strength."

He was right. She was only standing because he was holding her up. She couldn't drive. Besides she had said she would protect him in case the other vampires showed up. Ruby looked up at him reluctantly, "Alright." Gabriel leaned down slipping one of his arms behind her knees and lifting her into his arms. "What are you doing?" she asked looking up at him surprised.

"Well you seem to have stopped bleeding, and now you need some rest," he said heading for his room. "I don't have a guest room, and my bed is going to be more comfortable than the couch to sleep on." Ruby looked up at him doubtfully. "I can keep my hands to myself if you want," he said looking down at her.

"I should stay out here in case those other vampires show up. I said that I would protect you."

"Well then you will be right here beside me if they show up," he said gently setting her on the bed.

"You don't believe me," she said looking away from him. She didn't know why she said that, and she didn't know why it appeared to bother her.

Sitting down on the edge of the bed, Gabriel leaned over her so that she would have to look at him. "I saw how they went after you when you showed up, and I'm sure that had you not shown up they would have come after me. I'm very grateful that you showed up because I probably would not have fared as well as you did, but I'm still not sure I'm ready to believe they were vampires."

"You saw what their faces looked like, you saw their fangs, you saw how fast he moved, and I'm sure you realized how strong they were. For god sake, one of them had me hanging in the air by my neck."

"I noticed that didn't slow you down much either," he commented.

"That's because I'm not human."

"You're going to have to explain that later too. For now, I know what I saw, and you are probably right, but you are going to have to give me time to accept it," he said continuing to look down at her.

"What is it?" she asked softly. She could tell from his face that he wanted to ask her something else also but wasn't sure if he should.

"Well, it's just… you seemed to know him, and you did appear quite similar in dress and strength. You yourself just said you are not human, should I not be worried that you are a vampire too?" he asked nervously.

"I came across Lucien a few years ago over in Italy. I wounded him pretty badly, and would have killed him, but the others with him at the time swarmed me, by the time I was done with them he was gone. I searched the city over for him, but he had already fled by then. I had told him that I would catch up to him when they swarmed me, and I did tonight but that was not how I intended to catch up to him.

I can only imagine how many people have died because I couldn't kill him then," she mused upset with herself.

"Is that why you showed up tonight?" he asked curious.

"No, I told you earlier, I was there because I had sensed the danger the second you stepped into that place. I knew I wouldn't be able to forgive myself tomorrow when I read the paper, so I came as quickly as I could. I'm not one of those wretched things. I'm stronger and much more powerful than them, but they are still stronger than you. It is hard to explain exactly what I am, but I don't feed on blood like they do, and I kill things like them if that is any consolation."

"You said you came across him a few years ago, but when you were talking to him you said it had been nearly a century," he questioned.

"Yes, so I did. I guess I forget myself sometimes."

"So, it wasn't nearly a century ago?" he asked sounding relieved.

"Yes, it was nearly a century ago. What I meant was that I forget that a century is a long time to humans. A century is but a moment in time to me. I said a few years because to me that is how it feels, but I forgot that saying 'a few years' is understood differently to humans sometimes."

"You are saying you are over a century old?" he asked cautiously.

"I prefer to see it as a century *young*," she said tersely insulted by him calling her old. He was but a baby and he was calling her old. "And I'm well over a few centuries *old*, for your information."

"I'm sorry I didn't mean to insult you. It's just that you barely look older than twenty, the idea that you are... is incredible. You sure you are not a vampire?" he asked with a slight smile.

"I'm sure. If I was a vampire, I would not have saved you tonight. Speaking of those damn vampires again," she said closing her eyes and bringing up her hand. She closed her hand real tight quickly, and then opened it. He watched as she blew softly on her hand and then let it fall back to her side.

"What did you do?" he asked looking at her like she was nuts.

"I set that building on fire. I can't have them finding those bodies in the morning."

"Don't they burst into flame with sunlight?" he asked jokingly.

"Yes, but they weren't outside, now were they?" she asked raising a brow at him.

"You expect me to believe you set that building on fire from here," he said doubtfully.

"Believe what you want, it will be all over the news tomorrow. Four mysterious dark spots, about the same size, where the fire appears to have originated from, but no signs of accelerant, a lighter or even a match to go from. Makes a great alibi, doesn't it? There won't be a trace of them left," she said softly.

"You sound like you've done this before," he said still confused by what to think of her. Ruby began to laugh, until it began to hurt her abdomen. "Alright, alright calm down. I don't need you opening that cut back up." Ruby wasn't worried she knew it wouldn't open back up once a wound was closed it was closed it was just a matter of it finishing healing. "Get some rest, I'm going to go clean the towels up, and then I'll be back."

"Wait, what if they come back and I'm not in there with you?" she said sounding terrified of him leaving the room without her.

"I'll be fine. It won't take that long, and besides I get the feeling that you will sense them and be up long before they get to my apartment," he said softly. Ruby knew he was right, even though he didn't entirely believe it, but she still didn't like the idea of leaving him alone. "And you say I worry," he said as he stood up. "I'm not sure you would be able to fight them if they showed up anyways," he said leaning over slightly as he gently removed her shoes for her and set them down on the floor.

"Hurry back," he heard her say as he left the room. Once he had left the room, she began to pull off her pants. They were tight and uncomfortable to sleep in, and of course she was having difficulty getting them off. She would have asked Gabriel to help but given she didn't know him very well and after that kiss, she wasn't sure it was such a good idea to have him pulling off her pants. Ruby finally managed to kick them off and tossed them over the side of the bed towards her shoes, and then pulled the sheets up to her waist.

When Gabriel came back in the room, she was fast asleep. He noticed her pants lying on the floor and smiled softly to himself. He wondered how hard it had been for her to pull them off, as he walked around to the other side of the bed to lay down. He did as he had said and kept his hands to himself. He wasn't sure he would actually be able to sleep considering he had a gorgeous woman in bed with him with practically no clothes on, and that wasn't even taking into account yet his worry about her being pretty badly hurt and his concern as to how well she would get through the night.

* * * * * * * *

Ruby woke up to strong masculine fingers tracing the line of her wound. "I thought you said you would keep your hands to yourself," she said opening her eyes.

"Yes, I did say that, didn't I? It would seem I lied. You're awake," he said suddenly looking up at her. "Is something wrong? Do you sense danger coming?" he asked worried.

"The only danger I sense is that of the man that woke me with his hands all over me."

"You couldn't mean me. I'm as dangerous as a bunny."

"Sure. You might be as cute and as charming as a bunny, but I would in no way compare how dangerous you are to a bunny."

"This from the woman who threw me across the room."

"That doesn't mean you are not dangerous."

"If I am so dangerous, then why did you come rescue me?" he asked.

"Being a dangerous man and a good man are not necessarily mutually exclusive," she said reaching up to touch his face.

"I'll give you that," he said smiling softly.

"I'm guessing my wound has healed, otherwise you wouldn't be touching me, well at least not where my wound had been anyways," she said with a seductive smile.

"It's amazing," he said tracing the thin scar. "That was barely four hours ago and now it looks like a years old scar. How do you feel?" he asked looking back up at her.

"Still a little woozy. It's going to take a little longer for my blood volume to replenish itself," she told him.

"See, had we gone to the hospital they could have given you a transfusion and you would be fine now."

"Not likely. Human blood doesn't do much in the way of replenishing my system. Actually, my system would probably have started attacking it, making this take longer. Besides as amazed as you are, imagine how excited a doctor would be to see how fast I heal. I would be the government's new secret experiment to play with."

"Unfortunately, you are probably right." Ruby looked at him funny, surprised by his response. "I may have lied a little when I said I was a cop. I was with the military. I recently finished my tour. I was considering applying to the academy. I don't know why I thought saying that would scare you after you killed those four guys."

"I'm not surprised. You definitely look more military than cop. I've never seen a cop so handsome or strong in all my years."

"Really?" he asked looking up at her. Her response was a deep smile that caused her to blush a little too. He returned to tracing her scar.

"That really seems to fascinate you. I do have other scars. It's not like it is my only one." Gabriel looked up at her and seemed genuinely disturbed by the idea that she had other scars. "And even this one will fade more with time," she said softly.

"Somehow I don't find that comforting," he said gruffly.

"I appreciate your concern but given my age and my line of work it is actually surprising that I don't have more scars. I'm sure you have plenty of your own from the military."

"Not really, I didn't exactly go getting in knife fights, not that I don't know how to use a blade. I did get shot a few times though, which is kind of why they sent me home," he admitted.

"You were shot?" she asked looking worried.

"The most recent caught me in the upper back, it was a clean through and through luckily. That was a few months ago, it's healed now," he said gently, trying to comfort her.

Her hand slid down his neck and found the scar from the bullet near his right collar bone.

"I never liked guns," she said quietly. "I don't know why, it's not like I wouldn't heal just as well from bullets."

"It's alright," he said. She really seemed upset by him getting shot when she had just been wounded.

"No, it's not, you are not like me. That bullet could have killed you," she said running her finger over his scar.

"Why are you so concerned?" he asked softly.

"What?" she said distracted as she leaned up to brush her lips across his scar.

"It's just that you barely know me, and you seem awfully concerned that I was shot," he said confused.

"I don't know what it is exactly, but you seem like such a good man. You wanted to take me to the hospital, you took care of me and cleaned up the blood, you seemed genuinely concerned, and though you think some of the things I say sound absolutely crazy, you don't look at me like I'm crazy. You seem upset at the idea of me having this scar, not to mention the others. I've never found anyone so gallant before that would help someone they barely knew, especially in this century. I don't think I met anyone nearly this kind even in the years of chivalry, but then most saw women as property at that time and didn't care much for my... nature, if you will. Maybe it's that or maybe it's something altogether different. There is something about you though," she admitted unsure.

"What do you mean?" he asked curious what she meant by something about him.

"Well I don't know what exactly it is, but you know how I said I sensed you go in there?" she asked.

"Yes."

"Well it was strange, the feeling I had was incredibly intense, like something I would feel when a mass murder would take place," she told him.

"That's why you were so upset, isn't it?" he asked awareness dawning.

"Yes, I mean don't get me wrong, I don't regret helping you. I'm very glad I met... I just expected..." she trailed off unsure how to finish her thought.

"Something catastrophic," he finished for her.

"Well yes, and I was having a hard time understanding. It feels like there is more to it that I'm not seeing," she admitted.

"Do you think maybe it is because Lucien was there?" he asked trying to help.

"No, my feeling is related to the number of innocents in danger or at least usually. I don't know what it is, but I think maybe I was supposed to find you for some reason."

"Maybe the universe was trying to tell you, you need someone to take care of you." Ruby raised her eyebrow at him looking doubtful. "Hey, you can't blame a guy for trying. Besides you said you liked me," he teased lightly.

"It's not that I don't like you, or the idea, but you are human. You are handsome, strong, and very gallant, but you will be dead long before I even look twenty-five. I've never dated anyone before because of that, not that I've found anyone until now that I wanted to date anyways."

"You want to date me?" he asked liking the sound of that.

"I think you are missing the point," she said blushing.

"You can't even date me for a couple of years and find out if you really do like me?" he suggested hopefully.

"I get the feeling I would, but at some point, I would have to go on again without you because you will die eventually," she told him sadly.

"So, is there no one else like you?" he asked curious and feeling bad at the idea that she had no one else in her life.

"Not that I've ever met, but then I don't ever stay in any one place for very long. Unfortunately, the biggest give away would be how slow we age, and I really don't stay around long enough to see people age or not age."

"So, what are you?" he asked gently.

Ruby laid back on the pillow. "I can try and tell you, but as I said it's not easy to explain. Your human myths don't really mention anything like me."

"One quick question," he said interrupting. Ruby looked over at him and nodded her head. "Why are you telling me, all this?" he asked confused as to why she'd be willing to share so much when clearly secrecy would be of the upmost importance to keep her safe.

"I don't know, I guess because you asked isn't really a good reason," she said furrowing her brow.

"I think I know what you mean. I know I should have taken you to the hospital, but I don't know what it was. You asked me not to and I felt compelled to do as you wanted, but I mean… Well, I know now that you didn't need a hospital, but I didn't then, and I should have taken you to a hospital. If you weren't whatever you are…" he trailed off. "But I just…"

"Really?" she said more to herself than him. She could 'push' people, but she had been too weak at the time, and he was right that was kind of how she felt. Maybe his idea wasn't so ludicrous. The fates, should they exist, did seem to be throwing them together, but to what avail, he was still human, and she couldn't change that, at least not to her knowledge.

"I guess it doesn't really matter if I tell you anyways. Not that I think you'd tell anyone, but no one will believe you if you do. Anyways, the closest thing in human myths to what I am would be an immortal, but of course there are differences."

"You mean like the Greek and Roman gods and goddesses."

"In some regards yes, but not exactly. I was born well before their myths came about and I never met any of them, but I guess that doesn't necessarily mean they aren't real," Ruby took a shaky breath. "I'm not a god, as far as I know, but I guess if I was, I would be better than the one all you humans seem to pray to. I don't see him down here fighting the vampires and other things to save you humans."

"I know what you mean," he said softly.

"Really?" she asked turning her head and narrowing her eyes on him.

"Well, probably not as well as you do, but I was in the military and I saw people dying every day. No god ever jumped in and did something to help, and I didn't even know about the real evils out there at the time. I don't even remember the last time I prayed, not that I was raised exactly religious per se. I imagine it has to be harder for you though. Out living generation after generation and watching as we destroy ourselves and each other without any knowledge that things like vampires are also out there destroying us." Ruby's eyes softened as she reached up to brush a lock of hair out of his eyes. "I'm sorry, you were telling me about yourself."

Ruby smiled at him softly as he laid back down on his side with his head propped up on his elbow. "A lot of your myths surrounding immortals focus on them being eternally youthful, incredibly beautiful, and impossible to kill. It may be very difficult to kill me, but I doubt it is impossible. I however, have not always looked like I do today, and I will not always look like I do. Though I may age very slowly, I still age. I assume that I would at some point die of old age."

"What do you mean by assume?" he asked.

"Well I have never met anyone like me. I don't know exactly how I will age. I know I have always aged several times slower than humans, but my aging has actually been slowing down more and more as I've gotten older. I don't know if I will stop aging when I reach my peak fitness, if I will just continue to age slower until I die, or if this is only to prolong my peak fitness, and when I get past it my aging will begin to speed up again. Unfortunately, I have no idea. Without knowing really what I am or where I come from, I can only guess. I don't know if I'm a genetic anomaly and am really human. If my parents had been… If one of my parents had been a vampire it could explain some things, and the rest may have been explained by my other parent. Then again maybe there is an entire race like me living amongst humans that I've never met, but if that was the case then why have I never met my parents," she mused sadly. She hadn't thought about that in a long time and now here she was telling a stranger things she'd never tell anyone in the world.

"So, you raised yourself?" he asked watching her.

"More or less, I had a little help when I was really, really little, but that didn't last very long. People didn't exactly like that I had looked like an infant for nearly a decade."

"A decade," he said astonished.

"That was actually some of my much faster aging. After that, it took me nearly a decade to age about one of your human years until I reached… Well, it's hard to say exactly when or how long, I was really young developmentally so there is… limits to what I remember. I know it slowed down further as I grew, but I also know from what I've been told and what I remember my aging took a nosedive around the time I started looking five or six and then it slowed down drastically further when I started looking around ten years old. I've looked like this for nearly one and a half centuries. You know I don't mind answering your questions, but you look exhausted," she said reaching over to touch his face with her fingertips in a caress. "I get the feeling you didn't sleep while I was out earlier."

"No," he said softly.

"How about you get some sleep and I can answer your questions in the morning?" she suggested.

"I'm not sure I can. With such a beautiful woman that is barely wearing anything in my bed, the idea of sleep is silly, especially when I know you are still weak from your wound." The first he had said lightly but then he had become concerned remembering why he hadn't slept earlier.

"I'll be fine, I'm making more blood cells right now as we speak. Please get some sleep, if nothing else for me," she said leaning over to kiss his cheek lightly and lay back down.

"I can try, at least I know your wound itself is healed now," he conceded.

Ruby turned away from him and on to her side. Gabriel slid his hand over her waist bringing it to rest on her stomach. She didn't protest or move away from him, so he moved a little closer and continued to hold her to him while making sure not to hold her too close. He didn't want to make her uncomfortable, and he didn't want her to know exactly how much he liked her, not yet anyways. He didn't want her running from him.

* ◦ ◉ ◉ ◉ ◦ ◦

Ruby woke up sometime midmorning with Gabriel's arm still wrapped loosely around her. She'd never realized how nice it could be waking up in a man's arms. Slowly she began to realize he was absently tracing her scar again. "It really bothers you, doesn't it?" she asked softly.

"Yes," he said plainly.

"I have others. You can look at those too if you really want too," she said turning towards him slightly.

He looked down at her with troubled eyes. "I wouldn't mind seeing them at some point, but right now this one really has my attention. Maybe because I was there when it happened, and I saw how fast it healed. You wouldn't have gotten it if you hadn't been defending me. It's a shame."

"What that you're still alive?" she asked shocked. "You wouldn't be here if I hadn't jumped in and got this little cut in place of your death." The idea of him not being here horrified her. She should have been shocked at how much the idea of his death bothered her, but she wasn't, and she couldn't stand the idea of even imagining his death.

"No, I meant it's a shame you got such a big scar across such pretty and soft skin," he said as he moved to brush soft kisses over her scar.

"What are you doing?" she asked slightly breathless as she brought up her hand to tangle her fingers in his hair.

"I hope this won't stop you from wearing clothes like you were last night. You looked rather gorgeous and sexy, if you don't mind my saying," he said huskily as he continued kissing the length of her scar.

"I don't think anyone has ever said that to me before," she said with a catch in her voice. She was over a thousand years old, hell closer to two, and no one had ever told her that, until now.

Gabriel looked up at her suddenly. "Never," he asked softly. She shook her head slightly. He found it hard to believe that as pretty as she was no one had ever told her so. She was staring straight at him, but he could tell from the look on her face that she didn't see him. She was far away.

It was hard to believe she was lying to him and he quickly dismissed the idea. No one looked as tortured or as far away as she did when they were remembering good memories. No, she wasn't lying. She was remembering all those years of no one paying her complements or attention. How old was she really? How long had she gone without anyone ever telling her she was pretty?

Gabriel laid back down on the bed holding her tightly in his arms. She never cried, she just laid there silently in his arms. After a while, she began to come back around. "I'm sorry," she said softly, not looking up at him.

"Don't be sorry. You are very beautiful, and someone should have told you so a long time ago. I'm sorry they didn't, but you have every right to be upset about it."

"It's not that or at least not exactly, and I had never even realized it until you... How could I not have noticed it?" she asked softly.

"You seem like someone who keeps quite busy with what you do, and maybe you really didn't want to notice it. Who wants to look at and analyze the things that hurt them?" he asked softly.

"I haven't thought about the idea of a relationship since I was a few centuries old. You don't know how hard it was to be several times older than people would ever reach at that time in history, and yet I looked far less than 10 years old. The idea of dating anyone that was 'my own age' as people say was and still is ridiculous, impossible even, not that dating was exactly permitted at that time, it was usually arranged marriages back then. Nobody of a decent age worth dating would look at me twice, and of course I wouldn't age with them. I would stay looking a child while they grew old and died. No, no one would waste their time on me, nor should they have done so. I gave up on the idea of a relationship a long time ago," she admitted softly.

"I didn't realize how hard that had to be for you growing up," he apologized hating the idea of her having to come to such a decision at essentially such a young age. She deserved to have someone in her life. Being alone can be hard enough for humans, but she wasn't human. Centuries spent alone, no one deserved that.

"I know you didn't," she said as she moved to sit up. "You hinted at wanting to date me, but you don't realize how hard that would be for me. Watching you age and die, and then having to continue long after you are gone. And if we had a family, if we even could, I don't know if they would take after me or you. I like to think that since it would be me carrying them for all that time, they would end up like me, but I don't know. I could end up cursed to watch my own children and descendants age and die. I don't even know if I would carry a baby for only 9 months like human women or if it would be a lot longer, but then I guess that may depend on what I ended up giving birth to. The baby's normal development, whether human or immortal, may affect how long I was pregnant for, but then I guess it could also end up being somewhere in between," she mused sadly not looking at him.

"You want to be a mother," he said smiling softly at her with the realization.

"I never said that," she denied.

"No, you didn't have to. Only someone who wanted to be a mother would have thought about it as much as you seem to have," he pointed out.

"You wouldn't happen to have any food, would you?" she asked changing the subject.

"I think I can find something you will like," he said smiling sadly at but not commenting on her change of subject. He could only imagine how hard it must be, wanting family, and having none. Something usually so easily taken for granted. He did think she wanted to be a mother, but he suspected more than anything she wanted family. Somebody to turn to.

"Can I use your restroom?" she asked slipping off the side of the bed.

"Of course, it's over there," he said climbing out of bed and heading for the kitchen.

Ruby headed for his bathroom. Closing the door, she leaned over the sink bracing herself with her arms. She didn't know what it was, but it was disturbing. The way he looked at her, as if she was worth looking at and more than that he actually seemed to see her. He didn't ignore her like everyone else did, but they didn't ignore her, not exactly. More like they didn't even notice she was there at all. Yes, it was definitely disturbing. She slowly reached to turn on the facet. The sound of running water was always so comforting for some strange reason. Ruby splashed some water on her face hoping to clear her head. Turning off the water, Ruby reached for the hand towel to dry off her face. After hanging it back up, she headed for the kitchen to find Gabriel.

He had started making pancakes and eggs. Ruby shook her head slightly. "What?" he asked curiously.

"You cook too. It's a shame you are human," she said softly as she made light of it, but he knew she was serious. "Thank you for taking care of me last night, it's much better than passing out on urine soaked, rat infested streets."

Gabriel looked up at her horrified. She wasn't serious, was she?

"I'm sorry, I guess I can be rather blunt," she said softly. He didn't know what to say. "I hate to put you out, but you said you aren't working right now, right?" she asked hesitantly.

"That's correct," he said cautiously.

"Would you mind terribly coming with me to my place?" she asked. His answer was a slight rising of one of his eyebrows. "They are still out there. I can't exactly leave you alone, but I need a shower and a change of clothes."

"I guess I don't mind spending the day with a beautiful woman, human or not. Besides I get the feeling I really don't have a choice now, do I?" he asked not expecting an answer.

"No," she said softly. "I just want to make sure you are safe," she said walking around and pulling herself up onto the counter.

Gabriel watched her as he placed the last pancake on a plate and turned off the stove. He couldn't help but notice she hadn't put her pants back on. All she wore was his shirt and her thin lacy panties. The edge of another scar caught his eye.

Moving towards her, his hand reached out to trace the scar. Ruby didn't move away from him, she knew what had caught his eye. His thumb slowly traced the old scar from just above her knee that twisted around her leg and ended a few inches below her hip.

She found it interesting. He wasn't horrified by her scars like most people of this generation would be. He seemed intrigued by it like he couldn't take his hands off it, and she didn't know why, but he almost seemed hurt by it. It was as if her being hurt or scarred as the case may be actually hurt and upset him.

Ruby's hand reached up to touch his face. Gabriel looked up at her at her touch. He brought his hand up to cup her face as he leaned down to kiss her. He had expected her to stop him, but she didn't. His kiss was long and passionate, when he finally pulled away, they were both out of breath and just stared at each other for a time while they caught their breath. Gabriel gently placed his hands on her waist and lifted her back down to the floor.

He took her hand and led her to the table. Pulling out a chair for her, she sat down, and he returned to the kitchen to grab the food. Sitting down, he watched as she began to dig in. She finally looked up realizing he hadn't even started eating. "What?" she asked looking at him.

"Nothing," he said with a hint of a laugh.

"Healing takes a lot of energy," she found herself explaining herself for some reason.

"You don't need to explain yourself to me. I just find it nice that you don't pick at your food like most girls do," he said picking up his fork. "So, where do you live?" he asked.

"I've got a house on the outer edge of the city. It's surrounded by quite a bit of land and forest."

"Do you own the land and forest surrounding it?" he asked curiously. That's what it sounded like she had meant, but a forest that was a little hard to believe.

"Yes," she said with a soft smile. "I bought it some time ago. I like coming out here. It's really pretty and open, and quite serene, but then most of my properties sit on a few acres. I like to be able to get away from the noise and relax when I'm not hunting something."

"Properties, how many do you have?" he asked almost choking on what he was eating.

"A few, I don't keep track of how many exactly, and I don't visit some of them as often as the others."

"You must be loaded."

"I guess you could say that, but I'm also a few hundred years old, so when you think about it, it's not all that surprising that I've accumulated quite a bit of money," she said waving it off.

"So, what is it exactly that you do to earn this money?" he asked curious.

"Most of the time I do various things with business financials, stocks, real estate, sometimes the video industry, and things of that nature."

"You said most of the time. Why do I get the feeling that the other things you do are not as respected?" he questioned.

"I've never gone and killed anyone that didn't deserve it if that is what you are getting at. From time to time, I get hired to go retrieve some rich person's child, or catch a fugitive on the run, and sometimes I actually consult with the police, but I try to keep that to a minimum. Usually it depends on the situation. I've helped various kings and people of that nature over the centuries, but I prefer to keep to business that way I can pretty much do all my work anonymously."

"How do you keep up with all that and still find time to save people?" he asked astounded.

"Well as I said the two are not always mutually exclusive, and I do have various people that work for me. I don't have that much to do really to keep up with my business, but when something comes up, I delegate it out, with specific orders of course. I wouldn't dare just put my money in their hands and let them run with it, especially not after the great depression. You know it's funny I've never actually met any of them. That must be odd working for someone with my kind of money that you've never met or even heard of."

Gabriel just stared at her trying to take it all in. "I'm going to go try and rinse what blood I can out of my clothes. Blood tends to make the material quite tight and stiff. Hopefully I can get some of it out or at least loosen the material before putting it back on for the ride home," she said carrying her plate to the sink.

"Alright," he said softly, but Ruby wasn't sure he was actually paying attention after everything she had just told him.

"I don't mean to be rude, but I would like to leave soon, so if you wouldn't mind getting dressed…" she trailed off softly as she came to stand beside him.

Gabriel gently wrapped his arm around her waist and pulled her down to sit in his lap. Looking down into her face, he brushed his fingertips over her cheek in a gentle caress.

Ruby brought her arms up around his neck feeling oddly comfortable sitting in his lap. She wouldn't have thought she could feel this comfortable with a man.

"Do we really have to leave? I like watching you walk around dressed like this," he admitted watching her and enjoying having her in his arms.

"Yes," Ruby said softly as she laid her head against his chest. "My place is safer and away from innocent bystanders in case they come after you."

"And how long before we decide they aren't going to come after me?" he asked holding on to her.

"I don't know. Maybe you will just have to stay near me the rest of your life, that wouldn't be so bad, would it?" she asked jokingly.

"I guess that would depend, now wouldn't it?" he asked running his hands suggestively over her body.

"I suggest you pack some clothes for the next couple days, in case you end up staying with me while we sort this out."

"And what if I don't want to wear clothes?" he asked hinting at what he would prefer to be doing at her place.

"Well, that is your prerogative, but it might be a little embarrassing if we have to go out," she told him.

"Alright," he said laughing softly. "I know it's not the best fitting or the most stylish, but if it would be more comfortable, you are more than welcome to wear my shirt over to your place so that you don't have to put yours back on."

"That's alright. I already have to put the pants back on any ways. Besides I think my shirt managed to stay more blood free than my pants," she said as she slowly moved to get out of his lap. Ruby picked up her shirt from the coffee table as she headed back to his room where her pants lay on the floor.

Gabriel cleaned off the table and followed after her to pack his bag. He threw a few things into a backpack and found some clothes to throw on while she rinsed off her clothes. "I'm ready whenever you are," he told her as he pulled on a clean shirt.

"Alright, just let me grab my shoes," she said emerging from the bathroom in her clothes from last night. Ruby picked up her shoes and headed back into the living room to put them on. Gabriel slipped on his backpack as he followed after her. "Oh, do you have my keys and knife?" Ruby asked standing back up after pulling on her shoes.

"Here are your keys," he said pulling them out of his pocket, "and I've got your knife in my bag. I don't think you will need it to drive," he said heading for the door.

If he didn't want her to have her knife that was fine. She was quite dangerous without it and had plenty others at home. Besides she wasn't planning on hurting him anyways. Ruby followed after him, out to where he had parked her bike last night. Happy to see that it was still in one piece,

Ruby climbed on and started up the engine. Gabriel went ahead and climbed on after her. He hadn't a clue where they were going, but she seemed to keep things interesting.

Ruby quickly drove them into the city and back out the other side. As they passed the city limits and hit the open country roads, Ruby began to speed up the motorcycle even faster.

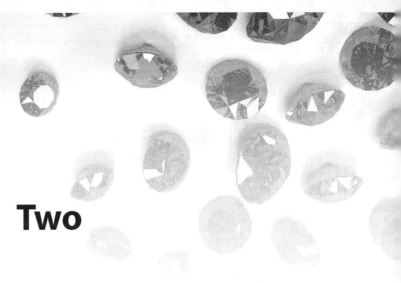

Two

After a while Ruby turned down an even more country road, if that was possible. There were fences on either side and the road barely seemed wide enough for two cars to pass each other going opposite directions. As they began to slow down for an electronic gate with a keypad, Gabriel realized why the road seemed so narrow, because it wasn't a road at all. It was the start of her driveway.

They never came to a complete stop though and Ruby never touched the keypad to input a code, she never even came close. They must have been nearly fifty feet away when Ruby waved her hand at the gate and it began to open. By the time they reached the gate it was open, and they drove right on through. The driveway was full of twisting curves that had been cut at sharp angles through what he would guess to be the outer edge of the forest she had been talking about, and of course she took them at a frightening, break-neck speed.

They finally came to a stop in front of a mansion, and Gabriel would have notice if it wasn't for the fact that his stomach was still back at the gate. Ruby turned the bike off and tried to get off, while Gabriel let his stomach catch back up to him, only to realize how tight his arms were wrapped around her. She could have broken his hold easily enough, but it didn't really bother her, and she was more interested in why he was clinging to her so hard. Ruby turned her head around to look up at him, and immediately realized she had taken the last few curves way too fast. Gabriel looked like he might be sick.

After a few minutes, he finally began to look around and realized she was looking up at him. "What?" he asked confused.

"Are you alright?" she asked grimacing slightly. "I didn't realize how fast I was going. I'm sorry, I don't usually take those curves with a passenger."

"I'm fine, now, but next time either you take those curves much, much slower or I'm driving," he said as he began to loosen his hold on her.

"Sure," she said climbing off the bike.

Gabriel turned to get off the bike and stopped as he finally caught sight of her house. "You call this a house?" he asked stunned as he continued to stare up at the mansion.

"I know it is a little on the small side, isn't it?" she asked pretending to be serious as she tilted her head and looked at the mansion with contemplation. After a minute, she turned back around to look at Gabriel with a big smile. "I was only joking," she said catching sight of the frown he was looking at her with. "It's not that big a deal. It was much cheaper in the olden days to build a house of this size than it is now."

"I guess being old has its benefits," he said walking over to her. Ruby frowned and narrowed her eyes at him in response. "Well, it does," he said as if that would make calling her old better. Ruby turned and began walking up the front walkway without saying anything. Gabriel followed closely behind her. She never bothered to stop to unlock the door, instead reaching right for the handle, and Gabriel was surprised when it opened. "You don't keep your door locked?" he asked.

"No, not usually. There really isn't much need. The gate is coded, and I can stop any intruder." The front door immediately opened into a large living room area.

Gabriel continued to follow her into the house. Gabriel caught her hand pulling her quickly into his arms and leaned down to kiss her. His kiss had started out slow and gently but had quickly turned desperate as his tongue swept into her mouth and his arms tightened around her waist. When Gabriel finally managed to lift his head from hers, they were both breathless and he realized with a small smile that at some point her arms had wound up around his neck holding him to her.

"How come every time I turn around, I find myself in your arms?" she asked shaking her head slightly as she looked up at him, never bothering to remove her arms from around his neck.

"It can't really be that bad. You never try to pull away from me, when I know you are plenty strong enough to get away from me if you wanted. And I could be mistaken, but you always seem to be kissing me back," he teased.

Ruby let out an exasperated sigh as she rested her head against his chest. "This isn't a good idea. We shouldn't be doing this."

"I can appreciate your view on relationships, but somehow I think that ship has sailed whether you like it or not," he said as he softly kissed the top of her head.

"I know," she said softly as if whispering it would keep it from being true. Ruby slipped out of his arms and turned toward the staircase.

"Where are you going?" he asked catching her hand again. This place was huge, and he didn't want to get lost or rather his real concern was losing track of her.

"To take a shower," she said without turning around. "Make yourself at home. Feel free to wander around, watch TV, or take a nap in any of the rooms."

"How will I find you back? Which room is yours?" he asked.

"Mine will be the one with the locked door, but I'm not going to help you find it." Gabriel had let go of her hand already, but she couldn't seem to make her feet move.

"Ruby," he said softly. "Are you alright?" he asked worried.

"No, I mean yes. I don't know. Nothing," she said confused.

"I can tell it's something, what is it?" he inquired.

"There's something I want to tell you, but I think it might offend you and that is not my intention." She knew he wanted to sleep with her or at least she had gotten that impression. Maybe she was wrong, what did she know about men. She couldn't deny that she liked the idea. Every time she turned around, he was pulling her back into his arms, and he was right she never once tried to pull away from him. She didn't want to. She liked being in his arms, but they couldn't sleep together.

"What is it?" he asked curious.

"Maybe later, I need a shower," she said finally getting her feet to start moving for the stairs again. She wanted to tell him they couldn't do this, maybe wanted was the wrong word, she didn't want to tell him that at all, which was why she hadn't. But she didn't know how to tell him, and she certainly wanted to… to be with him, but she knew she

41

couldn't… and he certainly deserved the truth. She needed to tell him. She couldn't… shouldn't lead him on.

Gabriel watched as she slowly climbed the stairs and turned left at the top. He wasn't sure what to do now. He didn't feel like watching TV, maybe because he didn't think he would be comfortable watching TV in her big mansion. He wouldn't mind looking around but was willing to bet he would get lost. Maybe he should get some sleep. He had spent all night up partly from insomnia but mostly because he was worried about her. She seemed to be doing fine now, but it still made him nervous to have her out of his sight.

Without thinking Gabriel slowly began to climb the stairs and took a left following the direction she had gone. He didn't want to bother her, but he hoped knowing where she was would help calm him down a little.

He didn't know which room she was in, but he knew she had turned down this hall. He slowly worked his way down the hall softly turning doorknobs one after another. He knew hers would be the locked one. He was careful not to make too much noise. He didn't want to alert her to the fact that he was looking for her or rather that he had found her by yanking too hard on the locked door. He was also careful to make sure that he stayed in sight of the staircase so that he could at least find his way back if he didn't find the locked door.

About halfway down the hall, Gabriel found the locked door. It didn't look any different from the others, but he knew she was in there. He stood there for a moment wondering what to do now that he knew where she was. There was another door directly across the hall from her. Slowly Gabriel opened the door to find a bedroom. He propped the door open with his backpack hoping she would notice it when she came out and would know where he was.

Gabriel briefly glanced around the room as he entered, but his eyes quickly fell on the huge bed and that was where his legs ended up taking him. He sat down on the edge of the bed. It was soft, extremely soft. He glanced over at the doorway and decided to lie down and relax a little while he waited for her to come back out. Surely, he would hear her when she came out of her room. She was only right across the hall.

He laid back against all the pillows on the bed thinking how soft and comfortable the bed was. He was asleep almost immediately after his head hit the pillow.

Ruby opened her bedroom door to look for Gabriel. She wanted to make sure he hadn't gotten lost and she was curious as to whether or not he had come looking for her. She felt much better after having showered and changed clothes, but she was still tired which made sense considering she usually kept nighttime hours and of course the blood loss. Ruby noticed Gabriel's bag propping open the door across the hall from her. Ruby couldn't help but smile to herself. Somehow, she wasn't surprised that he had come looking for her, but she was surprised by how happy it made her to know he had come looking for her.

Ruby walked further into the room and found Gabriel sound asleep. He hadn't even bothered getting under the covers. She knew he hadn't really slept all night and was happy to see him resting. Ruby knew she should leave and let him get some rest and probably get some of her own, but she found she couldn't force her feet to leave. She knew it was wrong, but she quietly climbed into bed beside him, careful not to disturb him. She laid down with her back resting against his side and her head on his shoulder and brought his arm up around her waist and held it there. Ruby took a deep breath and savored the smell and feel of him beside her. Within minutes if not seconds, she had fallen asleep.

At some point, Gabriel half woke up to find Ruby lying in his arms. Gabriel couldn't help but smile sleepily as he fell back asleep tightening his hold on Ruby's waist.

⋄ ◦ ◉ ◉ ◉ ◦ ◦

Gabriel woke to Ruby getting up from the bed. "Where are you going?" he asked as he caught her wrist in his hand and realizing she had somehow changed clothes since he had first woken up and found her in bed with him.

"Nowhere, I'm just getting back," she corrected.

"When did you leave?" he asked tugging on her hand to get her to sit back down.

"A few hours ago, you were sound asleep," she said with a soft smile.

"Where did you go? Are you hurt?" he asked sitting up suddenly alert at the thought.

"I'm fine," she said reaching up to brush her hand across his cheek. The urge to lean in and brush a soft kiss across his lips was so strong. Part of her just wanted to be able to touch him and the other wanted to reassure him that she was alright. Ruby tried to pull her hand away to try and stop tempting herself, but he held her hand to his face liking the contact.

"I just went out scouting for a few hours, I swung by your place for a few hours to see if they would come looking for you after sundown, they never showed up. I would have stayed longer but I wanted to check on you and make sure you were alright. I didn't want you waking up without me here and worrying something had happened when you couldn't find me. Worse I didn't want you to come looking for me and get yourself in trouble," she said looking away from him

Gabriel turned his head to brush a kiss across her palm and let go of her hand as he brought his hand up to wrap around the nape of her neck and brushed his thumb along her cheek forcing her to look up at him. She had expected him to kiss her at that point, but she was surprised when it was a soft tender kiss barely a brush against her lips and then he pulled back just to look at her. He had never had somebody care so much about him.

"You want to come downstairs with me to get something to eat," she said feeling foolish, when what she really wanted to ask was what was that for, what did that mean. She knew he liked her but... "I was just getting ready to go downstairs to eat when you woke up. You've been out for quite a while you must be hungry."

"Sure," Gabriel said letting his hand fall away from her face as he moved to stand up. "What time is it?" Gabriel asked realizing it was dark out as he followed her downstairs.

Three

Ruby pulled herself up on the counter and looked down at her hands that she clasped in her lap. They'd just finished eating while she'd answered more of his questions and told him more about herself. She looked up to watch Gabriel washing their dirty dishes as a thought occurred to her, she knew who he was. Ruby continued to stare at his backside in complete disbelief while he continued to quietly wash the dishes.

"What is it?" Gabriel asked not turning around but having sensed a change.

"I just realized this is the longest I have stayed in one place in... well... 25 years," she said tilting her head slightly to the side, watching him. "In fact, I do believe the last place I stayed in for any amount of time was here," she slowly said, thinking about it as she said it out loud.

"How long have you stayed here?" he asked curious. The way she had said that... it had seemed almost like an admission of something if he wasn't mistaken, but she also seemed confused by it.

"I've been here about a month now."

"Why have you not been staying put anywhere?" he asked softly. A month wasn't very long, and if that was the longest she had stayed anywhere in a quarter of a century...

He could understand her moving frequently because she aged so slowly, but more often than once a month seemed excessive. Even once a month seemed kind of silly in his opinion.

"I hadn't really thought about it until now, but I do suppose... I think I was running," she admitted watching his back. She hadn't realized it before now, but the reality hit home.

"From what?" he asked concerned.

"I do believe it is a whom," she corrected.

Gabriel waited quietly to see if she would continue.

"From you," she said barely above a whisper.

"From me," Gabriel asked stiffening and turning around to look at her.

"You are twenty-five, are you not?" she asked continuing to watch him closely.

"I'm not sure I understand what that has to do with anything," he said confused.

"You were born here, weren't you? In mid-May if I recall correctly."

"Yes, but how..."

"How did I know? I remembered when I left here last and why. It was the only other time I felt something as strong as I did the other night. It was that same draw I still feel when I look at you, and it terrifies me, which isn't easily done. It would seem at some point I forgot I was running from you... and I began running to you," she said closing her eyes tightly and shaking her head softly.

She knew exactly who he was. And this was wrong on so many levels. She had known his mother and father, she had held both him and his twin in her arms, but it had been him she had favored, and his name hadn't been Gabriel then but then hers hadn't been Ruby. It appeared he too, still favored her as he had as a newborn.

"Ruby," he began taking a step towards her.

"Don't," she said her eyes flying open and looking back up at him, stopping him in his tracks. Ruby slid from the counter but clung to it for support. Taking a deep breath, she forced herself to look away from him and at the clock, "It's four in the morning. I should... get some sleep if ..." she trailed off not knowing what to say, just knowing she needed space.

Gabriel nodded, not saying anything. He knew he was missing something.

"Don't leave the house," she said glancing up at him for a second before she turned and quickly headed for the stairs leaving him standing there confused.

Gabriel couldn't help staring after her looking at the stairs. Running from him. Him. Why? He'd never hurt her. Hell, he couldn't if he wanted to. Why on earth was she afraid of him? And 25 years ago... sure that's when he was born, but why would she run from him then. He would have been but an infant. He raked his hand through his hair confused. As she had told him more than once, he was just a human. He wanted to assure her she had nothing to fear from him, but... well, that seemed irrelevant. He was surely missing something.

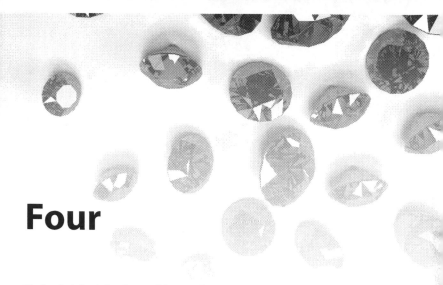

Four

Ruby laid in bed unable to sleep. She could hear Gabriel outside her door pacing. She had a feeling he wanted to come in, but he never attempted to open the door or knock probably thinking she was asleep.

Ruby rolled over on to her side facing away from the door. It didn't help all she could think about was Gabriel outside her door and how badly she wanted to let him in her room even though she knew that would probably be a big mistake. She wanted to feel his arms around her. Holding her tight. Feeling the warmth of his body. It made no sense which was probably why it scared her so badly, but she felt safe there. It was a weird sensation since she was fully capable of taking care of herself, had for centuries, but there was a different kind of safeness that she couldn't begin to understand or explain.

Ruby sighed deeply and not moving used her mind to pull back a corner of the comforter on the other side of the bed and opened the door to let Gabriel in. God help her it was probably the biggest mistake she could ever make, and she knew it, but... she did it anyways. She heard Gabriel stop when he had turned around to pace back in front of the door again. He had spotted the open door.

Gabriel didn't see Ruby, but the door was open. He hesitated before pushing the door open further and entering her room. It was dark in her room. Gabriel stopped trying to let his eyes adjust when a curtain was moved letting moonlight pour in helping light his way to the bed. Gabriel glanced over to the window, but no one was there. He didn't hear or see her moving back to the bed yet there she was lying in bed still as a rock.

Seeing the corner of the blankets pulled back Gabriel continued over to the bed and quietly got in beside her laying down on his back. He wanted to pull her into his arms, but he didn't. She appeared to be resting and he didn't want to disturb her, not after she had seem so upset earlier. He was just relieved to see her resting.

Ruby couldn't stop herself, she rolled over on to her other side facing Gabriel and snuggled up against him.

"So, you're not asleep," Gabriel whispered in the dark as he wrapped his arm around her waist to hold her to him.

"Neither are you," Ruby responded softly. "Why are you pacing outside my door?" she asked quietly.

"I was worried about you. I couldn't sleep and wanted to check on you, but outside your door was the closest I could get. Are you alright? I didn't keep you up, did I?" he asked realizing that as quiet as he had been, she could hear him outside her door.

"I'm fine," Ruby said softly not answering his other question.

"So, I was keeping you awake," he surmised.

"Yes, but not because of your pacing," Ruby admitted softly not wanting to lie to him. He had been the reason she couldn't sleep. Knowing he was in the house, knowing he was right outside her door, wanting him in her bed and knowing she shouldn't.

Screw it Ruby thought, she knew she shouldn't, but she didn't care. She leaned up to kiss him placing her weight on his chest and Gabriel responded as she had hoped.

Gabriel pulled Ruby closer to him and brought his other hand up to grasp the nape of her neck and kissed her long and hard. His hand slowly slid from her waist down to cup her bottom in his hand and pulled her on top of him so that she was straddling him. God, he wanted her like he had never wanted another person in his life.

She was only wearing a large t-shirt, his t-shirt he was sure, and panties. Somehow his pants had been pulled down in front setting him free. He could feel himself pushing at her wet entrance with only her thin panties between them. His hand slid from her bottom moving to push the offending garment out of the way. He wanted to take her slow and right their first time, but he needed her now and she was ready for him.

Ruby pulled away abruptly breaking their kiss. When Gabriel tried to follow her into a sitting position so he could continue kissing her she had held him down with her hands on his chest while moving off of him so that she was straddling his large thigh instead of his hips so that he was no longer pressing against her.

"We can't do this," she said gasping for air. Her eyes moved from his drifting down his chest to rest on his large cock that stood very erect very close to her thigh. She knew she should be at least a little afraid, he was huge, and she was tiny and doubted she could accommodate him, but she was excited, she wanted him in her. She shouldn't have done that. She shouldn't have moved to kiss him. This was dangerous.

"Sure, we can," he said huskily as he brushed his fingers across her cheek, trying to get her to look back at him even though he was pleased that she was enjoying staring at him. "We are both adults and we both want to," he reminded her. He reluctantly tucked himself back into his pants though he had no idea how he had been set free. He didn't remember moving his hand from her body to pull himself out nor her hands on him. Unfortunately, it didn't help much he was still wearing thin pajama bottoms that did nothing to hide how badly he wanted her, it simply made a tent out of his pants.

Ruby's eyes slid back to his, they were huge, and he swore she was on the verge of tears. Ruby realized she had been involuntarily rubbing herself against his thigh trying to find relief and forced herself to stop as she laid her head back down on his chest and shifted slightly to the side so she wasn't sitting on his thigh but her thigh still rested possessively across his. "No, I don't mean we shouldn't do this I mean we actually can't do this," Ruby said his arm still wrapped around her waist holding her to him.

This was not what she had wanted. This was not comforting. Being in his arms… it just hurt. She had known better and this… this wasn't going to change. He was human. She was just making this all harder on herself. She closed her eyes shaking her head against the realization.

"You're going to have to elaborate on that one, because I still don't see the problem," he said his hand moving the t-shirt she was wearing out of the way so his hand could rest against her bare skin. Gabriel could have sworn he heard her release a soft sigh in response and he also couldn't help but absently think about the fact that she was wearing one of his t-shirts though he wasn't sure when or how she had gotten it. Gabriel brought his hand up to brush his thumb across her cheek comfortingly and found it wet. He swore softly, he had scared her, he had to have scared her damn it what was wrong with him, she was innocent, she had never been with anyone and here he was thinking of his needs and not hers. Trying to… "You're crying," he said softly as he brushed away tears feeling horrible.

"No, I'm not," she replied. "I never cry.

"You are crying. I scared you, didn't I?" he asked softly, "I swear I didn't mean to."

"What? No," she replied bringing her hand up to wrap her finger around his wrist, but her fingers barely wrapped halfway around his wrist if that.

"Then why are you crying?" he asked confused not understanding what was going on. He could understand that he had scared her with his advances, but if he hadn't scared her as she claimed then… then why was he holding a crying Ruby that was breaking his heart. He barely knew her, and yet her tears… clawed at his heart. He didn't like them.

"I've never wanted anything for myself," she said softly.

"But you want this?" he asked brushing soft caresses against her cheek.

"Yes," she answered fighting back a new wave of tears. It wasn't fair.

"Then why can't we be together," he questioned confused.

"Gabriel, I'm a whole lot stronger than you," she said softly almost as if she didn't want to say it as she shook her head trying to deny it.

"Yes, I know that," Gabriel said.

"Yes, but I don't think you really understand just how easily I could hurt you accidentally," she told him.

"I trust you."

"I know you do, but you don't know half of how strong I am," she sighed. She didn't want to, but she knew she had to tell him. She couldn't have him, not even for a short time. She was ever alone. It was her curse. One that appeared never ending. She didn't know what she'd done to deserve it, but nonetheless… here she was.

"I'm willing to risk it," Gabriel said. He couldn't explain it, but he needed her, and she wanted him. He couldn't deny her or his desire to have her.

"I'm not, what you want… what we want to do… usually requires one to be… to be out of control and that would be extremely dangerous," she admitted.

"I trust you," he repeated.

"I don't. I don't want to hurt you on accident. Besides even if I could stay in control, which the whole point is to let loose and lose control is it not, there is still one very important muscle you are forgetting about. I've never attempted to be with anyone, and I don't even know if I physically can… I don't know if that muscle is stronger like the rest of my body or not, and I don't know how much control I would have over how hard I… well… squeeze," Ruby said getting ever quieter as she talked. She hated having to admit this to him, but she had to be honest with him. She couldn't lie to him. He deserved to know why they couldn't be together.

"You lost me," Gabriel said softly.

"That muscle you want to bury yourself in," Ruby said feeling her face flush in response.

"Oh… oh," Gabriel said suddenly moving his hand to rub against his erection as if just thinking about it hurt. "But you don't know for certain."

"No, but I certainly don't want to find out by risking hurting you," she said firmly.

"Then why did you let me in here?" Gabriel couldn't help but asking. He wanted to be angry at her letting him in like this when she knew they couldn't… but he couldn't. He couldn't be angry. His hand moved from his groin coming to rest on her thigh. He couldn't stop touching her, he was going to lose his mind. He just wanted her.

"I don't know. I like you holding me in your arms like this even if we can't… and I like the thought of you worried about me, but I didn't want you staying outside pacing worried about me if you didn't have to be. I wanted you in here," she said softly.

"So, I can still stay in here then," he said as he moved to pull the blanket up over them and then returned his hand to her thigh. He was crazy. He was definitely crazy. He should be trying to put distance between them, between temptation, but he seemed no better at it than her.

"Yes," she answered with a sigh as she moved closer to his body resting her hand on his bare chest since he wasn't wearing a shirt, which might have been because she had stolen a shirt out of his bag to wear to bed. She liked having the smell of him all around her but then she liked his arms around her and on her even better.

"Can I still kiss you?" Gabriel asked trying to find out where he should help draw the line.

"As long as that is all it is," she said softly.

"And what if my hands want to wander?" he asked trying to get as much as he could, but he knew it wouldn't be enough. He wanted all of her and he hated this. Being so close, being able to touch her and yet unable to have her. He needed to stop this insanity. Touching her was only going to inflame both of their desires further.

"I think they already are," she commented. "But within reason," she continued to answer anyways. She didn't have it in her to tell him 'no' like she should. She liked this, she wanted more, and she would take what she could get, but this was dangerous. She was tempting fate. And preparing her heart to be shattered and she seemed unable to stop it.

Every step she seemed to be taking was only going to make it worse in the end for her. He'd move on after she was gone. He'd have a family and kids, and she'd... Well, she'd still be alone.

"You sure there is nothing you can do to make me stronger?" he asked wistfully. God, he needed her.

"You could be a vampire," she said nuzzling his chest, "but then you'd be a vampire."

"What about those animal things you talked about, I can't be turned into one of them?" he asked trying to find a solution.

"They've only ever made weres- which I've only ever heard of going crazy and having to be put down. And even then, those are super rare. I'm not sure about the safety of attempting that and I'm not sure it would help in the long run. Besides, to be honest, I'm still a good deal stronger than all of them," she told him sadly.

"If those can change a human, regardless of the end result, why can't you?" he asked not liking the whine in his voice.

"I only said I don't know how, not that it's impossible, but it's not like I have anyone I could ask on how to change a human. Besides, being like me..." she trailed off not sure how to finish that thought other than 'being like her sucked'. "Do you think you will be able to sleep now that you know I'm alright?" she asked softly trying to change the subject.

"No, but I will certainly rest easier, painfully full and uncomfortable but easier. You?" he asked.

"No, I need a long hard run, or at least a very cold shower." She heard Gabriel groan softly in response. She wanted to run her hands over him. She wanted to resume kissing him. She didn't know how she had ended up straddling him, or remember pulling down his pants, but back in that moment was where she wanted to be. But she wanted it to end how it should have, not like this. She whimpered feeling the tears that streamed down her cheeks.

Gabriel kissed the top of her head comfortingly as he held her to him. He knew she wasn't trying to make him miserable, but he was highly uncomfortable with wanting her. And the thought of showers… he could use a cold one himself, but he would much more prefer a hot soapy one with her. But at least he could hold her in his arms, that was something, right?

Five

At some point Ruby had drifted off uncomfortably, but she was now awake again. She knew it was just after sunset, about eight in the evening, she had a good internal clock. It was time to go hunting. She needed to get rid of these vampires. She needed to leave. She should never have come back here.

Ruby slowly moved to get out of Gabriel's arms.

"Ruby," he called huskily as he tried to maintain his hold on her, which she easily broke without trying.

"You're awake," she said turning her head to look down at him.

"Where are you going?" he asked not wanting her out of his arms.

"Hunting," she told him flatly.

Gabriel sat up abruptly grabbing at her arm as she turned away from him.

"You can't stop me," she said softly as she moved to slide off the edge of the bed.

"How are you going to hunt them?" he couldn't help but ask worried about her, even though he knew she had been doing this for centuries and was completely capable of taking care of herself.

"I was going to go watch your place for a while, and then hit the clubs and usual haunts where they go to find a meal to see if I can follow them back to their nest," she said.

"I'm coming with you. I can help you stake out my place or be bait to help draw them out."

Ruby had whirled on him so fast he didn't know what had happened. One moment he was looking at her back and the next she was on top of him pinning him to the bed, her small but incredibly strong hand spanning his throat and holding him down. "You are not bait," she bit out softly but every bit of her fury showing in her eyes.

"I was going to be bait the other night," he managed to get out despite her tight hold on his throat.

Ruby growled in response.

Damn him, he couldn't help but think. He knew he should be afraid right now, but he was turned on and he knew she could feel him pressing against her when she gasped in realization and climbed off of him. "Fine, I'm not bait but I'm still coming with you," he said rubbing at his neck as he sat up.

Ruby stepped back near him brushing his hand away and replacing it with her soft touch and then her lips. There was no mark there, but she traced where she knew she had touched him. She didn't apologize but he knew she was sorry.

Ruby was angry with herself, she had lost control, she never lost control. What was it about him? She wasn't acting herself. Flying into a rage, crying for the first time in centuries, curling up in a man's arms like a kitten, acting like a cat in heat... god she needed to get away from him and soon. He was going to destroy her, she was going be stuck with the memories and the taste of him in her mouth long after he was dead and it wasn't like she could simply kill herself. Not that she had ever tried but she had an amazing capacity to heal and she wasn't sure she could self-inflict enough damage to kill herself if it was even possible.

"What are you thinking?" he asked catching shadows of something chasing across her face as she looked up at him.

"Nothing." She needed to hurry up and kill these vampires. She needed to make sure he was safe, so she could resume running from him. Part of her knew him being safe or not, didn't make a difference in the grand scheme of things. Anything could happen after she left, but she couldn't leave knowing they were likely after him. She needed to run. And cry.

"Liar," he said softly. He knew her well enough to know she was lying to him.

Ruby turned to walk away from him towards the bathroom to get dressed. "Just wondering when it will all be over," she said not completely lying but enough that he would know it was the truth.

Gabriel quickly followed after her confused. "You mean this situation with the vampires wanting to kill me, right?" he asked standing in the doorway of the bathroom.

"Ruby?" he asked when she didn't respond.

"No, I mean everything," she said lifting her gaze to look at him.

When she looked at him her eyes were cold, empty even whereas before they had been filled with rage, but there was something else. Sadness... no, it wasn't depression, she wasn't the type to be forlorn. Was it self-hatred? He knew she was angry at herself for losing control but that wasn't it. Was it self-mocking... self-deprecating is that what he saw in those eyes that stared up at him pleading, but for what? "Surely you don't mean that, you've done so much good for this world of that I'm sure."

He heard the soft snort of derision as she turned away from him "And what has it done for me in return?" she asked as she pulled his shirt over her head baring her back to him. Gabriel couldn't help the soft intake of breath, my god she was covered in scars. He could tell these were old, they had silvered and were nearly imperceptible and he knew they laid flat against her skin because his hand had rested there while she had slept never feeling a thing but soft smooth skin. "Given me a man I want for the first time in my long life that I can't keep, can't touch and will long out live." What had she ever done to have him dangled in front of her like this? "And made me extremely difficult to kill," she added with a sigh. Ruby pulled a cropped long sleeve shirt over her head and turned to look at him as she untucked her hair from the shirt and put it in a quick braid. "I told you I had more scars," she said softly, not sad nor angry, just a factual soft comment. She was old, and alone.

Gabriel wanted to pull her into his arms, but something told him not too. She had pulled back from him and he suspected trying to comfort her wouldn't go over well. But he was sure he knew what that look in her eyes had been... defeat.

"If you're going to come with me, you better go get dressed," she said looking him up and down once before turning and disappearing into her closet to locate a pair of pants.

Gabriel reluctantly left to get dressed, he was definitely going with her. She wasn't going out alone. Not in her current state. She wasn't even trying to continue fighting him on coming with her. Was all this because she had lost control? He knew about control, it was a fine line, but it seemed like there was more to it. She'd said she had been afraid of him, was this why? That look that broke his heart.

Had he broken her? But he was… he was nothing. Just a human, and one she barely knew at that. Gabriel quickly changed and met up with her downstairs.

* * * * * * *

Gabriel stayed in the shadows with her watching his place. She had ordered him to stay put while she had searched his apartment and then returned to him. They'd barely said two words. He understood they were on a stake out and didn't need to be holding any long discussions that could be overheard or draw attention, but the tension… well, it could be cut with a knife.

After a couple hours, Gabriel was surprised to see the couple that had slipped away arrive, he had figured it would be a whole lot longer if they showed up at all. Gabriel was about to point them out to Ruby, but she had already spotted them and held a finger to her lips.

Gabriel raised an eyebrow in inquiry confused as to how she knew.

Ruby tapped her nose softly and then tapped her heart and her ear indicating they smelled different and that she could somehow hear their heartbeat or lack thereof, then returned to waiting for their exit. Ruby told him to stay there hidden while she followed them back to the nest and if anymore showed up to take her bike and return to her house.

Gabriel wasn't going to do that, but he saw no reason to argue with her. Once she had taken after them, he followed after her. She may be able to take care of herself, but he questioned the state she was in and she was looking for a nest. If she found it… she was liable to get herself hurt and with no way to get herself home, and that was depending on just how severely she was hurt. He didn't care what she

thought at the moment, she wasn't going alone. If he died…
well, so what… he was human, and she'd be free of him
and any pain he had or would cause her. She'd be able to
move on.

Besides, what did he have going for him? He wasn't
in contact with his family, and he kept to himself. She'd
been the only good thing in his life in a long time, and he
suspected he'd only managed to hurt her since coming into
her life. He also suspected, no he knew, she'd leave after
this vampire thing was settled. And he was willing to bet
that would be tonight. Then, they could both return to their
lonely lives.

Ruby was already fighting a handful of vampires when
he slid into the room. He saw blood trailing down from a
slash to her thigh and to her hip but neither seemed to be
geysers or slowing her down. She was a whirlwind, spinning
from one to the next cutting slashes and debilitating wounds
but she never went for a kill. What was she doing? And he
swore he caught a smile on her face, was she… having fun?
Had she been itching for a fight? A release. An outlet for her
pain. He suspected she'd continue like this if not possibly
even participating in more reckless behavior after she left.

One of the vampires on the edge of the fight stopped,
sniffed the air and whirled towards him.

Ruby had nearly lost control, she had felt the awareness
the second he had entered the room nearly doubling her
over in pain. She had been having fun playing with them,
taunting them. It was hard for her to find a good fight and
she had needed an outlet for her energy. Hell, she didn't
need to touch them to kill them, but this always helped to
drain away some of the physical energy in an attempt to
help her find some sleep, that or a good wound with some

blood loss which always helped her sleep. She knew sleep was going to elude her for a long time to come unless she found it like this, and even then, she knew she'd regularly be doing something she almost never did... crying herself to sleep. Alone. Always alone. But first, she had to get out of here, out of this city, out of this state, and then... and then she could cry.

Ruby couldn't get to him. She couldn't reposition herself so that she was between him and the vampires, because she was already surrounded. What the hell was he thinking?

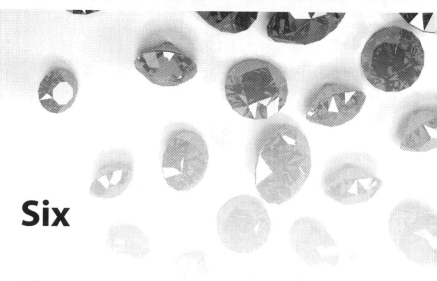

Six

Ruby rushed over to Gabriel in a hurry. He'd been attacked and bitten. He was already changing. "Gabriel," she cried kneeling down beside him.

Gabriel had insisted on coming with her to stake out his apartment for the vampires, but when they had showed Ruby had told him to stay put out of sight and that she was going to follow them back to their hideout when they left. Ruby had given him her keys and told him to go back to her house if anymore showed.

But apparently Gabriel hadn't listened and had instead followed her. She had felt him enter the room, and then spotted him fighting with a vampire while she was taking on a few others, unable to help him and hoping he could handle the one. But apparently a second had gotten involved and had thought it would be fun to turn him instead of killing him.

When Ruby had realized he had been bitten she had been filled with so much rage she had frozen the full room of vampires so that they couldn't move and then excited the energy where their hearts would all be located killing them all instantly with a fireball to the hearts so to speak. She didn't usually do that because it took so much energy and well it was less sporting, but Gabriel had been bitten there was no time for sport.

"Ruby," he said his body convulsing in pain, "kill me."

"I… I… I can't," she stammered her face twisting in pain at the sight of him in pain. Damn it why had he followed her.

"Why… not?" he nearly screamed in pain.

Ruby just shook her head vigorously in denial. She just couldn't do it, not Gabriel. She didn't have it in her. She'd sooner kill herself. And right now, she wanted to. Why hadn't he listened?

The pain was beginning to subside, he had to be nearing the end of the transition. "Ruby," he said softly as he reached his hand up to wipe the tears off her cheek.

"I won't," she practically whimpered. Ruby sat there and watched in horror as he turned into a vampire and yet she could do nothing.

"If you won't kill me, then leave." At Ruby's stunned and horrified look at the idea he added, "I don't want to hurt you, and if what I've seen of vampires is any indication, I think that is going to change. I don't want to hurt you, and I don't think you're going to defend yourself if I attack you."

"I'll heal. I'm not leaving you like this," she denied his request.

"Ruby," he screamed as a new wave of pain rippled through his body. Despite his protests, she never left, and his pain finally ended. He cautiously stood back up, now that the pain was no longer coursing through his body.

Ruby stood up with him, watching him carefully. "How…how do you feel?" she asked nervously.

"I'm not sure. I don't really feel different, except there is this weird pounding in by head," he said looking down at her. "I don't want to hurt you like I thought I would, though

I could use a drink, cotton mouth." Ruby's eyes widened slightly, but he didn't understand why.

Gabriel inhaled deeply, there was something in the air that he had never noticed before now. It smelled amazing. He tilted his head to the side as he looked down at her. It was Ruby he was smelling. Why hadn't he noticed before? "You smell wonderful. I don't know how I didn't notice it before."

Gabriel leaned in to get a stronger whiff and the pounding that he suddenly realized was in his ears and not his head got louder. His eyes became intent as he looked at her what was that sound. He caught sight of her beautiful soft neck. He could see the vein throbbing in her neck. *Huh, that was weird.* It was beating in time with the pounding in his ears and there was an incredible urge to lean down further and put his mouth on that exact spot.

Gabriel caught himself leaning in closer and pulled back quickly stepping away from her, but he couldn't pull his eyes away from the throbbing at her neck. *Dear god, he wanted to bite her.*

Ruby was suddenly hit by déjà vu. Why hadn't she remembered it before? He wanted to feed from her, and others had commented before on how good she smelled, but why hadn't she remembered. Only one person or rather vampire had ever managed to get close enough to bite her.

How could she have possibly forgotten the result of the one vampire that had ever managed to bite her? Why hadn't she thought of it sooner? He had asked her if there was any way to turn someone into what she was and she had said no. Sure she didn't know how to turn a human into what she was, but considering what had happened centuries ago she was pretty sure she knew how to turn a vampire into what she was. The information had never seemed important considering how blood thirsty and crazy they were, but maybe this could save Gabriel from having to live as a vampire. He was newly turned, he wasn't blood thirsty and crazed yet.

"Gabriel," she said stepping towards him. "Bite me."

"What?" he asked horrified stepping back from her again.

"It's alright. You have to trust me. Just bite me," she said following after him.

"No, I won't bite you," he said walking backwards, but she kept following after him.

"It will be alright," she said softly as she followed him.

"Stop," he said as he backed up against a wall.

Ruby placed one of her palms on his chest and stepped closer into him. Gabriel looked down at her feeling helpless. She felt amazing against him, just as she always had, and she smelled absolutely delicious. He groaned at the comparison. Ruby reached up on her tip toes to kiss him, and as much as he tried, he couldn't resist leaning down to kiss her. His body continued to betray him as he brought his arms up around her to hold her to him. Her kisses tasted amazing, but he wanted more. He slowly began to trail kisses across her jaw and down her neck. As his lips settled on the throbbing in her neck, he felt his incisors lengthen and the urge to sink them in her neck.

Gabriel pulled away horrified, but Ruby's arms were around his neck preventing him from pulling back too far. She leaned up to kiss him again hoping to distract him. She knew he wanted to bite her, but he was fighting it, which all things considered was kind of sweet in a weird way, but she still needed to get him to bite her. She just needed to keep him distracted from what he was really doing so that he would let his instincts to bite her take over.

He tried to fight it. He knew exactly what she was doing, but he couldn't. She felt amazing, smelled amazing, and even tasted amazing, but he wanted more. Before he knew what he had done, he had bitten into her throat exactly as she wanted.

Ruby ran her fingers through his hair, comforting while he drank from her. It wasn't long before he pulled back. He licked his tongue once up the length of her neck and then lifted his head to look down at her. For a while, he just stared down at her satiated, but then he began to come back around to the real world. As he began to realize what he had just done, he began to panic.

"Oh my god what have I done?" he asked dropping his arms from around her and pushing her back from him. "I bit you... I'm so sorry. I don't know what happened. I couldn't stop myself. My god... I bit you. Why didn't you stop me? You should have killed me. I bit you," Gabriel continued becoming hysterical.

Ruby had snorted when he had asked her why she hadn't stopped him. Why hadn't she stopped him? Because she couldn't kill him. Because she loved him. Because she knew she wouldn't be able to live with herself. And because she knew she wouldn't be able to kill herself when it grew to be absolutely too much to live with herself. But she wasn't going to tell him that. Besides he was too hysterical to really hear any answer she gave him.

"Gabriel," she said trying to get his attention, but he couldn't hear her. He just kept blathering on and on about the fact that he had bitten her and how sorry he felt. Ruby slapped him across the face, and he fell silent just staring at her.

Ruby couldn't take it anymore. She launched herself into his arms, wrapping her arms around his neck. *Oh, thank god*, Ruby thought holding on to him tightly. She felt his arms slowly come up around her and hold on to her just as tightly.

After a while, he spoke up. "You hit me," he said falling silent again.

Actually, I only slapped you, she thought to herself.

"You could have hurt me. You could have broken something."

No, I couldn't of, not now. Besides I only slapped you now if I had punched you, I maybe could have broken your nose, but that's about it, Ruby imagined saying out loud, but she didn't actually say a word. She didn't trust herself. *I'm just so happy you're all right*, she told herself. *I don't know what I would have done if...* she couldn't even think it to herself.

"Ruby, I'm so sorry I bit you. I... I couldn't stop it. I tried, but I couldn't. I can't believe I ..." he tried to stay calm, but he was starting to sound and feel hysterical again. Gabriel fell silent just holding on to her tightly.

It's alright, she thought stroking his hair softly as she held on to him. *It's alright. It's alright.*

"Stop saying that. It's not alright. I bit you for crying out loud and not like some weird kinky sex thing. I bit you and I was drinking your blood. God, I feel horrible," he told her.

I don't care. It's alright, she thought to herself. "You only bit me because I let you," she said out loud trying to make him feel better.

"How can you not care?" he asked. "I could have killed you. For all I know I might have turned you too."

How could he know she didn't care? She thought surprised. "I highly doubt you could have killed me or turned me," she said softly.

"Because you just said you didn't care," he said confused as he answered her question.

Ruby pulled back from him and he loosened his hold on her, so that she could look into his face as he set her feet back on the ground. "No, I didn't," she said confusion clearly showing on her face.

"Yes, you did," he said distinctly recalling her say 'I don't care. It's alright.'

"No, I didn't say that, but I don't care," she said confused as to why he was insisting she had.

"How can you not care? And I'm not insisting that you said you didn't care. You said it plain and simple. You said, 'I don't care. It's alright. You only bit me because I let you.'"

Ruby shook her head confused. *I didn't say that out loud, did I? I said the second part out loud, but I only thought the first part,* she thought confused.

"What are you talking about?" he asked confused. "I heard you say it out loud. I know what I heard, but more importantly I want to know why you don't care."

Oh, dear god, Ruby thought. *It couldn't be. No, it's not possible.*

"What isn't possible?" he asked completely confused as to where this conversation was going.

Oh god, what have I done? She thought horrified.

"What have you done?" he asked confused, "and why do I feel so horrified?" he didn't understand why, but all of the sudden he felt completely horrified and it made no sense like this whole conversation. He wasn't even sure why he was asking her, but her 'oh gods' seemed to indicate she had some idea as to what was going on.

Gabriel, she thought.

"Yes."

Look at my lips, she thought.

"Alright if that's what you want, but I don't know what that has to do with anything," he told her confused.

71

My lips aren't moving. I didn't say that out loud. I've barely said two words since you bit me, she told him mentally.

"Your… your lips aren't moving," he said horrified. "What do you mean you've barely said two words? You've barely stopped talking. Oh god, how do I know that? Ruby what's going on?" he asked his arms on her tightening to pull her back towards him for comfort.

"You're… you're…" *reading my mind somehow,* she thought since she couldn't seem to say it out loud.

"That can't be possible," he contradicted.

You just did it again, she thought as she let out a whimper. She leaned forward and rested her head on his chest. *What on earth have I done to him? Oh god.*

"I'm not human, am I?" he asked softly.

No, she moaned, but he wasn't sure whether or not she had actually said it out loud since he couldn't see her lips.

"And I'm not a vampire, am I?" he asked holding on to her.

No, I don't think so, she said with another moan.

"Then what am I?" he asked even though he already suspected the answer.

I think you are like me, she thought silently. *Or at least, I hope you are like me,* Ruby told him nervously as she continued to hold on to him.

"What does that mean?" he asked loosening his hold as she tried to put some space between them, but she didn't move away from him. She stayed near him resting a hand on his chest as she looked around them.

"We need to get out of here," she said her hand sliding from his chest and taking his hand in hers and beginning to head for the exit. She had already begun to excite the energy in the air with the intention of burning the building down.

"What are you doing?" he asked following her. He could feel it, he didn't know what it was, but he could feel the change in the air, and somehow, he knew it was her.

Burning the building down, she thought. *I can try and answer your questions, but we need to do it somewhere safe. Let's go back to my place.*

"Alright," he said trying to head for her bike, but she held on to his hand leading him away from the bike.

"Running will be faster," she told him.

"You are joking, right?" he asked seriously.

No, just run. Don't think about your speed, just focus on following me. Stick close, listen to the noises around you, and just try to feel or sense or imagine, if it helps, where I am. Watch out for trees, she thought as she let go of his hand and took off running.

"Are you nuts?" he asked, he assumed to himself as she began to disappear from sight.

Maybe, he heard her whisper in his head, and he was sure it was in his head. He felt halfway between absolutely sure that he would follow her and that he really hoped he would follow her, the feeling felt weird, not like it was him, but it was him, right? He felt great relief as he took off after her. He followed her all the way back to her house, and it was a lot faster than he thought it would be and it was a lot easier to follow her than he expected. He was surprised how easily he could hear her running ahead of him but he had a feeling that she wasn't making any sound and that he just thought he could hear her but yet he knew instinctually and definitively that he was accurately following her.

Ruby stopped outside the house. She had intended to go inside, but now that she was standing outside the house, she didn't seem able to go inside. It was too small inside. She could feel Gabriel approaching, he barely made a sound but then she had been intently listening for him. Anything or anyone else in the woods wouldn't have known he was there. She knew the second he stood behind her, but she didn't turn around. She forced herself not to. She wanted to so bad, she wanted to see his face she wanted to look at him, she wanted…

Gabriel reached out and touched her arm, "Ruby."

She closed her eyes tightly. She wanted to answer him to turn and look at him, but she didn't trust herself. She told herself it was okay he was reaching out to comfort her, which meant he wasn't mad, right? But what did he know? He was his own person, he could make his own decisions it was okay, she needed him, no it wasn't okay, she knew better he didn't, how could he think for himself he had her in his head.

"Ruby, let's go inside," he said as he shook his head as if trying to clear it. He had so many thoughts and feelings going through his head, but yet it was hard to grasp them. They all seemed opposite of each other and they all seemed to leave and come back just as soon as they entered.

"It's so small," she said shaking her head out just as he had done, but the funny thing was when she did it, it actually seemed to help clear his head the only thought he had was whether he meant his head or the house and he wasn't sure and he realized looking down at her that it was her it was all her.

I'm so, so sorry Gabriel, she thought to herself as she headed inside and a small voice inside her head said, *'no you're not, it's exactly what you wanted'*. *'But not like this,'* she argued with herself.

"Ruby," he called trying to get her attention. He could hear her arguing with herself and he knew that's exactly what it was he was hearing.

What? she thought softly.

"Look at me," he told her.

Ruby did as he asked, and he was immediately hit by so much happiness and so much shame. It made his chest physically hurt and he was surprised he didn't fall to his knees. Gabriel reached over and tightly grabbed the back of the couch to keep from falling. Ruby saw the knuckles of his hand turning white and knew he was struggling with her feelings. "I'm sorry," she said her face twisting in anguish. *He needs to sit down, we should sit down, I can't sit down, I should sit down.*

"Let's try and sit down," he suggested.

She nodded her head feeling like a child doing what she was told. She wanted to help him sit down but she was afraid that if she touched him it would make her feel worse and that would only hurt him more.

Ruby sat down on the couch not quite beside him but near him and definitely not across from him. She pulled her feet up under her and her knees into her chest trying to make herself feel smaller. She knew he was watching her waiting for her to say something. I don't know what to say. In her head she tested out saying, *I'm sorry*. No, he would know that wasn't entirely the truth. She was glad he was alive, and part of her was thrilled that she had turned him. Before she kept telling him that they couldn't be together because he was human but now, he wasn't. She had realized when he was turning that she loved him and didn't want to be without him. Sure, she'd felt the same way before, but she hadn't realized that... Ruby swallowed hard realizing that he could still hear her.

"I didn't mean to turn you like this. If I had realized I could turn you, I would have told you and given you a choice, well in a controlled environment, but I had forgotten, and even then, I'm not entirely sure if or how to turn a human. I accidentally turned a vampire once, it was so long ago back when I was a child," she rambled on trying to give some kind of explanation.

There was suddenly a flash of an image of a child that looked like it could have been her in his head and then it was gone.

"It was back before I started hunting," she continued unaware of the image he'd seen, "it was why I started hunting. She was a child, or she looked like a child."

Another flash.

"I didn't realize she was a vampire. We were out late playing I didn't think anything of the time of night or that her parents were nowhere around. It was a different time, I was a child, and I didn't have any parents and played where and when I wanted so it didn't seem strange. At least not until she bit me," she continued hurriedly.

Gabriel could see and feel it all like it was happening to him as she told the story, he knew she wasn't lying, and he knew she hadn't previously been lying to him when she said she couldn't turn anyone.

"I threw her off of me, and she came back at me saying, 'you smell so good', she kept coming back at me trying to bite me, I could sense her changing, I could feel her getting stronger as we fought. I ended up killing her. I still don't completely understand now that I think about it how I was able to kill her since I'm so hard to kill. But you..." she paused looking up.

"What about me?" he asked.

"I feel it. You are a lot more like me than she could ever be. It's like with you it's almost done, you're almost whatever I am but there are still a couple of slight things in you that are changing or are trying to change, finishing the process. But with her she was nowhere close, the change was going so much slower in her and it was different like it was wrong like it wasn't supposed to happen. But not with you, with you it was almost instant but there is something there waiting," she said looking at him funny. "I can feel it. It's not bad," she added knowing the way she had said that had to sound bad.

"Why?" he asked.

"I don't know maybe because I wanted to turn you, maybe because I let you bite me unlike her maybe because I let you drink until you stopped whereas I threw her off before she could finish," *maybe because of how I feel about you,* she thought, *maybe for the same reason I was drawn to you that first night we met I don't know...*

"Look you don't have to stay with me, I know you know how I feel," she knew she couldn't or wouldn't hold him but the thought of letting him go filled her with such sadness and darkness. It was like a pit of despair and she wanted to fall into it. She knew he could feel it and she wished she could shield him from it. She didn't want to let him go but she would have to find a way to let him make his own decision and she wanted him to make it without her influence.

"I know this is a lot to take in and I know I have no right to want or expect you to want to stay with me. I can show you how to use your abilities, I can show you where all my houses are and set you up with bank accounts and identities, you will probably always be connected to me so you will know where I am so you don't have to see me if you don't want to, you can use any of my houses and there will be more than enough money in the accounts that you can buy or build others if you want. I will try not to think about you too much I don't want to hurt you or make you uncomfortable, but I can't promise anything."

She couldn't help but think '*he will always know where I am if he changes his mind besides there is no one else like us*'. She couldn't help but feel incredible guilt at this thought. What had she done? What had she become? She was a monster. How could she have done this. She had only made things worse between them. He had seemed interested in her… well, at least physically. But how could he possibly want her, really want her… for keeps, and now he was connected to her. She wished she was dead.

"I can't and I won't stop you from trying to have relationships, but I caution you, you aren't human anymore it can be dangerous, and if you do decide you want to attempt to turn someone make sure it is the right person. Whatever we are, we are incredibly dangerous and in the wrong person we could destroy the world. Even if you don't want to stay with me, I know I didn't turn the wrong person I know you are a good guy and I know you would use these capabilities appropriately, so just remember that. It's not a turn and try and date them you need to be sure before you try and turn them."

The idea of leaving her filled him with dread or was that her.

"And of course, if you don't want to be around me long enough to learn your abilities and would rather learn them on your own that is your decision," she continued telling him.

"Ruby," Gabriel said after a while startling her.

Ruby quickly looked down at her hands. Somehow, she had ended up staring at him longingly and had stopped talking. Gabriel had been filled with such a feeling of warmth and love beyond imagine and yet such deep sadness as she had stared at him. Before he knew what she was doing she launched herself off the couch and across the room slamming her fist up to her elbow through the brick wall trying to distract herself. She pulled it out of the wall and looked down at it, all she wanted to do was breakdown and cry and have Gabriel hold her. She felt like a crazy person.

"Ruby," he said wrapping her in his arms and trying to pull her in against his chest wanting to comfort her. He hated being able to feel and know everything she felt and thought, those things were intended to be private.

"I can't," she said gently pushing out of his arms, "I can't do this. It's not right, it's not fair to you. I need some air," she said taking off for the door. "I'll be back."

She needed air. She couldn't breathe. She couldn't think or she was thinking too much. She honestly wasn't sure. He was there. She couldn't even feel pity for herself over losing him without him knowing, but then it wasn't like she deserved it. She didn't deserve that right, but that didn't stop her from wanting to just… hurt, and wallow in it. But she couldn't hurt without hurting him. She couldn't think. She needed to breathe. Why had she been drawn to him? Why hadn't she just killed him like he asked she thought wanting to cry at the thought. Why had she cursed him to the same life as her?

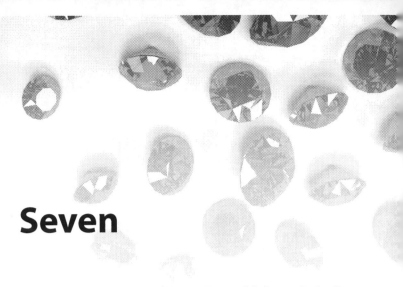

Seven

Ruby ran as hard and as fast as she could through the forest. She needed to clear her head, but she couldn't because she knew he could hear every thought she had. She was in agony. She loved him and didn't have a problem answering any question he had for her, but this was different. She had no idea how he really felt about her and yet he knew exactly how she felt about him. How much she loved him, how terrible she felt about turning him without his permission, how agonized she felt that he knew exactly what she thought and how she felt. Not to mention, how embarrassed she felt by the fact that he knew how much she loved him when she had absolutely no idea how he felt.

Ruby closed her eyes and shook her head vigorously, as if that would get him out of her head, but she never stopped running. She knew these woods like the back of her hand. She had no trouble running these woods, blindfolded or not, she couldn't get lost.

About another 5 miles ahead there was a river that took a sudden drop off a cliff into a large natural lake. The cliff had to be half a football field high, but to be honest Ruby didn't really care. With as fast as she could run, it wasn't long before she broke into the clearing at the top of the cliff.

Ruby didn't slow down as she continued to run full out towards the edge of the cliff. As she reached the edge of the cliff, she pushed off with enough force to put her easily 10 to 20 feet out from the edge of the cliff, but still well within the limits of the lake below.

As the wind rushed past, Ruby cleared her head and thought only of the lake far below while she positioned herself for a headfirst dive into the lake. Ruby entered the water with barely a splash and continued diving for the bottom of the lake.

Once she had finally reached the bottom of the lake, she moved to sit cross-legged on the bottom of the lake. The feeling of water all around her and the concentration needed to remain seated on the bottom of the lake helped clear her head. All she could see and think about was the calm, blue water of the lake. Time seemed to simply stand still for her. There was nothing. It was… peaceful.

* * * * * * * *

Gabriel had felt so overwhelmed. He couldn't stop it and he couldn't control it. Her thoughts just kept coming and coming. It was all he could feel. He felt horrible. These were her private thoughts and feelings. He didn't want to hear her thoughts or feel her feelings. They were hers and this was a horrible invasion of privacy, but no matter how hard he tried he couldn't stop it. And of course, to make things worse, the connection was so entirely consuming he was having trouble telling the difference between his feelings and hers.

He knew that before, whatever this was that had happened, he had liked Ruby a lot. He'd been at a loss to understand it. He could barely stand to be separated from her. A few times, he had even entertained the idea of how wonderful it would be if he was or could be like her. They would be free to find out what really was between them and live out their days together if that was what they chose. Ruby had told him that she didn't know of a way to change anyone, and he hadn't doubted she was telling the truth. Of course, clearly, she had been mistaken, but after hearing her tale, he knew she hadn't technically been lying, but that still left him unsure about how he really felt now.

He knew he cared for her a lot, more than made sense for the short time that he had known her, and he could have sworn he even loved her, but he could also feel how much she loved him. The emotion was overwhelming, and it made him doubt whether he really loved her or if it was her feelings for him that were clouding his judgment. And if he did love her, did he love her as much as she deserved? As much as she loved him.

He knew exactly where she was at this very moment, and all it would take was for him to get up and start running, and he knew he could find his way straight to her, but he also knew that was not what she needed or wanted at the moment. But then he also wasn't really sure that was what he wanted at the moment. What would he say? What could he say? He was still confused himself.

Suddenly the image of a river dropping off the edge of a cliff filled his mind. He had no idea where the image had come from, and it was all consuming. It was all he could see. All of Ruby's tormented emotions were gone and all that was left was the image of the cliff and a gut-wrenching fear.

It took him a moment, but he quickly realized that the fear belonged to him. Ruby wasn't afraid, she wasn't feeling anything. The only thing that filled her mind was a river that dropped off the edge of a cliff. He knew it wasn't far from her and he knew she was running straight at it.

He knew there was a large lake below. He had seen it pass through her mind. He had also seen how far the cliff dropped in her mind. It seemed like a mile to him, but he felt a thought absently run through his head telling him it was only really about half a football field.

He had no idea what she was planning to do. She was past thinking about it, she was doing it, and he had been too overwhelmed and too busy trying not to listen to know what she had decided, but he had the feeling she planned to jump, and he was terrified.

Gabriel took off running for the cliff. Everything was suddenly perfectly clear to him. He wasn't confused any more. The only thing that mattered was making sure she was safe. He knew, surely, no human could survive that high a jump. Sure, she wasn't human, but he had no idea what a fall from this height would do to her. Hopefully, it wouldn't kill her.

Gabriel was terrified for her, and the emotion was just as all-consuming as her feelings for him had been before the cliff had entered her mind. He was terrified of what would happen to her, that he would never see her alive again, and that he would never be able to tell her that he loved her.

He had known it the second he had realized she planned to jump. With the only thought in her head being that of the cliff, he was able to separate their feelings, and he knew exactly how he felt about her. He had been able to tell instantly that he did love her, and he was terrified of losing her. He had doubted his feelings before because having her thoughts and feelings in his head was so overwhelming and he had been shocked to realize exactly how she felt about him. He wasn't used to having more than one person's thoughts in his head, but he could see it clearly now. Her feelings hadn't been clouding his judgment before, exactly the opposite. They had matched his own, it was exactly how he felt and that was why it had been so hard to tell them apart. But he knew the truth now, and he wanted to tell her. He wanted to tell her that he loved her. He knew she wanted to hear it, more than that, he knew she needed to hear it. He needed her to know, he needed her to not be in pain because she didn't know how he felt.

Gabriel knew the second she pushed off the edge of the cliff, and pushed himself to run even faster, if that was even possible. He could feel the wind rushing past him as if he had been the one to jump, and he could see the lake flying up at him. It was strange he could see the lake in his head crystal clear as if it actually was right in front of him and he had been the one to jump, but it wasn't. What was even stranger was that he could still see the forest around him perfectly clear, and the image of the lake didn't interfere in any way with his ability to run through the woods towards her.

He knew he wouldn't be able to reach her before she hit the water. Even if he did, what could he do? He couldn't stop her mid-air. He couldn't prevent her from hitting the water. He just hoped that she could survive the impact. He wouldn't be far behind and he could pull her out of the lake. Surely, with the way she could heal herself… all he needed was for her to survive the fall. Surely her body could take care of the rest and heal her, it had to. He couldn't even entertain the idea to the contrary. He'd only just met her, and he hadn't even had the chance to let her know exactly how he felt about her. He loved her and he couldn't stand the idea of going on without her.

Weirdly he felt a strange calm invading his body. It made no sense, he wasn't calm, he was far from calm. It had to be her. How could she be calm? She was plummeting through the air, possibly to her death, and all she felt was calm.

Gabriel felt her hit the water. He didn't feel any pain, she didn't seem to be hurt. All he could feel was that strange calm. He could feel her swimming towards the bottom of the lake. He was still running towards her. He still had to tell her how he felt.

He was dry on land, but he could feel the water all around him. It was pressing in on him. She wasn't coming up for air. He could feel her still sitting on the bottom of the lake. He knew she was alive. He could still feel her calm and the strange sensation of the water pressing in around him. If it weren't for the pressing need to get to her and make sure that she was safe, he was sure that he would feel as if he was suffocating under all that water and begin to panic. What on earth was she doing? She didn't feel hurt, but then why wasn't she coming back up for air?

He knew she wasn't human, but she still needed to breathe, didn't she? He had felt her breathing in his arms all night. She could be injured, she bled, and she had felt woozy when she had lost all that blood. Surely, she needed to breathe. It was driving him nuts. Why on earth wasn't she coming back up?

He continued to run for her. It felt like hours before he finally broke into the clearing at the top of the cliff, but he was sure it had only been minutes. Gabriel didn't hesitate. He ran head long at the cliff just as she had. He pushed off at the edge and felt himself flying through the air. He knew she was still alive, and surely the same jump she had taken couldn't kill him if it hadn't killed her. He was sure he could have found another, safer, way down to the lake, but he was in a hurry to get to her and had no reason to believe he wouldn't survive when she had survived. Besides, he wasn't sure he wanted to if she didn't.

Gabriel broke through the water surface and dove for the bottom where she sat. Gabriel grabbed Ruby from behind and began pulling her towards the surface. Ruby began fighting him the second he had grabbed her from behind, but he wasn't human anymore so she couldn't just break free of his hold like she could have before. When they broke the surface, Gabriel turned her around in his arms so that he could look at her. Not realizing it was him, Ruby continued to struggle trying to get away from him.

"Stop it. Ruby, it's me," he said easily grabbing both her fists in one of his and using his other hand to bring her in against his body to prevent her from struggling. Ruby finally fell still once she realized it was him. Gabriel could feel her confusion and her racing heart. Gabriel released her hands, but she kept them resting in fists against his chest unsure what to do with them. Gabriel stared down at her not sure where to begin, he had been so terrified for her.

"Don't you ever do that again," he said quickly bringing his hand up to circle the nape of her neck unable to stop himself from kissing her. He knew she didn't understand what he was talking about or why he was kissing her, but she didn't care. She kissed him back anyways, she loved him and if he wanted to kiss her, she wasn't going to stop him.

"God, I love you Ruby. Don't you ever do that again," he said as she trailed kisses along his jaw.

Suddenly she knew what was missing, what she had been unable to explain to him. It was the other half of the connection between them. She felt fangs in her mouth, she had never had fangs before, and she wanted to bite him. Not for his blood but to finish the bond between them. She didn't know how she knew but she knew, and her body and heart craved it more than she could put into words. It was as if she needed it to keep on breathing. He was her other half and she didn't know what she would do without him.

"Do it, Ruby," he said holding her to him.

The sound of his voice helped bring her back to reality. "No, I can't. It's not fair to you," she said trying to push herself away from him, but she couldn't not anymore. "You don't understand what you are asking. There will be no going back. We will be bound together forever."

"I know that's what I want. It's what you want. It's okay."

"Gabriel?" she questioned doubtfully.

"Ruby, it's alright. I feel it in you, the need, the ache. I know what it will do to us. It will bind us together. Just as I know and feel everything in your mind, you will know and feel everything in mine. It's alright it's what I want," he reassured.

"How could you possibly know that is what you want," she said trying to push herself out of his arms again. *Please let me go*, she thought struggling. She needed air he was too close, and the need was too strong. She didn't trust herself. She wanted to be irrevocably bound to him, but if she was going to do that to him, she had to be sure. She had already taken away his choice to choose death, she couldn't take this from him. She already knew she was going to have a hard time living with herself, but if she... she wouldn't be able to live with herself. She wouldn't be able to live with the thought that she'd... she'd taken everything from him. His life was... over, and he had her in his head, and if she... if she... his mind wouldn't be his own anymore. How could she think she loved him and do this to him? She'd never destroyed someone so completely. She'd never been so cruel.

Gabriel loosened his arms around her but only because he knew she wasn't planning on running. She had thought about it, but she couldn't, more than anything she wanted convincing that this was what he wanted and that it wasn't because of her thoughts and feelings in his head. She needed this too much to run.

Ruby brought her knees up to her chest and used her feet to push off of him and flip herself backwards into the water. He felt her twist around in the water and swim a small distance away from him. She came up much closer to the edge of the lake, but she didn't make a move to get out. She had only moved close enough to the edge that her feet could touch the bottom. She was waiting for him to come to her. He could feel it.

Gabriel dove under the water and came up right in front of her. As he stood up, he towered over her. He felt her heart start racing and couldn't help but smile. She had never realized how big he was. She had known factually that he was a lot taller than her and that he was a lot more physically built than her, but she had never thought twice about it. She had known she was still stronger than him, the one in control, but now that she looked up at him, she realized that she wasn't. But her heart didn't race from fear, no, quite the opposite, it raced with excitement, to not be the one in control, to be able to let herself go, to not have to be in control, to be free.

Gabriel had to stop himself from reaching out to touch her. Wanting to pull her back into his arms, wanting to kiss her, wanting her. "Ruby, I love you, and I don't want to be apart from you. I want to finish this bond between us. I want you to know how I feel. I know that I love you and I want you to know," he said bringing his hand up to cup her face unable to stop himself, "I know you don't believe me that you think it's cause of my connection to you, but it's not. I was confused at first because it was weird being connected to you and not because I don't want to be but because I'm not used to it and didn't understand it, and it's still hard to get used to but I know how I feel about you. I know the only way you will believe it is if you feel it for yourself. Plus, aside from the fact that this is what I want, I think it will be easier on both of us once the connection is completed," he tried to convince her.

How so? she couldn't help but think.

"Ruby, I hate feeling your torment and so much of that is because you know I know how you feel about me, and your shame and embarrassment about that because you didn't get the choice to tell me it was taken from you. I think had you been able to tell me before, this wouldn't bother you nearly as much, I think you might have been slightly embarrassed because well it's weird having someone in your head, but not like you are now and I think once you know how I feel and believe me when I say I love you, you won't care anymore. And if you don't believe that, if nothing else then it will be fair. Just as much as I know your inner secret thoughts and feelings you will know mine and I won't feel nearly as guilty."

Except that I love you and to me this is a commitment. One there is no turning back from, she thought looking down at the water.

Gabriel's hand slid around her neck and he tilted her head up with his thumb under her chin so that she was looking at him. "Trust me, this is a commitment I want to make. And if you can't, and you truly love me like I know you do, you will respect me enough to do as I ask as opposed to me having to trick you into biting me as you did for me. Because I will if I have to." He knew that hurt her, but he did not intend to. He knew she had done it for him and not to him and he would do the same for her. As much as he wanted to finish the bond with her, he also knew that she needed it and it would be completed one way or another of that he was sure.

Ruby looked up at him nervously, she still wasn't entirely sure, but she could tell from the look in his eyes that he had made up his mind, he was sure it was what he wanted. She just hoped he didn't regret it later.

"I won't," he said looking down at her. She was going to do it. Gabriel stepped closer to her as he leaned down to kiss her. He knew she would do it she wasn't going to fight it anymore but the least he could do was help distract her. Besides he liked kissing her and was having a hard time keeping his hands off her. Ruby brought her hands up to fist in his shirt while he kissed her long and hard. Gabriel lifted her up and wrapped her legs around his waist. He felt her surprise and excitement at his obvious need pressing against her. God how he needed her, and it was driving him nuts. He felt her let go of his T-shirt and wrapped her arms around his neck as she bit into his jugular.

He was surprised, he thought it would hurt even if only for a second, but it didn't. There was no pain, only pleasure. He knew most but not all of it was because of her. The pleasure she got from joining them mentally together forever. There was also a deep feeling of satisfaction and completeness, and he knew that was both of them. He knew this was right that they were supposed to be joined like this. He had never realized anything was missing before but now being joined with her he knew he had been missing her.

Ruby licked her tongue up the column of his neck and raised her head to look at him. She didn't see or feel any repulsion or disgust but maybe it hadn't finished yet. Gabriel didn't give her any more time to think, he pulled her tighter against him and slanted her head for better access as he resumed kissing her. *I've never bitten anyone before, I've never wanted or needed to*, she thought to try and explain to him.

I know, he thought in response. She could feel it then an all-consuming hunger, a sexual hunger, one that matched if not surpassed her own. She had barely been able to control herself before around him and now knowing his feelings she couldn't and wouldn't. His need and hunger only made her need him more it drove her crazy. She slid her hands down his chest pulling at his shirt to find the hem. She slid her hands underneath so she could feel and touch him, skin to skin. Ruby slid his shirt up further, he knew what she wanted, and he helped her remove his shirt for her. She slid her hands over his chest outlining each muscle as he slid his hands under the edge of her cropped long sleeve shirt to cup her breasts in his hands. He more than heard her intake of breath he felt it as if it was his own. He kissed her deeply as he began gently massaging her breasts. He raised the edge of her top to expose her breasts to him. He broke his kiss to replace one of his hands on her breasts with his mouth. Ruby gasped in pleasure bringing her hands up to bury in his hair. She threaded her hands in his hair and held him to her.

Ruby moved to pull her top off, she didn't care that they were out in the open. She knew the panthers lived nearby and that any one of them, could have wondered past or heard them and stopped. All that mattered was Gabriel. She felt it the moment he realized they were out in the open. He had picked up on the fact that she didn't care. He hadn't seen anyone out here and he knew she hadn't either, but then neither of them had been looking. He didn't want to take her like this, out in the open where anyone could be watching, not for their first time, not for her first time, but he didn't want to stop, and she didn't want him to stop which didn't help. *Behind the falls*, she thought trying to help him as she continued to kiss him and run her hands over his body. At least then they would be shielded from any possible eyes.

Gabriel thought back to her launching herself off of him earlier and she knew what he wanted, he wanted her to head for the falls. But this time when she pushed off from him, he helped launching her in the air. She twisted around in the air, dove into the water, and immediately began heading for the area behind the falls. Unlike last time Gabriel didn't wait and watch her, the second she was out of his hands he took off after her. She barely had time to turn around before he was pulling her back into his arms. Gabriel helped remove her top the rest of the way. He couldn't help the sharp intake of breath as he stared at her. Ruby smiled at his response as she looked up at him.

Gabriel began to back her up towards the cliff face behind the fall. Ruby was relieved to find that this far behind the falls and close to the wall the water was shallow enough for her to stand in. The water only came up to just above her belly button. Ruby bumped up against the wall preventing her from going any further back. Gabriel pressed in against her as he lowered his head to hers. He could feel her breasts pressing in against his chest, he could feel her excitement, her need. They still weren't close enough, he needed all of her and he knew she felt the same way.

Ruby could feel his hard need pressing against her stomach. He had done his best to hold back before trying to protect her knowing despite how many people she had killed, just how truly innocent she was in this regard, and she couldn't help but love him more for that, but she didn't want him holding back she wanted him. She could feel his hard length rubbing against her uncontrollably as he kissed her. She could feel it, he couldn't and wouldn't hold himself back anymore, and she didn't have to hold herself back anymore. She could let herself want him and have him, and she didn't have to worry about hurting him.

Gabriel spotted a shelf in the wall a couple feet down. He moved them over so that he could lift her up to sit on the ledge. Gabriel's hands remained on her waist as he trailed kisses over her jaw and down her throat. Ruby arched her back and brought her hands up to hold on to his shoulders as he kissed his way between her breasts and down across her flat hard abdomen. His hands slid down from her waist to her hips and traced the edge of her pants around to the front until his hands met at the button. Gabriel looked up into her face to see if she would stop him. Or maybe rather if she would try because he wasn't sure he could or would stop even if she tried to stop him.

Gabriel didn't sense any hesitation in her, and he was sure she knew how little he was in control. He felt her use her mind to unbutton her pants. Gabriel unzipped her zipper and slid his hands inside her pants and slipped them around to the back to cup her bottom in his hands. *Dear god she wasn't wearing any underwear.* She could feel his shock and excitement at the knowledge. Gabriel lifted her up slightly to lower her pants down her bottom, he pushed them down her thighs and began to pull them off completely.

She could feel his need and hunger increasing as he revealed her to himself. Ruby couldn't help but feel complete happiness and incredible excitement at the knowledge of how badly he wanted her. His fingers trailed lightly over her calves then over her knees and across her thighs towards her hot need that burned for him. She wanted him to touch her, no she needed him to touch her. Ruby's hands slid down his chest to tangle her fingers in the belt loops of his jeans. Ruby tugged gently on his pants to pull him closer to her as she opened her legs to him so that he could stand between them and have complete access to her. One hand came up to cup her head in his hand as he leaned down to kiss her while the other slid between her legs.

Gabriel slowly slid one finger inside her testing to see if she was ready for him. He withdrew his finger and inserted two stretching her, she was so tight. *Gabriel*, she moaned in his head as she continued to kiss him, and her hands slid to the button on his pants. *I need you in me.*

You are so tight, my love, he thought withdrawing and reinserting his fingers slowly. *I don't want to hurt you.*

I know you would never hurt me. I trust you.

I know you do, but I'm not a small man and it's your first time. It might be a little uncomfortable at first, he thought as he continued stroking her.

It's okay, Gabriel. I trust you. And she did, he could feel it that and her need of him, but her complete trust was the only thing helping him stay in control enough to take it as slow as he was which he knew wasn't really all that slow but it was slower than both their desires wanted him to go and they both knew it.

Hello little one, is that you? I know someone is out there. I can hear you. Come out or I will drag you out.

Gabriel lifted his head from her and withdrew his fingers but maintained his hold on her as he continued to look down at her. *Who is that and why is HE inside my head*, he asked more than a little confused and for some reason infuriated? He knew she was surprised and upset that the mood was ruined but she wasn't confused. And she didn't seem surprised or afraid by his anger she seemed to understand why he was angry more than he did, and she felt apologetic, submissive even in response.

That's Felix, a panther, she answered him her eyes sliding from his to look at his chest.

You mean he is an animal literally and can speak like people? he asked watching her closely.

No like a werewolf or shapeshifter so to speak but a panther, she answered him weakly.

Why is he in my head or is he in yours and why? he asked more anger than he intended getting through. Who the hell was HE? He'd gotten the impression he was the only one who could talk to her like this.

Ruby continued to stare at his chest. He knew she could feel his anger and he could feel her response. She knew he wasn't angry at her directly, but she felt bad and was worried that he was upset with her and was going to start regretting his decision. She didn't want to lose him when she'd just gotten him. Her chest hurt. She could feel him slipping through her fingers. She really was cursed.

Ruby, he said forcing himself to soften his tone as he tilted her head up so he could gently brush a brief kiss across her lips. *I'm not going anywhere, now tell me what is going on,* he said trying to reassure her but for some reason he had taken an immediate dislike to whoever this guy was and it was making it hard for him to control himself, but he had absolutely no intention of letting her go.

He's in both our heads, some panthers in their animal form can project their thoughts for communication but they can't hear us, and I wouldn't or couldn't respond to him. He knows I'm out here and so he's projecting over this area, she told him still worried.

How does he know you are out here? he asked suspicious.

I don't know. He could have seen us or heard us or someone else could have told him. Gabriel, if I don't go out there, he will come looking for me, she told him grudgingly. He knew she didn't want to go out there and deal with him, she wished he hadn't shown up and interrupted them.

Alright, he said looking down at her, *but you are not going out there by yourself.* It wasn't that he was worried about him hurting her it was more that he just didn't like him and didn't want him alone with her.

I need my clothes, she told him glancing up at him from under her lashes.

I like you better without clothes, he said looking her up and down causing her to blush.

Yes well, I would imagine you would prefer I was wearing clothes when I go out to tell Felix to go away. They were both surprised when he growled in response. Ruby smiled up at him slyly, half wanting to chuckle at his response.

Gabriel stepped away from her to look for her clothes in the water, luckily thanks to the falls they were right where he had dropped them. Gabriel bent down to pick up her clothes and then handed her pants to her to put on while he held her shirt for her. He watched her breasts bounce as she slid from the cliff shelf and worked to pull her tight pants back on in the water. He was well aware that she knew he was staring at her breasts and he didn't care.

As soon as she was done, he pulled her back into his arms. *We're not done*, he said letting her know they would pick this back up later as he leaned down to kiss her one more time. It was like she couldn't decide what to say in response, he heard three different responses float at him all at the same time, *good, I know, we better not be*, but what hit him the most was her relief. He hadn't realized just how worried she was about his reaction and what it meant for them. Gabriel finally broke their kiss and handed her shirt to her. Ruby quickly pulled her shirt back on. *We need to find you my shirt to put on also.*

Gabriel, she asked confused.

Her shirt may have covered up her breasts, but it still didn't leave anything to the imagination. *That shirt is tight, and the water is cold,* he said staring at her erect nipples through her shirt.

I'll find your shirt on the way to the water's edge, she said blushing up at him and the ideas she could see dancing through his head, all involving her breasts currently.

I don't like this, he said as he watched her dive down into the water to go find his shirt.

I know. Ruby pulled on his shirt underwater and resurfaced in the middle of the lake.

Gabriel came up near the water's edge between her and Felix but he didn't get out he waited for her to come closer before he began to climb out. Once he was on solid ground he turned around and reached down for her hand to help her out of the water. His gaze couldn't help but linger on her. His shirt helped in some ways and not so much in others. It helped hide her breasts a little bit better but with his shirt being soaking wet it also clung to her curves emphasizing her waist and her hips.

"Who the hell are you?" Felix asked as Gabriel turned around to face him

"I don't like him, Ruby," Gabriel said looking him up and down like he was assessing an enemy for a fight.

"I don't care what you think," he said turning to look Ruby up and down as she was wringing out her hair. Gabriel was just about to take a swing at him when she looked up and froze them both in place.

Ruby let me go, he thought.

"In a moment," she said out loud.

Ruby? he questioned.

"Gabriel, I'm not going to let you kill him," she told him out loud even as she couldn't stop from thinking, *not yet.*

We'll see about that, he mumbled ready to kill the guy for looking at her.

"Gabriel this is Felix, Felix this is Gabriel, my..."

Mate, he said in her head. She didn't know what to call him and he knew that was the word she was wanting to use.

"Really?" she asked turning around to look up at him and forgetting for a moment that Felix was there. She struggled to keep from releasing him so that she could move back into his arms and resume kissing him. She had a mate she couldn't help but think smiling up at him.

Yes, he said imagining caressing her face with his hand. He could feel her happiness. He wanted her back in his arms. He didn't like her holding him away from her like this. He was her mate and he was going to kill Felix.

"My mate," she said staring at him a moment longer before forcing herself to turn back around.

Ruby released Felix just enough so that he could talk but not enough that he could move. She didn't need him doing anything stupid.

"Your mate, since when? I don't like him, and I don't need you to protect me from him, I can defend myself."

"Maybe you can defend yourself but not against him and certainly not against me," she said plainly as if it was a fact that they all knew.

"Ruby," Felix asked surprised.

"I can assure you he can take you and he will kill you. He really does not like you," she admitted easily.

"I'm not alone, the men are in the woods," Felix told her unfazed.

'Neither is he' she wanted to say but didn't, but Gabriel heard it and couldn't help but smile inwardly as she narrowed her eyes at Felix and asked "why?" menacingly.

"We came to help you."

"Me, do I look like I need help?" she asked sardonically.

"No, but Sheila said she saw you or someone she thought was you struggling with a man out here and she came to get me. I figured if it was you and someone was actually strong enough to struggle with you, I might need them."

"How is little Sheila?" she asked pleasantly as if they weren't having a conversation involving death threats.

"Pregnant which is why she came to get me as opposed to trying to help you herself."

"Really, who's the lucky father to be?" she asked curious.

"I am."

He has a mate, Gabriel thought at her. *A pregnant mate and he was looking at you like that.* Despite being frozen in place they could hear him growl in response. He was struggling against her hold and he would be able to break it sooner rather than later especially if he was already able to growl against her hold. She needed to hurry this along.

"Are you sure you are alright?" he asked doubtfully. "I don't like the look of him, and I certainly don't like the way he looks at you."

"Well the feeling is mutual. He doesn't like how you look at me either," she informed him.

"You're communicating with him," he said suddenly realizing why she hadn't released him enough to talk, she didn't need to.

"And I don't care whether or not you like how he looks at me, I like how he looks at me."

"Him?" he asked looking at him disdainfully.

This time she growled in response. "Yes him, and I suggest you stop questioning my decision and provoking him if you want to see tomorrow." *Gabriel, please stop struggling.*

He could hear the strain in her head. *Then let me go*, he told her unable to control his disgust for this panther as he continued to struggle in an attempt to get at him. The sooner she let him go, the sooner he could kill him and calm down, and resume kissing his mate.

"Not just yet. I need you to understand why I'm restraining you from killing him at the moment," she said turning her head to look at him.

"I told you I'm not alone," Felix piped up.

"And neither is he. He is my mate and if you provoke him or attack him, I will stand by him and I can assure you, we will be the ones to come out alive. Do you really want to sentence your tribe to that?" she asked him bluntly.

"You love him that much that you would wipe out my tribe?" he asked shocked unable to believe what he was hearing. Everyone knew how powerful she was and not to mess with her, but she'd never done anything out right malicious. She'd always been methodical, logical, but this was... insane.

"Yes, I have warned you. After this whatever happens is on you. And spread the word to the other tribes also and tell them to spread it too," she told him authoritatively. He may be in charge of his tribe, but all the tribe leaders knew that she stood above them. They existed because she let them. But now, Gabriel would be included by her side above them. He was her mate and they would respect that. And if not... well, then they ultimately meant little to her. Only Gabriel mattered.

Gabriel, she thought turning around to look at him. *I will stand by you, whatever decision you make, but please don't, not today. I know you don't like him, but I've known him since he was a child. I've known his entire line for centuries. I wouldn't call him a 'friend' per se, and I can't say I really even think of him as family, but I would hate to see him die especially at your hands. Please just not today, not the day*

I will remember as the time I first got to call you my mate, please, she pleaded looking up at him. *Give yourself some time to think about it, and if we run into him again, it's on him. He's been warned, and I won't stop you if you need to attack him,* she said knowing that didn't change the fact that it would still hurt her if he died. She'd protected not just the panthers but all the animals from the humans for a very long time and the thought of seeing any of them die at his hands hurt, but if it was what he needed to do... she'd standby him. She couldn't lose him but then maybe knowing how much it would hurt her would help him to restrain himself and if not... she'd hurt and then get past it as long as she had him.

Ruby let us go, he said gently.

Ruby nodded her head. She'd said her bit and now it was time to let the cards fall where they may. She released them and almost immediately began to collapse.

Gabriel caught her before she could hit the ground. "Ruby," he called to her. "Stay back," he hissed looking up as Felix tried to step closer to her. "What's happening? What do you want me to do?" he asked looking back down at her.

Take me home, she told him. *Our home,* she couldn't help but add as he took off running for the house. *Ours,* she sighed happily.

He didn't bother questioning how but he knew exactly how to get home. *Ruby, what's wrong?* he asked worried as he continued running.

I'm sorry, she thought to him.

Don't you dare say that.

I'll be fine, Gabriel, she reassured realizing he was worried about losing her. *But I am sorry. I didn't want to hold you like that and I'll never do it again, but I had to make sure that you both understood the decisions you were making before there was no going back,* she apologized softly.

That's what this is, isn't? It's because you were holding us like that, he accused.

There had been a number of things that had led to her current state, but that had been a big part of it. *And because you were struggling,* she didn't want to think it but she couldn't control it and she knew it made him feel bad which only made her feel bad cause she didn't want him to feel bad for caring about her so much. That's why he was angry and disliked Felix so much, because he loved her and didn't want or rather wouldn't lose her. He had no idea who Felix was or whether or not he was a challenge to his hold on her. It was all still so new, but she was his.

You are? He asked hesitantly but needing to know.

Of course, just as you are mine. I would let you kill Felix or anyone else you thought was trying to come between us. And I can assure you, I will kill anyone who tries to come between us including women, especially women. You are mine and I won't let you go, she admitted as she laid unmoving in his arms with her head resting against his chest as he quickly carried her through the woods towards their house. She wasn't going to give him up to anyone. He had chosen to let her finish the bond between them. He was hers. Any women that tried to come between them would have her to deal with.

That's why you thought I might regret it, he laughed softly.

Well not everyone likes their women being jealous murderesses, she told him shrewdly.

It doesn't bother me, but then I think it helps that all I want is you, he reassured her unconcerned since he knew there would be no reason for her to be jealous. He only had eyes for her.

Yes, but as you saw it's not just about what you want or do, someone looking at you the wrong way might be all it takes, she told him honestly. She was worried about how she might react in a similar situation. Or rather what he'd really think because she knew if she had been him, she'd have killed Felix.

I think I'll take my chances, he told her unconcerned. All he cared about was her being safe and happy and in his arms. *Are you sure you are going to be alright?* he asked worriedly as he redirected the subject back to her current state as he entered the house and headed for her room.

Our room, she corrected him, *and yes, I just need some rest. You're not human anymore and it takes a lot of effort to hold you like that especially when you are fighting it as much as you were. You may not know how to control it, but you are a lot stronger now. I was only able to control you for that long because you don't know how to control it, but it wouldn't have been much longer before you would have broken my hold. The prior events earlier tonight with the vampires didn't exactly help either,* she told him.

Gabriel laid her down on the bed before he realized she was still soaking wet.

I should be cold, shouldn't I? she thought remembering she was wet at his realization.

You're not? he asked worried.

No, I don't feel cold, she admitted.

I'll be right back. Let me get a towel and we'll dry you off. Gabriel grabbed a couple towels and his shirt that she had worn to bed last night that he spotted hanging off a door handle. She appeared to like wearing his shirt and he needed to get her out of her cold, wet clothes. All he could think about was her, he had no idea what was wrong with her, and even though he had only known her for a few days he knew he didn't want to live without her. He needed her to be alright, but she wasn't even cold. She should be freezing.

She should be shaking like a leaf. He couldn't lose her. He didn't know this would be the result when he'd ignored her when she'd told him to stop struggling.

Gabriel, he heard her call in his head and she sounded panicked. He ran back in the room to check on her, she hadn't moved a muscle.

What's wrong? he asked sitting down on the bed and pulling her into his lap.

It's not me, it's you. I can feel your terror for me. It's overwhelming. He pulled her closer against his chest as he tightened his hold on her trying to comfort himself. *I'm going to be fine, Gabriel. I just need some sleep, it's like when I was...* she couldn't even say it because she knew how he felt about it. All she could do was picture the wound she had gotten the first night they met. *I just need some rest so that my body can heal or rather renew itself.*

You're sure you will be alright? He questioned doubtfully.

Yes, she said softly as she imagined brushing her fingertips along his jaw.

Then why are you still awake? he asked wanting to know even though he wasn't really sure he could handle her going to sleep.

Because my mate is terrified and doesn't want me to go to sleep, she said softly.

Let's get you dried off, he hated that his wanting her to be awake was causing her to stay awake. If she needed to go to sleep to feel better, then he wanted her to go to sleep as long as she would indeed wake up.

Gabriel, I know that makes logical sense but that doesn't change the fact that I can feel your emotions. You're terrified of losing me and of what will happen if I go to sleep. I know you want me to ignore your feelings and go to sleep. That as long as I wake up fine, it doesn't matter how you feel right

*now you just want me to be alright, but I can't. I love you
and the thought of just going to sleep when you feel like this
is unbearable to me. I need you to calm down,* she told him
gently wanting to comfort him. It hurt to feel him like this
and know she was the cause of his distress.

Gabriel quickly finished undressing her and drying her
off. Pulling back the covers, he gently slid her into bed and
pulled the covers back up around her and brought his hand
up to her face brushing his fingertips longingly over her
cheek in a caress. When he looked at her it was like he was
seeing two different realities. In front of him in real life he
could see her lying in bed not moving at all it was like she
was already asleep or worse, but in his head he could see her
looking up at him lovingly, he could feel her fingertips on
his face he could feel her rest her hand on his arm, he could
feel her trying to make him feel better.

*How am I not supposed to worry about what will happen
when you go to sleep? What will it feel like when you go to
sleep?* he asked suddenly realizing a better question right
now he could feel her in his head and see the two different
realities because she was awake. What would happen when
she was asleep? The other nights when she had slept in his
arms he had felt her breathing but she had gone for some
time underwater without breathing did she need to breath
and when she couldn't seem to voluntarily move her body
and her body seemed to want to shut down. What would
happen to her breathing? How would he know she was still
alive?

Gabriel take off your pants and get into bed, she told him.

What? he thought shocked.

*I want you to hold me, I want to be in your arms even if I
can't feel them right now, besides you can, and you need to be
able to hold me right now,* she told him gently.

But are you sure you want me to take my pants off? he asked warily.

Yes, they're wet and probably cold, besides you're only worried about crawling into bed with me naked, because we didn't finish what we started out at the lake and you think it might make me uncomfortable.

It won't? he questioned wanting to be sure.

Gabriel, you are my mate and we will finish what we started out there, not right now, but we will and in the meantime I want to be in your arms and you need to be able to feel your mate in your arms right now, she told him trying to do the only thing she could think of to try and help comfort him. She wanted to crawl into his arms and hold on to him. She felt safe there and she knew it would be reassuring to him to have her actually move into his arms, but she couldn't. She was struggling just to stay conscious.

Gabriel quickly took off his wet pant and dried off and then climbed into bed with Ruby. He pulled her gently into his arms resting her head against his chest. In some ways, it felt just like yesterday being able to hold her in his arms and feel her breathing in and out, but he was still worried what would happen when she fell asleep, especially now that they were connected the way they were.

I can't pretend to have all the answers, Gabriel, but I shouldn't stop breathing, maybe if I was physical injured in a way that would affect breathing but I'm not. I'm still breathing now and even underwater I was breathing just not in a way you would recognize it might slow down a little more when I'm asleep but that's normal it shouldn't be too slow that you wouldn't feel it unless it actually ceased which it shouldn't, she tried to reassure him.

You were breathing underwater? he asked needing to know. If she had been breathing underwater that meant she definitely needed to breath.

It's hard to explain but yes, she reassured him.

That helps, he said, and she could feel it did, but she could feel he was still worried about their connection.

I don't know what will happen when I go to sleep. I don't know if you will see my dreams, I don't know if you can choose or not, I don't know if you will just feel how my dreams make me feel, or... she couldn't bring herself to say what he was worried about and that was not being able to feel her and mentally connect with her when she was asleep.

Gabriel, I don't know for sure, but I can't imagine that we wouldn't still be able to connect when we are asleep. And she couldn't, the bond they had was amazing, but even though they were connected she still felt the overwhelming need in both of them to be able to reach out and touch the other both mentally and physically to reconfirm that they were alright. *The need is just too great for us to not be able to reach out to one another even when one or both of us is asleep. I could even see me or whichever of us is asleep reaching out to know the other is there.*

You really believe that? he asked hesitantly.

You know I do, she said imagining bringing her hand up to rest on his chest.

Gabriel slid his hand down her arm to her hand and brought it up to hold against his chest since she couldn't really hold it there.

Close your eyes, she told him gently.

What? he questioned thinking the idea ludicrous.

Gabriel, I need to sleep and I'm hoping if you stop seeing me with your eyes and only feel me with our bond you might relax enough for us or at least me to go to sleep. She hated this. She knew it made him feel bad that she was staying awake because of him. She knew how he felt, and she knew she would feel the same way if it was reversed and she didn't want to make him feel worse. She wished she could stay awake until he was comfortable. She wished that she wasn't like this the first time they went to sleep while they were bonded, then they would know what to expect. Every second she stayed awake was a struggle and she wasn't sure how much longer she would last. She was hoping this would help him relax. It hurt to think of how he would feel when she finally hit that point that she could no longer maintain consciousness and passed out without warning.

Gabriel closed his eyes reluctantly. He could still see her right there in his arms. Ruby moved closer to him if that was possible, he knew he was already holding her pretty tight. He felt her brush her lips against his chest.

How? he asked looking down at her.

Because we are connected mentally and without you distracted by what you would actually see, you can see what I see in my head, what I wish I had the energy to do and I can see what you would do in response, she told him looking up at him. She could feel his surprise to find them suddenly dressed and standing as he continued looking down into her face relieved to see her beautiful eyes looking at him again.

Ruby stepped away from him taking his hand in hers. *Come with me,* she said walking towards the door.

Where are we going? he asked looking over her head to the dark hallway. He couldn't see anything even though somehow, he knew he had night vision.

Just trust me, she reassured him.

As they stepped through the doorway, they were suddenly falling. There had been no floor outside the door.

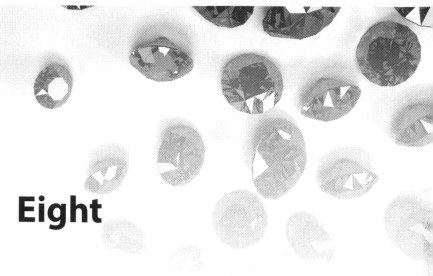

Eight

All the sudden they hit the ground or at least he did, he lifted himself up to see where they were at and to make sure Ruby was alright. Ruby was nowhere near him. He was laying in the middle of an open area of grass surrounded by forest with a brilliant star filled sky overhead wearing black jeans and a black T-shirt. "Ruby," he called standing up.

"Who are you?" he heard behind him and turned around to see Ruby there dressed in black leathers.

Gabriel ran over to pull her into his arms relieved that she was alright.

"Who the hell are you? Get off of me," she said twisting herself out of his arms.

"Ruby, it's me, Gabriel. What's wrong?" he asked worried.

"I have no idea who you are and who the hell is Ruby," she asked.

"This isn't funny, Ruby."

"I'll say. My name isn't Ruby, and I would like you to stop calling me 'Ruby' before I hurt you. And I want to know what the hell you are doing out here," she demanded.

"You're serious," he realized looking down at her not understanding what was going on.

"Deadly," she told him narrowing her eyes at him.

"I don't understand," he said running his fingers through his hair. "I don't know what I'm doing here. I just kind of landed here. One minute I was with Ruby at the house and then I was here. What is your name then?" he asked since she seemed adamant that she wasn't 'Ruby' as he looked her up and down.

"Flame and one doesn't just land here. We are in the middle of nowhere on private property."

"You're here," he said pointedly.

"Well, it's my property. Stop looking at me like that," she said launching herself at him and tackling him to the ground.

He looked up to realize they had landed with her straddling him. Gabriel took a strangled breath, god she looked like Ruby, he wanted to reach up and pull her down against his chest and kiss her. "Like what?" he asked after catching his breath as he continued to stare at her longingly. He started to reach up to touch her again unable to stop himself. He wanted his Ruby.

Flame's eyes opened wide and then she was gone in a blink of an eye.

Gabriel slowly sat up and looked around, he was alone again. But where the hell was he? And where was Ruby? Gabriel slowly got to his feet again and turned around to look around the clearing he was in and spotted a blonde wearing a red dress swaying in the wind, when she turned around, he realized she too was Ruby. "Ruby," he called quietly.

"Oh, a dancing partner," she said excited as she headed over to him. "What's your name handsome and what are you doing all the way out here by your lonesome?" she asked bubbly, clearly flirting with him.

Confused Gabriel looked down at her and discovered he was wearing a tux. "Gabriel," he said realizing this too wasn't

Ruby. "And who are you?" he asked trying to remain calm as his agitation was mounting at not finding Ruby, his mate.

"Well, I'm Scarlet of course," she said seductively. "And you are going to ask me to dance, aren't you?" she asked stepping closer and placing his hand on her waist not waiting to see if he'd ask or not as ballroom music was suddenly playing. Gabriel danced with her for a time until another Ruby showed up and interrupted them. What the hell was going on?

"You can leave now, Scarlet," she said dismissing her.

"And who are you?" he asked as he turned around, realizing his clothes had changed back to jeans and a t-shirt. This Ruby looked more normal, wearing simply jeans and a blue t-shirt with brunette hair. He knew instantly this wasn't Ruby, for several reasons. But she looked very serene, he wished this calm for Ruby. Where was she?

"My name is Serenity." He couldn't help but notice how appropriate her name seemed. "I'm sorry about Scarlet she can be a little brazen and well of course Flame can be a little hot headed. I'll leave you now." And she was gone in a flash right before his eyes.

It wasn't long before another Ruby appeared this one not as... pleasant or talkative. They'd scrimmaged for a while before she too finally left.

"Hello, Gabriel," a little girl he hadn't noticed before sitting in the grass called.

Gabriel moved to sit down beside her where she was picking flowers to make into jewelry that she was wearing. "And what is your name?" he asked more sadly than softly. He wanted his Ruby back in his arms where he knew she was safe.

"You can call me Rose," she said as she suddenly picked up a rose that was sitting beside her on the ground and turned it this way and that to look at and then handed it to him.

"That's a pretty name," he said taking the rose from her not knowing what else to do.

"I'm glad she is gone," she told him as she continued playing with the flowers.

"Who?" he asked confused.

"The last one, Lilith. She is mean and scary. The others are just different. Though to give Lilith credit, I think she just hurts, and wants someone else to feel her pain too," she told him almost confidentially it seemed like.

"She didn't seem so bad," he disagreed looking at the rose he was still holding. She hadn't seemed that terrible and he could certainly understand the desire to make someone else hurt when you were in pain. Though to be fair they hadn't really talked. She'd come straight at him immediately launching into an attack. She'd fought well… reminded him of Ruby now that he thought about it. He'd been too busy blocking her blows and sparing with her to stop and dwell on it. It had helped distract him even if only briefly from how much he missed her.

"Hmmm, maybe that's a good thing," Rose said tilting her head to the side as she looked at him curiously for a moment before returning her attention back to her flowers. "Hi, Jade," Rose called without looking up.

Gabriel looked around and found another Ruby or Jade as Rose had called her, she looked a little younger and kind of sad her hair was jet black with green highlights. "Hi, Rose," she responded. Gabriel watched as she walked across the clearing and then disappeared from sight.

"I don't understand, Rose, where is Ruby?" he asked somehow knowing this child knew, this child who he suspected was another Ruby also.

"We are Ruby. And you must protect her," she told him not looking up and sounding more like a weird fortune cookie than a child.

"I don't understand, what do you mean 'we are Ruby'? And I'm not sure that is really necessary," Gabriel said thinking how well she could fight, but he also had no intention of letting her go it alone anymore. He would be by her side no matter what whether she wanted him there or not.

"It is. She fights for everyone without hesitation or thought for herself, but no one fights for her, for us. No one keeps her safe. She struggles to keep us all together," she shrugged halfheartedly.

He could feel a sharp pain in his chest that he rubbed at absently, he knew the little girl was right she fought for everyone but herself. And he'd seen her starting to fall apart on more than one occasion. Trying to keep it all in, he suspected afraid to just breakdown, because as Rose said 'no one was fighting for her'. She didn't feel safe to be able to breakdown and cry. "I will, I swear, I won't let anyone hurt her, not ever, but I'm not sure I'm necessary or maybe I'm just not sure she'll let me," he admitted to the little girl.

"But you are necessary, and you don't need her to let you… or rather, she won't let you, but you mustn't listen to her. She needs you to protect her from herself, and from you. She may not look it, but she is delicate with only one heart that has already had to endure a lot over these long years, and whether you meant to or not you've already stolen it. You hold her demise in your hand."

"That's why she ran from me," he sighed knowing it was the truth. "I'd never hurt her, she knows that now," he whispered.

"There's knowing and there's *knowing*. She needs to *know*, she needs you to show her," Rose corrected him.

"You are very wise for one so young," he commented softly.

"I'm not as young as I look," she contradicted him while smiling.

"I'm still confused," he admitted.

"You followed her into her dreams, did you not?" she asked softly.

"Yes, but…" he looked up and Rose too was gone.

Was this her dream? This was a weird way to dream. Are these all parts of Ruby, but why would she dream of them like this, and why now?

"Gabriel," someone called softly. This time it was Ruby, he was sure. She was wearing his shirt and she walked straight to him.

"Oh Ruby, my love," he smiled reaching up to help her to the ground beside him.

She moved to lay her head on his thigh. "I'm so very tired, Gabriel," she told him with a yawn as she curled up beside him.

"It's alright. Get some rest, my love," he sighed brushing her hair back from her face, relieved to have her by his side again. His Ruby, but then Rose had said they were all Ruby. Were they all trying to meet him, in a manner of speaking? Were these pieces of her past, split personalities from being alone, or were they just figments? Had his Ruby only reappeared, because he'd met them and passed some sort of unofficial test? He knew his Ruby knew he loved her, but did she need him to see them, or had they needed to approve or make sure he'd protect them too? Or was he being crazy, and it was just a dream? Either way, his Ruby was here with him, and he would protect her, or all of them if need be.

He stroked his hand through her hair, then tangled his hand with hers that was resting on his leg next to her face. He discovered a tree trunk was suddenly right behind him and leaned back against it to rest as he watched her sleep using his thigh for a pillow while he made sure she was safe.

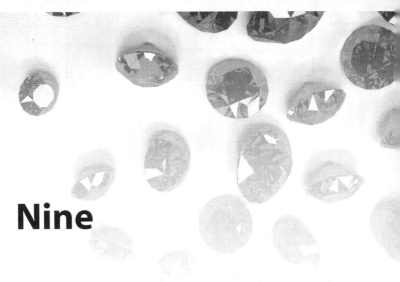

Nine

Gabriel knew the second Ruby was awake. "Ruby," he called softly.

"Gabriel," Ruby responded drowsily, she was still exhausted.

"Why are you awake? You need some more sleep," he chided sensing her exhaustion. "Are you alright?" he asked softly.

"I'm fine, I was just worried about you. I wanted to check on you. Are you alright? How long have I been out?" she asked realizing it was daylight now.

"About twelve hours," he answered kissing the top of her head.

"I'm sorry," she said slowly moving closer to him. "I didn't realize I would be out so long. How are you doing?" She asked worried about how he was after her being asleep for twelve hours.

"I'm alright," he said softly. "I'm just glad you seem to be doing better, but you need some more sleep. I can feel it you're still tired."

"I know," she said brushing her fingers against his chest. "What was it like?" she asked softly.

"What?" he asked.

"Being awake while I was asleep."

"Ruby, get some rest I can tell you about that later."

"I'm not sure I can wait," Ruby said anxious to know how her sleeping was affecting her mate.

"Well for a while I stayed with you while you dreamed, seeing what you dreamed. At some point, I must have dozed off, but I could still feel you beside me, and then when I woke up, I could still feel you. It wasn't like when you are awake and I can hear every thought, but I could feel that you were sleeping peacefully," he informed her.

"That's good to know," Ruby said closing her eyes again.

"Get some rest, my love," he said leaning down to kiss her head. "I'll still be here when you wake up," he reassured.

◦ ◦ ◉ ◉ ◉ ◦ ◦

Ruby woke up with a start running for her closet to get dressed. Someone was in danger and she knew it wasn't close by.

Gabriel knew what was going on, he could feel it in her head, and he was glad they were connected because she didn't seem to be stopping to talk to him as she got ready. Gabriel pulled on his jeans that were now dry and was about to pull on his shirt when Ruby turned on him.

"What do you think you are doing?" she asked.

"Coming with you," Gabriel said flatly.

"No, you're not," Ruby said with a soft chuckle.

"Yes, I am."

"Gabriel, I'm not letting you get hurt out there."

"I'm not going to get hurt, and I'm not going to let you go out there by yourself," Gabriel told her calmly.

"I can handle myself. I have been for almost twenty centuries."

"I know you can handle yourself, but I can't stop seeing you hurt the other day. I can fight and I'm stronger now. I can help as little or as much as you want or need but I can't stand the thought of you out there alone. I know you can do it, but you shouldn't have to," he told her.

"I get it and that's sweet, but I can't have you out there. What if something happens to you again? I don't know how well you heal. I don't know how much like me you are, but besides that, I just found you, I can't stand the idea of something happening to you."

"I'm coming with you," Gabriel said stepping closer to Ruby and pulling her into his arms. He quickly pulled one of the blades she had hidden away out and quickly in one smooth motion sliced open his arm from elbow to wrist.

"Gabriel," Ruby nearly screamed as she grabbed his t-shirt sitting on the bed and began to apply pressure to his forearm. "What the hell are you thinking?" she asked angrily as she struggled not to panic.

"You know exactly what I'm thinking," he said calmly.

"Not about me clearly. Damn it, Gabriel, if this doesn't stop bleeding… we are too far from a hospital and I can't stitch your arm shut. Damn it, Gabriel, you could die," Ruby said noting how saturated his shirt was as she bit at her lip anxiously. Gabriel started to sway slightly. "Sit down on the bed," she ordered.

"I'm sorry, Ruby," he said as he sat down.

"No, you're not, you would do it again in a heartbeat," she denied shaking her head.

Gabriel tilted her chin up so she would look at him. "I am sorry I hurt you, that was not my intention," he corrected her.

"Really, what was your intention, to die, to leave me alone for a few more millennia after I finally found you, my mate?" That stung him and she knew it, but she wanted him to understand how badly he had hurt her. She was terrified.

"No, I wanted to show you that you don't need to worry about me getting hurt," he said as he moved her hand holding his shirt away from his forearm to reveal a nasty cut that while still open was no longer bleeding.

Ruby brought her hand to her mouth and fought to keep from crying at the sight. Gabriel, her mate, injured.

Gabriel used his free arm to bring her in against his chest to comfort her. Ruby wrapped her arms around his neck and buried her face against his throat.

"Gabriel, is this how it felt?" Ruby asked her voice breaking.

"What?" he asked gently.

When I got hurt the other day, is this how you felt? she asked feeling horrible at the idea of putting him through this much pain and terror.

Gabriel didn't answer her, but he knew she didn't really need an answer. "I'm beginning to think you like keeping me shirtless," Gabriel said to distract her.

"What?" Ruby asked laughing.

"Well first you steal one of my shirts to sleep in which don't get me wrong I very much like you in my shirts, but then I think you intentionally used my shirt to apply pressure to my arm so that I couldn't put this shirt on," he teased.

"Well, I do like you without clothes," Ruby agreed softly as she brushed a kiss against his neck. She could feel his response to her, and she loved it. Ruby moved to straddle Gabriel lifting her head to look at him but careful to avoid looking at his arm. She knew he would be fine, but it hurt to look at his arm and it would take a couple hours for it to completely heal.

Gabriel leaned down to kiss her and slowly began to remove her weapons from her. Lifting his head from hers, he moved to take her top off. "Wait, what about where you were going?" he asked forcing himself to stop.

"What?" Ruby asked breathily. She was completely disoriented at this point only thinking of her desire to have her mate. She struggled to focus on his question.

Gabriel loved the way she sounded frankly he just wanted, no needed her now.

"Oh, I don't feel it anymore, I wouldn't know where to go."

"But it won't be good reaching you here at the house, will it?" he asked concerned.

"Probably not, but right now, I don't care. I need you," she told him honestly. The world could burn down without them, and well... she'd be okay with it. She'd spent her whole life trying to keep the planet from imploding. She wanted her mate. She didn't care if she deserved it or not, but right now he was what she needed. She needed... she needed...

Gabriel knew exactly what she needed, what she was afraid to admit. She needed to feel appreciated, she needed to feel loved, and he'd make sure she knew just how much he loved her. *I love you, my beautiful little love,* he told her brushing his thumb over her cheek as he stared into her face. *And I'm going to make sure you always know just how much I love you,* he promised her as he moved to take custody of her mouth again.

No, she most definitely didn't deserve him, but she was going to keep him anyways. He was bonded to her now and she refused to give him up. Ruby slid her arms around his neck to hold him to her as she continued to meet him kiss for kiss.

Gabriel moved to stand up having slid a hand to one of her thighs to hold her to him so he could continue kissing her and keep her in his arms against his chest. *Move the bedding,* he told her lifting his head from hers to look at her. He was going to have his mate. Ruby obeyed without hesitation using telekinesis to move the bedding out of the way so that he could blanket her as he moved to lay her down on the bed.

Leaning down to find her lips, he kissed her long and hard enjoying having her finally under him. *I like having you under me,* he admitted lifting his head to look down at her.

Good, because I intend to keep you right here. I'm not letting you go, she told him running her hands over his chest.

I'm not going anywhere, he swore leaning down to kiss her as he ran his hands over her. *I want this off now,* he ordered her beginning to move her shirt up wanting it off of her. He watched intently as she lifted up slightly to take off her top for him. *You still have too many clothes on,* he complained leaning down to kiss her trailing kisses along her jaw and down her neck and lower yet towards her breasts.

I… I think you know how to fix that, she gasped her hand sliding into his hair to hold him to her as his mouth closed over her breast. *Gabriel,* she moaned arching against him. *Please,* she pleaded wanting the rest of their clothes off. She wanted her mate.

Gabriel stood up to remove his pants and then slowly removed hers, taking his time enjoying the feel of caressing her legs, of having her in his hands and he enjoyed being able to feel her response to him. Gabriel slowly ran his hand up the inside of her leg caressing as he went. He leaned over her to capture her mouth as his hand continued up her leg coming to rest at her entrance that was already wet for him.

He slowly inserted one finger and then two stretching her for him.

Gabriel, Ruby pleaded pushing down against his hand trying to find relief, but she knew only he could supply that, it was him that she needed. She needed him and his solid weight on top of her and his hard length filling her. She needed him claiming her completely as his mate.

Gabriel moved to blanket her again settling his weight between her thighs. He slowly began to enter her allowing her time to stretch. It was hard to control himself, but he knew it was her first time and she was so tight. He knew she didn't care and just wanted him, but he could feel just how much he was stretching her and the last thing he'd ever do was hurt her.

Gabriel set an easy rhythm as he leaned down to kiss her trying to allow her body time to get used to accommodating him. He could feel her pleasure and he could hear her calling his name in his head as she held on to him tightly. He had started out slow trying to take it easy, trying to give her the romantic lovemaking she deserved for her first time, but it wasn't long before he was taking her hard and fast. He needed her desperately, and he could feel just how badly she wanted and needed him too.

There was no more controlling himself as he took her as both their needs demanded. Her body was heaven, being bonded to her was heaven. It was more than he could have ever hoped for in life. He was going to take her over and over and over and then he was going to take her again. He was going to do everything but build a shrine to her to show her just how much he loved her. Hell, he might just build a shrine to her too.

Gabriel, Ruby cried out as he took them both over the edge, emptying himself into her as her body clamped down on him. Gabriel collapsed on top of her wrapping his arms around her, holding on to her tightly as they both struggled to catch their breaths while shockwaves continued to pass through both of them. *I love you*, Ruby admitted truly choosing to tell him for the first time as she tunneled her hands in his hair holding him to her as he shifted to kiss her softly on the lips.

I certainly hope so because you're stuck with me, he teased her as he continued kissing her moving along her jaw and then down her neck letting his mouth wander where it chose. There was no way she was getting rid of him, but he probably should move off of her. He knew he wasn't light, and she was tiny. The last thing he wanted to do was hurt her, but he seemed unable to move from on top of her, not because he couldn't but because he didn't want to. He liked having her under him.

Ruby closed her eyes enjoying the feel of his lips on her skin. She knew he was thinking about moving from on top of her, but she didn't want him to move she liked the feel of him on top of her, in her, and she was relieved when he decided against it wanting to keep her under him. His weight on top of her was reassuring. It told her that he was there, and she wasn't alone.

You're not alone anymore, and you're never going to be again, he comforted lifting his head to look into her face. But she didn't open her eyes to look at him, in fact he felt a pain in his chest as she turned her face away from him resting her cheek on the pillow. He knew some of it was his, but more than anything he knew it was her. He knew the pain that felt like a hole in his chest where his heart should be was her pain. *Ruby, I'm not going anywhere*, he repeated tightening his hold on her.

He could feel her on the verge of tears. He didn't want her crying, he didn't want her in pain, but he also wanted her to know that she could turn to him, that she could trust that he was there for her. He didn't want her to feel like she had to try and hide herself from him. Or from herself. He loved how strong she was, but he also wanted her to know that she didn't always have to be strong. He wasn't going anywhere. She could fall apart. She didn't have to hold it all together. He was here for her. He could and would pick her up, hold her in his arms, and keep her safe. She didn't have to hold it in. He'd always be here for her.

Ruby tightened her arms around his neck as she buried her face in his throat. She wanted to believe him. She knew he meant it, but she'd been alone for a long time. She held on to him trying to keep from crying again. He didn't need to know just how broken and crazy she was just yet.

Ruby, you are anything but crazy. Though you'd have every right to be a little crazy after everything you've been through in your life and I know that I only know a very small amount of it at that. As for broken, I don't think you're broken, my love. You hurt and you're tired and lonely which is understandable, but that does not make you crazy or broken. It's alright to hurt, my love. You don't need to try and hide your pain or anything else from me. I'm not going anywhere. You can trust me, you know that. I know how strong you are in so many ways, but you're not alone anymore and you can lean on me for support. I want you to know that you can, you don't need to carry this alone anymore. Let me help, let me be here for you, he tried to reassure her gently. He wanted to roll over and pull her into his arms against his chest to comfort her, but he didn't. He knew she was finding comfort in his weight on top of her and he didn't want to take that away from her.

Gabriel, I do trust you. If I didn't, we wouldn't be here, but I've been alone for longer than I care to admit and I already depend on you a lot more than you realize, she admitted weakly as she continued to struggle to try and hold herself together.

My love, it's alright to fall apart. I'm right here with you, and that's where I'm going to stay, he told her gently.

Gabriel, I want to believe that, I do, but... Ruby trailed off holding on to him all the tighter.

It's the truth, Ruby. I mean it, he told her firmly.

I know you mean it. I know you have no intention of leaving me, but... Well, all the humans say that before they get married, and you know how high the divorce rate is.

Ruby, we're not human, he reminded her.

I know we're not, but... but you were. I know you love me, but you barely know me. Humans get divorced all the time, and they go into it usually saying how much they love the other, but they still go their separate ways, she told him sadly.

Ruby, I know there's a lot I don't know, but I do know you, I know I love you, and I know I'm never going to leave you. Me having been human has absolutely nothing to do with us. We're bonded together. You're my mate and I'm yours, and I'm never going to stop loving you, he argued gently.

I... Gabriel, you don't know that, she contradicted weakly.

You're afraid I'm going to stop loving you, he realized. She didn't answer, but he knew he was right. He'd found what was bothering her. *Do you think you could ever stop loving me?* he asked her gently even though he already knew the answer. She didn't answer but he felt her shake her head against his neck. *Then why do you so easily think I could stop loving you? You're not going to lose me,* he tried to comfort.

It's not that I... that I think... Even the best human marriages that last, at best get what 50, 60, maybe 70 years on the outside if they marry young and live to a ripe old age. Most humans don't even get to 30 or 40 years and that isn't because of death or a marriage found late in life. Gabriel, I know you love me, and it's not that I think that would change on a whim, but our life expectancy is nowhere close to that of humans, she told him pessimistically.

I'm not leaving you, he told her confidently.

Maybe not today or tomorrow or next year or even in a decade, but what about in a hundred years? Or two? Or five? She asked slowly pulling her face out of his neck to look up at him. *Or ten?* She asked one last time.

Ruby, he started bringing his hand up to her face and gently brushing away the stray tear he found there. *If I'm still alive in ten centuries, I'll be right here still holding you in my arms,* he reassured her confidently.

How can you be so sure? she asked quietly.

Because I love you, and I know that our love is nothing like what humans experience. What we have is so far beyond human imagination... in so many ways, including our mental bond to each other. And if I'm ever stupid enough to try and leave, I damn well expect you not to let me, you hear me, he told her.

I never said I'd let you leave, but that doesn't mean I want to hold you against your will. That's... that's not love, she sighed hurting at the thought, because she knew she'd do it anyways.

I'm not going to stop loving you. I know you don't believe it, but you will with time, my love. Give it some time. You've been alone a long time and you only just found me a few days ago, give yourself some time to accept that I'm not going anywhere, he told her leaning down to brush a soft kiss over her cheek in comfort.

When he lifted his head back up to look down into her face, Ruby stared up at him for a moment bringing her hand up to brush her fingertips over his cheek before she reached up to kiss him. Needing to lose herself in him again. Needing her mate to take her away and knowing he would.

She was going to enjoy every moment she got with him, and hopefully he was right. Hopefully, this would start to feel real at some point and she'd be able to believe that she wasn't going to one day find herself alone again, because she wasn't sure she could stop him from leaving. She wasn't sure she had the heart for it, but she also wasn't sure she'd have the heart to go on if he did leave her. She was tired of being alone.

* * * * * * * *

Ruby laid in bed with Gabriel still on top of her. She knew he'd been staying on top of her to help keep her calm and she didn't care. If anything, she appreciated it. Though to be fair, they hadn't really taken a break long enough for there to be a point in him moving off of her unless it was to have her on top of him, but they hadn't gotten there yet.

Gabriel's head was resting next to hers on the pillow. She knew he was watching her. She couldn't help blushing in response. She wasn't used to having anyone look at her, let alone the way he looked at her with such hunger. She could feel his intense desire and love for her. It was consuming.

She had one hand threaded in his hair as she absently trailed the fingers of her other back and forth over his neck, his shoulder, and his upper back. Her hand stilled on his neck as she brushed her thumb back and forth over one spot in a caress. She looked down to realize she was caressing the spot where she'd first bit him. She knew it was the same spot without a doubt.

They'd already exchanged blood a few more times since then while mating. They'd been at it for hours. Enjoying themselves and each other. Periodically feeling compelled to… Neither of them had been inclined to fight the sensation needing the connection, needing to remind the other that they were theirs.

Ruby didn't understand it in the least, she didn't pretend to, but she also wasn't going to look too closely at it. Her mate didn't have a problem with her biting into him and that was all that mattered. *Amica mea, mundus meus,* she muttered absently to herself as she leaned down to softly kiss that same spot.

What language is that? Gabriel asked as he watched her languidly.

Hmm, she questioned turning her head to look up at him.

I know what you said. I understood it somehow, 'My love, my world'. I know a number of languages, but I don't know that one. What is it? he inquired brushing a kiss over her lips as he brought his hand up to her face.

I didn't realize… she trailed off. She hadn't really been paying attention to her thoughts or words. *It was probably Latin,* she told him not really remembering.

Probably Latin? he questioned with a chuckle as he raised an eyebrow at her. *The dead language?* he asked doubting her.

Dead and buried, she agreed smiling.

But you just said it was probably Latin. And what in the world do you mean by probably? he inquired.

It wasn't a dead language when I learned it, she told him trailing a finger along his neck. *And I say probably because it was one of the first languages I learned. I speak many languages, very many, and if I had to hazard a guess, well…* You said I thought 'my love, my world', that would be 'amica mea, mundus meus',* she told him.

That's what you said. You speak Latin, he smiled surprised and amazed.

Yes, she agreed watching him. She loved his smile.

But how could I understand what you said? he asked curiously.

Ruby shrugged a shoulder casually. *I don't know. Though you are bonded to me, and I understand Latin. Maybe somehow that allowed you to translate or know the translation of what I said.*

It's impressive. I mean I understand that it's just another language to you, but still… he trailed off astounded.

A lot of languages came of Latin, a number of dialects, some died off and others continued to evolve and are still around today, she told him absently as she looked at her hand. A lot of things had changed over the centuries. She was always having to learn new languages, but luckily it was easy enough for her to pick up.

How many languages is very many? he asked gently.

I couldn't begin to enumerate them, she said distractedly.

What's wrong, my love? he asked gently turning her face back toward him.

Nothing, she told him smiling halfheartedly.

Something feels different, what is it? Talk to me, he pushed gently as he stroked his thumb over her cheek in a caress.

There's something we haven't talked about that… that we should probably discuss, she told him weakly struggling to meet his gaze.

What's that? he asked watching her intently. He didn't like how nervous and anxious she sounded and felt. He wasn't going to give his mate up.

Living arrangements, she mumbled biting at her lip.

There's nothing to discuss. I will be living with my mate and we will be sharing the same bed, he told her firmly. She was his and he would have access to her.

That's… that's not what I meant, she struggled to get out following his thoughts of wanting to claim her again.

What else could there possibly be to discuss? he asked.

Gabriel, we can't… I can't stay here, she told him reluctantly as she slid her hand around his neck to hold on to him.

Here being in bed? Gabriel questioned brushing a lock of hair back from her face and trailing his hand through her hair down her back. He ran the back of his knuckles over her side caressing her. Bringing his hand to rest holding her breast in his hand, he enjoyed feeling the weight of her breast in his hand and the response he felt when he brushed his thumb over her nipple. He had no intention of letting her out of bed.

No here, being the city, she gasped struggling to focus. She knew exactly what he was doing, but she needed to get this out. *I've been here long enough, it's time to… to move again and… and I assume you will be coming with me…* she finished nervously. He was her mate, but they had yet to discuss moving or her way of life.

Gabriel could feel her holding her breathe she was worried he wouldn't agree to come with her, but there was something else. *There's something you are not telling me,*

Ruby, he inquired as he wrapped his arm back around her comfortingly wanting to know what the other thing he was feeling was.

I… I don't just want to leave. I was wanting to go… to go far from here to one of my houses that is… is quite secluded. I was thinking it… it would be a good idea for several reasons. It would allow us to be alone if… if you agreed. And it would be a location where I… where we wouldn't have to worry about going fighting and either of us getting hurt. We could… I could have a break. It would also give you a place far from other people to… to learn to use and control your new strengths and abilities. Well, I… I assume you'll have all the same abilities as me. I mean you healed just as well. I guess that would be a good thing for us to figure out.

And I… I won't go out fighting anymore without you but I… I want to see you fight first in a controlled environment. I need to know you can defend yourself because I can't stand the thought of you getting hurt and I know you don't want me to get hurt from being distracted worrying about you. I mean I know I'll worry regardless as I would imagine you would about me, but there's a difference I hope between how much I would worry in general and how much I would worry not knowing how you fight. It would also allow us to better learn each other's fighting style and how to fight together, she struggled to get everything out. Trying to defend her reasoning. Afraid he'd want to stay or think her request irrational and unnecessary.

Alright, he accepted nodding his head.

That's it, that easy? she questioned surprised.

Ruby, I love you. When I started to fall in love with you, I accepted that if I was lucky enough to be with you, life might be isolated and nomadic, but as long as I have you that's alright. I just wanted to know what you weren't saying.

Besides, it's not like I have many ties here anyways. I could pick up and leave in a heartbeat and no one would notice, he reassured gently.

I would, she thought moving her hand to his face caressing his cheek lovingly.

When do you want to leave? He asked leaning in to kiss her.

Soon, but I think we can spare a few more hours here, she told him biting at her lower lip as she smiled at him.

As long as I can take you back to bed when we get there, he added as he lifted his head to look down into her face as he shifted his weight more fully above her.

Definitely, she agreed excitedly knowing he was preparing to take her again.

Good, he agreed leaning down to capture her mouth again as he shifted his hips to feel her response. He could feel her muscles squeezing on to him as she arched up against him. He felt her body protest his withdraw as he pulled back in order to push back into her. He set a vigorous pace needing her desperately, she had made him nervous when she had brought up living arrangements.

Ruby moved her hair for him knowing he intended to feed again. She hadn't realized she had scared him. It hadn't been her intention, but she could feel his need to claim her as his as he pounded into her. Filling her. *Gabriel,* she gasped or maybe it was more of a sigh as she felt his teeth sink into her neck. She held on to him as he took what he wanted, what he needed, what was his.

◦ ◦ ◦ ◉ ◦ ◦ ◦

We should get dressed, Ruby told him softly as she trailed her fingers over his chest.

He could feel her lack of enthusiasm at the idea as she laid resting in bed with him. Her head was pillowed lightly on his chest while she was cuddled up against his side with her leg still draped across him from when she'd collapsed beside him after the most recent time they had made love. They had been at it all night and well into the day. He didn't know how they had kept up the momentum, but even now he knew neither of them wanted to stop.

You don't sound very convincing, my love, he told her trailing his fingers over her back in a caress as he looked down at the top of her head.

Ruby tilted her head back to look up at him. She knew he wanted to kiss her again. Her hand sliding up his chest to his neck as he slipped his tongue into her mouth again exploring, claiming. *Gabriel,* she moaned arching against him.

She was however surprised when he lifted his head from hers leaving her feeling bereft. She looked up at him pleadingly. She wanted more and she knew he was more than ready to take her again.

I love you, he told her bringing his hand that had been resting lightly on her leg up to brush his fingertips over her face. *You are beyond belief my gorgeous little Ruby,* he told her as he watched the light blush that stole across her cheeks at his words. He loved how easily she responded to him, and how happy she felt being in his arms. He knew without asking that she'd never felt like this before, and he was pleased that it was because of him. He felt the same about her, but he also knew he didn't have the same number of years of loneliness that she had experienced.

Gabriel, I don't want to get out of bed, she told him, even though she knew he had to already know that.

Then let's not. I like our bed. It's soft and comfortable, and better yet it has you in it and it's ours, he told her brushing a kiss over her lips softly as he tried to tempt her to stay in bed.

To be fair, the whole house is 'ours', she told him knowing he liked it being their bed.

I know, but… it just…it doesn't feel quite the same, he admitted looking down at her. This room, this bed more than anything felt like theirs. The rest of the house… was still an unknown.

Not yet, but we'll fix that with time, she reassured him resting her head on his shoulder.

Why am I still feeling an inkling of you wanting to get out of bed? he questioned kissing the top of her head.

Because we need to leave, she sighed closing her eyes. *We'll start with making a different house feel like home first, and… we can come back to this one in a few decades, or a century or two,* she told him softly.

My love, you don't need to be worried. I told you I will follow you anywhere, and I know with time wherever we are will feel like home, he reassured her brushing a lock of hair back from her face.

I know. It's just that… I also know that… While we are connected now, I know it's only been a few days and now I'm asking you to leave everything you know behind, she told him imagining how hard that would be for him… for anyone.

Ruby, it's not hard at all. I love you, and I'm not human anymore, it's not like I can exactly continue to pretend otherwise. And what would be hard, would be being separated from you or putting you in danger by getting you to change routines that have kept you safe for centuries. He understood her concern, but he wasn't most people for one, and two when it came to her, he'd do anything to keep her safe and happy without blinking an eye. The only thing he needed was her.

Gabriel, it's not just moving, this means no more family, she whispered weakly. He had said he was alright with leaving with her, but she wasn't sure he really understood what that entailed. She wasn't sure if his parents were still alive or how close he was with them or any of his siblings, but things were going to change a lot going forward.

That's not true. I have you, and you, my mate, are definitely family now. And somehow, I got the impression you wanted little Rubys and Gabriels to chase after one day, he told her.

Gabriel, I meant... I do one day, and you are... you are family, she agreed shocked at the realization she had family now, *but I meant...* She meant that he wasn't going to be able to see or contact any of his family ever again without putting all of them at risk.

I know what you meant, my love, and I told you I will follow you anywhere. You're what I need just as you need me, he reassured her.

You're sure, she asked opening her eyes to look up at him from under her lashes.

You know I am, he answered her easily. *I go wherever you do.*

Alright, she sighed happily. She couldn't believe it. *We can swing by your apartment and grab whatever you want to keep before we leave. Maybe some more clothes at least, if nothing else,* she suggested.

I'm not sure what would be the point, I don't intend to wear them, he assured her.

Ruby couldn't help but chuckle to herself at his honesty though she wasn't exactly surprised. She did intend to spend a good deal of time sleeping with him and she knew he had the same intentions. *You don't have to, and of course, we can always buy more clothes when needed, but it might be convenient to have at least a few more outfits that you can wear if needed. And I have become fond of wearing your shirts if you don't want to wear them,* she told him with a seductive smile.

While I do like seeing you in my shirts, he smiled remembering how she very blatantly looked like his in his shirts. *I also much more prefer you in nothing,* he told her running his hand down her bare side making sure to caress her breast possessively and suggestively. *But we can stop and pick up some clothes,* he conceded gently. He knew she was comfortable like this in bed with him, but he knew this was all very new for her too. He got the impression that while she was comfortable nude in bed with him, she was uncomfortable, anxious even, at the idea of walking around the house nude. She wanted to be able to wear his shirts when she wanted to feel covered but not necessarily 'dressed'.

He kissed the top of her head gently. He was more than happy to concede. He wanted her feeling comfortable, and it wasn't a big deal. He did like seeing her in his shirts, and it would be easy and quick to undress her when he wanted access to her. He could feel her reaction at the thought of him pulling his shirt off of her to take her whenever he wanted.

Somehow, I don't see us getting out of bed often, or for long, she added feeling silly knowing she was blushing again.

Pink looks good on you, he reassured her.

Come on, the sooner we get out of here, the sooner you can take me back to bed, she told him knowing it would be their first destination when they got to the other house.

My love, why don't you get some sleep first? I know how tired you are, he told her gently.

That's why we haven't gone again, isn't it? she asked looking up at him realizing why he had been holding himself back.

I know I've thoroughly worn you out at the moment, and I know you were still a little tired when we started, he told her honestly.

I still would have… You know I still want you, and my body's still… reacting, she told him weakly as her gaze slid from his.

I know, my love, but I have no intention of taking you when you need rest. I love you, and I'm going to always put you first. We've got the rest of our lives, but right now you need a break and I'm not going anywhere, he reassured her unconcerned. *Now how about you get some sleep?* he suggested again.

Gabriel, I think it would be better to go now. I'm tired, sure, but I still have enough energy for us to get up and leave. If we go to sleep, it will be much harder to restrain ourselves to leave when we wake up than it is now, she told him softly.

He couldn't argue with her logic, and he knew connected as they were, he could keep an eye on just how tired she really felt in case she felt inclined to wave it off. *Very well,* he agreed. *So, how are we going to get where we are going, or are we going to take your bike there?* he asked curious.

No, we'll take the helicopter out back. It will be faster and easier for landing where we are going than the bike, she told him. *Besides, we kind of abandoned the bike the other night at what is undoubtedly now a crime scene. It wouldn't really be realistic or safe to retrieve it.*

You have a helicopter, he asked smiling at her like an excited little boy.

We, she corrected him.

Cool, he told her kissing her excitedly.

So, do you fly, or are you wanting to learn? she asked knowing it had to be one of the two.

I learned in the military, but I never owned a helicopter before, he told her smiling.

Ruby couldn't help but shake her head at his excitement. It was refreshing and uplifting feeling his all-encompassing joy when she'd spent so long without those feelings. *Well, you do now. Do you want to fly us out of here?* she asked smiling up at him.

I don't know our destination, he told her hesitantly.

No, but I do, and I'll be sitting next to you, right? she asked him teasingly.

One way or another, even if I have to haul you out there and strap you in myself, he told her leaning down to kiss her.

You needn't worry, I'll come quite willingly for you, she reassured him brushing her fingertips over his jaw as she reached up to brush another kiss over his lips.

As much as I can't believe I'm saying this, let's get up and get dressed to leave, he sighed shaking his head.

You'll have me back in bed before you know it, she tried to reassure him as she moved to sit up beside him. She couldn't help looking down at him longingly. It wasn't even so much that she didn't want to get out of bed, she didn't want to leave his side. Right here in bed like this with him, she knew where she stood. She knew what he meant by this bed felt like theirs. Maybe it was herself she was trying to reassure that he'd have her back in bed. She wanted it all to feel like theirs, but it felt safe here. This bed was an island, their island.

Yes, I will, he agreed knowing she needed reassurance. He reached up threading his hand around the nape of her neck pulling her down towards him as he leaned up to capture her mouth again. *Now, go get dressed, Ruby, before I have to pin you back down and have my way with you again,* he told her letting go of her neck for her to sit back up as he laid back down.

Ruby sat there biting at her lip with her hand resting on his abdomen. She couldn't remember why she needed to get dressed as she sat staring at him. She much more preferred his idea and she didn't want to get out of bed.

It's alright, my love. Go get dressed and then we can go to my apartment before we leave. It's alright, nothing is going to change between us. We may be going to another house and another bed, but it's still us, he reassured gently.

Ruby nodded her head silently.

Ruby, I'm right here, and I'm not going anywhere without you, he reassured her feeling her anxiety about leaving the room or maybe more specifically about leaving his side.

She reluctantly slipped out of bed to go get dressed. She felt Gabriel's eyes on her tracking her movements to the bathroom. He was struggling to let her go get dressed and to not pull her back into his arms. She quickly changed clothes and started packing her small bag of things that she took with her from house to house. While everything in the house was hers, and everything in the house they were going to was hers. There were usually a few things and outfits that it was just easier to bring with her place to place.

She knew Gabriel was already dressed and waiting for her as she headed out of her closet and back through the bathroom turning out the lights as she went. *You don't need to do that,* she told him as she stepped back into the bedroom. He had started remaking the bed while she'd been packing her bag. *I've never liked how that bed looked more than I do now,* she told him shyly. It looked very well used. Something none of her beds had ever looked like before now.

He tugged the last corner of the comforter back into place and turned around to look at her. *Come here,* Gabriel called wanting her back in his arms and knowing she needed to be back in them. He wrapped his arms around her tightly, holding her to him as she pressed a cheek against his chest and fisted a hand in his shirt. He could feel her sigh of relief at being back in his arms.

How did you do this to me? she asked confused.

Do what? he asked unsure what she was asking.

Turn me into this simpering little female, she muttered weakly against his chest.

Gabriel couldn't help but chuckle at her accusation. *My love, you may be little, and you are definitely female, but…* he trailed off as he moved to lift her chin for her to look at him as he continued. *You are in no way simpering,* he corrected her before he leaned down to capture her mouth once more. *As for the bed,* he told her reluctantly lifting his head. *We don't know when we'll be back, so I rather make it so it's ready for us to mess up again next time. And we can and will mess up the bedding in the other houses just like we did this one,* he reassured her.

I don't know. I've felt utterly ridiculous and fairly unhinged ever since the other night when I stumbled upon you, she disagreed.

He knew she was still on the simpering female thing. *My love, I know a lot has happened… a lot has changed in the last few days. You fell in love and found a mate. Which in itself is a lot to take in after a long time alone and not really having anyone in your life. And I don't mean just a mate, I mean anyone like family or friends. That in itself is plenty to adjust to, but you also spent all that time alone not knowing anyone else like us and not knowing you could turn anyone, not that you necessarily wanted to. You spent all that time thinking you'd always be alone, didn't you?* he asked gently.

Ruby weakly nodded her head in answer fighting the knot in her throat at how spot on his assessment was.

I know you feel a little off kilter after everything. I think that's fairly reasonable and not ridiculous. You are not some simpering little female. You are however absolutely amazing. You fell in love making me the luckiest man in the world that it was me, but that's a lot of change after thinking you'd never have anyone. After finding me and being afraid and hurt by how you felt about me when I was only human. You're still you, just you with a mate you love. I've not changed you and you know that, but this is a new side to yourself that you didn't know and that can be scary but it's alright and I will always be right here with you, my love, he reassured her.

I love you, she told him looking up at him. She was relieved that he always seemed to know her so well and just how to calm her down. And she knew it wasn't just their bond. He 'saw' her when no one else did. He was her mate, bond or not.

* * * * * * * *

Ruby sat cross-legged in the middle of the bed at Gabriel's apartment watching him pack. She hated being out of his arms or at least touching him. She kept having to remind herself that he was right here in the room with her as she watched him intently to keep track of him and to help her know he was alright.

Breathe, my love, he told her coming over to sit on the edge of the bed as he took her hand in his and brought it to his mouth to kiss in reassurance.

What? she asked tightening her hand on his.

You're holding your breath, he told her. *You need to breathe. I'm right here.*

I'm sorry, she apologized looking at their hands. *This is hard for me,* she admitted even though she knew he already knew that. That was why he'd sat down and stopped packing.

It's alright, my love, he reassured her. *And you're not alone. I don't like having you out of my arms either,* he comforted. He had a feeling that was part of the reason they were struggling. They were both feeling the same way and feeling each other's identical feelings which was serving to intensifying their sensations or rather discomforts. *But if you want to leave, I need to finish,* he told her gently.

I know, she nodded.

Which means I need you to keep breathing. No holding your breath, he said reaching over to trail his fingers through her long hair.

I'll try to remember that, she said with a small smile.

Gabriel reluctantly stood back up after brushing a small kiss over her lips. He turned and started to head for the closet but stopped turning to look at her. He'd already packed a few more shirts and pants to add to the couple he'd originally packed when going to her place. He now had about a week's worth of clothes. He didn't want to pack any more. It wasn't realistic, he didn't need to carry around a ridiculous amount of clothes and he knew the intention was to make it more or less look like he'd just disappeared into thin air. An empty closet or one that was clearly missing a good deal of clothes would be suspicious.

I guess I shouldn't bring any of my weapons, he asked. He had a gun and a handful of knives that he kept in his bedside table.

If you have something particularly sentimental you want to bring, I don't think it'd be a big deal, but otherwise no. You were in the military, it'd be almost expected to find some amount of weapons in your place when it's discovered. I have plenty of weapons and we can buy anything else you might want, she reassured him. *As for the gun, it's got a serial number. We don't need a weapon that's in the system and can be tied to the old Gabriel that will be essentially dead when we leave here. You do realize once we leave, I'll be creating a new identity for you, right?* she asked looking up at him.

As long as I have you, I don't care who the hell I am, he reassured her. *I'd imagine you change identities and move fairly regularly, but you also said you've been on the run since I was born, so how often do you... are we going to move around?* he asked curious.

Where... where we are going now, is... is more isolated so we can get away with being there for a while, but usually a couple years to maybe five or seven on the outside depending on where I go and the age I set on my identity when I initially move. I can pass for quite young, but I don't really seem to age so I have to be careful. When I was younger, I moved more often, because... well children tend to age quickly. It was usually a year or two, she informed him. *I think I tend to average three to five though. Sometimes I move a lot sooner if I feel I need to whether I can put my finger on the reason for the urge or not. Sometimes I just get tired of a place. But right now, we just... we need to disappear. I know you say you're not close to anyone, but right now you exist, and some people might know you or at least recognize you. We need... I need you to not exist in the human world,* she told him hesitantly. She knew he said he was coming, and she knew he meant it, but she was scared to lose him. She needed to see it.

I understand. It makes since, Ruby. Let me grab my laptop, he told her turning towards the living room. He could feel her hesitation in regard to the laptop. *I'm just going to clone the hard drive,* he assured her coming back into the room with the laptop and a backup drive. *I'm not bringing it with me.* He knew a missing laptop would be unusual since most people owned one, but there were family photos he wanted on it. He had no problem leaving with her and he knew he'd never see them again, but he wanted the photos he had to remember them by.

Ruby had scooted closer to him resting her head against his shoulder wanting to be closer to him when he'd sat down on the bed. He kissed the top of her head in comfort as he turned on the computer. He quickly copied what he wanted and then did the same to his cellphone. He knew he'd need to abandon his phone too. He closed the laptop. He'd put it back in the living room on the charger when they left to make it not look out of place and the cellphone he reached over and put on the charger on the bedside table making it look casually forgotten and in a normal place. He reached into his back pocket pulling out his wallet and his front pocket for his keys and set them on the table next to the phone which was where he kept them when he slept. He wasn't going to need his keys or ID anymore and credit cards were trackable.

You ready, Ruby asked tilting her head back to look up at him.

Gabriel couldn't resist pulling her into his lap as he leaned down to capture her mouth. He loved the dazed look on her face when he lifted his head from hers. *There's just one more thing I want to do before I disappear,* he told her brushing his fingers over her face in a caress.

Me? she asked excitedly as she bit at her lip in anticipation.

He couldn't help chuckling lightly at her response leaning down to brush a soft kiss over her lips. He could feel her confusion in response. She wanted him to take her again. *I would love nothing more than to have you again, but we both know we'd be at it for hours and we are trying to leave to go somewhere else where I will take you again over and over,* he assured her. *Besides, when they realize this apartment has mysteriously gone vacant, this bed probably shouldn't be covered in our DNA,* he reminded her.

Fine, she agreed unhappily.

I'll make it up to you, he promised.

Then what is it you're wanting to do? She asked struggling to focus and fight the urge to reach up and kiss him as her eyes wandered over his body. She wanted to wrap her arms around his neck and turn into his arms to straddle him.

Marry me, he told her trying to ignore her thoughts.

What? she asked her thoughts slamming to a stop as her eyes jumped to his face.

I want you to marry me, he told her again running his hand over her back comfortingly.

What? Why? she asked confused as to what was happening.

You're my mate and I love you. I also assume that as you change our identities it would make the most sense to create two identities that are married to each other, no? he asked watching her.

I… I suppose, she agreed hesitantly. She probably would have done that when she started creating them, but she hadn't really thought about it yet and right now she was still confused as to where this was going.

I told you where it's going, he thought laughing at her thought. *I want you to marry me. I want one time before you start creating all these identities over the years to come where you actually marry me. I want a ring on this hand,* he told her as he took her hand in his and then brought it up to his mouth to kiss.

Gabriel, you... you know that you can't... I mean this you that we're disappearing can't... there can't be a record of you marrying someone and then just disappearing, she argued struggling to form a coherent thought.

We both know you could create an identity really quick for you to marry me with, he corrected her.

I guess, sure, but I still don't understand why. I mean it's just a ring and a piece of paper. Hell, probably ultimately hundreds if each of our new identities from this point further are married, she argued.

If it's just a ring and a piece of paper, then why are you fighting marring me? he asked gently. *I know it's not because you don't love me.* He watched as her eyes fell from his face. *You're afraid this will change something between us,* he realized. *My love, we've talked about this. I love you and we're bonded to each other. Nothing is going to change that,* he reminded her gently.

Then why do we have to get married, she asked weakly. *I'll wear a ring, but...*

I know I'm not human anymore and I know you have a poor view on marriage, but I love you and I'd like to know that you married me for real once. That it's not just papers you faked along with our identities and some random ring that I didn't put on your finger. Please Ruby, he asked tilting her chin up to look at him, *do this for me. I will only ever ask this of you once.*

Alright, she agreed weakly nodding her head. He was giving everything up for her, scared or not she could do this for him. *But we don't have any wedding rings,* she informed him as she reached over and pulled his laptop into her lap to create his fake identity to marry her with. She knew he wasn't talking anything fancy which was more than fine with her, but they would still need some kind of rings.

We can stop off somewhere between here and the courthouse and grab something that will work for getting married, but I assure you at some point we will find something nice that you like to put on that finger, he told her watching her fingers fly across the keyboard.

I don't usually where jewelry, she told him absently as she paused typing to glance at her hand.

You will from now on. You're my mate and I want that clear to everyone, he told her firmly yet gently.

Alright, she nodded. It would be an adjustment, but she'd wear it for him. *It's done and I also created and back dated the documents we need to get married, and then deleted the history of me using your computer. All we have to do is...* she trailed off looking up him.

Then let's go, he told her standing up holding her in his arms and lowering her feet to the ground to stand. *I'll be right beside you. I'm yours forever,* he reassured her leaning down to brush a kiss over her lips. *It's just a ring and paper,* he told her trying to make her feel better.

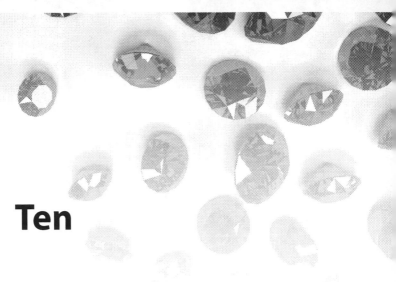

Ten

Ruby and Gabriel were enjoying being out at the cabin style house she'd built centuries ago into the side of a mountain to help hide it and keep it secure as she had similarly done with a number of houses. They'd spent most of their time in bed, but even when they were out of bed, they usually seemed to be making love. It was hard to keep their hands off one another.

The bond between them made it hard for them to be physically separated even just in different rooms, so they usually stayed close to each other. Even in the same room, it was difficult for them not to be next to each other where they could touch each other and reassure themselves that the other was alright. They usually seemed to be in each other's arms to at the very least be close to each other. Though it didn't take much for the energy to change and for them to end up mating not that either of them cared.

They'd been out there for about a decade and a half. They were in an extremely isolated area and had been keeping to themselves. When they needed to go into town, they had a few towns that while not exactly nearby by human standards were close enough and were in fairly equal distances in different directions around them. This had allowed them to stay in one spot for as long as they had without anybody getting suspicious and had been part of the reason she'd built this house where she had and had chosen here to come to spend time alone with him.

In between mating, she'd worked with him on learning to use telekinesis. It had been especially hard in the beginning. At one point she started to wonder if that was an ability that she hadn't passed on to him. Once they had managed to trigger to get him to use it the first time it had helped, but it had still been slow progress for a few years. He'd been so used to doing everything by hand. It had taken time to retrain his brain to know that he didn't have to use his hands.

Hell, even Ruby did half of what she did with her hands out of habit because of interacting with the human world as much as she did and needing to keep a low profile. That and it did take energy to use telekinesis. She understood that that would all apply to Gabriel too, but she wanted to make sure he knew how to switch back and forth when he wanted or needed. She also wanted to make sure he was in control of it so that he didn't accidentally trigger or use it without his intending to which could end up being dangerous for any number of reasons.

She'd also attempted to work on assessing his fighting ability since she had agreed that she wouldn't go hunting without him. Though to be fair she wasn't sure either of them could tolerate that much distance apart even if she wasn't fighting. However, attempting to assess his fighting style had been interesting. Aside from the fact that it had taken a lot of convincing on her part that he wasn't attacking her and that he wasn't going to hurt her, it had ultimately ended up more or less being a game of mental chess. Before either of them could make a move, the other already knew what they had decided to do, and they could in turn just as easily see what they were going to do in response which had left them both standing there not really sparing. It had been interesting and not what she'd been going for but it had at least allowed her to see, even if it was only mentally, what he would do in response to various attacks which was what she'd wanted to assess to feel comfortable with him beside her when she went hunting.

Ruby had just finished scrolling through an alert that had sounded on her phone drawing her attention. "Pack your bag," she told him reluctantly. She didn't really want to leave. She liked it out here alone with her mate, who it felt like she'd still just found yesterday.

"Where are we going?" Gabriel asked unconcerned but curious.

"D.C.," she told him as she set the phone back down.

"As in the capital? I'm not sure that is such a great idea," he told her hesitantly as he tightened his arms around her holding her back against him.

"Yeah, I never am either, but nonetheless that is where we are going," she sighed turning into his arms to rest her cheek against his chest.

"Ruby," he questioned confused. He knew she knew how to take care of herself, but he wanted to know more before they left, like whether or not he should be trying to talk her out of this. He wanted her safe. He needed her safe. He understood that was kind of a difficult task, a bit of a contradiction with her lifestyle, their lifestyle, but he didn't want her taking unnecessary risks. She was his mate, and he couldn't live without her. Hunting was one thing, but this... he knew this wasn't hunting. He wanted more information.

"We're going to the CIA," she told him knowing he wouldn't like it.

"We're just going to the CIA. Like no big deal, just what, going to walk right in the front door," he asked looking down at the top of her head doubtful and liking this less by the moment.

"Actually yes. We've kind of been invited," she told him cautiously.

"Kind of," he repeated raising an eyebrow in inquiry. "How exactly does that work?" he questioned watching her closely.

"Well, I told you I was wired into all government information, black ops and otherwise," she started not looking up at him.

"Yes," he agreed wanting to know where she was going with this.

"Well, the CIA just sent an internal memo to a few high-ranking members saying, 'bring her in now at all costs'," she told him.

"Her who," he asked confused.

"Her me, that is always how they refer to me since they don't know my name. Giving them my name would be… well, ill advised to say the least," she informed him.

"I don't understand. How do they know about you? And the message implies they would know how to find you, which I know you well enough to know that is not possible. So, why on earth would you go walking in the door giving them exactly what they want?" he asked not liking this in the least.

"I told you I have infiltrated all levels of government to keep an eye on them. I also told you sometimes I do retrievals and sometimes I help with serial killers and sometimes I do that for a government. I'm whispered of as an urban legend among the elite because only the elite of the elite even know that I am actually real. Hell, even they question it because information is passed down by word of mouth over a significant amount of time, nothing about me is written down or recorded. They are told when things seem absolutely desperate to send that memo and I will come. They don't know how I'll know, but they also know not to question it," she explained casually and then looking up at him shrugging.

"And they don't question the fact that this info gets passed down generation after generation. They don't stop to question that you might be dead?" he asked her still confused, but at least starting to feel a little more reassured that they wouldn't be necessarily walking into an ambush.

"Yes... and no," she told him shaking her head in a wishy-washy manner. "I know the information has been passed along that I am ageless. Over the centuries a few have been fortunate enough to see me in their younger years and unfortunate enough to see me again in their older years. It usually scares the crap out of them," she smiled up at him in amusement at the reminder. "I am sure they have doubts and hesitations but, in the end, I still see this memo come across when they need help. I'm just glad this is so much easier to monitor since the invention of the computer."

"But how will we just walk in the door?" he asked still a little doubtful that this would be as easy as she made it out to be.

"A small targeted device to shut down cameras and alert my arrival usually does the trick, and then we calmly walk up to the desk and tell them that she is here to see the director," she informed him unconcerned.

"You're sure about this," he asked looking down at her worried.

"Gabriel, it's alright. Really," she tried to assure him. "I know it seems a little crazy, but this is far from the first time I've done this. It's as safe as anything else I do. Besides, I'll have you there with me this time, won't I?" she asked partly to reassure him by reminding him she wouldn't be alone, but also to make sure that he would be with her. She still wasn't quite used to the sensation of not wanting to be alone, but she didn't want to go without him. She didn't want to be without her mate by her side.

"I told you, you are not going anywhere without me. This is very new and a little extreme for me. I just wanted to make sure that you are sure. You are the one with experience in this department, not me, but I will be right there with you," he reassured her leaning down to kiss her. He had his doubts and concerns, but he could feel that his mate felt comfortable and he would be by her side.

* * * * * * * *

Oh, this looks good, Ruby told him mentally unable to hide her amusement spotting the guy coming towards them.

He stopped before them looking her up and down, she felt Gabriel ready to punch him in response. She knew the only reason he didn't was because he knew the guy wasn't looking her up and down in a sexual manner. He was attempting to assess her and they both knew he was underestimating her. "You're her," he asked skeptically.

"Yes, you got a problem with that," she asked looking him up and down. "What's your name?" she asked unconcerned knowing she had the upper hand whether he knew it or not.

"Phillip," he replied intentionally not mentioning a last name.

"Well Phil, I suggest you take us to the director," she suggested calmly while still managing to make it sound like she was the one in charge. They could both tell he didn't like her calling him Phil, but he didn't bother correcting her.

She knew that made Gabriel happy. He wanted to torture the poor guy who had no idea what he was in the middle of.

Phil began to lead them down a back hallway coming to a stop before a private elevator. "You're going to have to wait here," he said looking at Gabriel.

"That's not going to happen," she said ignoring Phillip's order and scanning her finger to call the elevator.

"My orders are to bring you to the director, not you and your friend," he said trying to hide his surprise that her fingerprint worked.

"Gabriel is my husband and he is coming with me," she told him firmly.

"Either he stays here, or you don't go up," he told her still unaware who was really in charge.

"I'm more than happy to leave. I didn't have to come in and I don't honestly care. You're the ones who asked for help. Feel free to go ask your director if he would like me to leave but I think you know the answer," she told him pointedly. "Besides, that's not exactly what your orders were now were they? They were to bring me in at all costs and well... I believe that means, he is coming with me. That is if I'm not mistaken," she pretended to ask smiling tightly at him. "Besides, he cares more about your country than I do. He was a part of your military, I wasn't," she said unconcerned knowing he wouldn't be able to identify her mate. She'd seen to that years prior.

"You served," he asked looking up at Gabriel.

"Marines, and let me guess you were a ranger," Gabriel said knowing he was right. He could read it in the way he carried himself.

"So, what is your decision, Phil?" she asked enjoying the tick in his jaw in response to her calling him 'Phil'.

"Get in the elevator," he said frowning clearly not liking having his arm twisted.

Gabriel placed his hand at the small of her back as he let her in ahead of him. Ruby stood close to him brushing up against his side while his hand stayed at the small of her back. It was hard for them not to stay close to each other or physically touching, but it was hard when they knew Philip was watching and neither wanted it to look like she was weak or that she needed him there to protect her. Not that Gabriel wouldn't step in if she needed help, because they both knew he would.

Even after all the time they had spent out at the house together, it was difficult not being close. They could barely keep their hands off each other. It was more than just a desire to stay in close proximity, it was a true need. Even though they were mentally connected, neither of them would have been able to tolerate it if he had stayed on the first floor. They had both thought that with time they would get used to the feeling and it would be easier, but they had now been together for a good deal of time and they had gotten used to the feeling. However, it hadn't really gotten any easier for them to keep their hands off each other, though honestly, they weren't sure they wanted it to but they did want to at least be able to behave in public when they needed which was easier said than done.

They both knew Gabriel was having a hard time keeping his hand from wandering and it wasn't helping that all Ruby could think about was wanting his hand to wander. She at the very least wanted to be able to stand closer to her mate. She wanted to be able to lean into him resting her head against his side with his arm wrapped around her waist, not this barely brushing against his side and his hand at her back. She knew... they both knew they needed to show a front of professionalism and strength, but she suspected this small distance between them was teasing their desire to be closer together and was part of what was making everything so difficult for them. Not being able to casually stand closer together with their bond was pushing their need for each other further in an attempt to make up for it. It was like some weird reverse psychology, the further they were from each other the closer they wanted to be to each other and right now a few inches felt like miles.

* * ● ● ● ● * *

Gabriel stood with his arms crossed staring out the window listening as Ruby and the director discussed why they had called her here. Her focus on the conversation with the director was helping to distract them both from the fact that she wasn't in his arms. His mate and the director were currently pouring over a map. Apparently, the current president's son had gone missing overseas in a war zone. He was with the army and his unit had been ambushed. He had been cut off from his unit and they hadn't heard anything from him. They didn't want to risk a full-on assault to get him back when they didn't know his status, MIA or KIA, or where to start looking for him, but it was the president's son, so they had to attempt to do something. So, they had called in the best, which meant his mate. The director was indicating last known coordinates and where the troops on both sides were set up.

Ruby looked over her shoulder at Gabriel, he was staring out the window and appeared to be withdrawn and not paying attention, but she knew he was listening. "Thomas, can you give us a minute?" Ruby asked looking back up at the director.

"It's my office," he reminded her. He wasn't going to be asked to leave his own office. He was in charge after all.

"I know," was all she said in response not moving and completely unfazed by his displeasure at being asked to leave his own office.

Thomas sighed heavily and quietly left the room unhappily.

Ruby turned around completely to look at Gabriel. She knew even though he was here and listening, he wasn't here. He was overseas in a war zone a number of years past, hearing the shells and seeing the blood and destruction and smelling the seared flesh. He hadn't even realized she had sent the director out of the room or that she was watching him.

Ruby walked over to him and softly placed her hand on his arm. *Gabriel*, she asked looking up into his face.

Gabriel blinked a couple times and looked down at her. He could easily see the worry on her face, which was nothing compared to what he felt from her through their bond. *I'm fine*, he tried to reassure her as he brought his hand up to cup her face in his hand.

Gabriel, we don't have to do this. He is one boy, the world will go on, besides they don't know if he is even still alive, she continued trying to play it down even though she could already feel his protest.

Ruby, it's not right and you know it. Besides, you want to go. You already know the story and the details, and I know if you don't go and find out one way or another, it will torture you. And I can't have that, he told her worried about her.

Gabriel, that may be true, but things are different now, I have you in my life, she argued. Ruby knew better than to suggest that she could go by herself, aside from the fact that she didn't want to, she knew Gabriel wouldn't let her. Either they went together or not at all. Besides, it's not like it would make much difference, if he didn't come, he would still see and feel everything she went through without actually being there. Which just meant things would be worse, because on top of dealing with the difficulties of going, they would also have to deal with the separation from each other and he would struggle with her not having someone watching her back whether she needed it or not.

You're not going by yourself, Gabriel said reinforcing her thought.

I know, but I don't want to put you through this. I can see the flashes in your head. I know this is a lot to ask, she said feeling horrible at the thought of him having to deal with the pain of going overseas again because of her.

My love, it's really not. We're in this together, and I would do anything for you. If that means going overseas then so be it. I'll be fine. I'm sure, he added answering the question he felt her already wanting to ask as to whether or not he was sure. *Besides it's not like we will be there for months on in, and I won't be worrying about keeping a whole unit alive and dealing with inevitable losses. It will be just me and you backing each other up and we are not so easily killed,* he reassured her.

I know, Gabriel, but this will be different for other reasons. Gabriel, when we are over there some things will be the same. The same smells, sounds, and sights, but you won't be human like you were before. You won't be a marine. You won't be there to help end a war. It will be just me and you sneaking in and out along enemy lines to find one person. We won't be able to stop for every fight, ambush, and raid we see or hear. We won't be able to stop and attempt to save every wounded soldier we come across. And you, like me, will feel everyone in that area that is in need, she said rubbing at her temples at the thought of it, because she knew it would leave her with splitting migraines and feelings of pain and guilt. *And when I say everyone, I mean everyone, not just those you consider your country men, but also their enemy. They are hurting too and are just as much in need. You will feel them too whether you like it or not and you will be just as much compelled to help them as the men you think of as your own. Do you understand?* she asked doubting he fully understood what the circumstances of being over there would be like.

Gabriel had seen her rub at her temples, and he knew what she wasn't saying. How much it would hurt her to be over there, and not be able to help. He knew on one hand she wanted to help them, but he could also feel her deep-down suppressed thought of 'why bother' and he knew why. Sure, she was strong enough to end a war nice and quick, but she would feel them all. Every death. Which side did she choose? How could she choose a side? And she couldn't make them settle on a peace they weren't ready for, so in the meantime, what was the point of her getting involved? She could fight and fight and try to save people, but to what avail? She would still feel the pain and those she saved would only live to die anther day.

Then why bother to go at all, Ruby? he asked not wanting her in this kind of needless pain when it would ultimately be unproductive and not solve anything.

Because I wouldn't be going over there for the war. I'd be going for one boy, and I know I'm not going to mess with shifting the balance of the war. I never do unless absolutely necessary, she explained.

I get that, but you're still going to expose yourself to all that energy and you will end up feeling guilty for not helping after feeling their pain. And all for as you say for one boy, he said questioning her logic.

Gabriel, even if I don't go, they're still over there fighting and I'm not helping, she reminded him gently.

Yes, but you're not feeling them, and you are not feeling needlessly guilty about it, he corrected.

Maybe not about the war but you know I will about that boy, she admitted weakly not wanting to push him into going over there but also not wanting to lie to him, not that she could. He would know whether she said it or not.

I know, he sighed. *But is it worth going over there and easing the guilt over one boy with that of several hundred if not thousands?* he asked not liking this situation. He wished they had just stayed at their house.

It will suck, but that's a feeling I've felt before and I know going into it there is nothing I can do. I will get over it and I will just have to deal with the pain while we try to find the boy. I'm just worried about you. I want you to understand what to expect. I can handle myself and I don't need you to worry about me. I need to know that you will be able to handle it, she said concerned about him. She knew she could get through it, but she wasn't alone anymore. It wouldn't be just her having to 'get through it'. He would be dealing with the same feelings as her and feeling her going through it.

Ruby, I told you I will be fine, and I will help you through it however I can, he reassured her. He would do whatever he could to help her with the pain and guilt she'd be feeling over there.

Gabriel, I don't think you are getting it. Everything I feel, you feel. It won't be just me in pain. You will feel all of it too, and you've not been there like this before, I have, she said still doubtful he fully understood the situation.

We will figure it out, he reassured her. *But I will be going with you,* he repeated to make sure they were clear on that point.

Alright, she reluctantly agreed still worried about him. She was always going to worry about him, but this was going to be a lot and it probably didn't really help that this was the first time they were venturing out into dangerous territory of any kind since they had first mated. Though if she was going to continue hunting with him by her side, they were going to have to start somewhere, but this was kind of like jumping in the deep end of the pool. But then if they could handle this together… well, that certainly would be reassuring for the future.

Come here, he said wrapping his arms around her and pulling her in against his chest as he kissed the top of her head. He could feel her relief at being back in his arms and he knew it wasn't just her. He had missed having her in his arms even if it had only been for a short time. He didn't care for it.

Go ahead and call him back in here, Gabriel sighed heavily.

Ruby looked up at him in question. She didn't want to get out of his arms, and she knew if she called him back in the room, she'd have to extricate herself from his hold.

The sooner you finish talking with him, the sooner we can get out of here and stop worrying about their eyes on us, he attempted to comfort her as he leaned down to brush a kiss over her lips before reluctantly letting her out of his arms.

⁕ ⁕ ◉ ◉ ◉ ⁕ ⁕

"Are there any supplies you'd like, or do you have everything you need?" Thomas asked looking at her as she folded up the map on the desk to take with her.

Ruby glanced over at Gabriel and talked with him mentally for a minute discussing supplies. They had plenty of weapons. No guns but then that was for the best since the plan was for a stealth exfil. Their phone had GPS that was more accurate than the government. She had clothes and shoes packed in the chopper that would suit the situation.

She looked back at Thomas. "Some stealth wear in his size," she said indicating Gabriel. "A few days' worth of MREs, and a couple sleeping bags or blankets," she finished.

"You don't want any weapons or anything else?" he questioned confused.

"We're good," she assured him.

"Very well. I'll have Philip escort you out the back to take you wherever you want to go, and I'll have someone meet you on the way out with the supplies," he told her as he picked up the phone to call Philip back in the room.

Usually Ruby wouldn't have let them drive her anywhere, but they were only going to be taking them to the air strip where they'd landed the chopper which was untraceable, and they already knew the direction they'd be heading in. So, it wasn't like it would be revealing anything they didn't already know to let them drive her and Gabriel to the air strip, but it would allow them time to be able to be next to each other before the long flight overseas and after the difficulty of being watched and scrutinized by other people they needed that time.

Ruby moved into Gabriel's arms as Philip loaded the few supplies, she'd asked for into the back of an SUV which had heavily tinted windows and a partition between the front and the back. She knew it was one of the vehicles they used for extra security for special circumstances.

Gabriel couldn't resist leaning down to capture her mouth as she looked up at him. He didn't care if Philip saw them or not. He needed to taste his mate. He didn't like them struggling to keep each other at arm's length. He reluctantly lifted his head from her at the sound of Philip repeatedly clearing his throat to get their attention.

Opening the door for Ruby to slide into the back, Gabriel told Philip which air strip they wanted to be taken to and told him to take the long way as he slid in beside his mate. He'd seen the specs of the vehicle in her head and knew there was a privacy partition. He knew she hadn't initially been thinking of taking advantage of it for anything more than to be able to lean against him with his arm around her on the trip to the air strip, but he knew she was now since the thought had passed through his mind. He needed her and she needed him, especially if they were going to tolerate a long flight overseas.

As soon as he'd closed the door behind himself, Ruby moved to straddle him. He didn't hesitate to recapture her mouth relieved that she wasn't trying to resist her need for him or feeling uncomfortable with his intention.

Ruby sat back slightly as she continued kissing him in return so that she could get at his pants to undo them. *Do it,* she told him knowing he was wanting to tear the sides of her skirt that she was wearing to create slits so that she could straddle him better giving him better access to her.

Gabriel slid his hands to the hem of her skirt on one side and struggled to control his strength as he began tearing at the material. He wanted to create a slit on each side, not tear the thing off of her when she had nothing in the vehicle with them to change into. He had found it unusual when she'd initially put on the skirt at their house. It hadn't seemed like her, though to be fair, he seemed to usually keep her half naked, but he had to admit he was relieved she'd worn a skirt because this would have been significantly more difficult with her in pants.

He slid his hands under her skirt to help push the material higher up her hips towards her waist to give her hips more freedom to better accommodate him as she sat back up pressing herself against his chest. He knew she wanted to be skin to skin with him, so did he, but now unfortunately was not the time. He moved his hands that were still under her skirt to tear off her panties to get to her. He quickly tucked the shredded scrap of material in his pocket to keep them from getting forgotten in the car and discovered by someone else.

Taking hold of her hips, he helped settle her on to him. He loved how tight she always felt around him. He maintained control of her hips, raising her up and pulling her back down on him as he felt her wrap her arms around his neck to hold on to him as he set a vigorous pace. They needed each other, and they couldn't spend the same amount of time mating that they would if they were at home.

He could feel her getting closer and closer, her body tightening in anticipation as he continued pulling her down on him. He knew it wouldn't take much more. She was almost there, and she always took him with her when her body clamped down on him demanding all of him.

Gabriel, she cried tightening her hold on him as he pulled her down on him again one last time, pushing her over the edge. Collapsing against him, she held on to him riding the aftershocks with him as her body continued to milk him dry.

I got you, my love, he reassured her letting go of her hips and wrapping his arms around her as he kissed her temple. He was never going to get enough of her. He held her tightly to him while they both tried to catch their breaths.

Ruby reluctantly sat up knowing they were at the air strip. She knew they had arrived a while ago, but she didn't yet move to get off of him. She didn't want to move, she liked being exactly where she was.

Gabriel leaned down to brush a kiss across her lips in comfort knowing she didn't want to move, but unfortunately, they were going to have to move shortly.

How do I look? she asked worried she looked like a complete mess and knowing Philip, a complete stranger, would see her when she got out of the car. She loved being with Gabriel, but she didn't want anyone except him to see her like this.

You look amazing, he told her brushing a stray lock of hair back from her face.

That is not what I meant, she groaned resting her forehead against his chest.

Your skirt may be sporting some new fashionable slits up the sides and your underwear is in my pocket, but your beautiful French braid is still intact, he teased lightly.

Well, as long as the braid is still intact that makes up for everything else, she told him sarcastically as she rolled her eyes at him even though he couldn't see them since she still had her forehead resting against his chest.

You look fine, my love, he reassured her kissing the top of her head. *Besides, I think he already knows what we were doing. He's not stupid. I told him to take the long way, and we've been in here a good deal longer than we needed to be since the car came to a stop. I also don't think he's stupid enough to say anything to upset you and if he is, well, I think he'll end up with at least a black and blue eye,* he reassured her knowing he was very unlikely to be able to control himself if Philip upset his mate.

Ruby nodded her head slightly and reluctantly moved off of him to readjust her skirt and shirt while he refastened his pants.

Come on, my love, let's get out of here. The sooner we locate that kid and get him home, the sooner we can go home, he reassured her before reluctantly moving to open the door to get out.

* * ❋ ❋ ❋ ❋ ❋ * *

Ruby laid resting peacefully in Gabriel's arms on the couch. She'd fallen asleep and he didn't have the heart to risk waking her up by carrying her to bed. He knew she'd settle back down and quickly go back to sleep once he got her to their room, but she was sleeping so peacefully, and he could feel how tired she was after the night they'd had… and technically day. They'd been out hunting quite productively all night and then come home and spent the day in other much more pleasurable pursuits.

It had been a few months since they had gone overseas on behalf of the CIA. They had settled at a different house this time than before. The first few days they'd spent in bed breaking another bed in as theirs and settling back in after the difficulty of being overseas. Then they'd spent the rest of the week making the house feel like home before settling into their current pattern.

Sometimes, they'd go out hunting for a night or two in a row and other nights they stayed home. Sometimes preferring to just stay in bed and other times just not caring about going out and hunting. It didn't seem to matter though how their day or night started or was spent it always ended the same way with them in each other's arms after at least a few hours of mating.

Gabriel leaned down to kiss her head lovingly before closing his eyes to join his mate in sleep. He had to say he liked their life and he loved his mate just as he knew she loved him. He looked forward to centuries of this.

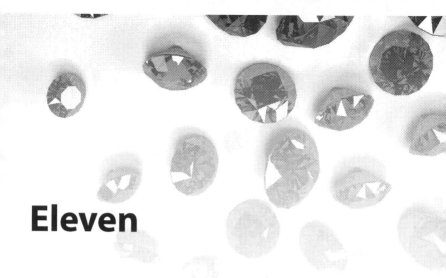

Eleven

Ruby sat back against one of the two doors to the bedroom with her knees pulled up to her chest. Resting her head on her knees, she wrapped her arms around her legs holding them to her, trying to comfort herself.

She knew Gabriel was coming, she couldn't get him to stop, though to be fair she wasn't entirely sure she wanted him to. she missed him and hated being separated from him. She wasn't entirely sure how she had managed to get this far away from him. She was past holding it together. She'd been crying into her knees wishing they were her Gabriel. Wishing to feel his arms around her, but that only made her cry harder. This was her fault and she knew it.

While she'd been still holding it somewhat together, she'd pleaded with him to stay where she'd left him, but he hadn't. And then she'd asked him to turn around and go back once he'd started chasing her, but again he hadn't listened to her. She'd tried to tell him to wait for her that she'd be back at the end of the year, but he'd ignored her and kept coming.

It hadn't been a long conversation. He'd made up his mind and she'd barely been holding it together to start with. She couldn't keep talking with him continuing to try and convince him to stay away. She didn't have it in her. And a big part of her didn't want to deter him. She wanted him back by her side. She needed her mate, but then that was the problem at hand and she feared if she kept trying to talk him down... she feared one of two different things occurring the first being that she might succeed which while it would suck and would hurt, she'd fix it next year, she hoped. Or two which in some ways was worse, she'd turn and run back to him to apologize and beg his forgiveness.

Her only choice was to stop talking to him and continue running, and hope he'd forgive her next year. She did her best to shut off her mind from him, but that... that was impossible. The only thing she could do was cry as she felt his pain and ignored him and his pleas for her to come back.

She'd ran for hours on in until she couldn't keep running. It hurt too much it was killing her. She'd only managed to keep up running long enough to get to where she sat now. To one of her houses... one of their houses that Gabriel had never been to before that had also been relatively nearby. She'd just wanted to rest for a moment before resuming running, but she couldn't get up and she couldn't stop crying. She didn't want to run any more. Hell, she was doing good just to keep herself glued to the floor where she sat crying instead of turning and running back to him. She wasn't entirely sure she wouldn't before it was all said and done.

She wanted to explain her decision, but she couldn't there was no excuse for her behavior. Hell, she hadn't made a decision she'd just... she didn't know what. What was she doing? What was she thinking? She wasn't thinking, that's all there was to that. She was doing her best to shut off her mind all together as she cried into her knees. Everything hurt and ached and needed. She didn't want to think it just made it worse and he was in her mind. All that left was crying.

And he was still on his way to her, she could feel him growing ever closer. What was she going to do?

* * * * * * * *

Gabriel sat down on the other side of the door she wasn't sitting against. He had been angry when he had woken up without his mate in their bed with him, but more than anything he had been hurt and using the anger to hide it. He didn't understand why she had left him, especially when he could so badly feel her need to be in his arms.

On the long trip back to her side, the anger had quickly fallen away and left him in pain. He didn't understand how she could do it, but he would have her back in his arms, she was his mate and he wouldn't let her leave him.

It was a while before he ashamedly realized he wasn't the only one hurting. He had been so hurt by her leaving that he hadn't stopped to think about how she was feeling. He had just wanted her back in his arms, and he had wanted her to tell him why, but she wasn't answering.

He had come to a dead stop nearly collapsing to the ground grabbing at his chest, she hurt so much. How had he not noticed? How had he focused on his own pain making her feel worse and not trying to help her? She was his mate, he wasn't supposed to be hurting her, he should have been comforting her. He still had no idea what was going on, but he knew he needed to get to his mate.

He forced himself to resume running redoubling his efforts. He could feel her still trying to tell him to stay away, but he could feel her pain at being this far away from him, not being able to see him, and worse not being able to touch him. She needed to be back in his arms just as much as he needed her back in his arms. What he didn't understand, and what she wasn't telling him is why she was fighting the urge, the compulsion to be back in his arms, fighting it itself was causing her more pain. He knew she wanted to run back to him, he knew she felt horrible for leaving, he knew she needed him. He didn't understand why she was fighting it. They had been together for years, she knew he loved her and had no intention of leaving her, ever. Why after the last two decades they had spent together was she fighting her need to have him take her? Sure, her need and desire for him had never been like this, it felt like she might die if he didn't take her, but then they had also never been this far apart since they had mated and that couldn't be helping given how possessive they both were of each other. He needed his mate, he needed to give her what she needed, which right now was him.

"Ruby, my love," he said softly from the other side of the door, hurting. He needed to ease her pain, but she didn't want him in the room, and even though he knew he could force the door open and she would be relieved to be back in his arms, he couldn't hurt her like that. He knew there was a reason for her behavior, and he needed her to tell him.

"Gabriel, please don't," she whimpered.

"My love, I need you to talk to me. Tell me what is going on, you hurt so much. It's killing me, it's killing both of us. You need me, my love. Please," he implored closing his eyes.

"I can't," she sobbed fighting how enticing it would be to just give in as he wanted her to do. "This is different, we can't."

"Why not, Ruby? Nothing has changed between us. I love you, I always have, and I know you still love me."

No, no, no, we can't, no, not this year, no, she chanted more to herself than to him. She wouldn't let him touch her, she couldn't, not this year. She needed him to stay away, he could have her back in a year, not right now. She needed to keep him out, which she knew wasn't going to be easy when every nerve in her body was craving his touch.

"My love, what is different about this year? Why not this year?" he asked turning his head to look at the other door she was leaning against. He absently brought his hand up to caress the door where she sat. He knew exactly where she was sitting, and if it wasn't for the damn door, he would have been caressing her back attempting to soothe her.

"What?" she squeaked. "Why did you ask that?" she barely whispered.

Because you were thinking not this year, he told her mentally to gently remind her of their connection.

No, Gabriel. Please, I can't, we can't, don't make me. Please Gabriel, she sobbed moving to lay curled up on the floor with her back still against the door.

My love, I'm not making you do anything, but I need help understanding what is going on. Please love, why are you putting yourself through all this pain? I know you need me, why won't you let me help my mate, my love? You are hurting both of us. If you want me to help you keep putting yourself through this, I need a reason, my love, he told her gently.

I don't want to get pregnant, she whimpered softly in his head.

Nobody said anything about getting pregnant, my love.

I did, I'm not ready, I don't want to be pregnant. Please, Gabriel...

My love, I don't understand. I would never make you get pregnant, but I don't understand why you are bringing this up now. We've been together for a little over twenty years now, and you've never once been worried about getting pregnant and it's not like we've been exactly careful or abstinent. Why are you concerned all of the sudden, my love?

It's not all of the sudden, it's been fifty years.

We've not been together fifty years, my love, he gently reminded her confused.

No, but it has been fifty years since the last time I had a fertile year, she sniffled.

My love? he asked confused.

This year.

I still don't quite understand, my little love. I know your body like the back of my hand, but this I don't know. Help me understand, he encouraged gently.

Gabriel, I wasn't concerned about getting pregnant before because I couldn't.

And this year you can, he questioned making sure he was understanding what she was saying.

She nodded her head even though he couldn't see her. *Every fifty years, this... this... fun year,* she scoffed.

Ruby, I'm not sure I understand the problem.

I don't want to get pregnant, Gabriel, she whimpered.

I thought you wanted children, my love? he asked confused.

I do, but... she opened the door still laying on the ground so she could look at him. He leaned his weight back against his hand so that he could look down at her, but he didn't touch her, he knew she didn't want him to, despite what her body told both of them. *Are you ready for children?* she asked awkwardly looking up at him.

What? he asked shocked.

Do you want me to get pregnant? she repeated.

Ruby, that's not what I said.

I know, Gabriel, but I'm asking you, do you want me to be pregnant? Are you ready to start a family? she questioned.

I... I... I don't know, I hadn't really thought about it.

Me either, I've enjoyed having you to myself. We've not once stopped to talk about a family. I'm not... we're not ready for me to be pregnant, she told him weakly.

My love, you're sure it's not me, he questioned worriedly.

What? Of course, I'm sure. I love you, Gabriel. You are the only one I want children with, but not yet. Gabriel, I've been alone for so long, I just want time to be with you alone, she admitted.

Ruby, why didn't you mention this before? he asked gently. Gabriel reluctantly moved knowing she wanted the door closed again.

Ruby closed the door with her foot. She couldn't have the door open it was too much temptation, but then it's not like closing the door changed anything, he was still right there, and she still needed him. *I don't know, Gabriel. I obviously planned to at some point, but I... I don't know, it just hadn't come up and I hadn't thought about it. I wasn't concerned about getting pregnant, and I... I got lost in time. Being with you... I guess, I just forgot, I lost track of when... I meant to tell you, Gabriel, I don't want to hide anything from you, and obviously it impacts us both, but I...* she trailed off.

Ruby, what happened? Why did I wake up alone? Why didn't you getting out of bed wake me like it usually does, especially considering the circumstances? he asked gently.

Because I hadn't intended to leave when I woke up, I didn't stop to pack anything, I had just gotten up to get a drink and then I was coming back to bed, she swore.

But you didn't come back to bed, he countered.

I'm sorry, she sobbed.

My love, you don't need to be sorry, I just want to know what's going on. I want to know how I can help. Why didn't you come back to bed? he questioned.

Because I knew if I came back to bed, my need for you would have woken you and we would have… I didn't want to get pregnant. I was afraid, Gabriel. I had felt it downstairs when I was in the kitchen, she struggled to explain.

Felt what? he asked gently.

I felt it start. The need, the craving, I knew it had started. I had never thought about it before, but suddenly feeling it now. It was all different, it was the same, but different. It made sense, but at the same time, I knew if I stayed, we'd get pregnant.

My little love, I need you to help clear that up a little. I'm missing something here, he coaxed gently. It was like pulling teeth. He knew it wasn't her fault, she was trying to explain, but it wasn't easy for her and his knowledge was limited.

Every fifty year it would happen, this… this… horrible year, she started telling him. She sounded so forlorn and far away to him, he could feel the pull like she was taking him back through the ages or maybe more like she was going back without him and their bond was stretching trying to keep them together trying to ground her. *I don't know how to explain it, it's like all of the sudden all of my hormones turn on, just for a year sure, but there they are all laid out and feeding on me. It's not like human hormones, it's different they're so much stronger, so consuming. You know what I mean, we're not like humans,* she pleaded for him to understand.

Gabriel nodded he knew what she was referring to, their bond, their need for each other. They mated so much harder and so much more frequently than humans did.

But this is more, she continued. *I know you feel it, I know you know it feels stronger, more urgent, more demanding. It's the hormones*, she told him.

Ruby, what about before me? he asked hesitantly. He could feel her need for him, but if it was like this every fifty years, and they had only been together for twenty... He wasn't sure he wanted that answer.

It was the same, but different. Before you, I didn't have you. In some ways it was worse, a lot worse. There was the clawing need, an ache, a void that needed filling, but I didn't know what it was... I... I... I wasn't me, I was anxious and angry, and I needed... I didn't know what I needed. It ate at me, I was out of control, I would have to isolate myself for the year to keep from... I don't know what, I just... I wanted to make others hurt and feel what I felt, I felt crazy... and now you're bound to me. I don't want you to feel and see me like this, Gabriel, she sniffled wiping at her face.

His heart was breaking for her, he hated to think of her going through that every fifty years without him. He could feel the pain time after time. He could feel it ripping through him as she remembered the emotions, and he knew it had only been magnified by being alone and being lonely. *But you said something made sense now, my little love*, he asked gently.

I know what I needed, I know what I couldn't figure out, what I couldn't find and why, she told him sadly.

My love, he prodded softly wanting her to continue her thought.

Exactly.

What? he asked confused.

Your love. It's you, you're what I was missing, what I needed, but I didn't know you, I didn't have you, and I couldn't find you because you didn't exist, yet, she explained.

But I do now, and you have me now. Let me help, my little love, it doesn't need to be like the past anymore, he tried to comfort her.

I said in some ways it was worse, but in one big way this is worse. Now, I know what I needed, and you're here, she whimpered.

Ruby? he asked worriedly.

It's you I need, but this year it's you that can get me pregnant, she told him pointedly.

Ruby, please. We'll just have to be careful then, he tried to reassure her softly.

Careful… careful… she laughed. *Gabriel, we go at it all the time as it is, and I can feel the difference, so do you. This will be worse, it will be more, I wouldn't have thought it possible, but I can feel it. The need. If we… We won't be able to stop until the year is out, I can feel it. We will spend the year in bed, there is no careful. I need you to leave for the year,* she pushed.

No, my love. I can't do that, and we both know that is not what you really need, he gently disagreed. He couldn't leave her like this. It wasn't going to happen.

What I really need will get us pregnant, she told him.

Would that be the worst thing, my little love? he asked gently.

What? she asked scared.

So, we… so we get pregnant, would that be the worst thing ever? You're my mate, and I'm yours. I know you want children at some point, and there is no one else either of us wants to have them with. Would it be such a horrible thing if we got pregnant now versus, I don't know when down the line? he asked gently.

Gabriel? she whimpered not liking what he was suggesting.

Ruby, we both know we can't keep this up for a year.

Gabriel, I'm not ready, she argued.

Ruby, I know you are terrified, but I think we both know that's not going to go away. Neither of us knows what to expect when we have a baby, but we will be together, he reassured.

I… I know that, but I'm still not ready to give up having you to myself. And neither of us knows how to do an ultrasound or anything else, she argued.

What? he asked confused.

Gabriel, we're not human. How would we even know when I was due? she asked scared. *We don't know…* she trailed off. *Do you really think I'll only be pregnant for nine months?* she asked him.

I… he trailed off unable to think of anything to say.

Ruby could feel his silence. That thought hadn't even occurred to him, but then he had grown up human. He had just assumed it would just be a pregnancy and they'd go to a human doctor like they were just… normal. No big deal, but there were so many things to consider involved with her getting pregnant.

They weren't normal.

Gabriel, I know we will be terrified when we have our first baby, but I don't want it like this. I'm not ready, we're not ready. We've not talked about having children at all other than before I turned you and you realized for both of us that I wanted children, but there is a difference between wanting them, and wanting them right now, she told him.

I know, my love, he said gently.

Do you? she asked gently not sure he really understood.

I do, my little love. I just… I don't know what to tell you, I don't know how to fix this, he admitted feeling horrible.

Leave for the year, she said softly.

My love, you know I can't do that.

I know, she whimpered hating admitting the truth.

Ruby, please let me come in the bedroom, he requested gently.

No, she told him shaking her head.

Please, I want to… I need to be able to hold you, to touch you, he imagined brushing his fingertips over the side of her face, holding her hand, bringing her hand to his mouth to kiss in comfort. *I need to at least be able to see my beautiful mate's face, my love. I hate having this door between us*, he told her his heartbreaking.

Gabriel, if I let you in here, she said shaking her head. *I know right now you just want to comfort me, but you'll want to touch me to hold me, and then… Gabriel, you know I already want, need more than that. You know how much I'm struggling. If I feel you touching me, even if only to comfort me, Gabriel please…* she trailed off hurting.

My little love, we can't keep this up for a year. I know how much you are struggling and I know how much pain you are in because of it, but I also know that you know how much I'm struggling not to tear down this door to be by your side when you feel the way you do, and I know how much you need me and I don't just mean sexually, I know you also need to just be in my arms and feel my reassuring touch.

I know, but… she knew it would lead to more.

My love, I don't think we can even keep this up for a couple days let alone even a week, I can't take much more, he admitted even though he knew it wasn't what she wanted to hear.

Gabriel, please…

Let me in, I won't touch you, please. He could feel her thinking about it, he could feel her struggling, she didn't like feeling the pain he was in being separated from her, but then he felt the same from her which was why he wanted in the room so badly. *My love, please. What is the point in trying to delay letting me be by your side, even if you can keep me out here for a week there are fifty-one more in the year? There is no point in us being in this pain, please let me in, my love,* he repeated.

Gabriel, she protested still not wanting to get pregnant, but nonetheless reluctantly opened the door with her mind.

Gabriel leaned over her as he leaned back into the room to look at his mate. She looked so tiny curled up in a ball on the floor like this. She was small, yes, but this was different it was like she was trying to curl into herself until she could disappear altogether. He started to reach for her with his hand, wanting to caress her face, needing to touch his mate, but he managed to stop himself. He needed her to come to him, he needed her to accept the situation they were in, especially in case they did end up pregnant, he couldn't have his mate hating him, blaming him.

I don't hate you, Gabriel. I couldn't. I love you, she told him hating herself for what she was doing to him. Making her mate question that she loved him.

Gabriel scooted back further into the room so that he could lay down on his side on the floor beside his mate without touching her. *My little love,* he crooned softly watching her fight the urge to look at him, to touch him, to move into his arms.

How can you accept this so easily? she asked struggling just to breathe.

It's not easy, love, but what choice do I have, what choice do we have? he asked trying to stay calm headed for both of them.

To fight it, she told him firmly.

For a year? Besides is it really so bad being with me? he asked softly trying to conceal his hurt.

Of course not, she told him unable to keep from looking up at him to make sure he knew that she loved being with him.

Gabriel started to reach for her again, but stopped himself, clenching his outstretched fingers into a fist and setting his fist on the floor between them. *Ruby, I obviously don't know how, but there has to be a way for us to control whether or not we get pregnant,* he suggested adamantly.

There's not, Gabriel, she told him sadly.

You don't know that, my love. Have you ever been through this mated? Have you ever been through this with anyone else? Have you ever talked to anyone who has? he questioned gently trying not to hurt her further.

Of course not. You know I've only ever been with you, and I don't know anyone else like us, she sniffled.

Which means you don't know, not that there isn't a way, he gently corrected her.

I suppose, but, Gabriel, that doesn't mean there is a way, she pointed out the flaw in his reasoning.

I think there is, there has to be, he told her. There had to be a way for them to get through this.

Why? she asked. She knew he wanted to be right, she wanted him to be right too, but that didn't mean he was right.

Because we're not human, he reminded her.

Gabriel, we may be able to do many things, but control procreation… that seems a little… she trailed off.

Farfetched? And the fact that we are talking in our heads, that we can move things with our minds, we can set fire to things at will, that I just ran here from, well I don't know how far away, that's not a little farfetched? he asked raising an eyebrow at her.

Yeah, but…

Just because we don't know how, doesn't mean we can't.

Gabriel, I understand what you are getting at, and I know you are trying to make me feel better, but we've been... intimate for decades now, don't you think if there was a way that we would have felt or sensed something to indicate that we could, she disagreed doubtful.

Not necessarily, neither of us was thinking about getting pregnant. You weren't concerned, because you knew you couldn't at the time. Maybe neither of us felt anything like that because we weren't looking or maybe because we can't feel it or do anything when it's irrelevant, like it has been until now, he suggested.

That's a big maybe, Gabriel.

Maybe, but it's all we've got, my love, he told her gently wishing he had a better answer.

Gabriel, she protested shaking her head not liking any of this.

Besides, my love, if we couldn't control it, don't you think there would be a lot more of us, he suggested.

What do you mean? she asked confused.

My love, if we can't control it, no matter how long your... our pregnancy would be, at some point soon after you deliver, we would resume this cycle of fifty years and then one year where we can get pregnant. And you are right with the frequency with which we mate, if there is not a way for us to control it, there is every likelihood we will get pregnant which would mean...

Oh god, Ruby thought bringing her hand to her mouth.

Ruby...

Oh god, we'd be swimming in kids in just a couple centuries and with how we age... they'd all be babies. Oh god, Gabriel, she cried starting to hyperventilate. She was already feeling lightheaded. She wanted children, sure, but... she wanted to be able to have time with them to raise them, to watch them grow, not be overwhelmed and surrounded by them. How would she ever be able to be a mother to them? And her mate. She'd found her mate, and had been happy, but it was going to be over. Her world was shattering. She was going to be an incubator never getting to just be happy with her mate.

Breathe, my love, breathe, he tried to calm her down reaching for her hand and surrounding it in his larger hand. He squeezed her hand gently and brought it to his mouth to kiss and then rested their hands between them on the floor. *Ruby, it's just not logical.*

Gabriel, she whimpered. *What does logic have to do with anything? We are what we are.*

Yes, but from an evolutionary standpoint, that doesn't make sense. For us to be capable of what we are capable of but to uncontrollably reproduce like that. It doesn't make sense, and at some point, it would be unrealistic for us to be able to take care of all those babies until they've had time to grow, and it would be unrealistic for us to be able to take care of them and still mate like this, like our bodies demand, especially during this year. It wouldn't make sense for our species to be this advanced, but yet...

Gabriel, we are hardly a species, it's just the two of us, she argued struggling not to just scream and start pulling her hair out. She knew she was screaming in her head. She had to be, how could she not be? This was so much worse than she thought.

Gabriel struggled to ignore her panicking so that he could attempt to calm her down and comfort her. It wasn't easy but giving into and getting stuck in her panic wasn't going to help her. *As far as we know, my love, you came from somewhere, from someone. And seeing as how you know you scared a lot of people shitless as a baby, I'm guessing you were born this way and not turned as a baby. Besides, when you turned me it started the bond between us, if someone had turned you, don't you think you or both of us would have noticed the presence of someone else's thoughts all this time.*

Yeah, but…

So, you came from someone. I don't know who would abandon you or why, but if we can't control having children, then I would think you have a whole hell of a lot of siblings out there and I find it hard to believe that it wouldn't have made a noticeable dent on the world or at least a presence you could have detected, he suggested calmly.

That's a fair assumption, unless I was the first of us, if I was some kind of genetic mutation or jump in evolution.

Well, now you're just grasping at straws, he teased lightly.

Gabriel, you are trying to apply logic where there may not be any, she said shaking her head sadly.

I know, my love, but I have to believe that the fate that pulled us together, that allowed you to sense me, did not do it for this to be the end result. You don't deserve that. You thought it had pulled us together for no reason when you didn't know how to turn me, you thought the world had finally given you something good only to really just taunt you with it, but here I am now. I can't believe fate would give me to you only to hurt you like this, he hoped like hell she was wrong. He swore he'd never hurt her and this… this was killing her. She had to be wrong, because this… this was cruel and wrong… very wrong.

Gabriel, Ruby took a deep breath. *I love you.*

Ruby? he questioned softly feeling something odd in her words.

If after everything, all I got were these twenty years alone with you, I want you to know that I love you and love being your mate, and I always will no matter what, she tried to apologize.

My love, I feel like you are telling me goodbye, and I don't like that, he told her worried. More than worried, scared.

Neither do I, she agreed.

Ruby, I'm not going anywhere, he reassured her.

I know, and neither am I, but I don't know what is going to happen, and I need you to know how happy you've made me, just how much I love you, she told him. Even if it was all over now, she'd had a few years of happiness and it was because of him. He didn't deserve what she feared was to come, but he'd loved her and made her happy and she'd never forget.

I already know, my love. Just as I can't begin to describe how much I love you, he reassured her.

Gabriel, she said reaching up to touch his jaw. *I'm sorry for whatever I may say or do this year, know that it's not… it's not entirely me,* she tried to warn him as she leaned in to kiss him as she stopped fighting the need. She let it consume her and thus him. She knew they would resurface at some point, but she wasn't sure how he would feel at that point or whether or not they would be pregnant.

But she couldn't fight anymore.

Ruby pushed him back against the floor as she moved to straddle him. Fisting her hands in the middle of his shirt, she began pulling. Tearing it in two down the center to expose him to her. She needed him in her now. Ruby reached down to find the hem of her top and pulled it off tossing it aside as she leaned down to kiss him as she ran her hands over his chest.

Sitting back up, her hands moved to the front of her pants and started undoing them. She didn't have time to stand up to take them off. She needed him in her now. Once she had the zipper down, she used her strength to begin tearing at her jeans. Ripping them apart to expose her entrance so that she could take in her mate. She didn't care about the clothes. Intact, shredded, on, off, whatever, but she needed herself accessible to his hard length so that she could have him in her.

Ruby, Gabriel struggled to think with her lust and need clouding their minds as he reached up to pull her down against his chest for him to capture her mouth. *I know you need me, but at some point, this year will end, and these are my only pants here at this house,* he informed her as he continued kissing her.

He didn't care about his clothes. Hell, part of him really wanted to see her shred his clothes to get to him, but they would need to be able to leave the house at some point and he hadn't exactly stopped to pack when he chased after her. They had been leaving a few clothes for him at each house they stayed in. Ruby wanted the closets to start becoming more reflective of the fact that he was her mate and to not just contain her clothes. But they had yet to visit this house otherwise he'd be encouraging her to tear his jeans off instead of attempting to try and keep them intact because otherwise at the end of the year she'd have to leave the house without him to locate pants for him and he knew how much they both hated being separated from each other.

If you don't want them hanging in taters, you better quickly get what I need available, she told him forcefully as she trailed kisses down his neck and across his chest as she moved to sit back up to look down at him.

Gabriel rested his hands on her thighs as he watched her remove her bra for him while he used telekinesis to unbutton and unzip his pants to set himself free for her before she shredded his pants. His hands slid to her hips to help steady her as she shifted lifting up so that she could settle herself on him. He could feel her relief as he stretched her.

Ruby reached back resting her hands on his thighs to help balance herself as she started riding him trying to sate her need. She couldn't help the anger she felt feeling his thighs clad in jeans. She wanted to feel her mate. He was hers. All of him. She struggled not to shred his jeans to get to his thighs moving her hands instead to his washboard abdomen where she could feel his skin under her hands.

Gabriel fought to maintain any kind of awareness as he watched his mate ride him. He knew she was lost in sensation. He knew she'd given up any hope of not getting pregnant, but she was beyond caring at the moment just needing him. He knew if there was something to find or feel to help keep them from getting pregnant, he'd have to be the one to figure it out. He hoped he was right, and he hoped he could muster enough focus to figure it out because right now he felt just about as lost in her need as she was.

He'd felt her orgasm as he'd emptied himself into her. She didn't stop riding him, she couldn't. She'd barely paused long enough to milk as much as she could out of him before she'd started moving her hips again in a vigorous rhythm needing relief. Needing more. But she could ride him until her heart's content, he'd found the information he was looking for, what they needed to know to make it through the year.

❖ ❖ ◉ ◉ ◉ ❖ ❖

Gabriel wrapped his arms around Ruby holding her to him. She'd finally passed out from exhaustion. They'd been at it for days mating nonstop. The last time before she'd passed out completely, she'd collapsed on top of him still needing him but unable to move to keep riding him as her body demanded. He'd done the work for her. Holding her hips in his hands as he'd lifted them up and pulled her back down on him over and over again while she rested on his chest until he felt her clamp down on him pulling them both over the edge as he released in her yet again.

Now that she'd finally passed out, Gabriel kicked off his shoes and struggled to lift his hips to use his mind to push down his pants and remove them. He knew she had hated them staying on him and had struggled not to destroy them, but she'd been unable to stop long enough for him to dispatch with them. He knew once she woke up, she'd still need him. He could feel it. So, he got rid of his pants for her which wasn't an easy task. They were both exhausted.

He struggled to pull the blanket off the bed with his mind to cover them. He didn't have the strength to stand up or get her to the bed. Gabriel ran a hand lovingly through her hair as he kissed the top of her head. Tightening his arms around her he laid his head back down on the ground and closed his eyes. They'd get through this he tried to remind himself.

* * * * * * * *

Ruby had woken up crying in his arms which had woken him. He could feel how weak she still was. They both were. Her fear over getting pregnant had cut through her deep sleep and woken her, but her being awake had also stirred her need and craving for him which left her crying at the combination of the two. Though her need was quickly winning roaring its head despite her tears that still fell and her inability to move in her weakened state.

Gabriel, she pleaded needing him to take her again. She couldn't move, but she now had too much energy to pass out with her need for him riding her.

I've got you, my love, he reassured her as he rolled her onto her back so that he was on top of her. *And you don't need to be afraid about getting pregnant,* he told her gently not wanting her needless fear to continue keeping her from getting rest. *We're not going to get pregnant,* he assured her gently.

What? she asked looking up at him as her thoughts managed to break through her need, but only just barely.

We won't get pregnant, he repeated bringing his hand up to brush away her tears.

You're sure, she asked doubtful and still plenty scared.

I promise, my love, he reassured her as he leaned down to capture her mouth feeling her need.

Faster. Harder, she demanded digging her nails into his back to hold on to him as he pounded into her. She needed relief.

Gabriel struggled to give her what she needed nearly as exhausted as she was. He could hear her scream his name in her head as their orgasm took her over the edge and he released himself in her.

Thank you, she sighed her arms falling from holding on to his back as she closed her eyes passing out and succumbing to the darkness.

◆ ◇ ◈ ◉ ◈ ◇ ◆

Ruby grabbed at her lower stomach as she closed her eyes against the pain. She'd been watching Gabriel make her breakfast. The last few days had felt normal. She knew the year was far from over and she was still plenty emotional, but she'd managed to string thoughts together and to stop screwing Gabriel's brains out for the moment. She knew the need would come back and from the pains in her stomach she was willing to bet soon. They'd probably get a few more days of rest first before her body demanded they resume their previous activities.

What's wrong? Gabriel asked dropping what he was doing to pull her into his arms back against his chest as his hand slid to her stomach where hers rested.

Nothing's wrong. It's normal, she tried to reassure him as she turned towards his chest bringing her other hand up to hold on to his side.

This doesn't feel normal. You're in a lot of pain. What's going on? he asked worried about his mate.

I'm not pregnant, she sighed relieved.

That's what this is, he asked realizing what was going on. Ruby nodded her head in answer against his chest. *I had promised you I wouldn't get you pregnant when you'd woken up crying at the beginning of all this,* he reminded her gently as he kissed the top of her head in comfort.

I know... I... I know you meant it, but I... I was scared, Gabriel. I still am. I was afraid to believe you could... keep from getting me... pregnant... in case you were wrong. I know how badly you wanted to make me feel better, to reassure me that we could keep from getting pregnant. I know you weren't lying, but I also know that I was... not all here, and I know I was affecting you through our bond, she told him struggling not to start crying. She didn't want him thinking she didn't believe him and that she'd thought he'd been lying to her because it wasn't true. She loved him. She knew he wouldn't lie to her, but she was terrified of getting pregnant.

It's alright, my love. It's alright. I know how much this scares you, but I'm right here with you and you're not pregnant, he reminded her gently as he held on to her. *Is there anything I can do to help?* he asked feeling her continuing pain in her lower stomach. The pain was excruciating.

A *hot bath*, she told him wrapping her arms around his neck and burying her face there as he scooped her into his arms.

You got it, he agreed carrying her upstairs to their room to take a hot bath.

She could feel his worry. He didn't like her being in pain and he still wasn't entirely sure what all was going on exactly. This year was a very new experience for them. *It'll only be for a few hours. It's not like humans,* she tried to tell him wanting to make him feel better and trying to help him understand what was happening.

What? he asked confused as he sat down on the side of the tub holding her in his arms as he used his mind to turn on the water for them.

The pain... the bleeding, she struggled to admit feeling embarrassed. *It will only be for a few hours. It won't last a week like it does for humans. We can... we can stay here in... in the tub until it's over if... if that's alright with you,* she asked worried about his reaction. Worried that he might not want to stay by her side while she was... while she...

I'm not going anywhere, my little love. I'm staying right here by your side. And if you want to stay in the tub in the hot water, that's exactly what we will do, he reassured her as he turned still sitting on the side of the tub to put his feet in the water. Holding her in his lap with one arm, he moved to untie her robe so that they could slip into the tub. He knew she would have preferred to be wearing one of his shirts, but she'd shredded the only one he'd had, the one on his back when he'd arrived.

He floated her robe over to hang off the hook on the wall and slid into the water still holding her in his arms. He was relieved to feel the hot water helping her cramps as he set her down in his lap. *I know you're scared, my love, and I know telling you not to worry won't stop your worry, but you don't need to worry. I don't know how to explain it, but I can feel it. We're not going to get pregnant. You don't need to worry. We won't get pregnant until we decide it's what we want and that we are ready to have children,* he tried to reassure her as he kissed the top of her head in comfort.

Ruby nodded her head against his chest as she closed her eyes and let herself drift. She'd still been recovering from the last several weeks, they both were, but she needed rest. She was relieved to be in his arms and the hot water was helping with the pain. She felt him kiss her head again as she slipped to sleep.

Twelve

"Ruby what's wrong," Gabriel asked coming up behind her.

"Nothing is wrong," Ruby denied softly as she continued staring out the window in their bedroom.

"I know something is wrong and you've been denying it. I haven't said anything about it until now because I thought once you figured it out or had had some time to think about it that you would come to me with whatever it is and talk about it. But you've been intentionally trying to keep yourself from thinking and you haven't come to me to talk. It's been nearly five years since I started feeling whatever this is that is bothering you. Talk to me," he encouraged gently.

"It's almost time."

"I know," Gabriel said wrapping his arms around her waist to pull her back against his chest while kissing the top of her head gently in comfort. "But I'm not going anywhere, and you know that. I'll be here for you just like I was last time, and the time before, and just like I'm going to be here every time from now on," he reminded her.

"I know," Ruby said softly.

"Then what is it? There is more to this that you're not saying," he pressed wanting to know what was bothering his mate.

"Gabriel, we haven't talked about it since last time. We said we would, and we never did," she said turning around and burying her face against his chest.

"I take it 'it' is referring to more than just your ovulation period," he guessed shrewdly tightening his arms around her comfortingly to hold her to him.

"We both agreed last time that it was too soon to look at having children, we weren't ready, and that was after I had… well… panicked the time before at the idea of getting pregnant," she struggled to admit. She didn't like remembering how badly she had panicked the first time she went through her fertile year after mating him. "But we said that we would spend some of the time until now discussing what to do this time, but we never once talked about it."

"I know. I guess we were just too distracted with everything and never really took the time to sit down and discuss it," he agreed apologetically as he kissed the top of her head and rested his chin there as he continued to hold her snuggly against him.

"I think I want a baby, Gabriel," she said barely audible.

"Ruby," he questioned lifting his head to look down at her even though she still had her face buried against his chest.

I think I… I'm ready for… for us to try, she struggled to get out unable to talk out loud.

"You want to try and get pregnant this time," he asked running a hand comfortingly over her back continuing to hold her to him.

I… well, not this time. I mean we haven't really talked about it or done anything to prepare. Next… next time, if… if you want… want to have a baby with me, she barely got out weakly worried he might not want to get her pregnant.

"My little love, you needn't worry about me wanting to get you pregnant. I'd love to see your belly growing with my baby in it," *my seed,* he couldn't help but think unable to stop the unbidden thought. The possessive streak in him when it came to her. He was relieved when he felt her sigh and happiness at his thought. She liked his possessiveness and liked that he wanted his child in her.

"But Ruby, my love," he crooned softly kissing the top of her head. "I'm not sure I see the need to wait until next time to try getting pregnant. I mean if you're ready to try now… unless you're not sure and want to wait until next time… That's alright, I understand. I want you to be ready before we try for children. It's a big decision expanding our little family," he told her softly.

I… I am sure, she reassured him tilting her head back and resting her chin on his chest to look up at him. *But I think there are some things we need to talk about. Things we need to decide on and do before you get me pregnant. I want us to be prepared.*

"My love, the only thing we need to do to prepare is start setting up nurseries in our houses which we can do while you are pregnant. And whatever houses we don't manage to set one up in before you deliver we can set one up in as we move around, or we will set up a child's room if we need to at that point depending on how big our baby is when we get there. Our baby is going to grow, we will undoubtedly be having to make periodic updates as we move around. And depending on the frequency at which we get to certain homes, sometimes it will be a dramatic change to update our baby's room to a more age appropriate setting. Besides, I'm not sure we should be setting up a nursery until we know if we are having a boy or a girl, which we won't know until after I get you pregnant," he finished teasing lightly.

"Gabriel, a nursery or several is not what I'm worried about," she assured him.

"Then what is it you are worried about, my love?" he asked trailing a hand through her hair.

"Well, for one, where do you think I'm going to deliver our supernatural baby?" she inquired.

"Supernatural," he asked chuckling.

"Well, what else would you call us? It's not like we are human, and it would be our baby. I'd expect it to be like us, wouldn't you?" she asked

"Of course, I would, my love. I just… I find it a little funny to hear you actually call us 'supernatural' that's all," he reassured her gently.

"So, where am I going to deliver our baby?" she asked him again.

"I'm not sure I understand, Ruby. We can deliver anywhere you like. I don't care what country, territory, state, or city. We can go to which ever home is in whatever location you want as we get close to delivery, and when it's time we'll go to the hospital and have our little baby to take home," he answered her.

"Gabriel, do you really think we can go to the hospital?" she asked shaking her head in disagreement as she looked up at him.

"Why not?" he asked confused. "Ruby, I know you don't have a fondness for hospitals, but they are the ones that would know how to deliver a baby and our baby would have to come out at some point," he assured her.

"And that is one reason we need to talk about how we are going to prepare, because there are several reasons we can't go to the hospital," she disagreed with his plan.

"I'd like to know these reasons first, Ruby," he asked scooping her into his arms and carrying her to the bed to sit down.

"Fine," she agreed as he sat down on the bed holding her in his lap.

"Ruby, it's alright. We have time to talk about this," he reassured her. He knew she was worried about the encroaching start of her fertile year. "It doesn't start today or even tomorrow. We both know we have about a month. It's alright to take time right now to talk, and when it is time... if we haven't finished talking about this, we will wait until next time. That's alright. I swore to you, I wouldn't get you pregnant if it wasn't what you wanted, and I meant it. I know you're ready in some ways, but whatever this is we need to discuss... I know it needs to be discussed and settled before you're fully ready. Before, we're fully ready to get pregnant. So, let's talk, and if we need to, we will pick this up in exactly a year and a month, maybe two months if we need some rest first," he promised kissing her temple as he played with her hair to calm her down.

"I love you," she sighed looking up at him. Reaching up she brushed her fingertips over his jaw, and then briefly kissed him on the lips.

"Of course, you do. Why else would you agree to carry my child?" he teased lightly.

"So, you don't leave me when you find out I'm cheating on you," she teased him unable to keep a straight face at her own attempt at humor.

Gabriel's hand slid to the nape of her neck as he leaned down to capture her mouth. *You know I'd never leave you. I'd just kill your lover,* he told her frankly. *You're mine, and mine alone,* he told her brushing one more soft kiss over her well kissed lips before lifting his head to look down at her.

Ruby couldn't help smiling up at him as she bit at her lower lip. She loved his possessive streak for her. He had absolutely no reason to be jealous. She'd never lie to him, cheat on him, or leave him. She didn't have it in her to hurt him. But nevertheless, she loved how possessive he was of her.

Gabriel brushed his thumb over her cheek in a caress and then slid his hand down to her hip to hold on to her. He was always relieved when she wasn't upset by his animalistic possessiveness of her, but it wasn't really his possessiveness that she loved, or maybe 'just' was more appropriate. It wasn't just his possessiveness she loved. She loved belonging to him. Knowing she belonged to someone, with someone. She had a family in him, and she knew just how much he loved her and that he'd never hurt her.

"Tell me what's wrong with the hospital," he encouraged gently as he watched her.

"Well, there is the small issue of us very much living off the grid. I may have tons of false identities as do you now, but I… I technically don't exist. But living off the grid is what we need given who we are. We can't have our son or daughter's birth being recorded and put on the system, especially given as long as we live," she pointed out calmly.

"Yeah, that… that wouldn't be such a good thing," he agreed not wanting to put any child they had in jeopardy.

"And what happens if I need a c-section for whatever reason, like my cervix doesn't dilate. I mean we heal well, and the natural state of a cervix is closed. That could make things difficult if my body keeps trying to heal to 'closed'. Though that might also be a good thing to help prevent me from going into early labor," she continued.

"Ruby, you just continued on getting very detailed about something and you lost me. Let's back it up to your question or point you were trying to make again," he told her.

"What happens when I need a c-section?" she asked.

"Well… then you'd be in the right place for a c-section to deliver our baby," he told her.

"Yeahhh," she drew out slowly. "And how about you explain to me how you see that going?" she asked concerned.

"Well, I mean… they'd do a c-section. They do an incision to get into your uterus to deliver our baby and then you'd… I mean I know you'd have to heal from a c-section but that's to be expected and I'd be there helping you take care of our baby especially while you're recovering," he said not entirely sure what exactly her concern was regarding a c-section.

"Gabriel," she interrupted. "I think you are missing a big part. Exactly how long do you think it's going to take me to recover from a c-section?" she asked.

"I don't know, a few weeks, but we'd have our baby," he answered thinking she was concerned about recovering from a c-section.

"Gabriel, how long did this take to heal?" she asked moving his hand on her hip so that she could roll over his arm that was resting across her waist to look at the underside of his forearm. As she looked at the scar there, she couldn't stop herself from running a finger over it down the length of his forearm remembering the terror she felt seeing him carve it into his arm trying to prove to her that it was safe for him to back her up.

"Ruby, you know the answer to that," he told her gently knowing she was reliving the memory.

"Humor me," she told him forcing herself to look away from his arm to look up at him.

"A few hours," he estimated shrugging.

"And how about this one?" she asked raising up his shirt that she was wearing to show him the scar across her midriff that she had received the night she met him.

Gabriel ran his thumb over the scar. Over the years it had further healed to the point that he could no longer feel it just like his arm, but he could still see it, just as she could see the one on his arm. "A few hours," he answered sadly as he looked up into her face hurting at the memory.

Ruby let go of the shirt bringing her hand up to his neck as she reached up to kiss to distract him from the pain, and to remind him that she was okay, that she was safe.

Gabriel kissed her thoroughly before breaking their kiss. Before completely lifting his head, he brushed one last soft kiss across her lips thanking her.

"Now remind me how long you think it will take me to heal from a c-section?" she asked looking up at him intently.

"Shit," he muttered shaking his head as he caught her meaning. "About as long as this wound," he said lifting up his shirt to look at her stomach again.

"Gabriel, that's hardly the only problem with me having a c-section in a hospital," she informed him gently.

"What do you mean?" he asked confused.

"Well, aside from how quickly they had completely healed, think about how fast they stopped bleeding," she suggested.

"Extremely, almost immediately," he said thinking about how quickly his arm had stopped bleeding. "But I don't think that's necessarily a big deal in the circumstances you are talking about. I mean a c-section should hopefully be a relatively controlled surgery, so there should be a limited amount of bleeding regardless," he said confused what her question had to do with anything.

"Gabriel, they stopped bleeding because they were trying to heal. My concern is not my blood loss or lack thereof. My concern is my body trying to actively heal while they are trying to cut into me to get to our baby. Aside from the fact that it won't be hard to miss their incision closing and shrinking as they are trying to progress which would have its own repercussions for us, and I mean all of us because at that point they would have strong suspicions about you and our baby having the same abilities, especially our baby since it would be related to me... aside from that aspect, my concern is for our baby. If we are having to do a c-section, it's because something is not going the way it's supposed to such as our baby being in trouble. I don't want some asshole stopping to investigate or acting hastily while trying to get to our baby and hurting him or her or putting their life in danger," she told him.

"I'm liking this conversation less and less," he muttered not liking how nice and calmly she was enumerating the problems with them attempting to have a child or rather specifically delivering their child.

"Yes, but you wanted to know the problems with delivering in a hospital and I'm not done," she told him.

"Great," he griped unhappily.

"Well, I know you've noticed our metabolism is also different. To which I'm specifically referring to how well we metabolize alcohol, but I assure you we also similarly metabolize drugs. How well do you think anesthesia would work?" she asked him as she looked at his hand she was holding on to.

"I'm guessing not well," he begrudged unhappily.

"I could... I could fake it and hold still if I had an epidural in place that they thought was working, but there would be no reason for me to get an epidural if it wouldn't work. And I assure you I would fight them if they tried to put a tube down my throat. I can handle a c-section without anesthesia, but I don't want them attempting to induce general anesthesia that would have limited or no effect on me and may or may not hurt our baby," she told him running her fingers over his hand.

"I get it, a c-section is off the table, so let's stop talking about it because I'm not enjoying this. Besides, we don't know that you would even need a c-section anyways you're getting a little ahead of yourself," he told her.

"I don't think I am. I think we should be prepared for all possibilities. And as for a c-section, well yeah it would be better to not have to have one, but we don't know what is going to happen and they have their place. If I need one for the sake of our baby, I damn well want one," she proclaimed.

"Ruby," he sighed. "You just got done telling me a ton of reasons why that would be a bad idea."

"No, I just got done telling you why that would be a bad idea in a hospital," she argued quietly.

Gabriel's eyes widened as he looked down at her in shock. "And where the hell else would you suggest doing a c-section?" he asked not really wanting an answer to that question, but knowing she planned to ultimately give him one.

"Let's come back to the question," she suggested barely audibly knowing he wouldn't like her answer and he was already unhappy.

"Sure, why not?" he answered sarcastically like it was no big deal to ignore the question when it was clearly a relevant question that needed addressing.

"I'm... I'm going to let that go," she hedged quietly. "Gabriel, if things started to change and I suddenly needed a c-section and we were in a hospital, well it's not like we could just leave," she told him not looking at him.

"No? You want to bet. If you say we're leaving, I assure you I will make sure we get out of there," he told her firmly.

"Yes, and make a big scene in the process," she chuckled looking up at him from under her lashes. She found the thought slightly amusing, but also reassuring because she knew he would do it. But it would also create other problems too.

"Gabriel, hospitals have a lot of rules and if they tried to prevent you from being at my side at any point… well, I don't think either of us would handle that well," she admitted.

"No, I suppose not," he agreed.

"And aside from the fact that I just don't like hospitals in general, they tend to have a lot of people there," she said weakly.

"Ruby, I'm not sure people are a valid argument against hospitals," he questioned her reasoning.

"Gabriel, we hear well, very well. We'll be able to hear everything going on in that hospital nonstop for who knows what kind of duration we'd be looking at. Long enough to drive us crazy, and… and I'd also be in pain throughout that duration until I delivered, which means you'll be in pain too." Ruby peered up at him for a moment before she looked back down at their hands to continue. "I know I'm old, and for the most part have good control over my abilities, but…"

"You're worried about my control," he interrupted when she hesitated.

"No, I mean I don't know… I probably should be, but no, I was speaking about me. Gabriel, that's going to be a very volatile situation in which my limitations will be pushed in many ways and I can't begin to imagine how anxious I'd be in regard to our baby. Gabriel, you know just how powerful we are, but you have no idea what I was like as a child when I discovered my abilities with my emotions. It was… well, let's just say the animal tribes had reasons to be afraid of me. And that's not even taking into account our just plain strength," she added shaking her head. *Gabriel, it wouldn't be safe there, for any of us,* she confessed highly doubting her ability to control herself and she hadn't even thought about Gabriel controlling himself when he'd be feeling everything she felt too.

My love, where are we going to have a child then? he gently asked moving his hand she was still holding onto to tilt her chin up to look at him.

Anywhere you want, country, state, providence, territory, but not a hospital, she answered meekly.

Are you mocking me now? he asked narrowing his eyes at her.

Ruby shook her head vigorously. *No, I mean it. I don't care where, but not a hospital. Though to be fair I was kind of thinking it would make the most sense for it to be in one of our houses,* she told him worriedly as she looked up at him.

"And who exactly is going to be delivering our child?" he asked raising an eyebrow at her.

"Well…" she started as she tugged on his hand that she was still holding on to so that she could look at her lap again as she meekly continued, *one of us should probably go to medical school.*

"One of us?" he asked raising her chin back up.

Well, it would probably be best if it was you. I mean I'd go with you of course, but it might be a little tricky for me to deliver our baby, she admitted with a half-smile.

"You don't say," he agreed shaking his head. "So, you want me to go to med school," he questioned.

Well, you're plenty smart, and there's only one area we really need expertise in, and you won't be alone. I mean two brains are better than one, she grinned ear to ear. *And it probably wouldn't be a bad idea to do a residency program in obstetrics. I mean that way if you felt uncomfortable in any way after med school, it would be good practice. It would also allow you to get plenty of practice with ultrasounds since I would imagine we would need to do serial ultrasounds plotted against a human growth pattern if we have any chance of predicting when I'll deliver and to monitor the pregnancy. I mean I imagine there will be a lot of learning that still has to be done while I'm pregnant when it comes to… to our baby since we have no idea what a normal pregnancy would look like for us. I guess it's possible it'd only be nine months, but I think we both suspect that is unlikely. I don't know if it will be the same rate just slower or if there might be some kind of curve variation. But it would probably be best to attempt to map the growth with ultrasounds, so at least one of us should be comfortable with that since it's not like we can have a human scanning my stomach over and over again attempting to do these calculations for us.*

"Now, I see why you said you wanted to prepare," he said shaking his head.

"Does… does that mean… no?" she asked nervously. She knew she was asking a lot of him.

"No, I'll do," he informed her still shaking his head. He couldn't believe his own ears.

"Really?" she asked weakly.

"I have no idea how, but yes. It looks like I'm going to med school," he said sounding both surprised and confused by the declaration as he leaned down to kiss the top of her head. "And I don't care how smart you think I am, I'm going to need your help… a lot. Especially in obstetrics if I'm going to feel any degree of comfortable with the idea of delivering our child."

"Of course," she told him smiling up at him ecstatically. "And I can hack into whatever institution we decide to go to in order to make sure we're in the same classes. There will have to be a lot of planning that goes into setting up back stories and records. I don't think it would be a big deal if we are always seen together, and not really seen at all outside of classes, but we might have an issue creating identities for us with the same last names like we usually do unless it's like an extremely common last name. Though it still might be seen as weird at some point and it would be better not to draw attention. I only suggest this because in pre-med school it's not a big deal, and even in med school itself it probably wouldn't be an issue depending on the school and class size, and so what if they thought we were married. I mean you did officially marry me that one time, but residency if we decide we want to go will likely be a whole lot smaller pool, and they probably won't want a married couple no matter what strings we pull to arrange things. Whereas if they just chose us separately or thinking we were individuals, I think it would be less of an issue if they discovered down the line that we were in a relationship that we chose not to fully declare to..." she shrugged.

Ruby, you're rambling, he told her as he leaned down to capture her mouth and thoroughly interrupt her moment of what seemed like one long massive sentence.

Ruby stared up at him dazed once he finally lifted his head from hers. *I'm sorry. I got excited,* she confessed once she managed to find her thoughts back.

"I know, and that's okay. I'm happy you're excited, but you needed air," he teased with a chuckle. "We can work all that out after this year, and we can calculate when would be the best time to implement it, so that we have time for any speedbumps and also end up finishing close to next time so it's fresh in my memory."

"I love you," she smiled up at him.

"Good, because now I feel like…" he trailed off as his mouth came down on hers and he felt her arms slowly come up around his neck to hold him to her. Sliding his hands under his shirt that she was wearing, he took hold of her waist in both his hands and lifted her up to straddle his lap. *Practicing,* he told her mentally finishing his sentence as he continued kissing her. They were going to practice all night, and maybe then some.

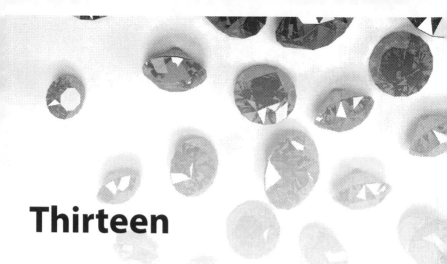

Thirteen

Ruby continued watching the crowd while she danced with Gabriel. They had been cooped up inside for nearly a year since she had gone into her fertile year, but it was over now, and she was itching for a fight. She was happy to be out in public.

Sure, there were times when she needed to get away from it all, but then it was her choice whether or not she was out in public. However, when she was in her fertile year her system was flooded with hormones and it wasn't safe for anyone, including herself, for her to be out in public. She was so much more volatile and emotional. Her mood was incredibly labile. It wouldn't take much to set her off causing her to unintentionally hurt someone or get herself hurt because she was acting emotionally instead of logically. Which meant she had to hole herself up somewhere until it passed. With Gabriel there it was easier than it used to be, but it was still difficult.

I can't believe how happy you are, Gabriel thought as he trailed his fingers over her hip and leaned down to kiss the side of her neck.

It's just nice to be out of the house for a change, she thought as she leaned back into him.

I didn't think it was so bad. I love being alone with you, and besides we spent most of the time in bed, Gabriel thought as he trailed kisses up her neck.

Ruby tilted her head back and to the side, so that he could kiss his way along her jaw to her mouth. Gabriel kissed her long and hard, taking her breath away and reminding her of what they had been doing in bed all that time. Ruby inhaled breathlessly as Gabriel lifted his head from hers. *I love being alone in bed with you, but... well... I need to be able to get out and run around once in a while or at least know that I can. I know you were feeling it to. I know you love being alone with me just as I do with you, but after a point cabin fever starts to set in, and not because I want to go outside, but because I know I can't. It's one thing to stay home with you because I want to and another to stay home because I have to because it would be dangerous for me to leave. Besides going out in public once in a while reminds me just how much I prefer to stay home alone with you*, she thought smiling up at him.

I guess maybe it's just not quite as hard on me because I choose to stay home with you. Gabriel wrapped his arm around her waist and held her against him as they swayed with the music.

Thank you, she said softly as her hand slid down to rest on his forearm.

For what? he asked confused.

For staying home with me. I know you don't have to and believe me I know that after a short time that year starts to feel like several and I know I tend to be a little bit more all over the place during that time. That is when I'm not just riding you over and over again needing you, she admitted.

You know there is nowhere else I would rather be, he thought as he leaned down and placed a soft kiss on top of her head.

I do and that is one of the reasons I love you so much. I just want you to know how much I appreciate it, because I know I'm not always so grateful when my emotions are going up and down like that. Ruby wanted to turn around and wrap her arms around his waist and bury her face in his chest, but she didn't. They were out in public at a bar and she didn't like getting distracted. They never knew who they might find lurking out and about, and she didn't want them to be caught off guard.

It could be dangerous if they were both distracted or focused on each other and not paying attention to their surroundings. Though it didn't matter who it was that was watching their surroundings because they would both know immediately, but it usually seemed to be Ruby. She was so used to watching her surroundings intently that it was hard not to, besides when Gabriel was on watch he usually found any guy that looked her way for too long suspicious. Plus, her looking around while he fondled her on the dance floor was usually more inconspicuous than the other way around. Plus, the other way around usually resulted in more women trying to cut in because they thought he wasn't interested in her, and Gabriel knew how much that hurt her, whereas the men never dared to approach her with Gabriel present.

I feel how happy you are that I'm there when you get the occasional moment of clarity and I feel how hard it is for you not to be able to control yourself. I know that more times than not that you react more quickly and strongly than you intend, and I know you feel bad afterwards when you say or do something you don't intend to. I know it's hard for you and I love being there to help you get through it, he reassured her.

I love you, she whispered in her head to him.

I love you too, he said wrapping both his arms tighter around her to pull her closer to him. *So how much longer do you want to stay out before calling it a night? It's nearly four and most of the creepy crawlies will be starting to go to bed before too long.*

I guess we can go ahead and call it a night, just let me run to the ladies' room before we head home, she told him.

Alright, but hurry back, he said reluctantly pulling his arms from around her waist.

Ruby was washing her hands when some blonde bimbo with boobs pushed all the way up to her neck approached Gabriel out on the dance floor. For some reason the gall of this woman infuriated her, she had been dancing with Gabriel all night and it was clear that they were together. Gabriel chuckled at her reaction, usually she just found it irritating when women tried to hit on him.

Ruby tried to remain calm while she dried her hands and headed back out to the dance floor. On her way, she heard the blonde tell Gabriel, "You deserve better than someone that's going to ignore you all night. If you were with me, my attention would be focused on you all night long." The blonde leaned in towards Gabriel placing her hand on his chest. "We could have a lot of fun together. I could pleasure you like you wouldn't believe, so what do you say we get out of here before that red head comes back?" she propositioned him.

Gabriel laughed out loud as he caught sight of Ruby over the blonde's head. She was failing miserably at remaining calm.

"You find this amusing?" the blonde asked.

"Actually, I do, but my wife isn't nearly as amused," he informed her.

Ruby snatched the blonde's hand off of Gabriel's chest and gave it a twist as she stepped in between the two of them and sent the blonde sprawling to the floor. *Gabriel, I think I'm going to need you to hold me back,* Ruby said as she tried unsuccessfully to step back away from the blonde and closer to Gabriel.

Gabriel stepped closer to Ruby instead and rested his hand softly on her hip.

"You bitch," the blonde screamed up from the floor. "You broke my hand."

Suddenly they had an audience. The people that had been dancing around them had stopped and had backed away slightly leaving them room. Gabriel used his mind to freeze them. He didn't need them coming any closer and getting in the way, doing anything stupid like calling the cops, or even watching which is why he also blurred their perception of what was going on.

"That's not all I'm going to break," Ruby said lunging at her. Gabriel's hand had slid from her hip to around her waist at the same time that she had lunged at the blonde. Ruby fought against his hold in an attempt to get at her.

"I wouldn't do that if I were you," Gabriel said as the blonde began to struggle to get to her feet without using her broken hand.

Ruby used her mind to clamp invisible hands around the blonde's throat. The blonde's progress immediately halted, and she fell back to the ground grabbing at her neck for hands that didn't exist.

Ruby was past the point of being talked down, but Gabriel had an idea. He didn't know when or exactly how, but at some point, he had found himself aroused by Ruby's jealousy. The fact that she was fighting for him had hardened him like steel. Gabriel pulled her in closer to his body so that his erection was pushed against her backside. There was no talking her done at this point, but maybe he could swing her emotions from anger at the blonde to lust for him. He followed her reaction as she became aware of his arousal both physically and emotionally because of her jealousy.

Gabriel leaned down and gently kissed her throat. Ruby rested her head back against his chest giving him better access to her neck. Ruby's hold slowly lessened from the blonde's throat as her attention shifted to Gabriel. Ruby turned around into Gabriel's arms as she finally let the last of her hold on the blonde's throat go. Gabriel found her lips with his and began kissing her voraciously as he lifted her up so that she could wrap her legs around his waist. He heard the blonde thank him as he headed for the back exit with Ruby in his arms. He couldn't help but laugh inwardly, he hadn't stopped her for the blonde he had stopped her because he knew his mate needed him to because she would hate herself when she realized what she had done.

Gabriel continued kissing her as he ran in the direction of their house, and he didn't stop running until he was far enough into the dense forest that surrounded their home to block them from prying eyes. Gabriel let his hands begin to wander feeling and caressing. She was his all his and she was willing to kill for him, and not just to protect him but for him. The thought would have bothered most people but not him. He loved her more than anything and he knew exactly how she felt and had more than once wanted to kill someone over her, but he had never seen her like this. He knew she loved him as much as he loved her but to see her like this, willing to kill someone who would even dare to attempt to try and take him away from her it made his heart soar. He knew it was wrong to feel this happy about it, when he knew that when she calmed down she would be upset about something that had him over the moon.

Ruby's hands slid under his shirt outlining the definition of his muscles as she continued kissing him. As the thought crossed her mind that she wanted his shirt completely off, Gabriel reached down between them for the hem of his shirt and begun to lift it over his head breaking their kiss. Gabriel tossed his shirt on the ground and took the opportunity to remove her shirt before he brought his hands back up around her. One arm wrapped around her waist holding her to him and the other wrapped around the nape of her neck tilting her head back to give him perfect access to her mouth. Gabriel trailed kisses along her jaw and down her throat as his hand slid from around her back to cup her generous and now bare breast in his hand. He continued to kiss his way down to her other breast as she arched her back to provide him the better access she knew he wanted. Ruby gasped and reached up to fist her hands in his hair as he sucked her nipple into his mouth. *Gabriel,* she moaned as she held him to her, *I need you.*

Take off your damn pants, Gabriel growled as he lifted her from around his waist to stand on the ground. Ruby did as he asked removing her pants and then stepping immediately back into his arms, her eyes fixing on the hard bulge in the front of his jeans. *Do it,* he said knowing she wanted to unbutton him and set him free. Ruby brought her hands to the front of his pants as she raised her head to look him in the eyes. Ruby bit at her lower lip at the look of hunger in his eyes. She always loved seeing that look in his eyes.

Gabriel leaned down to kiss her while he placed his hands on her hips and picked her back up. Ruby wrapped her arms around his neck and her legs around his waist. Gabriel slowly lowered her on to him, he felt her gasp as he stretched her. He loved how damn tight she was, she was exquisite and all his, only his. Gabriel gave her a second to adjust before he raised her up and lowered her on to himself again. He started out slow but that didn't last long, never did, before he was pumping into her hard and fast. He needed her desperately, like air. Ruby threw her head back arching her breasts towards him giving him a great view of her breasts bouncing up and down with each thrust. Gabriel brought her up against his chest to capture her scream with his kiss as he sent them both over the edge.

Gabriel leaned back against a large tree nearby while continuing to kiss Ruby while holding her in his arms, but these kisses were different still just as hungry but softer, not nearly as desperate, not because he needed to kiss her but because he didn't want to stop. Gabriel kissed her one more time and then raised his head to look down at her.

I love you, she said brushing her hand along his jaw. *Let's go home*, she said reaching up to brush one more kiss across his lips.

Sure, he said lowering her to the ground and holding her up for a minute to make sure that she was steady on her feet. Gabriel watched her backside as she slowly walked away from him to pick up his shirt to put on.

Gabriel, Ruby said with a tremble as she turned around to look at him without putting his shirt on.

Oh, god, she's going to start crying over that stupid blonde in the bar he couldn't help but think. He hated to see Ruby cry and that girl certainly wasn't worth her tears. Gabriel quickly zipped up his pants and pulled her into his arms against his chest.

I think I'm pregnant, she told him weakly.

What? Gabriel asked looking down at her. That certainly wasn't what he was expecting to hear.

It's the only thing that makes sense.

How do you figure? he asked confused.

"Well, I'm not normally like this. That is the nearly murdering bimbo sluts part, not the wild crazy sex with you part," she added when he raised an eyebrow at her. "Gabriel, you know I've gotten jealous over you before, but I don't usually act on it I could have killed her I nearly did. Thank you," she said looking up at him

"Ruby," he said reaching down to take his shirt out of her hands and helping her pull it over her head. "That doesn't mean you are pregnant."

"Doesn't it? These hormones are the only reason I would act so violently on my jealousy and if I'm not pregnant, they should be out of my system by now. That was why we went out for a night on the town, because they were supposed to be out of my system. I was supposed to be able to control myself which clearly, I can't," she told him.

Gabriel wanted to argue with her logic, but he couldn't. He didn't know if she was pregnant, but he had nothing definitive one way or another. "Ruby, even if you are pregnant, isn't this a good thing? Isn't that what we were aiming for?" he questioned gently.

"Yes, I just didn't realize I would be like this for the entire pregnancy," she said beginning to cry and switching to talking in their head. *It's bad enough being like this for a year and being unable to go out in public but to do this for the entire pregnancy, however long that may be. Gabriel, I nearly killed that bitch,* she sobbed.

"Ruby, it's not like she was entirely innocent. She knew I was with you and yet she was hitting on me anyways. She is a homewrecker, and someone needed to teach her a lesson. It's not right for her to go around trying to hit on men who clearly already belong to another woman. She was bound to get herself into trouble one day. And this doesn't mean we can't go out in public, we'll just go to places that are safer and less likely to have inappropriate skanks that will upset you. We weren't having any problems until she came over. We'll just go to finer establishments instead. Besides, it will be nice to just spend some time relaxing and enjoying each other's company."

Are you sure we can? she asked doubtful.

"I think we can. We've never had a problem when we've gone out for a nice quiet night or to any of the banquets. Worse case, I just drag you out of there again," he assured her. Gabriel bent down to pick up her clothes and then stood back up to lift her into his arms cradling her against his chest.

Ruby wrapped her arms around his neck and laid her head against his shoulder as he headed for home. *Gabriel, she said that I didn't care about you. That I was ignoring you all night.*

"Ruby, we both know that isn't true. She had no idea what she was talking about," he comforted her.

But that's my point. We were together dancing and talking all night, and she couldn't tell that I cared about you, she said sadly hurting at the fact that anyone could question how she felt about him.

"My love, I can tell how much you care about me, and that is all that matters. I don't care about some stupid human that has no concept of who and what we are, and neither should you. I know you love me," he reassured her as he entered their house and headed for their bedroom.

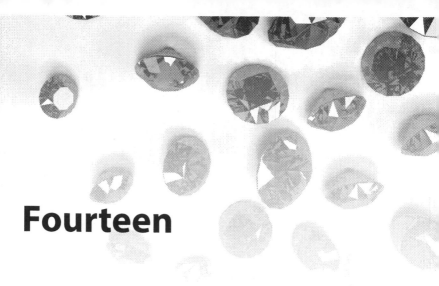

Fourteen

Ruby ran for the bathroom, she was going to be sick again. Despite her speed and her sense of balance and her body's ability to metabolize alcohol, usually, Ruby was drunk off her ass and nearly fell on her face twice on the way to the bathroom. Gabriel followed after her to make sure she was alright even though he knew he didn't need to in order to know how she was. He was in her head and he knew she had been throwing up periodically over the last few weeks, but then he knew she had been hitting the liquor pretty hard, not that he wasn't. Ruby didn't look at him as she used the walls to support herself as she moved to the sink to splash some water on her face and rinse out the taste in her mouth. She leaned into her hands resting her forearms on the counter as she watched the water running for a moment, just slipping through the air and down the drain. Ruby took a deep breath and signed heavily as she turned the water off. Ruby knew Gabriel was watching her, she knew he was worried about her, just as she was worried about him. He had never seen her like this. He had seen her drink and party and fight, but never like this.

But neither of them was saying anything. Neither of them was ready to deal with the fact that she had miscarried. So instead they were both drinking, fighting evil, screwing each other, and worrying about each other. Anything but talking. Ruby turned around and slid down the cabinets of the sink to sit on the floor.

"I'm sorry, Gabriel," Ruby apologized feeling horrible.

Ruby had miscarried a few months prior. She had woken in the middle of the night cramping and got up to find she was bleeding significantly. Gabriel, of course, had been there instantly not saying anything as he pulled her into his arms to comfort her.

He didn't know what to say to comfort her and he didn't know what she needed to hear, but then neither did she. So, they had spent months barely talking to each other and definitely not about the miscarriage.

"What on earth do you have to be sorry about?" he asked quietly as he moved to sit beside her on the floor.

"For losing our baby," she said softly.

Gabriel wrapped his arm around her and leaned down to kiss the top of her head, "My love, that is not your fault. Not at all."

And she knew he meant it, she could feel it, but she still felt like it was her fault. It had been her body that had been carrying their baby and it had been her that had lost the baby.

It's still not your fault, he thought trying to reassure her. If it was anyone's fault, it was his he couldn't help but think to himself.

"How on earth could it be your fault?" she asked hating the idea of him blaming himself.

"I was the one that got you pregnant and I'm supposed to be your doctor so to speak for the pregnancy and look at what a wonderful job I've done. We haven't talked in months," he pointed out.

"We are talking now, and it's not like time isn't different for us," she said moving to lay down with her head in his lap.

"Ruby, I can't do this again. At least not right now. I wanted a baby with you but... but I don't know what happened. How can I take care of you when you are pregnant after this?" he questioned not wanting either of them to go through this again.

Ruby wanted to correct him to make him feel better, but she didn't know what to say. She knew where he was coming from and understood his worry. Besides, she wasn't ready to try again. "That's alright. I'm not ready to try again right now," she tried to reassure him.

"Ruby, I may never be ready to try again. I don't know what caused you to miscarry and I don't know how to stop you from miscarrying again. I just want you to understand..." he trailed of hating what he was telling her when he'd always sworn, he would do anything for her.

"It's alright," she said softly.

"No, it's not," he argued. He knew how excited she had been, how excited they both had been about the baby as the initial terror at being pregnant had worn off. She wanted children, a family with him, and now here he was denying her. Denying her the one and only thing she'd ever asked him for.

"Gabriel, I love you and I don't blame you and this probably is nothing and might not happen again just like with humans but I'm not ready to try again and I might not ever be even if you are. I'm not sure I can do this again. It's not your fault, but I lost our baby and... Gabriel, it hurts so much. I want a family with you, but I just... I'm not sure I can risk going through this again. I didn't think anything could hurt this much but... At least, I have you that is all that matters to me. I know I can get through this as long as

I have you here beside me," she said weakly. It just hurt so much, and she wanted anything to not feel the pain. She would have happily taken a thousand knife wounds over losing their baby. She'd never hurt so much in her life.

"I understand, my love, and I'm not going anywhere. I'm staying right here beside you no matter what. I will always be here for you," he reassured her hating how much his mate was hurting. He wished like hell that she hadn't miscarried. He never wanted her in this kind of pain. And he hated that there was nothing he could to do, that this wasn't a wound that could just heal like all the others she'd gotten fighting.

⁕ ⁕ ⁕ ⁕ ⁕ ⁕ ⁕ ⁕

Ruby woke up running to the bathroom yet again to throw up. It didn't make any sense she had cut back on the drinking since talking to Gabriel, but she was still getting sick. If she didn't know better, she would think she was actually sick with something, which she had never been in her life, or...

Oh god, Ruby thought heading back into the room to grab a swig from the open bottle of whiskey she had left at her bedside table. Ruby quickly took a good long swig before Gabriel realized something was up and she probably shouldn't be drinking.

"Gabriel, I think I might be pregnant," she said moving to take another swig when Gabriel grabbed the bottle from her, stopping her and took a swig instead.

"Then you shouldn't be drinking," he told her.

"How do we know for sure if I'm pregnant or not, if we don't know if the human pregnancy test would even work on me or when the correct time to take it would be compared to humans if it did work," she asked him scared.

"For now, better safe than sorry so we will just assume you are, so no liquor," he informed her worried. He didn't know what else to do but he wouldn't risk it. If she was pregnant... "No liquor," he repeated at a loss to help his mate.

"Then if I want to drink, I need you to drink for me so I can feel the effects through you," she told him desperately wanting to get drunk. She understood why he didn't want her drinking and she wouldn't, but that didn't change how much pain she was still in.

"If that's what you need," he reassured her.

"Gabriel, are you alright with this?" she asked slowly.

"It's not like we have a choice. If you're pregnant, you are pregnant."

"I know, but that doesn't mean you have to be alright with it. I mean... well frankly, I'm not sure I'm alright with the idea to be honest," she admitted softly wishing she was in Gabriel's arms but not moving any closer to him.

Gabriel set down the bottle of whiskey and pulled Ruby into his arms holding her tightly. "I don't know how I feel, Ruby," but they both knew they both felt terrified after what had previously happened.

Ruby began to cry burying her face in Gabriel's chest. She wasn't a crier or at least she hadn't been but since getting pregnant and the miscarriage she would sporadically break down in silent tears. She knew it broke Gabriel's heart, but she couldn't help it. It was all just too much to handle.

I don't even understand how I got pregnant again, Ruby thought as she continued to cry.

"I don't know, my love. You must have ovulated somehow without us realizing it," he said softly.

I guess but I would have thought I would have noticed if my hormones had started up again, she questioned confused.

Would you? I mean are you sure they ever stopped? They were still going when you were pregnant to maintain the pregnancy and then you've been crying a lot more than you usually do. Maybe that wasn't just the grief, Gabriel thought softly. He surely would have understood and had thought it was just the grief of losing their baby but maybe it wasn't. "Maybe you've been ovulating this entire time," he questioned not liking the idea, but it would explain her being pregnant.

"But... but..." Ruby wailed feeling crazy. *You're supposed to be able to control whether or not you get me pregnant. You said you could, and you always have,* Ruby thought as Gabriel picked her up and carried her to the bed and sat down holding her in his lap.

"I thought I could I mean I can, but I don't know maybe without realizing it I've been thinking about getting you pregnant again. Or maybe it's... I know we both wish you were still pregnant maybe that's all it took to override my control. I'm sorry, my love. I know we both agreed we weren't ready to try again," he apologized holding on to her tightly.

"Gabriel, I'm scared. What if it happens again?" she cried terrified of miscarrying again.

"Hopefully it won't, but I will be here either way, I'm not going anywhere, and we will get through this together, my love," Gabriel said trying to comfort her. He'd be by her side no matter what. He knew they didn't know for sure whether or not she was pregnant, and while the idea terrified them both deeply, he knew there was a small part of both of them that hoped it was true.

They had both wanted a baby and they had both more or less given up on having one. Neither of them was willing to try getting pregnant again, but then they hadn't been trying this time. He hoped like hell, if his mate was pregnant like she thought, and she had been right last time, that they didn't lose this pregnancy. He didn't think his mate could handle losing another pregnancy so soon, especially when he knew she still blamed herself.

* * * * * * * *

Ruby ran for the nearest bathroom feeling nauseous. She knew Gabriel was right behind her which was a relief because she knew she was going to need to be in his arms shortly.

Oh, my love, he sighed entering the bathroom headed straight for her. She was sitting on the floor beside the toilet with her cheek resting on the seat. He kneeled down beside her running his hand gently through her hair in comfort.

Gabriel, I'm pregnant, she told him sadly as she continued trying to catch her breath.

I know, my love. I know, he agreed with her assessment as he brought her hand to his mouth to kiss comfortingly. It had been a few days since she had suggested that she might be pregnant, and he'd made her stop drinking. Up until now she had been fine, but this definitely wasn't from drinking, his little love was pregnant again.

Gabriel, she whimpered holding on to his hand.

Are you still feeling nauseous, my love, or are you... do you think you are done for now? he asked gently caressing his hand through her hair soothingly.

I... I hope so, my sides hurt and my throat burns. I don't like throwing up, she admitted weakly.

That does seem to be the general consensus, he agreed.

It's not like it looked fun, but... she trailed off. She was trying to focus on keeping her breathing slow and calm to keep from upsetting her stomach further which was still a little wishy-washy but had seemed to settle a little for the moment. Though to be fair she highly doubted she had anything left to throw up.

Just keep breathing nice and slow, my love. I think you got everything out, but dry heaves aren't fun either, he comforted gently worried about her. He continued to watch her closely. He wanted to pick her up and carry her to bed to rest, but he also wanted to make sure she was done for the time being. *You've never thrown up before,* he realized watching her and her emotions that this was a new experience for her.

No, she agreed weakly trying to shake her head, but she still had her cheek resting on the toilet seat.

I mean... ever, he questioned. Strangely wanting to confirm his suspicion that before the last few weeks that she had been vomiting on and off for, that she'd never vomited before.

No, she confirmed softly. *Gabriel, I... I think I'm done for now,* she told him knowing he was waiting to pick her up until she felt a little more settled and she wasn't honestly sure she could stand up at the moment. Besides, she wanted to be back in his arms.

Come here, my love, he comforted moving to scoop her into his arms cradling her against his chest as he stood up while using telekinesis to flush the toilet for her. Kissing the top of her head as she rested her cheek against his chest, he carried her out of the bathroom off the living room and headed for their room so that she could rest.

Gabriel, she weakly said stopping him as he tried to head for their bed after entering their room. *Could you... could you take me to our bathroom?* she asked not looking up at him.

Are you feeling nauseous again? he asked worriedly as he quickly headed for the bathroom.

No, I mean… well, my stomach is still a little… but I was… I just wanted to wash out my mouth and maybe brush my teeth. My mouth tastes horrible, she told him scrunching up her face at the taste.

Let's fix that, he comforted carrying her to the sink. He kissed the top of her head again as he set her feet on the ground, but he didn't let her out of his arms as he turned on the sink for her not wanting her out of his arms and knowing she didn't want to be out of them.

After rinsing out her mouth and brushing her teeth, Ruby turned back into his arms burying her face against his chest.

It's alright, my love, he comforted tightening his hold on her.

No, it's not. I'm pregnant, she whimpered.

I know, he sighed picking her back up and carrying her to their bed to sit down with her in his arms.

I had… I had hoped I was wrong, but… but I should have known better, she sobbed pulling on the comforter to pull a corner of it into her lap to fist her hands into and hold on to as she leaned hard against her mate for comfort. *I've… I've never been sick a day in my life, and… and… we metabolize alcohol very well,* she sobbed. *I should have known it wasn't the alcohol.*

Ruby, you had no way of knowing. We had absolutely no reason to think that you were pregnant. And to be fair, we… we were drinking a good deal, he said softly as he rested his head on hers while he held her to him and ran his hand up and down her back in soothing caresses. *It was reasonable to think that it might have been the alcohol.*

No, it wasn't. I know you've never seen me drink that much, but… but it's hardly the first time I've drank that much.

I was… I was… I was being stupid, she sobbed pulling the comforter over her head to hide.

Oh, my love, you're not stupid, he tried to comfort her as he looked down at his mate hiding under their bedding in his lap.

I can't do this, Gabriel. Not again, I can't, I can't, she cried.

I'm sorry, my love, he apologized gently pulling the bedding from over her head so he could kiss the top of her head. He wrapped her tightly in his arms as he rested his head on hers as he hurt for his mate. He had never intended to get her pregnant again. This was his fault. He was the reason his mate was hurting so badly. He'd been unable to keep her from losing their baby and then he had gotten her pregnant again against her wishes whether it was his intention or not.

I should never have asked you to get me pregnant, she sobbed wishing none of it had ever happened.

My little love, I am terribly sorry that we lost the baby and that you are now pregnant when you don't want to be, after we had decided not… not to try again. But my love, I… I don't think it was wrong for us to try the first time. We had no way of knowing how things were going to turn out. Besides, we wanted a baby and there is only one way for us to get one that is ours and like us. I knew back when I first mated you that you wanted to have a child someday, you had told me as much. If it hadn't been this time, it would have been next time or the time after or… My point is at some point you were going to ask me, and we were going to try. I am sorry, my love, but I don't think it was wrong for us to want a baby. Can you really tell me honestly that you wish we weren't still pregnant with…? he asked trailing off as he took one of her hands in his.

No, she sniffled. *Of course not*, she cried squeezing on to his hand. *I'd… I'd been so excited. I mean sure I was scared, but I'd… I'd also been excited. But Gabriel, this isn't that… it's a different… and I'm not excited. I'm just… I'm just…* she trailed off choking on her sobs unable to get her sentence out as she clung to him. She was just terrified now. She didn't like it and there was nothing her mate could do to make it go away.

I know, my love, he hurt for her, even though he knew she already hurt more than enough for both of them. She couldn't even say the word 'baby' because it hurt too much. Each time she had been trying to say a sentence where before she would have said 'baby', now she'd pause and did her best to continue talking skipping over the word knowing he would know what she meant.

I just… I just wish… she trailed off pulling the blanket over her head as she held her hands over her ears and curled up in a tight ball in his arms trying to block the thought that wanted to come.

Please stop doing that, my love, he asked tugging gently on the blanket to uncover her hiding in his arms. *What do you wish, my love?* he asked running his hand through her hair as he looked down at his mate curled up in his arms with her knees pulled in against her chest and her face buried against them as she leaned against him.

Ruby tugged the blanket back out of his hand and pulled it back over her head afraid of his incriminating judgement as she answered his question. *I… I wish I'd lose it already*, she admitted.

You… you don't mean that, he said stiffening at her words as he stared down at their bedding covering her head.

I… I do, she whimpered hurting more at his reaction. *I don't like this waiting to… to… lose… again, and have my heart ripped out all over again. I'd… I'd rather just… lose it now before… before… I'm not going to get a… a… a baby to hold. I just want it out,* she sobbed hurting. Her heart had already been ripped out and now she was waiting to watch it be crushed.

Gabriel let out a heavy sigh feeling her increased pain at his reaction. He hadn't intended to hurt her further, but he'd been shocked and confused at her words and hadn't been able to control his reaction. *Ruby,* he called gently as he pulled the comforter off her which took a little effort since she was doing her best to hold it securely over her head, but she was also tired. *Ruby look at me,* he told her even as he moved to raise her head up cupping her face in his hands.

Ruby shook her head not wanting to face him, but unable not to look at him as she continued crying.

Gabriel wiped at her tears with his thumbs repeatedly as her tears continued to fall. *My love, I know we're both still hurting deeply over the loss of our baby. I know this was unplanned and I… I know you're not in the least excited about being pregnant again and I… I am sorry, very very sorry, but we are pregnant again. I know you're scared. Beyond scared, petrified, so am I. I… I know this isn't the same baby, but I know you don't want to lose this one any more than you did the last one. I wish I could promise you it's not going to happen again, and I can't, but we also don't know for sure it will happen again. I know you still want a baby. Why else would you be afraid of this breaking your heart again? Because it's still what you want, what we want,* he corrected. *I know we're scared and have absolutely no idea what we can do different, but that doesn't mean… There is still every chance that this pregnancy can be successful and that you will have a baby to hold at the end of this,* he attempted to reassure her.

You don't know that, she told him shaking her head in his hands.

No, I don't, but I'm certainly going to hope like hell and do everything in my power to make that be the outcome, he told her trying to comfort her.

I know, she sighed sadly looking at him. She knew he'd do everything possible to help keep the pregnancy. *Gabriel, I'm scared that I… that I already want to keep it too much,* she admitted weakly.

I know, my love, he comforted pulling her back in against his chest. His mate was afraid to want their baby, afraid she already did when she was terrified that they were going to lose it. He knew whether she wanted to or not, she already wanted their baby. She'd never stop wanting their baby.

Ruby cried silently in his arms for a while before a thought occurred to her. *Oh god, Gabriel, how long have I been pregnant for?* she asked lifting her head from his chest to look up at him panicky.

Ruby, you know I can't answer that question any better than you can, he told her gently.

Gabriel, she whimpered getting upset again when she had been starting to settle down or maybe it was more just wearing herself out. *I've been throwing up on and off for weeks,* she realized.

I know, my love. I've been right here with you this entire time, he answered confused as to why that was upsetting her further.

It's been… it's been… I've been pregnant for weeks, she sobbed.

It's… it's probably more like months, my love, he corrected gently.

What? she asked shocked.

229

It's probably been a good month, month and a half since you started periodically throwing up. Maybe a little longer, it's hard to say it started out so slow and infrequent. But if that was all the baby, and I would estimate at the very least another couple weeks between us conceiving and the morning sickness starting, so I'm thinking more like 2 or 3 months give or take, probably more give than take to be fair, he told her softly. She'd been pregnant for a while and neither of them had realized it. He realized thinking about it, it appeared he'd gotten her pregnant much sooner after the miscarriage than he had initially realized. He was willing to bet it had been almost immediately after...

I am going to lose it again, she sobbed harder realizing how long she'd been pregnant for.

You don't know that, he argued.

Yes, I do. I've... I've been drinking heavily ever since it happened, she sobbed.

We both have, my love. Which is understandable, we've been hurting, he comforted reminding her she wasn't alone.

Yes, but you've not been pregnant for the majority of that time. I'm going to lose it and all because I was drinking because we... we lost the first one, she sobbed.

Ruby, we don't know that we will lose this one. You're still pregnant now, and you've been having progressing morning sickness for weeks despite drinking, he reassured gently.

I'm going to lose it, she sobbed again.

Ruby, if we... if we... I don't think it would be because of the alcohol. My love, as you said we've been drinking hard for months and it does appear you've been pregnant for most of that time. If you were... if you were going to lose it due to drinking, I would think that would have already occurred by now. Ruby, you're still pregnant, and you're not drinking any more, he reassured gently.

You don't know that. I can't imagine drinking has been good for the pregnancy, and I've been throwing up. Hell, we just left the bathroom, she sobbed. *Besides even if I don't lose it, what kind of damage do you think all that drinking will do to the... the...* she trailed off unable to finish her sentence.

My love, as you said earlier, we metabolize alcohol well, and I think that has helped protect the pregnancy and hopefully the baby. You are still awfully early. I know it's already been at least a couple months, but we both know there is no way a pregnancy would only be nine months for us. I think both those factors will help us, or at least I certainly hope so. And as for the throwing up, you know morning sickness is a normal part of pregnancy, my love, he reminded her gently.

You don't know that's what this is. I didn't... I didn't throw up before with... with... and I had been about this far along, but I've been throwing up for weeks. You... you don't know this is morning sickness. What if something's wrong? she whimpered.

You weren't throwing up, he repeated going over her words as he realized she was right. She hadn't thrown up once before. *You're right,* he said smiling.

Yes, I know. I was there. Now stop smiling about me throwing up. It's not a good thing, and certainly isn't fun, she told him getting angry, but it did at least seem to be helping her crying for the moment, but she was willing to bet that would only last for so long.

Ruby, I'm not smiling because of you throwing up. Well, I mean, I am, but not because I find it amusing. I wish I could make you promises, but I do think this is actually a good thing, he tried to explain gently.

How on earth do you think me trying to puke out my guts is a good thing? she asked looking up at him bewildered.

Because morning sickness is a normal part of pregnancy, and I do think that's what this is. It's linked to the hormones that maintain the pregnancy, and… and last time you weren't having any which I didn't think much of but considering… I think it's a good sign that you're having morning sickness, he tried to explain his reasoning.

You think… you think me not throwing up and me losing the… she trailed off glancing up at him, *could be related,* she asked doubtful.

I think it's a possibility and if nothing else, this is different than before which is good, right? he asked looking down at her.

I… I don't know, she told him weakly.

He knew she'd wanted to say, 'I hope so', but he also knew she was hurting and didn't want to be hoping for anything, let alone admitting to it. Gabriel ran his hand through her hair in a caress as he leaned down to kiss the top of her head. *Hang in here with me, my love. We will get through this together one way or another and hopefully in another month or two… hopefully, you will still be pregnant and we will find it just the littlest bit reassuring that you are much further along than we got before,* he tried to comfort her.

I'm not sure I like the idea of being reassured by that. I know what you're saying, and I get it, and you might be right, but you know as well as I that there is a fallacy in that logic. I don't want to be lulled into a false sense of security, she told him sadly.

I know, Ruby. I get that, but surely you can agree that at some point, if everything is going alright, we'll reach a point that we feel reassured that the pregnancy is going alright. I mean, I know it won't be anytime soon, and I know we would both undoubtedly be anxious and scared throughout, but I can't imagine there isn't a point that if we reached it, after watching the pregnancy progress, and being able to do repetitive ultrasounds and seeing the baby grow and develop like normal that we'd feel relatively safely reassured.

Sure, but if we can even get there, I guarantee you that isn't going to be anytime soon. Depending on how slowly or quickly I progress... would progress, she corrected not wanting to be overly optimistic. *That's going to be several months to a year or two, maybe three,* she told him.

And I will be here with you every day no matter what even if that means we spend a good deal of that time just like this, he reassured her referring to her crying and him holding her and comforting her. He'd be here no matter what. He hated her crying, but he also knew there was nothing he could do to make her pain go away, but that wasn't going to stop him from being here to hold and comfort her.

I think I'm going to need that, she told him sadly and appreciating the reminder that he'd be here with her.

How's your stomach feeling? he asked gently since she thankfully hadn't resumed crying again. He knew she needed rest, but he also wanted to make sure her stomach was relatively settled.

It's... I think it's alright, but I'm tired, she told him rubbing her cheek against his chest.

Let's get you some rest, and we'll worry about food later, he comforted. Ruby nodded her head slightly as Gabriel picked her up again and shifted to lay down. Setting her down beside him on the bed, he held her against him while she rested her head on his chest. He could feel her eyes quickly drifting shut from exhaustion after the vomiting and crying. He hoped like hell that this puking was indeed a good sign, and he hoped they'd have a baby for him to give his mate as opposed to further shattering her already broken heart that was trying to heal.

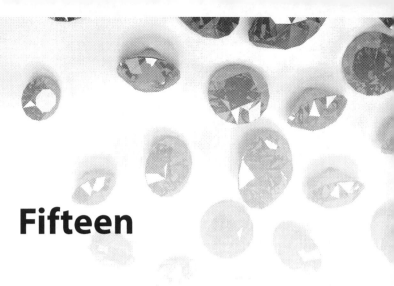

Fifteen

Ruby was now six months pregnant, from best they could determine since they weren't sure when she actually got pregnant, and Ruby felt miserable. It'd been four months since they'd realized she was pregnant and then plus the estimated minimal two month that she'd been throwing up for before they'd realized she was pregnant... six months.

The morning sickness was still going on which made sense, since she expected her pregnancy to be longer than a human pregnancy, but that didn't make it any easier to tolerate. The nausea had progressed, and she was throwing up a lot more often. She knew Gabriel was worried about her and anxious for the morning sickness to end and wishing he could estimate a normal duration for morning sickness but since they didn't know how long she would be pregnant it was kind of hard to estimate.

She knew Gabriel was worried that she wasn't putting on weight in fact she was losing weight because she couldn't tolerate anything other than crackers, ginger ale, and chamomile tea, but yet somehow, she was starting to get the slightest of baby bumps. It made her so happy to see it and she knew it made Gabriel happy even though he didn't say it. She knew how worried he was with her pregnancy.

But both were happy that she had made it this far. She was a good deal further than she'd been when she had lost the first baby. She'd never been able to even hear the baby's heartbeat. It had still been so little. She hadn't started hearing this one's heartbeat until a couple of weeks ago and at first when she had started hearing it, she wasn't sure what it was, but Gabriel had done an ultrasound and had confirmed that they were hearing the heartbeat for the first time.

Ruby came walking downstairs, she could smell Gabriel cooking. She knew it smelled amazing, but it just made her nauseous. Ruby sat down in the living room watching him cook and trying to get away from the smell. She always found it soothing to watch him cook, that and now listening to the baby's heartbeat which she seemed to do at least a few times throughout the day. Ruby opened up the pantry door across the room and floated the saltines to herself and forced herself to try and eat some.

Gabriel finished cooking and set his food down on the table and then came over to the couch to check on her. "I'm sorry, my love, I know the smell makes you nauseous," he apologized as he handed her a cup of tea to go with her crackers.

"It's alright. Gabriel. You have to eat. I can't have you losing weight too," she told him setting the cup of tea on the table beside her.

"I know but you're supposed to be putting on weight," he said worried.

"Don't worry, I will when the morning sickness stops and the cravings start, and then I'll have you cooking all the time," she said leaning over to kiss him on the cheek. "Go eat and then we can go for a walk in the woods," she told him softly.

At least it shouldn't be too much longer until the morning sickness stops. It usually stops in the second trimester, thirteen weeks for humans, and they start hearing the heartbeat at ten weeks so if we do the math… another month or two Gabriel thought to himself sadly, he wasn't sure he could handle another month or two of her not eating.

Ruby took his hand and placed his hand over the small bump she had developed. *Gabriel, I love you and we are going to be alright no matter what happens*, she thought holding him there for a moment. *And you will tolerate this morning sickness as long as I do*, she added firmly trying to reassure him but also needing him to stay with her on this. She couldn't handle it if he stopped hanging in there unable to handle her being sick.

Gabriel leaned down and kissed her softly on the lips. *I'm not going anywhere*, he reassured.

* ◦ ◦ ◉ ◦ ◦ ◦

Gabriel walked up behind Ruby, brushing her hair over her shoulder he leaned down and kissed the nape of her neck. Ruby had known the second he had entered the kitchen, but then she had known when he had gotten up, showered, put on his pajama pants that he only ever wore to breakfast, not to bed, and when he had headed down stairs looking for her.

Gabriel trailed his fingers down her arm and wrapped his arm around her waist pulling her back against him as he trailed kisses up her neck.

Ruby flipped the omelet she had been making over and then tilted her head back opening her mouth to Gabriel as she moved the pan to the back burner and turned off the stove with her mind.

Gabriel turned her around pulling her into his arms. He needed her and she knew it. He had woken up needing her without her beside him. He had known she was downstairs cooking, so he had showered and put on pants before coming down to find his mate and make love to her.

Gabriel slowly pulled his shirt that she was wearing up her thighs and then over her waist and then pulled it off over her head. Gabriel brought his hand up to cup her breast while his other went to the small of her back pulling her in against him so she could feel his need for her although he knew she already knew he was hard for her.

Ruby's hands came up to bury in Gabriel's wet hair as he trailed kisses down her neck to her breast. Gabriel picked her up for her to wrap her legs around his waist and Ruby did as she knew he wanted while he sucked her nipple into his mouth.

Ruby's hands moved down Gabriel's neck feeling the muscles in his back outlining each one enjoying the feel of him suckling at her breast. Ruby used her mind to lower his pants, she needed him inside of her and she needed him now.

Gabriel didn't hesitate stabbing into her hard and deep. God she was tight, and it was wonderful. He waited a second before pulling out and thrusting into her again. Ruby threw her head back moaning arching her back and forcing her breasts closer to Gabriel's mouth.

Gabriel set a fast, desperate pace. Quickly taking both of them over the edge. Gabriel set Ruby down on the edge of the counter, staying inside of her. *I love you*, he thought to her while still trying to catch his breath.

I love you too, Ruby said between gasps of air.

Let's go take a shower, Gabriel thought removing himself from her. He knew she hadn't showered yet, and he wanted her again. He wanted to lick the water from her body and run soap all over her.

Ruby chuckled softly, something she knew Gabriel loved hearing, as she leaned up to kiss him softly on the lips. *That sounds wonderful, but I'm starving, my love*, she told him turning down a hot soapy shower with him.

Then we bring the food upstairs to bed with us, Gabriel said just realizing that it was the first time in months that she had cooked. He was thrilled that she had an appetite and not morning sickness for the first time. He wanted to focus on his excitement over that more, but he needed her. Maybe the reason he needed her so bad was because she was feeling better more energized and Gabriel felt it too.

Could be, she agreed reading his mind. *And alright we can eat upstairs but I need food before we go again*, Ruby thought wrapping her arms around Gabriel's neck to kiss him again.

You are not helping, Gabriel thought kissing her long and hard.

I didn't say it was what I wanted, I said it was what I needed, she apologized not intending to tease him because she did need him right now, but she needed food more. She was so hungry.

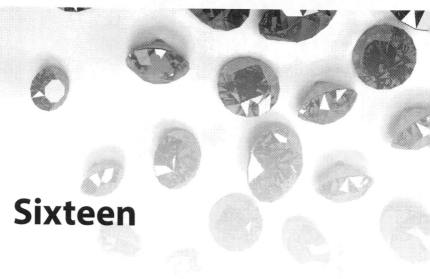

Sixteen

Ruby was lying in bed on her back asleep with Gabriel's arm gently draped over her swollen belly while he laid on his side beside her. She had been pregnant for nearly five years now and looked to be about seven and a half months pregnant in human terms.

Something suddenly woke Ruby. For some reason, she felt restless and agitated. She needed to get up to walk around. Gabriel moved his arm from around her and rolled over. Ruby knew he had felt her wake up and her need to get up, and knew that even in his sleep he had rolled over so that she could do so.

Ruby moved to sit up and slid her legs over the side of the bed. Something wasn't right she couldn't stand this. She got slowly to her feet and took a step away from the bed. She realized her heart was racing and her respirations were fast. What was going on? She tried to take another step forward and found she couldn't move. It wasn't like she didn't have the strength, no not at all. It felt as if she had been frozen in place.

Ruby began to panic. What was happening? Her already fast respirations began to speed up. She was starting to hyperventilate, and she knew it, but there was nothing she could do to stop it. Something was wrong.

Gabriel had felt her beginning to panic and was instantly awake. He raced around the bed to see what was wrong and found himself stopped about three feet away from her. *Ruby,* he mentally asked her confused and thinking that she had stopped him, but he could feel her fear increasing further at the realization that he was now frozen too.

Gabriel, he heard her whimper in his head.

He tried to fight it. He tried to reach her, but it didn't do any good. He had to call her name a half dozen times in his head before she finally seemed to realize he was trying to get her attention.

He could tell she was still panicked but he felt enough of her attention shift to him to try and talk to her. *Ruby try reaching for the baby,* he told her mentally. All of their talking was going on through their mental bond, they couldn't actually move their lips even to talk, but at least whatever was going on wasn't impairing the bond.

What? she asked confused.

Like you reach for me to talk like this, try reaching for the baby, he said trying to remain calm, but he was on the verge of panicking also.

She couldn't help but think, *Why?* What he was saying made absolutely no sense.

Ruby, something is clearly not right. We're being held hostage and it started with you. The baby is the only other person here. Something isn't right, try talking to or listening to the baby, he suggested trying to figure out what was going on.

Ruby tried reaching for the baby, but it wasn't easy. She was still terrified which made it hard to focus and the baby wasn't a familiar mental path that she was used to using like she was with Gabriel. When she finally managed to reach the baby, she was flooded with fresh flood of terror. The baby didn't know what was going on and was terrified by her panicking. Ruby instantly felt bad and tried to calm down. She didn't know what had happened she hadn't intended to terrify the baby.

Ruby try talking to her. Try getting her to at least let you sit down, he encouraged her gently.

Baby, she thought softly feeling close to tears. She tried bringing her arms up to wrap them around her belly and the baby. She found she could move her arms, but only very slowly. It took her a couple of minutes, but she was finally able to wrap her arms around her belly. *Baby, it's... alright. I'm just going to sit back down, alright?* she asked their baby. She was trying to sound calm and soothing, but it came out as a stutter. When Ruby went to try and sit down, she found that she could move again, and it wasn't like with her arms. She was able to move at a normal speed to sit on the edge of the bed.

"Gabriel," she was finally able to say out loud as she looked up at him, but he still hadn't moved. She had hoped that since she could move... but clearly, he was still frozen. She tried to stifle it, but she could feel herself beginning to panic again. She needed Gabriel. She needed to be able to touch him, but the baby wouldn't let her.

It's alright, Ruby. This is progress. She's listening to you. Try and get her to let me come to you," he suggested gently trying to help keep her calm. He knew he was right they were making progress, but it was driving him nuts. He wanted to be right there by her side just as much as she needed him by her side. It was hard to remain calm, when he was just as terrified as Ruby was, but he knew that she was barely hanging on and that it wouldn't take much to push her back to panicking. He had to be patient for all of them.

"Baby, sweetie," she said softly out loud to the baby. "It's alright. Gabriel isn't going to hurt us. He isn't going to hurt you," she reiterated knowing the baby was scared. "Please, let him come to me," she pleaded. Ruby knew the second he was free, but he approached slowly afraid of startling the baby and them ending up right back where they had started.

Gabriel knelt down on the floor in front of her. He took the hand she offered him and placed his hands on either side of her belly while still holding her hand. "It's alright, little one," he said out loud. "It's alright now. You're safe. We won't let anything hurt you," he told their baby as he brushed a kiss over her stomach.

Ruby thought he sounded much more convincing than she had sounded talking to their baby. She knew there was no danger to her baby here, but she'd still been terrified by what was going on, especially since she didn't know what was going on. She still felt kind of panicky and she tried to control it, but she was still so confused and felt close to tears.

Gabriel was still worried about Ruby. He knew she was still on the verge of panicking and he wanted to pull her into his arms to comfort her, but he couldn't, not yet. Ruby could control her powers and he wasn't worried about what she would do. Their baby was the one that had been holding them hostage. As much as he wanted to comfort Ruby, he knew he needed to make sure that their baby was completely calmed down first and wasn't going to continue attempting to control them before he could comfort his mate.

Gabriel continued to mumble words of comfort to their baby as he reached for their baby mentally following the path Ruby had taken to connect to their baby. Ruby could feel him sending the feelings of warmth and comfort to the baby. It was all he was thinking about, and she knew he was trying to overwhelm the baby in an attempt to calm her down.

Ruby knew what he was doing, and she knew it was working, but for some reason she felt hurt that he was comforting the baby and not her. She knew he was right, that calming the baby was the priority, but for some reason that didn't help. She could feel the tears welling up in her eyes. She tried to stop them, but she couldn't. She hated these hormones. She knew logically that he was right, but that didn't seem to matter. She wanted her mate's comfort.

Gabriel reached up absently to wipe the tears off her cheek while he continued to focus on the baby. She knew he was trying to apologize and that only made it worse, because he shouldn't have to feel the need to try and apologize. Ruby held on to his hand. She knew it was working, she could feel their baby beginning to calm down.

Gabriel began to mix in feelings of sleepiness and exhaustion. He was trying to lull the baby to sleep. He didn't want the baby awake to get upset again if his attempt at comforting Ruby didn't work. "She's asleep," he said unnecessarily, they both knew the second she was asleep.

"I'm sorry," he said looking up at her.

"Don't be sorry," she said softly through her tears. "You did the right thing," she said leaning forward to wrap her arms around his neck. Gabriel lifted her easily into his arms and moved to lay down with her on the bed. Now that whatever had happened seemed to be passing, Ruby wanted to understand what had just happened, but it was too soon. She began to panic again looking at the memory of what had just happened.

"Ruby, it's alright. Don't think about it right know. Everything is fine and we can talk about this later," he said gently.

She could feel him directing his feelings at her to calm her down like he had done for the baby, and she didn't care. She slowly began to relax into Gabriel's arms. "You said 'she'," Ruby claimed suddenly looking up at him.

"Yes, I could feel it when we were talking to her. Besides, we already knew from the ultrasounds that it was a girl," he reminded her gently.

"Yeah, but… I mean ultrasounds can be wrong and… and this felt different when you said 'she'. A baby girl," she sighed rubbing her hand over her belly. "Are you sure?" she asked looking back up at him.

"Yes," he said with almost a chuckle. "Now get some sleep," he said pushing at her to feel sleepy and exhausted as he had with the baby. He knew she knew what he was doing, but she didn't fight it. He had a feeling that what he was pushing her to do was exactly what she wanted to do, but she wasn't in control enough to do it on her own. She needed and wanted his help calming down.

* * * ● ● ● * *

"Gabriel," Ruby said waking with a start.

"I know," Gabriel said already pulling on a pair of pants. "I was listening. Are you alright?" he asked not wanting to leave her alone after earlier.

"Yes, I think so," she said glancing down at her belly.

"Ruby," he said softly.

"She's not afraid, she doesn't seem to be controlling me, and I think she is still asleep," she said trying to assess how their baby was doing.

"Ruby, I asked about you not the baby. Are you alright?" he asked her again.

"Considering, I'm relatively alright. I'm still a little shaken from earlier, but my heart's not racing and I'm not hyperventilating. I'm not feeling panicky," she tried to reassure him. The mention of the word panicky briefly had her questioning whether or not that was true and nearly careening back towards panicking. Ruby took a deep breath to steady herself. She was fine, just shaken, but she couldn't, no she wouldn't let herself start panicking again.

Gabriel looked at her doubtfully. "It's just nerves," she insisted still trying to reassure him reaching for his hand. "You need to go, they need our help and I promised you I wouldn't... I wouldn't fight or put myself in danger while I was pregnant. I know you're worried about me, but at the moment I'm fine and they need you more. Besides, I know you will be listening and watching me carefully even when you are gone, and I know you'll be back in a flash if anything starts to change for the worse," she reminded him knowing she was right.

"I hate this," he said strapping the two knives he tended to carry around his waist. "I hate leaving you like this," he admitted looking at her.

"I know," she said so softly it could barely be called a whisper. "I hate this too. Just be careful and come back safely and quickly," she ordered him.

"I will," he said leaning down to kiss her goodbye. "I won't let anything happen to me. I know you're worried and it's hard to be apart, but please try to take it easy and go back to sleep if you can," he said concerned about her and their little girl. They had already been through a lot tonight.

Ruby kissed him goodbye again and held on tightly to his hand. She tried to hold on, but her hand slipped out of his as he moved for the door. She tried to stay calm and breath through the sadness that struck as he closed the door. He was still only just on the other side of the door and he would be back within an hour or two, but still she was filled with sadness at being separated from him.

Ruby didn't understand it. It wasn't reasonable. He would be back soon, and he knew how to take care of himself. And while it would have been nice to blame it on the pregnancy hormones, it had been like this even before she was pregnant. It didn't matter why they were apart, how safe or how dangerous what they were doing was, how far apart they were, or for how long they would be apart, being apart was horrible it filled them both with such sadness, but then maybe that was part of the problem. They both hated being apart and their feelings fed off one another making it that much harder to handle.

Ruby, he thought softly in question feeling her overwhelming emotions.

I'm fine. I just miss you when you're not with me, she replied.

Are you sure that's all it is? he asked worried. *I can come back,* he told her without hesitation. She was his mate and she was carrying their baby. They were all that matter to him. They took priority over everyone and everything.

No, don't. Just... just keep talking to me, she said softly.

Alright, he agreed reluctantly but continuing to keep a close eye on her. He wouldn't hesitate to change his mind and turn around and head straight back to her side.

It's easier when I can continue talking to you. It makes it feel like you're still right here beside me, she thought trying to keep the conversation going.

So, what can you tell me about what you saw or felt? he asked trying to help keep her talking to him and distracted from him not being beside her holding her in his arms.

They're not human. I'm not sure what they are but it's not human, she said confidently.

You mean there is something supernatural in danger? he questioned doubtfully as he continued running towards town.

Yes, she confirmed.

That is unusual. We're usually helping humans, he said confused as to what was going on.

It gets more unusual. The female is pregnant, she informed him as she slowly moved to get out of bed.

Are you sure? he asked surprised.

Yes, and that is part of the problem. If she goes into labor or gets further in her labor, I'm not sure which it is from here, but things could get nasty. And she is close to quickly moving that direction, she told him sure of that much.

Great, he said sarcastically.

And I think she might be in a hospital. Her mate is nearby but he isn't with her and he is starting to get panicky, which could create another problem, she continued talking.

I guess I'll find him first to get him to keep from going crazy while I get her out, he said continuing to talk with her. He could feel it helping to keep her relatively calm.

That would probably be best, she agreed.

We don't usually do labor and deliveries, he mused.

No, we don't, and I've got a theory, she said softly.

Oh, really, he questioned curious.

Yes, I don't think it was me that felt them, she told him.

Oh really, he said doubtfully.

Well, at least not originally. I think the baby connected to them somehow. I think that might be why whatever happened earlier happened and I didn't understand what was going on. It wasn't until later that either I had the same feeling, or she managed to share what she'd felt with me once we'd both calmed down, she told him sharing her theory.

That is an interesting concept to say the least, he said not sure what to think of her idea.

Yes, well in some ways it actually makes more sense, she said.

How do you figure? he questioned.

Well think back, when was the last time I had a vision or feeling or whatever you want to call it? she asked him.

Gabriel really had to think about it. He hadn't realized that she hadn't been having any lately he had been focused on the pregnancy and to be honest he had been grateful there hadn't been any. *It was before the pregnancy, wasn't it?* he asked surprised.

Yes, and then all of a sudden this happens, and the victim happens to be pregnant, she said raising an eyebrow at him in question even though he couldn't see her, but she knew he'd still know as connected as they were to each other.

So, it could have been the baby connecting with someone her own age, in a manner of speaking, or your hormones directing your visions towards another pregnant couple, he asked.

Or maybe it was both, our baby connected to the baby and I connected with the couple. Maybe between the two of us that's why we panicked and why everything seemed to come through clearer than usual, she told him.

Well I think I found her mate, there is someone pacing around outside the hospital like he is ready to lose it, he said as he stopped running but continued approaching the hospital.

Gabriel walked up to him calmly planting himself in his path so that he had to stop and look up at him. "I'm here to help," Gabriel said watching the agitated male closely.

"Excuse me," the male said looking at him like he had lost it.

"I know what you are, I can smell it and I know that your mate is inside," Gabriel told him.

Gabriel, you should bring her back here, Ruby interjected. *You could deliver the baby for them,* she supplied wanting to help.

I know, Gabriel replied in his head. *I guess it will be good practice,* he couldn't help but think smiling inwardly to her.

"What are you?" he asked as he looked Gabriel up and down hesitantly.

"Hard to say but I'm here to help. I'm going to go inside and get your mate. I can get her without being detected, but I won't be able to stop and talk to you on the way back out. Can you track my scent even when I'm running fast?" Gabriel asked still watching him closely.

"Yes, no problem," he agreed.

"Good stay here and don't do anything stupid. When I come back out follow as fast as you can without causing a scene or getting hurt," he ordered the male.

Gabriel turned and headed inside to get the pregnant wolf. He could still feel exactly where she was from the connection Ruby had made to her. He knew she wasn't on this floor, so he headed for the elevator distorting camera images as he went. He couldn't get caught on camera kidnapping a pregnant woman that wouldn't go over well.

Once he was in the elevator, he guessed that she was on the third or fourth floor and hit both buttons. He could determine for sure which one when the elevator stopped, and the doors opened. Gabriel stepped out onto the third floor and immediately took a right down a corridor. When he came to the locked doors leading to the labor and delivery ward, he blurred the camera at the entrance and triggered the doors to open so he could enter. He moved quickly through the halls so that none of the nurses or doctors could see and he hoped there was no one in the woman's room as he moved closer but he blurred his image as he entered the room anyways just in case there were other people in the room with her. Luckily, she was the only one there, he unblurred his image so that she could see him.

The woman nearly screamed in shock at him suddenly appearing in the middle of the room, but she caught herself clearly realizing whoever or whatever he was... he was clearly not human and alerting the humans to his presence was not a good idea. "Who... who are you?" she stuttered.

"My name is Gabriel, I'm here to help get you out of here. I'm going to take you somewhere that you can deliver safely, and your mate will be right behind us on the way there, but I need your word that you are not going to fight me," he said firmly.

"Why?" she questioned worried.

"Why what? Why don't I want you to fight me? Because I plan to carry you out of here very quickly and you are pregnant. I don't want anything to happen to you or your baby, so I don't want you trying to fight with me. Also, because I would like to get you out of here as fast as possible which means I don't want to waste time fighting and arguing with you," he informed her calmly.

"No, I mean why are you helping us?" she questioned suspicious of his intentions.

Gabriel looked confused for a moment and then said, "Why not?" repeating more or less what Ruby had said when they had first met. He had always thought her answer a little bit vague and funny and yet somehow that simplicity had made him trust her. Now being on the other side of the question he really understood where she had been coming from. He really had no good or easy quick answer, and he certainly did not have time to have a conversation on the topic that would ultimately probably lead them nowhere. Actions spoke louder than words and when she had no actions on which to trust his words, there was no point in trying to explain his motives, which left him with a short simple non answer.

The woman still looked nervous. "Where is my mate?" she questioned looking him over hesitantly.

"He's right outside the hospital, he's going to follow us," he tried to reassure her.

She wants to know why he's not there in the room with you, Ruby said in his head trying to help him with getting her to let him take her out of the hospital.

"He wanted to come in. He is worried sick about you and he knows we need to get you out of here. He was trying to figure out how, but people don't tend to take kindly to pregnant women being kidnapped or taken out of here when they are in labor," Gabriel told her gently.

"But you are going to do just that," she asked unsure.

"Yes, I'm much more powerful than you and your mate. Now are you coming or not. I know you don't want to hurt anyone, but these are humans and you know that is a risk the further along you get in labor and I won't let your mate in here for fear of him adding fuel to the fire. He's having a hard-enough time controlling himself and we don't need anyone getting hurt," he told her. "So, what's your answer?" he asked.

"Yes, I'm coming. Can I get dressed first?" she asked tossing the hospital blanket off of herself.

"If you can do it quickly, I know it can be difficult getting dressed when you are pregnant," he said.

She raised an eyebrow at him in question at his statement.

"My mate is pregnant too," he explained.

"It won't take but a second," she said pulling a dress and some sandals out of a patient bag.

Gabriel turned around to give her privacy as she quickly pulled out her IV, took off the patient gown, put on her loose cotton dress that very clearly emphasized her baby bump, and slipped into her sandals.

"I'm ready," she said placing her hand on her stomach.

Gabriel couldn't help but notice how she caressed her belly both for comfort and a need to protect her baby. He loved seeing Ruby do the exact same thing. "Let's go," he said stepping forward to pick her up. Gabriel carried her through the unit at the blink of an eye unlocking the doors before they got there so that they were open by the time they reached them. He kept going straight through them, pulling an empty elevator up to their floor as he continued moving quickly. The doors to the elevator opened just as they got there. The only thing he couldn't control was how fast the elevator went.

"What are you?" she asked as they waited for the elevator to reach the ground floor.

"Don't actually know, and who are you?" he asked looking down at her.

"I'm a wolf," she said.

"I know that, I said 'who' not 'what'. You have a name don't you," he asked her.

"Amber," she said blushing in embarrassment.

"It might be easier for you to close your eyes as we get out of the elevator. I'm going to run even faster as we leave the building and I don't want you getting sick. We'll probably be going too fast for you to see your mate, but he will be following us. He knows our scents and I will be able to hear him behind us," Gabriel informed her.

"Alright," she said closing her eyes as they reached the ground floor. Gabriel took off headed back to Ruby picking up speed once he was outside the hospital and he didn't have to wait for any more damn doors to open.

Gabriel slowed down as he approached the house, and the front door opened, he knew it was Ruby. She was standing on the stairs about halfway down. Gabriel began climbing the stairs towards her carrying Amber. He stopped leaning down to kiss Ruby on the cheek and then continued the rest of the way up taking Amber to the nearest guest room.

Her mate wasn't far behind. He stopped at the front door entrance looking around until he spotted Ruby on the stairs.

"She's alright. Come on in, she's right upstairs," Ruby tried to reassure him.

He slowly entered the house closing the door behind him. He headed up the stairs towards Ruby. He stopped when he reached her waiting for her to turn around and head upstairs.

"You don't have to wait for me," she said turning around and heading up stairs. "I'll be there shortly, it's the first door on the left," she informed him.

"I wouldn't feel right leaving you alone, especially on the stairs, when your mate is taking care of mine," he admitted waiting while she took her time carefully climbing the stairs to lead him to both their mates.

"Alright," she said softly leading the way to the room Gabriel had entered.

Ruby entered the room and stepped aside for Amber's mate to enter who immediately went to sit on the edge of the bed at Amber's side.

"Are you alright?" Ruby asked moving to stand behind Gabriel who was sitting on the other side of the bed. She rested one hand on her belly and the other on Gabriel's shoulder needing the physical contact with her mate.

"I think so…Well other than the contractions that is," Amber said lightly as she took her mate's hand and held on to it.

Gabriel stood up taking Ruby's hand from his shoulder and moving her to sit down where he had been sitting while retaining hold of her hand. He didn't like her on her feet for long periods of time and he definitely didn't like her up when she should be sleeping.

"How did you end up at the hospital?" Ruby asked carefully.

"We were on our way to the wolf midwife when another car hit ours and the ambulance brought me to the hospital, and I was separated from Antonio somehow. Thank you for helping us," she said glancing at them with a small half-smile and then looking back at her mate Antonio.

"No problem, happy to help," Ruby reassured her. "Oh, and my name's Ruby by the way, and you've already met Gabriel, my mate," she said still holding on to his hand. "Gabriel trained to be my obstetrician, so if you would like, you can stay here during your labor and he can deliver your baby for you, or we can try and help get you to your midwife before you deliver. It's up to you," Ruby told her gently.

"Ruby," Amber said softly, "As in... you're her, aren't you?" Amber asked.

Ruby didn't say anything in response. She knew she didn't need to.

"But the stories say you went by 'Ruby' some three or four hundred years ago. The one thing the stories always have in common is you always change you name, and you never use the same name twice. And I know I heard a story of you going by 'Daisy' after you went by 'Ruby' though I've never heard any stories that occurred after that other than the wild tell about you mating. Why did you go back to 'Ruby'?" Amber asked curiously. Amber couldn't help but notice how the way Gabriel was looking at Ruby suddenly changed, and he let go of her hand like it hurt to hold it.

"Excuse me," Gabriel said quietly turning to leave the room.

"I just put my foot in my mouth, didn't I?" Amber asked softly.

"It's alright. It's not your fault, its mine," Ruby replied.

"He didn't know, did he? That your name isn't Ruby. What is your name? Wait... he's the reason you went back to Ruby, isn't it?" Amber asked realization dawning.

"Yes," Ruby admitted softly.

"I guess you finally found a name you liked."

"A name I love," Ruby said moving to stand up. "Excuse me. Oh, let us know what you decide. Gabriel or I will come back and check on you shortly," she told her as she moved to leave.

Ruby knew Gabriel was upset with her, but she also knew he had also only moved to sit on the floor outside the door with his knees pulled up and his arms resting on his knees. Ruby moved to kneel down beside Gabriel using the wall for support and was surprised when he reached up to help her down. Gabriel wrapped his arms around her waist and pulled her to him resting his head against her tummy.

"Gabriel, I'm sorry," she said resting her hands on his head.

"How could you not tell me?" he asked letting go of her and allowing her to move to sit all the way down on the ground.

Ruby leaned against his leg and rested her head against his knee as she looked down at her hands on her belly. "There was nothing to tell," she said weakly.

"Then why didn't you tell me?" he asked watching her.

"I don't know," she said with an aching in her heart that she knew Gabriel could feel.

"You're lying to me, Ru..." he started to say her name and stopped. "I don't even know your real name. You're my mate, you have been for almost two centuries and I don't even know your name," he said bitterly.

"Yes, you do. My name is Ruby," she said weakly.

"No, it's not that's just what I've been calling you," he denied.

"Then I don't know what to tell you because it's the closest thing to a name that I have," she said barely able to get the words out.

There was something about the way she had said that that struck Gabriel. "What do you mean?" he asked watching her.

"Nothing," she denied.

"Ru…" he fell silent he couldn't bring himself to say her name. "Tell me," she could hear the *damn it* in his head as much as he didn't want or mean to cuss at her he was angry and hurt.

"I don't have a name," she admitted weakly.

"Of course you do, everyone has a name," he disagreed.

"Which is given by who?" she asked barely loud enough to call it a whisper.

"Oh," Gabriel said realizing what she meant. She didn't have any parents. She had raised herself and he had known that. "But what about the tribes that took you in?" he asked. "They had to call you something."

"Yeah, they did. I was 'little bit' 'little one' 'wild thing' 'wild one' and of course as you heard Amber say 'her', but no one dared to name me. They knew how powerful I was," she said still looking at her belly unable to look at him.

"Until you started giving yourself names," he realized.

"But none of them felt like me until…" she trailed off caressing a hand over belly trying to sooth herself.

He knew what she meant, until him. But it still hurt that she didn't tell him.

"What was I supposed to tell you? I finally had a name that felt like home, but… 'Hey, that's not my name. I don't really have one but if you would keep calling me *Ruby* that would be swell'…" she trailed off kicking herself. How was she supposed to tell him?

Gabriel took one of her hands on her stomach in his and rested their joined hands where her hand had been against her belly. "I don't know…" he trailed off wanting to say her name but he couldn't bring himself to do it.

"Gabriel," Ruby asked on the verge of tears. She needed to know that he still loved her, that he wasn't going to leaving her. Her mate couldn't even say her name anymore.

"What?" he asked hearing her thought. "How could I not? Of course, I still love you, but that doesn't change the fact that it hurts. I wish you could have found a way to tell me," he said.

"In a way, I thought I had, I told you I never met my parents, how could I possibly know my real name, but at the same time it just hurt to think about the fact that I didn't have a real name, so I didn't. And I loved the way you called be 'Ruby', it just felt right. I didn't want you to want to call me something different, but I can change my name again if it's too hard for you, as long as I still have you," she said holding on to his hand as if her life depended on it. Because it did.

"I'm not going anywhere. You are pregnant after all," he joked but he knew she didn't find it funny. He knew that she was worried that was why he would stay and he knew by joking about it she would know it wasn't why he was staying. "I love you and I'm not going anywhere, Ruby," he forced himself to say her name knowing she needed to hear him say it.

Ruby could feel the pain it caused him to say it and it hurt to feel how much it hurt him to say her name.

"I'm sorry, my love, but I'm going to need time," he apologized knowing she was feeling his pain and causing her pain in return.

"I know. I just hate how much it hurts you. And I hate knowing I'm the cause of that pain," she said weakly.

"I know and its times like these I hate how closely we are connected but I can't change that, and I wouldn't change our connection even if I could because most of the time I love it, but this is going to take some time, my love," he apologized.

"I know," she said softly.

"Let's get you back to bed," he said moving to pick her up in his arms as he stood up. Gabriel carried her to their room. He could feel the name 'Peter' floating in his head, but he wasn't sure if it was her or him.

"You know," he said looking down at her as he set her on the bed.

"Of course, I know your first name is Peter and not Gabriel. You know I knew your parents and met you as a baby. Why wouldn't I know?" she asked.

"Because I never said anything. You never said anything," he said watching her.

"What was there to say, once I realized who you were? 'Hey, I know we're mated, and I know you've been lying to me about your name'. It's not like I had any ground to stand on. Besides, I understood, Gabriel was and is your name even if your parents named you Peter. Gabriel is who you are."

"Did you know Peter?" Gabriel asked watching her closely.

"Yes, I knew Peter. Why do you ask?" she asked moving her hand over her belly.

"I don't know. I never understood why my parents named me after him," he said running a hand through his hair.

"When your brother was named after your father you mean," she asked. "Your mother wasn't sleeping with him," she said answering the question in Gabriel's mind knowing what was really bothering him.

"You sure about that," he questioned doubtfully.

"Very, I remember the way your parents looked at each other. It was what I hoped to have one day," she said taking his hand in hers with her free hand. "But I got so much more. I love you. Now either get into bed with me or go check on Amber and hurry back to me," she told him.

"Alright, I'll be right back, my love," he said leaning down to brush a kiss across her lips.

Gabriel went to check on Amber and her mate. "Are you alright?" Gabriel asked Amber coming into the room. He could hear the baby's heartbeat just as he knew they could, but he had put her on the fetal monitor for a few minutes any ways to get a visual representation of the heartrate and her contractions. Gabriel moved to look at the strip, which looked beautiful, so he went ahead and took her off the monitor. "I'll put you back on the monitor for a few minutes in a couple hours or sooner if I hear anything concerning in the heartbeat," Gabriel said. "Otherwise just try and relax."

"Thank you, we're fine but are you two alright? We couldn't help but overhear. I feel horrible," Amber apologized.

"It's alright, it's not your fault. You don't need to worry about me and my mate. As I said, 'I love her and I'm not going anywhere'," he told Amber.

Gabriel visited with them a little longer and then returned to Ruby who had settled into the bed but was still awake. Gabriel climbed into bed with her and pulled her into his arms as he kissed the top of her head comfortingly.

"Yes, I think I know why they named you Peter," Ruby said answering his unasked question.

"What?" Gabriel asked and then "Why?" realizing of course she knew he had been thinking about it. Sometimes it was easy to forget the other was in their head when it seemed so natural after all these years.

"Peter helped save your parents' lives and since your mother was pregnant at the time you and your brother's lives also. Peter was there for your parents. As was I," she told him.

"You knew my parents?" he asked not realizing that she knew them more than just from a distance or from meeting them in passing.

"Yes, one of the governments or rather organizations I infiltrated years ago was the 'Agency'," she told him.

"You mean the FBI, so you met my father while you were working there and what? He introduced you to my mother," he asked running his hand over her belly.

"No, I mean the Agency, I had infiltrated the FBI long before that almost back when it was first created. Your parents belonged to the Agency. The Agency was an organization, granted one created for the greater good, but still an organization nonetheless that was created though not technically sanctioned by any of the governments involved."

"Governments, as in plural?" he asked raising an eyebrow at her.

"Yes, many," she told him shaking her head in disbelief.

"How many?" he asked curious by her reaction.

"More than I care to think about. I mean they've done a lot of good, especially since they have pulled their resources in regards to government accesses and resources and aren't strictly bound by any governmental laws, but I don't necessarily like this consolidation of power even if it has allowed me easier access to government information."

"You expect me to believe that my parents were secret spies for some secret mysterious Agency? My father worked for the FBI and my mother worked for the CDC," he told her firmly thinking this whole conversation ridiculous.

"Technically, but only as a byproduct of their covers," she told him calmly unfazed by his disbelief. She knew it would be a lot for him to take in.

"What exactly did this organization do?" he asked humoring her.

"Mostly they take out people and criminal organizations that need to be taken out, ones that most if not all governments aren't even aware of," she said calmly.

"Take out?" he questioned not liking where this was going and the fact that she felt so… factual… honest. It didn't in the least feel like she was lying not that she'd ever lied to him, but he certainly had a feeling he was going to wish she was lying.

"Assassinations."

"You want me to believe my parents were assassins? My father I can kind of get I mean I thought he was in the FBI and I knew he was in the military from there it's not a huge leap to sniper and then assassin, but my mother? She was a genius," he denied her comments fervently even as he gently caressed his hand over her growing belly having moved up the shirt she was wearing so he could touch her skin to skin.

"Yes, she was, which was part of the reason the Agency wanted her. Your parents were two of the best. I was there when they were training your mother, she was amazing. Her skill with weapons, her quick thinking, her ability to see things others couldn't. She was good, I really liked her," she admitted.

"You want me to believe my mother was a killer? No, my mother wasn't a killer," he told her hotly.

Ruby slowly got out of bed which wasn't easy given how pregnant she was currently. Walking over to the balcony to open the doors, she pulled her shirt back down over their baby. She needed air.

"Come back to bed," he told her gently having not restrained her from getting up as he'd been inclined to do.

Ruby shook her head as she stepped outside without looking at him. She was trying to be patient, she knew this wasn't easy for him to hear, but... She needed air. He knew she wasn't lying, and she wanted to be patient, but she was also loaded with hormones and this night kept getting longer.

"Come back to bed, my love. It's freezing out here. You and our little girl don't need this," he told her gently pulling her into his arms. Holding her to him, he ran his hands gently over her as he let his body heat help keep her warm.

"I need air," she told him as she leaned against him and rested her head against his chest. Even as she struggled with him not listening to her, she needed to be in his arms.

"There is air in our bedroom. Air that isn't freezing cold and possibly harmful to you and our child," he told her gently. He wanted to pick her up and carry her back inside but held off. He knew it would go over better if he could talk her back inside. And he knew if it came down to it, he could heat the air on the balcony up to keep her warm, but this wasn't in the least like his mate, even pregnant and hormonal.

"There's not. I can't breathe in there. I need..." she trailed off briefly glancing up at him from under her lashes. She didn't know what she needed. She felt overwhelmed. She thought she'd left these memories behind. "I'm... I'm not lying to you, Gabriel. I'm not. I swear. You know I'm not. I wouldn't… I… I…" she trailed of gasping for air.

"I know, my love, but you want me to change my whole view of my whole childhood. Please be patient with me," he told her gently.

"I… I…" *I can't. I'm trying but I can't. Gabriel, I can't breathe*, she gasped looking up at him for help.

Yes, you can, my love, he reassured her scooping her into his arms and carrying her back inside. Sitting down on the couch in their room, he set her down in his lap as he brought his hands up to her face cupping her face in his hands as he brushed his thumbs gently over her cheeks in soothing caresses. *You can breathe, my love. It's alright*, he cooed gently trying to calm her down. He could feel her hyperventilating. He took a quick second to check and make sure their baby was still asleep, before their baby started reacting to Ruby panicking too. *Ruby look at me, my love*, he coaxed gently. *It's alright*, he reassured her. *You're alright, my love. You're safe and so is our baby girl. It's alright, Ruby. Everything is good. We're fine, better than fine, we're perfect, my little love. Shhh, calm down*, he continued to reassure her gently. *It's alright. There you go, my love. Give me another slow deep breath, Ruby. I know you can do it*, he encouraged softly.

You… you called me 'Ruby', she started to sniffle knowing she was going to start crying.

Because you are. You're my little Ruby, and you always will be. I'm sorry, my love. I guess you panicking helped remind me of that, he comforted her softly.

I'm sorry, she sobbed wrapping her arms around his neck. *I swear I didn't do it on purpose. I wanted to give you time*, she blubbered.

I know, my love. I do. It's alright, Ruby. You don't need to worry, we're perfect just like we have always been together. You aren't ever going to lose me, no matter what, he reassured her holding her in his arms as she clung to him while she cried. He knew that's what all this was about. She was terrified she was going to lose him between the name thing, and knowing his name, and things he didn't know about his own family. He couldn't make out any of the memories, but he got the impression there were a number involving his parents and she was worried that she'd lose him, but she also had no intention of lying to him and with the pregnancy hormones… It had all hit her too hard.

Ruby slowly loosened her choke hold on her mate as her crying slowed down too. *I'm sorry, Gabriel,* she sniffled resting her head on his shoulder.

Ruby, you have nothing to be sorry for, he told her gently as he ran his hand soothingly over her back.

I… I don't think I should have told you about your parents, she sighed feeling guilty.

My love, we don't keep secrets from each other, he corrected her.

But they're not my secrets to tell, and I… I didn't mean to, but I've been keeping them from you for nearly two centuries. There was never a reason to shed light on… It never came up… I didn't see a point, but you were hurting and… it slipped out without even thinking about it, because I love you and I've never set out to intentionally lie to you. but I'm not sure I should have… they're their secrets, she told him awkwardly not feeling like she'd made any sense.

Ruby, you are not responsible for keeping my parents' secrets. If they were alive, I'd make them tell me the truth, but I can't. I want to know the truth. Besides, I know you don't consider it your secrets, but it is still your past, is it not? he asked gently.

I suppose, she agreed reluctantly.

Then tell me about my mate, he encouraged gently.

Gabriel, are you really sure you want to know? I mean we're talking about your parents being killers, she asked worried. She didn't like the idea of taking his childhood away from him.

I don't know, my love, but I don't like knowing I don't know the truth about my human life. It feels like we're talking about someone else from a long time ago, he sighed.

In a way, we are. That was more than a lifetime ago, she told him gently.

Tell me about my killer parents, he told her swallowing hard as he laid his head back against the back of the couch and looked up at the ceiling.

Gabriel, is it really such a terrible thing that they were accomplished killers? she asked softly.

Gabriel lifted his head back up to look down at her hearing a sad note in her voice, but she wasn't looking at him. She was looking down at her belly and drawing circles on it with one of her fingers from her hand that had slid down from around his neck. *What do you mean, my love?* he asked caressing his hand along her belly but not getting in the way of her circle drawing.

Well, I… I'm a killer, and I have been for centuries, and… and you… love me, don't you? she asked softly.

With all my heart. I never thought it possible to love someone as much as I do you, my little love, he reassured her.

It doesn't bother you that I'm a killer, but you don't like that your parents were… killers, she questioned.

Ruby, you never once lied to me about being a killer. Hell, the very first thing you did when you came into my life was kill four vampires, he told her.

So, it's not so much that they were killers, but that they had lied to you about being killers, she pushed wanting to know.

Ruby, what's wrong? he asked gently feeling there was more to it that was bothering her.

It's just… we're… both… killers too, she said weakly.

So, what, he told her unconcerned. He knew that didn't in the least change how much they loved their unborn baby.

I was just… wondering… what that meant for our baby. I had… I never stopped to think about it before, because… it… it… Yeah, you were raised by two killers, but Gabriel, I love who you are, and I love you. I never stopped to think… she trailed off. Ruby lifted her head to look up at him, *what about our baby?* she asked tears swimming in her eyes.

My love, he started gently bringing his hand up to caress his fingertips over her cheek. *Our baby is going to be more loved than she knows what to do with it. She is going to be the safest and most protected baby in the world. And if earlier is any indication, also very powerful just like her mother,* he reassured.

But…

No, buts, my love. Our baby will know the truth about us. We're not going to shield her from who we are or what we do. It wouldn't be fair to her. She will grow up knowing it's normal, not unaware of who her parents, that already love her very much, really are, he told her firmly.

You're sure, she asked.

Yes, I'm sure we both love her very much, and I know we'd do anything to keep her safe.

I meant…

My love, I think we both already know that it's a strong possibility she grows up to follow in our footsteps, and I don't think that is a bad thing. We will raise her to know right from wrong, and I think that should include honesty. How can she learn that and know that she can trust us, if we aren't honest with her? I'm not saying we tell her all the gory details when she's little, but... he trailed off looking down into her face. *Our baby is going to be just fine,* he reassured her. *You said I turned out alright, right?* he asked reminding her.

You turned out better than alright, you're amazing, she told him smiling up at him happily.

You're the amazing one, he contradicted leaning down to brush a kiss across her lips. *Now,* Gabriel said settling back against the couch back again as he continued to hold her in his arms resting her against him. *Tell me how my parents met. Did they meet in this 'Agency'? Did they work together, or did they meet in training?* he prodded finding at this point he was more curious than anything. Like Ruby said, it was a lifetime ago, and it didn't change who he was or that he had his mate who was pregnant with his child.

Did your parents really never tell you how they met? she asked surprised as she rested peacefully against him.

How could they have if they met in this Agency? he asked looking down at her confused.

Gabriel, your parents didn't meet because of the Agency. They met in high school, she told with a half-smile.

You're telling me my parents really were high school sweethearts, he asked surprised.

Those two, no, she said chuckling. *They were just friends in high school, and then they went their separate ways when they were separately recruited into the Agency, but then I didn't know them at that time. I got to know your mother a little during her training. She was amazing. She was a genius, shy, but could handle herself with confidence, and damn was she deadly. She was not a woman to be messed with. I think she felt more comfortable with a blade in her hand than trying to deal with people. I think there was a lot of hidden anger and pain there, but your father seemed to help with that later. She was one hell of a woman*, she said shaking her head slightly in disbelief.

You liked her, he realized kissing the top of her head.

Yeah, she was a good woman who had deserved an easier path in life, she sighed remembering so many of the glimpses she ultimately got into her life. She'd had a hard childhood.

You saw yourself in her, didn't you? he realized.

I guess, I did, she agreed slowly. *She was probably the closest thing I ever had to a friend*, she admitted. *But she had what I thought I never would*, she admitted feeling guilty at the memory of her jealousy and pain at seeing her get something she never would or at least that's how she had felt at the time. But there had also been some weird kindred thing that she had hoped his mother could at least have the happiness she feared she never would.

I'm sorry, my love. That's a hard way to live, he apologized hating all the pain he knew his mate had gone through without him and the rest of the pain he knew he couldn't begin to comprehend over her existence.

It's why I tended to keep my distance from the humans. It just hurt. A reminder of everything that… wasn't mine, she sighed.

Well, it is now, my love. You're not alone anymore, Ruby. You haven't been for some time. You have me, and I swear to you, I'm not going anywhere, Ruby, he reassured her.

I know, Gabriel. I do, but I… I can't go back to that, not after having you in my life, she told him.

You're not going to, I'm right here, he comforted kissing the top of her head.

I just… I know we weren't exactly friends, your mother and I, but I… I mean I was two millennia old and had lots of secrets, but I still feel like I'm betraying your mother.

By telling me about her and father, he questioned.

No, *I mean yes, but… also by… taking you from her,* she admitted the guilt she'd been denying and avoiding since the day she realized exactly who he was. She should have left that day. She should have called his mother and told her he was in danger and left.

No, you shouldn't have, he told her interrupting her panicked thought. *My love, I was an adult and had every right to make my own decisions and I did. I followed you to that warehouse of my own volition and I do not regret that decision. You let me make the decision whether or not to stay with you after you turned me, and you know I have never once regretted mating you. My mother had no place in what happened between us, and it would have left both of us in pain we didn't need to be in, and you for… a hell of a lot longer. I hate to think what would have become of you, as I know you do too. My love, you did nothing wrong,* he told her gently.

I fear you're wrong, she denied softly.

What do you mean? he asked feeling something he couldn't place.

I think… I think I might have… somehow… played an indirect role in… your existence, she struggled to admit.

You mean helping keep my mother alive while she was pregnant, he said remembering what she had said earlier but confused by her feelings.

No, I mean in regard to your conception, she blurted out in a hurry.

Ruby, that makes absolutely no sense. Last time I check, which we both know was recently, you are female. You are after all carrying my offspring. I'm pretty sure you did not play a role in my conception, he contradicted her confused.

I think maybe you are right, I need to tell you the story of your parents, she sighed fearing he would leave her, but knowing she couldn't not tell him. She realized now, she'd been wrong. It wasn't just his parents' secrets she'd been keeping. It was one she'd never even admitted to herself until now.

Somehow, I suddenly think you were right. I didn't need to know this side of my parents, he sighed. *I'm not going to like this, am I?* he asked worried, but yet still somehow more worried about his mate who sat terrified in his arms.

The Agency was a little different for reasons we can get into later, but your... Well, your mother and I had kind of parted our ways after she'd been trained. I hadn't exactly been close with her and well, that's not what either of us was there for. A couple years later I was tasked with a surveillance mission, she paused taking a deep breath.

What kind of surveillance mission? Gabriel prompted gently for her to continue.

There was an agent that had... well, returned after a very long undercover mission that had gone sideways a number of months prior, and he hadn't made it out until about a week or two before I was given the assignment, during which time he was recovering... well, physically from... the undercover operation.

You're talking about my father, aren't you? He was tortured, wasn't he? he asked not sure he wanted the answer even though he was pretty sure he already knew it.

I didn't know it at the time, that he was you father, I mean obviously, you didn't exist yet. They were worried about his ability to readjust. I was tasked with keeping an eye on him from a distance for his safety. He never knew, Ruby told him.

My love, I'm not sure what this has to do with anything, he questioned.

It wasn't long before I became aware of his connection to your mother. Neither seemed to be aware of the others status, and your mother had honestly seemed quite unhappy to see him. I still don't know if he had sought her out intentionally or if he just took advantage of the opportunity to...

Don't say it, he interrupted her having a feeling he knew where she was going, and he didn't want to hear her say it.

Well, any ways it wasn't long before they were practicing... she trailed off

Practicing what? he asked confused.

Practicing making you, she said unsure how he was confused.

Ugh, I said not to say that, he told her.

Come on, you had to know they did that at least once, she smiled up at him. That was after all how she got her mate.

Ruby, he protested.

Well, anyways, it came time for me to decide what to do, she said softly.

What do you mean? he asked confused.

Well, I was supposed to be reporting on him, but... I mean... I know they were only practicing. But I... I knew the Agency's stance on... I could tell even though neither of them admitted it and they never went out in public... I could tell how much they cared for each other. If any two people deserved to find a little happiness, it was them. I didn't want to get in the way of that, but they also... they were in denial about it... and they deserved to know that they were both agents. But I feared any decision I made could negatively impact them, and I couldn't explain my weird desire for them to...

To keep practicing, he finished for her.

I mean it wasn't so much that, but… yes. There was a weird need to see them happy and I just knew somehow that they were meant to be, she trailed off.

What did you do, Ruby? he asked gently as he moved his hand up to her hair, holding her head to his chest as he kissed it softly. He knew how much she was hurting, but he also knew she needed to get this out.

I… I did the only thing I could. I knew it would get out eventually, and if it wasn't me, it'd be someone else. It would be better to get out ahead of it. Either it would save them pain in the long run, or they would fight for each other, or… or there was a third option that seemed highly unlikely, but none the less… I had to report the discovery, she admitted.

I mean clearly, they chose to fight, but what was the third option? he asked curious.

Well, your mother was after all a genius. They had been trying for some time to get her to agree to a bodyguard. There was an unlikely scenario where the agency might have tried to… she trailed off aware he knew where she'd been going. That they might have tried to use his father as a bodyguard whether he was aware of it or not.

They didn't exactly choose to fight, did they? he asked.

Not at that time, no, she agreed.

This is where we are getting to the part I won't like, right? he asked needing no answer, but feeling her shake her head in response anyways.

They knew he'd never agree to continue lying to her once he knew she was an agent, and she'd break it off upon realizing he'd been told to protect her. No matter how real his feelings were, or that he'd have done it anyways, she said.

Please tell me they did not somehow implant my mother with embryos with their DNA, he told her closing his eyes.

I…

Ruby, he started trying to hold his emotions in check, but he was not liking where this was going.

I don't think they could have pulled that off... she trailed off again.

But, he prompted.

But they wanted me to swap out her birth control, she told him hesitantly.

They wanted her pregnant, he questioned.

I guess they figured... if she was pregnant, he would feel compelled to protect her further, or at least insist on proximity. That is him insisting from her, so that he could be near her and could keep her and... well, you safe, and she might feel inclined to agree, she explained.

But that would require her to decide to keep the pregnancy, he observed.

Yeah, that's the only problem with that plan, she told him rolling her eyes.

Ruby, why did my mother need a bodyguard at all? You said she was a killing machine, he questioned.

She was, and she didn't, but she was a genius and they didn't want to lose their asset. She didn't just kill for them. You'd be surprised some of the things your mother came up with. Hell, our computer system was built off of some the technology she created, granted its undergone generations of updates but... Suffice to say they wanted her alive, she shrugged. *Gabriel, you're avoiding your real question. Just ask,* she told him.

Did you? he asked.

No, I told them it was unethical and left, but I... I don't know what happened after that. Just because I refused doesn't mean they couldn't find another agent that would agree to substitute her pills, she told him.

Why do you feel confused? he asked.

It's just... it was quite a while before they ever reached out to me for help. If they had swapped them, there would have been no reason to delay the tactic, and as much as they... I would have expected a call sooner... she trailed off thinking.

But? he asked confused

But I didn't get one. So, I don't know if they really got pregnant despite birth control, or if it took that long before they got pregnant, but neither of those would exactly explain...

My brother, he surmised what she meant.

No. I mean it's possible, but... no, I can't help but wonder if after a while her pills were swapped for fertility meds, she told him feeling guilty.

But you don't know for sure, and it was never you who swapped them out, he tried to remind her.

No, but they only knew about them because of me, she told him.

Ruby, that's not your fault. You couldn't have known that they would plan something so underhanded, and once you did you refused to help. What more could you have done? It's not like you could have stalked them until they figured it out, whether it was that they loved each other or that they were both agents or that they accidentally got pregnant on their own. That would have been ridiculous, he told her gently.

I could have told them the truth, she sighed.

You could have, sure, but what would that have helped. I know you liked the idea of them happy, and you would know better than me their states of minds at the time. If you had told them, what do you think would have happened? he asked gently.

I think I wouldn't be pregnant, she said sadly.

You still have me, Ruby, he reassured her knowing she was unsure whether or not she still had her mate after everything she'd told him. *But what do you think would have happened?* he pushed gently.

Your mother would have run away. She never would have fought for him, not at the time. She wouldn't have gotten pregnant and married your father. None of us would have had any happiness, she said sadly.

And she was happy after all, right? he pushed trying to make her feel better.

Ruby shook her head in a wishy-washy method. That was a complicated question, but, *yeah, she was happy with your father,* she agreed.

I know you feel guilty, but I think it still somehow worked out the way it should have, he reassured her. *I have to say I know I'm happy with my mate that I wouldn't have otherwise.*

You sure, she questioned looking up at him timidly.

Very. I love you, and I hate to think of you without me for a number of reasons including our baby girl you're carrying, he reassured her brushing away the stray tear that had slipped out as he caressed his fingertips lovingly over her cheek.

I love you, she sighed relieved.

Get some rest, my love, he told her gently feeling her eyes drooping heavily after everything. She was worn out, and now that she'd told him what she needed to and he hadn't left her, it was hitting her hard.

Gabriel, she yawned softly. *I love our little girl too,* she told him needlessly as she snuggled against him.

I know you do, my little love. Now, I want you to get some rest for me and our little girl. I can feel how tired you are, he coaxed kissing the top of her head soothingly as he floated a blanket over to him to cover her with as he felt her drifting off to sleep.

That still didn't answer all of his questions, but he was good for now. Right now, he needed his pregnant mate to rest. He could ask questions if he needed to later, but at the end of the day he had his mate and that was all he cared about.

* * * * * * * *

Gabriel, Ruby called frightened as she felt herself being set down on the bed.

Shh, shhh, it's alright, my love. I'm right here, he reassured her as he sat down on the edge of the bed beside her. He gently brushed her hair back from her face and then caressed his hand over her stomach comfortingly to help her settle back down. *Go back to sleep, my love.*

Why aren't you laying down with me? she whimpered wanting to be back in his arms.

I'll be right back, Ruby. I was going to go check on Amber really quick, he told her gently.

What? Who's Amber? she asked her eyes flying open to look up at him.

Gabriel could feel her flash of jealousy and loss of recollection of the name. *Amber is the pregnant wolf in our guest room with her mate,* he reminded calming her down.

Oh, yeah, right, she agreed reaching out to rest her hand on his leg.

I'll be right back, he tried to reassure her again feeling her anxiety at him leaving her side. *I'm not even leaving the house,* he reassured her as he leaned down to kiss the top of her head.

Hurry, she told him. She knew he should check on her, but she didn't want to be alone. She never liked being apart from him, neither of them did, but she was still extremely anxious about being apart from him after everything and she could feel his swirling emotions which wasn't helping.

Of course, my love, he told her brushing a kiss on her stomach and then standing up as he brushed a soft kiss over her lips. *Try and get some more rest, my love.*

No, promises, she told him softly even as her lids closed.

He knew she didn't want to sleep without him, but he could feel her drifting off anyways. He couldn't help leaning down to kiss her temple one more time before leaving. He had no desire to leave her side, but the sooner he left the sooner he could have her back in his arms.

* * * * * * * *

Gabriel could feel Ruby frequently checking on him as he spoke with Amber and her mate. She was drifting in and out of a light sleep, but never fully waking up as she checked on his progress. Though he suspected she was only really checking on where he was and not so much on the conversation.

"I think we are going to go ahead and try getting together with the midwife again," Amber's mate told him calmly as he looked at her for confirmation. "We appreciate all your help, and your offer, but we don't want to impose."

"It's your decision. We just wanted to make sure you were safe and help however we could. If that means, helping you get to your midwife that's perfectly fine."

"I... I know how emotional pregnancy can be at times, and all the animals know how much you and Ruby like your privacy. I wouldn't feel right intruding on that especially not at a time like now," Amber told him apologetically as she glanced at her mate nervously.

"It's alright, Amber. We appreciate the consideration, and we just want you to be comfortable. You are the one in labor after all," he told her gently not wanting her to feel bad.

"We know our midwife better, and well… she knows our species better," her mate told him.

"I don't follow," Gabriel asked confused. He was in no way offended or trying to protest just simply curious.

"I… I thought you knew," he said looking at him funny, but continuing when Gabriel shook his head with a slight shrug. "It's just… well, we are wolves. When it comes down to it, we never know which form we will deliver in, and I'm willing to bet you didn't practice delivering wolves."

"No, I didn't," Gabriel agreed knowing he meant in case she delivered in wolf form.

"The midwife knows how to deliver in either form. Besides, she's early right now, but as she gets further in labor it can be dangerous as the need to shift back and forth asserts itself and the pain can be disorienting. I wouldn't… neither of us would feel right being here with your mate pregnant, and as you can imagine it's also a bit of a private matter for us too," he informed him.

"I didn't realize. Ruby had mentioned it could be dangerous, but she hadn't had a chance to elaborate," he confessed.

"Honestly, I'm not sure how much she knows anyways other than that it can be dangerous," Antonio added.

"How can I help you two get to the midwife? I know we're not terribly far from one of your towns out here, but I don't like the idea of the two of you trying to make that journey alone with her in this condition," Gabriel said moving to the problem at hand.

"If you have a phone, I can call the midwife. She was expecting us, so she is bound to be worried. She'll come with her mate and another male of the tribe to help escort us safely," he told him as he glanced lovingly at his mate.

"Of course," Gabriel told him pulling out his and Ruby's phone. There was never any need for them to have more than the one. They were almost always together, and if not, he was after all bonded to her. Gabriel logged into the phone in protected mode so that all he could do was use it to call, and then handed it over to them.

He felt more comfortable with the idea of them making the journey with the midwife in case she did progress and the fact that she wasn't coming alone. He didn't want them unprotected, not that he doubted the wolf's ability to protect his mate, but she was after all in labor and he didn't need to be distracted from her and also worried about the midwife's safety.

"They'll be here soon," Antonio told him as he hung up and handed him back the phone.

"Sounds good," Gabriel told him.

"You can go back to your mate while we wait, if you'd like. I'm sure you're worried about her," Amber told him softly.

"If it's alright with you, I'd rather stay here and make sure you all get off alright. He said they'd be here soon, and I'd rather not have to leave her side again if I don't have to, and this way I won't have to. Besides, I know exactly how she is doing and if she needs me," Gabriel assured her.

He did want to be back by his mate's side, but he knew she was resting, and he didn't want to have to leave her side shortly when the other wolves showed up. And while he knew they were coming to help, his mate was pregnant and he'd rather be able to greet them as they arrived to keep an eye on them and to keep them away from his pregnant mate.

It wasn't long before he felt their approach. He suspected they had been covering ground as fast as they could. "They're here," he told them aware from their behavior that they hadn't yet heard their approach. He waited to escort them outside as Amber's mate stood up and easily scooped her into his arms to meet them.

They stood outside in the clearing around the house as they exited the forest line. The three wolves including the midwife fell into formation around them as he moved forward carrying his mate.

"Thank you for helping me get back to my mate," Amber told him softly.

"Of course, and best of luck to you," he wished them off. He stayed outside for a little bit tracking their movements away from his mate before he moved to go inside and return to her side.

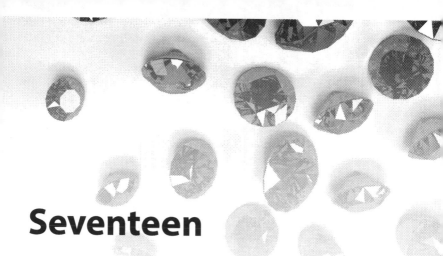

Seventeen

Gabriel, she sighed as he picked her back up into his arms and got into bed holding her to him. *Why were you gone so long? You said you'd be quick,* she questioned as she snuggled against him.

I'm sorry, my love. I was seeing the wolves off, he apologized.

Off, she asked confused as she opened her eyes to look at him.

They wanted to deliver with their midwife, he told her gently.

And you just let them go, she asked shocked.

Ruby, I wasn't going to hold them against their will. She felt more comfortable with her midwife, and if we could help her reunite with her, I saw no reason not to let her. I know you would be uncomfortable with anyone but me, he told her softly.

No, I meant she's contracting and pregnant. You let them go out there alone. We're still a good distance from their village, she questioned.

Of course not, my love. We had the midwife and a couple other wolves come out and help escort them. She will be fine, he reassured her knowing she was just worried about the pregnant wolf and her baby.

I never even felt them, she said worried.

You're tired, my love, and you know you are always safe with me here. I could feel you checking on me whether you realized it or not, and you know I wouldn't let anything happen to my girls, he reassured her.

I know you wouldn't. I had... I kind of liked the idea of getting to hold a baby, she admitted sadly.

Ruby, you don't know that they would have let you hold their baby, and besides, you will be holding our little girl before you know it, he comforted her gently as he ran his hand over her stomach.

You know at some point we will have to talk about names, she sighed as she closed her eyes.

I think not. It's a girl, and I am not stupid. I will not be suggesting any names and risking upsetting you, he knew she would be wanting to know where any name he suggested came from and would likely be angered by it regardless of there being an origin or not.

Gabriel, I want you to like our baby's name, she said sadly knowing where he was coming from.

My love, I will let you know if I don't like any names you think up, but you will be driving this train and you know that just as we both know the situation would be reversed if it was a boy, he told her.

I suppose I do, she agreed.

Now, sleep, my love. We can talk more later, he commanded gently.

I do like that you won't have to leave to check on her, she admitted ashamed of herself.

Me too, my love, he agreed pulling the bedding up around them. Normally, they both would have slept in a lot less clothes, and given that the wolves were gone, they could, but he didn't want her out of his arms again to help her undress or to undress himself. He'd worry about that later.

* * * ● ● ● * *

What's wrong, Gabriel? Ruby asked drowsily as she shifted slightly in his arms.

Nothing is wrong, my love. Go back to sleep, he encouraged.

It's not nothing, she sighed shifting slowly to his side to sit up needing a change in position. *You're thinking way too hard for nothing otherwise I'd still be asleep, and you'd be asleep and not awake. Now, talk to me, Gabriel. What are you thinking about?* she asked watching him carefully as she slid her hand under his shirt to rest on his hard abdomen needing contact with him skin to skin.

Gabriel reached out to caress her belly. He loved seeing her pregnant with his child. *I'm sorry I woke you, my love,* he apologized wanting her to get the rest she needed.

Gabriel, I'm fine, she reassured him. *I'm pregnant and occasionally emotional, but I'm not sick or injured. We have no plans for today that I need to be particularly extra rested for, and we know I'm not going fighting or anything else crazy. Besides, I was able to get some rest and our little girl is fine. Whereas you, my mate, have not rested, and I know you are just as tired as I was if not more so, because I've not left the house and I got some sleep. Now, stop stalling and start talking,* she told him bringing her other hand up to rest on his on her stomach. She knew he found it reassuring to be able to touch her belly, to know her and the baby were okay.

I was thinking about earlier, he told her staring at their baby.

Gabriel, I'm going to need you to be a little more specific, she told him gently, but also worried. A lot of what had happened earlier had had her in tears.

You said… you said my parents loved each other, but then… it sounds like… they only got married because she got… pregnant, he struggled to get out.

Ruby moved her hand trying ineffectively to cover her stomach more not liking him staring at her belly while talking about his parents getting married because they were pregnant. She knew the two were unrelated, but she was after all pregnant and had been terrified earlier about losing him. *Gabriel, that's not true,* she started telling him gently and trailed off as she watched him reach across the bed for one of the small decorative pillows.

He handed her the pillow to cover her belly. He knew she was feeling sensitive, but she had managed to stay on topic it appeared knowing their pregnancy was unrelated to his concerns.

Thank you, she smiled softly at him as she took the pillow. She hesitated waiting for him to move his hand that had never left her stomach so that she could hold the pillow to her.

Gabriel shook his head at her. *I'm not moving my hand, my love,* he told her adamantly.

Very well, she accepted easily as she held the pillow in her lap. It didn't bother her in the least if he wanted to keep his hand on her stomach. He wasn't the only one that found it reassuring to have his hand on her belly. *Gabriel, your mother may have been pregnant at their wedding, but that in no way means that she was marrying him just because she was pregnant.*

Doesn't it? he questioned.

No. Gabriel, your mother was a strong woman. She never would have married your father just because she was pregnant. She might have been willing to move in with him or have him move in with her, but marriage... no, she denied adamantly.

You don't know that. Humans do stupid things when they get pregnant, he argued.

You know what, right now I very much wish your mother was alive so you could argue that stupid point with her, she told him bluntly not liking the insinuation that pregnant women make stupid decisions.

Ruby, you know I was not in any way implying that you are stupid, he told her gently.

"No, just your mother," she snorted.

Ruby, he sighed. *I did not call my mother stupid though I'm not entirely sure why that should upset you. She's my mother not yours.*

"Because I'm pregnant and apparently that makes me stupid," she sniffed removing her hand from his abdomen and crossing her arms over the pillow she was holding.

Ruby, please. I think we've moved off topic. I do not think you or my mother are stupid, but I do still have doubts about them not getting married because of the pregnancy, he told her trying to redirect her. Feeling her still struggling despite trying to get back on topic, Gabriel sat up without hesitating to wrap his hand around the nape of her neck and capture her mouth. He slowly lifted his head from hers but had to stop to lean down and brush a soft kiss over her lips as she looked up at him stunned.

Why? she asked confused.

You feel calmer now, he told her gently brushing his thumb along her jawline.

Nikki Crawford

I'm sorry, she told him looking down at her lap. She hadn't meant to get so worked up. She had been trying to help him feel better.

Ruby, my love, you have nothing to be sorry for, he told her sliding his thumb under her chin to lift her head back up to look at him. *You are my mate. I will always do anything I can to help make you feel better just as I know you would for me. Besides, I enjoy kissing you*, he teased smiling down at her.

Thank you, she told him reaching up to kiss him.

Any time, he reassured her.

So, other than me telling you that your mother was already pregnant when they got married, have you ever had any reason to not believe that your parents loved each other? she asked raising an eyebrow at him.

Well, no, he agreed reluctantly. *But apparently my parents were accomplished liars for a living*, he finished.

Gabriel, I followed your father for a significant amount of time. Aside from them getting together frequently to... Gabriel, you know how good our hearing is, I could hear everything...

Please stop, he interrupted laying back down not liking the idea of 'hearing' more.

Gabriel, your parents did more than just practice making you when they got together, she continued ignoring his request. Gabriel moved his arm he'd covered his eyes with to look at her questioningly. *Gabriel, I told you your parents had been friends in high school. I'm guessing best friends. They would talk about anything and everything. The only thing your parents never talked about was... well, them*, she admitted sadly.

I think you are making my point, my love, Gabriel said.

Not at all. Your father was determined to bring your mother back into his life. I think he'd realized what was important during that mission, but your mother was hurt and having him come back into her life... wasn't easy. She was afraid to lose him again, and your father was doing everything he could to keep her. Sure, talking might have been smarter, but not necessarily easier when you're terrified. Your parents loved each other. Hell, I wouldn't have been surprised to find out they did already love each other in high school, she said.

You really think so, he asked unsure.

My love, I think them getting pregnant was the best thing that ever happened to them. I think it forced them to talk. When your mother called asking for help, I moved in for the remainder of her pregnancy. Your mother was clearly happy. I mean she was terrified and anxious, but she was happy too. You could see it in how they looked at each other, and I could hear it in how they talked and behaved with each other even when they weren't visible to their... guests. You were a good thing, you in no way forced them together, she reassured him.

Well, that's good, I guess, he sighed sadly as he moved the pillow she was holding, to see her belly holding his child.

Gabriel, she questioned softly as she scooted up closer to him. *My love, your words and your tone don't match,* she told him as she brushed a lock of hair from his forehead and then trailed her fingertips down the side of his face to caress his jaw lovingly.

I'm sorry, Ruby, he apologized glancing up at her and looking back down as he caressed his hand over the product of their love, her stomach.

You don't need to apologize. I know I've given you a lot of information. You're allowed to hurt. I just... want to... understand, she reassured him gently.

I am happy for them, or I guess I mean, I'm happy to know they loved each other, because they're obviously long dead... he trailed off thinking about that for a minute. He'd never really stopped to think about the fact that they were dead.

I'm sorry, Ruby apologized feeling bad.

It's not your fault, my love. It's not like you killed them or anything. They... they lived their lives, he comforted her gently.

Yeah, but I robbed you all of the time you could have spent together, she said weakly still feeling bad about taking him from his family.

My love, you and our baby are my family, he clarified.

I know but, she interrupted.

There is no 'but', my love. Sure, it would have been nice to know how their lives finished, and it would have been nice to introduce them to the love of my life, but obviously that second part would have been fraught with issues. But Ruby, I was at a point in life where I didn't live at home, and I only saw them on occasions. My life would have regardless been what it has been about and that's my family. Ruby, I love you, and I've only ever loved you, well until now, he told her caressing her belly. *I want this here with you, I don't regret my decision. I do wish my parents could have been able to meet our daughter, their grandbaby, but even if I had gotten you pregnant the first time that was a possibility they would have been in their seventies if they were even still alive and they might very well have died during your pregnancy. I'm not in the least upset with how things have turned out for us,* he reassured her.

I'm sorry, I've side lined us again, haven't I? That's not what you're hurting about. There was a 'but' coming after you said you were happy for them, wasn't there? she asked still worried about her mate.

It's just... it makes me wonder if they really loved... or more the pregnancy because it helped bring them together. I mean it was an accident after all. They weren't trying to get pregnant, he sighed. He was a mistake after all.

You are not a mistake. Your parents loved you. They may have gotten pregnant on accident, but they chose to keep you, she reassured him hating to hear that he thought his parents didn't love him when she loved him so very much and she knew how much his parents had loved him. He wasn't a mistake. He was her other half without which she would be nothing.

No, they chose to keep him, and they got me too, he denied. *It's not like they could keep one and not the other.*

That's not true. Your parents loved both of you, she denied adamantly. *Is this because he was named after your father?* she asked confused.

Gabriel shrugged his shoulders but didn't say anything.

Gabriel, he was first out. That is the only reason he was the one named after your father. It could have been either one of you. Your parents had agreed it would simply be first out. Your parents spoke multiple times on this in private. Your father did not like the idea of naming either of you after him for this reason, but your mother had insisted she wanted to name one of her babies after him. She couldn't very well give you two the same name though I assure you she suggested it. She loved your father, but she also loved you, both of you, she argued not liking this silliness. His mother had chosen to keep the pregnancy because she wanted him.

Ruby, sure she chose to keep the pregnancy, but she had no way of knowing she was carrying twins at the time. She chose to keep one baby, the first one, the one they named after my father, not me. I was the accident they were stuck with. How could they possibly have loved me? he asked hurting.

289

I… I… I need air, she told him as she started to panic and bolted off the bed for the balcony.

Gabriel followed quickly after her. *Ruby, you have to stop this running outside. It is freezing cold and you are pregnant,* he chided her gently as he pulled her into his arms, but she didn't respond to him. She was hyperventilating and struggling to breathe. This was way worse than last time. *Ruby, please, my love, I need you to breathe. You're scaring me.* Ruby shook her head adamantly. *Please, my love. What's going on?* he asked scared. He'd never been so afraid in his life.

Our…our… baby… accident, she struggled to think with her hyperventilating.

No, our little girl is not an accident, he corrected her.

Yes… yes… yes… she… is, she continued gasping.

No, my love, she's not. We were trying to get pregnant, he reminded her.

No… no… she shook her head. *We… we… lost… She… is… an… accident,* she told him gasping for air unsure how she was still standing as she was now feeling faint. She had known their baby was an accident, but it had never once bothered her until now.

Ruby, she might have been a surprise, but we wanted her. This is where we'd be if we hadn't… he trailed off hating the reminder of the miscarriage. He could hear the word accident running through her head on a loop. Gabriel cupped her face in his hands forcing her to look at him. *Ruby, I don't care if she was an accident or not, I love our baby and I know you do too.*

But… but… but…

Are you really going to try and tell me you don't love our baby? he asked knowing she was panicking because she thought their baby wasn't loved. Ruby shook her head. *And are you going to try and tell me that I don't love our little girl?* he persisted.

Ruby shook her head again. *But you said,* she whimpered.

Forget what I said, I was wrong, he reassured her wrapping her in his arms as he kissed the top of her head.

I did it again, she whimpered wrapping her arms around his waist.

What, my love? he asked resting his cheek on her head.

I was trying to make you feel better, and instead ended up freaking out, she sniffled.

Ruby, I don't care about that. I care about you and our baby, he told her gently.

Gabriel, she loved you both. She might have been caught off guard, but she loved both of you. That's part of why she wanted to name both of you after your father, but he told her that was ridiculous. Gabriel, you know how dangerous it can be having twins. Your mother risked her life to keep both of you, even after she found out it was twins. She was terrified of losing either of you. She loved you both so much, she told him.

I know, my love. It would seem I panicked a little myself with all the information you told me. If it helps, your panicking helped put that in perspective for me, he told her gently.

I think you would have preferred me not melting down again, she denied weakly as she held on to him.

Well, there is that, he agreed. *Will you please come in out of the cold now?* he asked kissing the top of her head again.

Ruby nodded her head against his chest. *Gabriel,* she said softly as he lifted her back into his arms.

Yes, my little love, he inquired looking down at the top of her head.

I don't want our baby to ever know she was an accident. I know we love her, but...

I understand, my love, he reassured her gently.

I don't want her to ever doubt that we want her. I know how hard that is, and it seems you do too, she told him remembering going through life unwanted and never having parents herself. *I don't want that for her,* she told him.

Our baby is only ever going to know how much we love her. I assure you of that, my love, he told her setting her down on the bed and moving to take her shirt off.

What are you doing? she asked looking up at him tired.

Taking my mate back to bed, so we can get some sleep, he told her as he took his shirt off and helped her put it on as a nightshirt. Helping her stand up, he helped her off with her pants and then helped her back into bed under the covers. Quickly relieving himself of his pants, Gabriel climbed into bed beside her and pulled her into his arms. He knew she was tired. He'd woken her up not long after going to sleep, and then he had proceeded to continue riling her up. *I love you,* he reassured her gently.

And I love you, she told him drowsily. *Promise me you will actually get some sleep this time,* she told him worried.

I will, Ruby. Talking to you helped. It always does, he sighed closing his eyes as he pulled the comforter up around them to keep her warm.

* * * * * * * *

"What are you doing?" Gabriel asked glancing at her over his shoulder.

"Nothing," Ruby said looking over at him.

"And the juggling knives," he questioned raising an eyebrow at her.

"It's not me," she told him innocently.

"I'm aware. Why is our daughter juggling knives?" he questioned.

"Because I showed her how," she told him smiling impishly. *Good girl*, she whispered to her as she caressed her belly.

"Why?" he drew out bewildered at her decision.

"Well, we're not using the silverware yet, you're still cooking after all," she told him playing dumb.

"Ruby, why are you teaching her to juggle, and does she really need to be juggling knives?" he asked worried.

"It was entertaining, and after the other night I was curious to see what all she could do even though I'm still pregnant," she finished slowly.

"Alright, but knives. Is that such a good idea?" he questioned.

"They were handy. Besides, it's not like she's juggling them with her hands. Gabriel, calm down," she told him gently. "I'm keeping an eye on her and the knives. She's safe, and so am I," she added knowing his real concern was her getting hurt because he didn't want her hurt and their baby was fine unless she was hurt.

"Ruby, please pick something else. Something safer," he clarified. "Hell, there's a bowl of fruit sitting right there next to you on the table, and yet you went for the silverware." He knew she was having fun playing with their little girl, and he knew she was watching her, but that didn't dampen his terror.

"Alright," she told him apologetically feeling bad for making him worry needlessly. "Sweetie put the knives down on the table for me. You're making daddy nervous," she told their little girl.

Daddy, he questioned turning around to look at her surprised.

She watched as the knives settled on the table before she turned her full attention to him. *Well, yeah. You are her father after all*, she thought to him confused by his surprise.

Yeah, but...

But what, Gabriel? she asked unsure what was going on.

I... I don't know. I guess I was just surprised. It's... new. I mean I know we're having a baby, obviously, but I apparently seem to have missed the part where I'm going to be a father, he told her surprised at his own surprise.

Really? she asked unfolding her legs and sliding off the table to walk over to him knowing he wanted her closer. *I've already been pregnant for five years, I'm as big as a house, and you are just now realizing you are going to be a father*, she questioned exasperated.

Gabriel shrugged slightly as he leaned down to kiss her. *Apparently*, he agreed. *I'm going to be a father*, he told her smiling goofily at her.

Ruby shook her head slightly as she stepped closer to him. *You do realize you kind of already are, right?* she asked him.

I...

I'll take that as a no, she said as he trailed off. *Let me finish lunch*, she told him taking the spatula out of his hand. She knew she had stunned him with the realization which seemed to have locked up the gears in his head. *Try not to think too hard about it, Gabriel*, she told him gently as she took over cooking. She was hungry. "I think I broke your father, little girl," she told her stomach.

"I... but I mean... I..." Gabriel struggled to think.

"Stop that," Ruby mumbled.

"Stop what?" Gabriel asked.

"Not you," she told him pressing her hand against her stomach.

"What's wrong?" he asked worriedly as his hands came around her, one finding the same spot she was pushing against.

"Nothing is wrong, my love," she reassured him as she turned her head back to look up at him and reaching up to place a kiss on his cheek. "We're fine, she's just stretching. It's just unfortunately also stretching the limits of my uterus with her, and it's… uncomfortable," she told him trying to calm him down. He was fretting over her like a nervous mother.

"Am not," he contradicted.

"Are to," she argued. "Can't I be the mother?" she asked teasingly.

"I don't know, you were teaching her to juggle knives after all," he asked laughing at her. "You might be better suited to being the dad that gives her bad ideas," he teased back.

"Oh thank god, then you can take over carrying this bowling ball that's still growing somehow," she told him easily.

"We both know you love carrying her," he told her kissing the top of her.

"I do," she agreed smiling up at him happily. *I can't imagine life without her,* she admitted.

You don't need to. She's not going anywhere, he reassured her gently.

Gabriel, do you want another one? she asked flipping over a pancake.

Another what? he asked confused.

Another child, she said softly.

I don't know, he told her holding her back against him as he watched her cook resting his chin on her head.

You don't want another, she said trying to keep her voice from cracking and surprised at the pain the thought brought.

I said 'I don't know' meaning I really don't know. I wasn't saying no, my love, he comforted her kissing the top of her head. *But Ruby, you are still pregnant after all,* he told her caressing her stomach for emphasis.

I know. Trust me it's kind of hard to forget. You won't let me fight, I'm not allowed to play with knives, you hover over me like a mother hen, and I am as big as a house, she told him.

You are nowhere near as big as a house. You have a cute little pregnant belly. As for the rest, I feel it's all very reasonable, he argued.

Yes, yes, reasonable, she said rolling her eyes as she continued. *Gabriel, I know how worried you are, and I would never do anything to hurt our baby any more than you would which is why I haven't fought you on it.* She felt Gabriel raise an eyebrow at her in disbelief. *Fine, I haven't fought you too hard,* she acquiesced. *Though I think you'd rather put me on a shelf and pull me out when it's time to deliver,* she grumbled.

Or tie you to the bed, he agreed wanting to have regular access to her.

That I might agree to, she told him smiling.

It can be arranged, he told her leaning down to kiss her neck suggestively.

Ruby turned off the stove and set down the spatula. Taking one of Gabriel's hands off her stomach she moved out of his arms and led him out of the kitchen still holding his hand in hers.

"Ruby, where are we going, I thought you were hungry?" he questioned following after her as she led him to the couch in the living room.

"I am. My appetite has just... changed right now," she told him reaching on her tip toes to kiss him. Gabriel took the opportunity to slip his tongue into her mouth as she knew he would. Ruby stopped him as he started to pull her into his arms and pushed him to sit down on the couch which he didn't fight her on as she smiled at him mischievously. She bit at her lip in anticipation as her eyes settled on his lap with his very evident desire for her.

Gabriel watched her eagerly as he offered her a hand to help her knowing exactly what she was thinking. Ruby used her mind to shift his pajama pants he was wearing to set him free as she used the hand he'd offered her to shift to her knees in front of him. She could feel his balls tightening expectantly as she settled her hands lightly on his thighs.

Sliding one of her hands along his thigh, she grasped him firmly in her hand as she leaned forward and lightly blew on his tip. Ruby smiled as his length jerked in response.

Ruby, he pleaded, aching needing relief. He watched desperately as she stared up at him from under her lashes and leaned forward to seductively lick his tip. He could feel the soft rasp of her tongue throughout his entire body. He fisted his hand in her hair needing to hold on to her. He thought about seizing control from her. He knew he could, and she wouldn't hesitate to let him. It wouldn't be the first time either, they could both be quite impatient when it came to them mating, but he didn't. He enjoyed seeing her like this. Watching her in control, pleasing him, teasing him.

Ruby smiled to herself feeling him struggle to not take control as she closed her mouth over his tip. It always varied how long he'd let her stay in control, but ultimately, he'd always take over. She never cared. She liked him wild and needing her. She loved how much her mate wanted and needed her and she trusted him completely. She knew he'd never hurt her.

She stroked him with a firm hand as she alternated between sucking on his tip and using her tongue to find the sensitive spots under the brim of his large blunt head. He knew she loved feeling his reactions and used it to guide her ministrations, finding his most sensitive spots.

Ruby, he gasped as she slid her hand to his base and moved to take him deeper in her mouth. She could never take his entire length in her mouth, he was too big for her, but she always loved to try wanting to please him knowing he loved her mouth on him. But then he loved having her any way he could take her. She always got the furthest when he took control, but he was always careful with her, not wanting to hurt her and knowing when he reached her limit.

He couldn't help thrusting into her mouth as she moved up and down taking him in while her hand stroked in rhythm what she couldn't take in. He was losing control. He needed more. He needed her. *Come here,* he told her tugging gently on her hair to get her to stand up. He needed to be in her, and he knew she needed the same thing. *Take off the shirt,* he told her as she used his thighs to help her push up from the floor. Lifting his hips to move his pants down his thighs to free himself more, he watched as she obeyed and took off his shirt she was wearing.

Ruby struggled to focus her eyes still riveted on his hard length and wanting nothing more than to sit on him. She had missed the part where he'd told her to take her panties off. Instead he gave up trying to get her to remove them, opting to do it himself.

Placing his hands on her hips, he leaned forward placing a gentle kiss on belly, and then slid her panties down her legs dropping them to the floor. Coaxing her to move one of her feet out with his knee, he brought his hand to her entrance. She was drenched with need for him, he knew she would be. He loved feeling how wet and ready she always was for him. Slowly inserting two fingers, he watched the feelings that played through her as he stretched her, but that was nothing compared to when he filled her. She was always so tight and fit exquisitely on him. He loved feeling how much he stretched her and the pleasure she got from it.

Gabriel, she pleaded bringing her hands up to fist in his hair to hold on to him for support. *Please,* she begged wanting to straddle him. Wanting him filling her beyond belief. She still couldn't believe he could fit, but she knew he would. He always did, stretching her endlessly.

Come here, he told her withdrawing his fingers from her and kissing her belly one more time before helping her to straddle him. He did, however, continue to keep her from impaling herself on him. He heard her whimper his name. He could feel her aching with need with his blunt tip pressing at her entrance. He could feel her body clenching in anticipation.

Gabriel leaned down to capture her mouth as he rammed into her. Filling her, stretching her. He could feel her gasp at the intrusion even as she continued to kiss him in return. He didn't give her any time to adjust immediately pulling out and slamming back in just as hard. He set a hard-fast pace needing her and feeling how badly she needed him.

Yes, Ruby moaned meeting him thrust for thrust as she held on to him. She reluctantly broke their kiss trailing kisses along his jaw. Before she knew it, she had continued kissing her way down his neck to sink her teeth into his throat to feed.

Gabriel struggled to force himself to change rhythm, slowing down to allow her time to feed and so she wasn't straining as hard to hold on to him. He could feel her resistance to the change in tempo. She wanted him still slamming into her, but she continued to feed despite it, needing the secondary connection to him. Needing her mate.

Faster, she requested as she lifted her head from his throat. *Please,* she pleaded looking up at him desperately. She was relieved when he captured her mouth again and resumed his previous speed for her. *Do it,* she told him feeling his desire to sink his teeth in her in return.

Ruby, you're pregnant, he struggled to resist his desire to feed on her as he usually did.

This is not a debate, Gabriel, she gasped out each work in rhythm with his thrusts. *I need you, all of you,* she told him. *Please,* she pleaded needing him.

Gabriel didn't hesitate biting into her as he held her to him. He changed rhythm again as he fed taking her even harder. He pounded into her, filling her with his hard length. Burying himself up to his balls over and over again. Needing to take what was his. He could feel her arms around his head holding him to her as he fed. He lifted his head as he felt her clamping on to him. He knew she was there. He captured her mouth and her scream as he slammed into her one more time sending her over the edge taking him with her. He held on to her as she clung to him as he emptied himself into her. Her body milking him for every last drop.

I love you, he told her reaching up to brush a lock of hair from her face as the aftershocks of their lovemaking subsided.

I love you too, she agreed resting her head on his shoulder to catch her breath.

Should we be worried about the baby during this given her ability to connect with us and freeze us in place and juggle knives? he asked curiously as he ran his fingers gently over her back as his other strayed in her hair.

I don't know, maybe, but right now… I don't care. I'm horny and I need you, she told him lifting her head to look at him and moving to capture his mouth. She needed him again. She'd worry about their daughter's exposure to their mating later.

Gabriel continued kissing her as he slid his hands down to take hold of her thighs to hold her to him as he stood up knowing she was holding securely on to his neck. He never broke their kiss or removed himself from her as he moved to lay her down on the plush faux bear skin rug in front of the fireplace.

He continued to hold one of her legs bent up for better access as he started an easier rhythm taking his time. He let go of her leg as he felt her move to hook it behind his back to hold him to her while her other had slid down along his resting her ankle on the back of his thigh. He enjoyed having her writhe beneath him in pleasure as his hands wandered over her finding and caressing her sensitive spots while he let his mouth wander a different path.

Her hands were threaded in his hair holding him to her as he kissed and nipped and licked a trail over her enjoying his mate. He felt a hand stray from his hair trailing down his neck to his back her nails digging in to hold on to him and then she'd alternate hands occasionally trailing her fingers along his biceps instead of his back, but her hands always seemed to return to his hair holding his mouth to her as she writhed calling his name in his head as she pleaded for relief. He could feel the tension slowly building in her muscles. He took his time riding his mate. Enjoying the slow climb as he lavished attention on her body.

Please, Gabriel. I need... she trailed off gasping as she tugged gently on his hair to get him to return his mouth to hers. She continued lifting her hips to meet his thrusts without hesitation, without fail needing him in her. She could feel her muscles tightening. She knew they'd get there eventually, but he was taking too long, he was going too slow. She was impatient, she wanted her mate taking her harder. Even when they went at it hard and fast it was by no mean a short adventure. They had stamina. It took a good deal of fun time and effort to get relief. But right now, he was torturing her. She loved his hands and his mouth and him in and on her, but at the leisurely rate he was taking her... She was going to be writhing under him for hours before either of them got relief and while she didn't mind being under him for hours... hell, she loved being under him for hours, but she preferred when he'd let them have multiple orgasms as opposed to torturing her as he was doing now. She knew he enjoyed it, he knew exactly what he was doing to her, and she did enjoy the pleasure he got from it, and of course she did enjoy it otherwise he wouldn't... and he wouldn't enjoy it as he did, but she was relieved that he didn't do this to her every time. He usually gave in giving them the release they both needed, especially since she'd gotten pregnant.

Gabriel captured her mouth as she wanted. He could taste her desperation. She was overwhelmed with sensations and pleasures. She needed air, she needed release. He changed pace quickly pushing her higher. He could feel her relief mixed with her pleasure. He didn't have the heart to torture her with pleasure, not when she was pregnant. Besides, he rarely had the control to do so being just as impatient and needy as her.

He felt her dig her nails into his back as he pushed them over the edge emptying himself into her. His. His mate. He used a forearm to help support his weight as he held on to her with the other brushing soft kisses over her lips as she smiled up at him happily as the aftershocks continued to rock over them her muscles still clamping down on him.

Ruby couldn't help the whine that escaped as he reluctantly removed himself from her and settled on the floor beside her on his side. She knew he didn't want his weight on the baby, but she also still wanted him in her. Gabriel leaned over to kiss her softly in apology as his hand moved down to caress her belly lovingly.

Has your appetite for some food returned yet? he asked teasingly knowing their food had long since grown cold.

We can always heat it back up or make more, she sighed reaching over to caress his jaw softly knowing that he actually was a little worried about her eating. *Gabriel, we never finished out conversation. We got a little side-tracked,* she smiled not in the least upset by the detour. It had been a great afternoon, and she could see the sunset streaming in through the large windows.

What conversation was that? he asked stroking his thumb over her skin gently his hand still resting possessively and tenderly on her stomach with no intention of moving.

About another child, she asked sliding her hand down his arm to come to rest on his forearm.

Ruby, I love our little girl and I'm sure I would love any other children that were ours, but I… I just don't know. It was rough getting here, my love, and she's doing well, but you are still pregnant. I know how much we both love her, but in some ways, we also haven't done much to take care of her like we will once she's born. Are you wanting another baby already? he asked a little nervously.

I… I don't know, she told him her eyes sliding from his face. *When I brought up getting pregnant, I… I never really thought past…* she trailed off her hand sliding to rest on top of his over her belly. *I mean I love her, so very much, and of course I don't want to get pregnant right away. Hell, I'm still pregnant and we both know it's going to be a while yet before I deliver. And I would love to have time with just the three of us. To get to know her, and figure out how to… well, everything,* she thought knowing they had a lot to learn yet. *But I… I don't know, I guess before we got pregnant I… I might have been afraid to think past…*

Afraid we couldn't get pregnant, he asked not realizing just how afraid she'd been about not having a baby.

I mean… maybe… I mean it's not like we exactly knew what to expect when we decided to have one, she admitted. *I think I was afraid to think past this here and now if…* she admitted.

Oh, my love, he sighed hurting for her as he leaned over to kiss her forehead in comfort and scooted closer to her.

But… but we have her, she nodded weakly.

My love, why do you still feel so terrified then? I know you've been scared when it comes to our little girl, but this… he trailed off worried about her.

Gabriel, I love her so much, she whimpered.

I know you do, my love, he reassured.

But I… I'm not sure I can do this again, she admitted looking away from him.

You're afraid I want more, he realized watching her as she nodded her head weakly in answer. Sliding his hand out from under hers, he brought it up to her face, turning her head to look at him as he brushed his thumb gently over her cheek. *Ruby, I love you, and we will make any decisions together as we move forward just as we always have. I'd never expect you to have children if you didn't want them,* he told her.

*It's not that I don't want them. I mean I'm sure I'd love…
I mean how could I not they'd be ours*, she told him softly
bringing her hand up to hold on to his.

What is it, my love? he asked gently. *I know you've loved
being pregnant with her, and I know you don't mind too
terribly bad the things you were complaining about earlier.*
He wanted to know what was bothering her.

It's just… Gabriel, I love her so much, she repeated.

Ruby, he interrupted her. *You don't have to keep saying
that to defend how you feel, my love. I know how much you
love her, and I'd never question that. It's alright, I just want to
know what's going on that's all, to understand*, he assured her.

Before we got pregnant with her, after I… she looked up
at him not wanting to say it and he nodded knowing what she
was referring to, the miscarriage. *We both agreed we couldn't
do it again because of…* she glanced down swallowing hard.
*And we… we probably wouldn't have changed our minds. I'm
glad we have her, but Gabriel, nothing has really changed.
We still don't know what happened. I mean… you said you
didn't want to try again after…*

Gabriel brushed his thumb over her cheek one more
time before sliding his hand away to rub over his face as
he shook his head slightly. *Ruby, you've got me confused. A
second ago you're afraid with me wanting to have you have
more kids, and yet you're also now having me not wanting to
try for more. Do I have this right?* he asked trying to hide his
amusement.

Yes, she whimpered not liking his amusement at her
mixed feelings.

*Ruby, I'm sorry, really, I am. I know it's not funny, and
I don't think it's funny 'ha ha', it's funny…* he wanted to
say ridiculous, but that certainly wouldn't help. *It's funny*

weird. I'm sorry it's a poor knee jerk reaction, he apologized brushing his fingertips along the side of her face feeling bad.

I know it's ridiculous, she cried turning on her side and moving into his arms wrapping hers around his neck. *I'm pregnant and hormonal and it makes no sense. I know, but I can't help it,* she sobbed.

Oh, my love, he comforted gently wrapping his arms around her to hold her to him. He realized suddenly why her emotions were so mixed. His mate did want more children, but she was also afraid of trying to have them and her ability to say no and afraid he wouldn't want to try. *Oh, my love,* he repeated kissing the top of her head. *Ruby,* he sighed. *I know we still don't know what happened, and unfortunately, that's never going to change, but one thing has changed since we both said we didn't want to try again,* he told her gently.

What? she sniffled.

Ruby, you're pregnant, very pregnant, with our little girl, who is doing well, he reminded her.

So, she sniffled not sure how that changed anything.

My love, we said we didn't want to try because we didn't want it to happen again, but I think we were also afraid that… that was the only option, that we couldn't have a baby. But my love, we are having a baby, and god forbid, we had to deliver you right now, our baby girl would be fine. I'd see to that, he assured her. *You are far enough along with her and everything has been going well with the pregnancy and her growth, I assure you no matter what I won't let anything happen to our baby girl.*

I know, I know you won't, Gabriel, she told him tightening her arms as she continued, *but you don't know it won't happen again.*

No, my love, I don't. You're right, there is every possibility that it could happen again, but we also know that we can be successful. *My love, I don't know what happened, I wish I did, but I… I don't think… I don't think I'd be against trying if you wanted to, but only if you wanted to,* he assured her. *I don't want you going through that pain again, I know neither of us do. If we lost another…* he sighed. *I know it would be a risk, my love, but you wouldn't be alone. I'd be by your side every day just as I am now, and god forbid it happened again, we still have our little girl. But my love,* he told her kissing her head again. *I will never ever force or encourage you to get pregnant again if it is not what you want. I will stand by you if you chose to take that risk, but I won't force you to take it. I just couldn't,* he finished. It had torn them both up inside losing their baby. They'd never even heard the heartbeat, but their baby girl was living proof they could have a baby, and if his mate could risk going through that again… well, then so could he. He knew at the end of the day they'd still have each other to turn to for comfort, and they'd have their little girl to hold and hug to help comfort themselves.

I… I don't know, Gabriel, she whimpered shaking her head against his neck. She knew he was right, and he'd be there, but she wasn't sure she could risk it.

It's alright, my love. You don't have to make a decision today, or tomorrow, or next year. Hell, you don't ever have to make a decision. I know you don't want to try currently, and that's okay. But the only decision that exists is if you change your mind, and you can change it at any time or… not. That's alright, my love. You don't ever have to make that decision if you don't want to, but you might change your mind after a few centuries of chasing after our little girl, and that's okay too. Ruby nodded her head slightly against his shoulder knowing he meant it. *And, my love,* he started hesitantly.

Yes, she whimpered.

I know it's a lot, and I suspect you won't want to think about it for a while, but I want you to know that you don't need to be afraid to think about this and debate about this if you need to from time to time. It would be a big decision to make this choice, and I know that. I would expect you would need to think a good deal before doing so. You don't need to be afraid to think about it, and I'm here if you want to talk about it. And while I said I would expect you would want to think about it, and I do, it would also be just as okay if you one day walk up to me, or turn around and look at me, or wake up next to me, or just look at our daughter, and decide there and then without even thinking about it that you were ready to risk it, he reassured.

Really, she sniffled.

Of course, my love, he reassured her running a hand lovingly through her hair.

"She's hungry," Ruby half laughed through her receding sniffles as she felt their baby reach for her mentally and kick her.

"I suppose we should feed you then," he chuckled sliding his hand down to caress her stomach. Ruby nodded smiling. "What do you want to eat?" he asked knowing the pancakes were long since cold and it was dinner time.

"I still want pancakes," she whispered lifting her head from his shoulder to look at him.

"What is with you and these pancakes? You wanted pancakes for lunch which we didn't eat and now you are insisting on pancaked for dinner," he questioned.

"I'm the pregnant one, and I want pancakes," she told him firmly.

"But it's dinner time," he reminded her.

"I don't care, I want pancakes. Besides, we didn't get up until noon and I didn't get my breakfast lunch," she told him.

"We would have been up for breakfast if you didn't keep me up all night," he told her suggestively as he leaned down to kiss her.

"I'll remember that next time," she told him when he lifted his head from hers.

"Please don't," he pleaded.

"That's what I thought," she smiled brushing a kiss over his lips. "Besides, we rarely get up before noon, and I still like pancakes no matter what the time of day. They're good," she told him moving to sit up and relieved when he helped her.

"Very well," he told her sitting up.

"Don't," she weakly whispered grabbing on to his hand knowing he intended to get up to make her pancakes. She floated the plate of pancakes into the microwave and turned it on. She didn't want to get up and she didn't want him leaving her side even if she would still be able to see him.

"Ruby, I'd rather make you fresh pancakes," he said gently.

"And we'd rather you stay right here," she whispered including their baby.

"You know they're better fresh," he persisted.

"No," she shook her head.

"Alright," he gave up running his hand she wasn't holding through his hair. He shook his head slightly as he laid back down exasperated. He knew she preferred fresh pancakes, but if she didn't want him to get up, he wouldn't.

"Thank you," she mumbled knowing he thought it was ridiculous.

"You know I'd do anything for you, my love, but I expect you to eat those soggy pancakes then. You need food," he told her turning his head to look up at her.

"I will," she smiled weakly scooting closer to him to sit right beside him her hip and knee brushing his side as she sat with her legs crossed Indian style. She opened the microwave and flipped the pancakes over and traded their positions around before she stuck them back in to finish heating them up. She picked a fork and knife up from the table and started levitating them across the room to them as the microwave went off and she started doing the same with them. Taking the plate out of the air she set it down on his abdomen.

"Really, you're going to use me as a table," he questioned.

"Well, you do have a very nice hard abdomen," she smiled biting at her lip as she looked at his stomach around the plate. Even if she couldn't feel him, which she could, she could see his very apparent reaction to her gaze and thoughts.

"I need a kiss," he groaned.

"You need way more than a kiss, but I promised to eat some pancakes," she smiled at him wickedly. She couldn't help but laugh at him as he growled at her unhappily. She knew he wasn't too seriously upset, he wanted her to eat and he knew he could easily have her later.

"What is it?" he asked as she looked at the pancakes debating.

"They're missing something," she said thinking.

"Syrup," he asked.

"Mmmm," she moaned looking up at the fridge.

"That is not what I meant," he told her shaking his head as he watched her grab a bottle of chocolate syrup out of the air.

"I know," she agreed. "But it is missing."

"Keep it off my pancakes," he told her knowing she planned to share the large plate of pancakes with him.

"If you insist," she shrugged beginning to pour syrup on one side.

"I insist," he sighed. Ruby began cutting up the pancakes, alternating giving him bites from his side as she ate from hers. "What now?" he asked as she looked up at the fridge again and paused eating.

"Raspberry syrup," she smiled looking at him.

"You're nuts," he teased her.

"Yeah, but you still love me," she agreed even though she knew he was teasing.

"I must be nuts," he sighed watching her add the raspberry syrup.

"Yeah, but I still love you too," she admitted happily as she resumed eating and continuing to feed him too.

Ruby began to slow down starting to fill up having already eaten a significant amount of her portion of pancakes. She handed him another bite on the fork as she ran a finger through the syrup on the plate.

Gabriel swallowed watching her play with the syrup on the plate. He held his breath as she brought her finger to her mouth. He knew she wasn't trying anything, but that didn't stop him from feeling his cock jerk in response as she licked the chocolate from her finger. He knew she had seen or at least felt it when she turned to look at him smiling.

"I thought you wanted me to eat," she questioned teasingly.

"No, she's the one that wanted you to eat. Besides, we both know you're nearly done," he said watching her.

"So, you would have been okay with me not eating," she asked raising an eyebrow at him.

"That is not what I said," he argued.

Ruby couldn't help laughing at him as she leaned down to kiss him, but stopped last minute pulling back and putting another bite of pancake in her mouth.

"Ruby," he demanded surprised. He could feel her laughter in her mind as she chewed looking down at him. He waited for her to swallow and reached up without hesitating to wrap his hand around the nape of her neck and pulled her down towards him so he could reach up to kiss her without knocking over the pancakes. He could feel the laughter quickly fade from her mind as he thoroughly kissed her peaking her desire.

That's not fair, she gasped as he let go of her letting her sit back up. She looked down at him shocked while he smiled up at her like the cat that ate the canary.

"I'm okay with that," he told her pleased with himself as he tenderly ran a finger over the length of her belly.

She looked down at her belly at his touch. She'd gotten distracted eating and teasing him, and his hand hadn't been on her stomach like it usually was. But feeling his touch had brought it all back to her attention. "I'm scared, Gabriel," she told him staring at her stomach.

"I know, my love," he told her gently. He did know. She'd been terrified when they'd first realized they were pregnant again, and she'd openly admitted it, but once they had gotten to a certain point in the pregnancy, she had kind of settled down. She'd never admitted it again since then until now, but he'd felt her fear throughout the entire pregnancy. It had wavered up and down, but it had never completely left. "It's okay to be afraid," he reassured her taking the knife and fork from her hand to set them on the plate and moving them to the floor above his head. "Come here," he told her gently no longer intending to attempt to maul her.

Ruby uncrossed her legs and moved with his assistance to lay down with her head resting on his upper abdomen looking up at him. "You're not afraid," she realized.

"No, our baby girl has been making good growth with no issues. I'm not going to let anything happen to her or you," he agreed.

"That's not what I'm scared about. Sure, I'm worried about that, though I know you won't let anything happen to us, but that's not what I'm scared about," she admitted.

"What are you scared about, my love?" he asked gently.

"I'm scared of having a baby, Gabriel. I don't know what to do with one. I have no idea how to take care of a baby or raise a child," she whispered running a finger nervously over his chest. "Doesn't that scare you?" she questioned.

"No," he told her gently caressing her stomach gently in comfort.

"Why not?" she questioned softly.

"Because I have you, Ruby. We're a team. We always have been. I know how much we both love her, my love. I know neither of us will ever let anything happen to her. I know it's going to take some adjusting to figure things out from time to time, especially in the beginning, but I know we will have each other's backs. I know we will do everything we can to raise her right teaching her right from wrong, and we'll teach her to use her abilities, and we'll worry about schooling when we get there. I know we will figure it out together, my love," he comforted her gently.

"What if we break her?" she questioned.

"My little love, do you forget the part where she is our daughter? Ruby, as much as I loathe to admit it because I fear so much for the safety of you two, we are both extremely difficult to hurt and even when hurt we heal quite well, I can't imagine that our ability to heal won't be passed on to our baby girl. Besides, I suspect it will be a long time before we know either way, because I know neither of us will let anything happen to her. We'd never in our life drop her or hurt her, and I know we'll both be keeping a close eye on her. She's our baby and we will keep her safe," he assured her confidently.

"I meant… I didn't just mean physically. What if we mess her up? She deserves to have a normal life," she sighed hurting.

"Oh my love, what is normal?" he sighed caressing her stomach. "I don't think I know anymore, but I'm guessing what you mean by normal does not fit us and thus will never fit our baby. She may not have a normal life, but so what? She will have us. She will be loved, and cared for, and protected like no other child on this planet, except maybe any others we may choose to have in the future. We will raise her right, and she will be normal for our child.

"If we're lucky, she will take after her mother. She will be strong, and she'll know how to use her abilities. She won't have a care in the world, and she will know just how powerful she is, and yet, I can't imagine she wouldn't want to take after us helping people, especially after her reaction with the wolves in trouble. And would that really be such a bad thing?" he paused looking at her.

"I suppose not," she mumbled.

"She may scratch her knees, or even break a bone on occasion growing up running through the forests around our houses, but she will always be safe, she will always be loved, and we will make sure she knows it. She will know she is loved, and at the end of the day, I think that is the only thing that really matters. The rest we will figure out with time. Besides, I think you are forgetting one very big thing, my love," he coaxed gently.

"What?" she whispered peering up at him.

"You are still pregnant with her. Let's not worry just yet about messing her up when she's still inside you, and even then, she's going to grow very slowly. We've got time to sort things out," he reassured her gently.

I feel like a fool, she whimpered. *What you say makes sense, I know it does, but I still don't understand how you aren't afraid. It doesn't matter what you say, Gabriel, I'm still scared.*

I know, my little love, and I don't expect that to change, he told her softly bringing his hand up to her cheek in a caress as he kissed the top of her head.

What? she asked looking up at him shocked.

Ruby, it's our baby girl we're talking about. I think I'd be worried if you weren't afraid. This is all very new for both of us. Maybe I am being a bit of a mother hen, but that's not going to change, my little love. You are growing our child…

You mean the bowling ball I've been hiding, she interrupted caressing her stomach.

"That is not a bowling ball," he chided her.

"Gabriel, I'm huge and my boobs are the size of melons," she groaned.

"Yeah, they are," he smiled looking down at them as he slid a hand to caress one.

Gabriel, she whimpered distraught as she moved his hand back to her stomach as she turned her face into his chest.

I'm sorry, my love, he apologized his hand encompassing her growing belly.

Gabriel, I love her, but… It's all so confusing. I'm relieved to see her this size, I am, but… "I've got a bowling ball for… for… for a stomach," she broke down sobbing.

It's alright to be confused, my love. Your body is not your own right now, he comforted her gently.

It hasn't been mine in a very long time, she couldn't help but think. She was his after all.

I know, my love, but this is different and we both know it. I know how happy you were when you could first see the slightest of baby bumps, and we've both loved watching her grow, but that doesn't in the least diminish how hard this is for you, he said gently.

My stomach has always been flat, she sobbed. *Always. And now... now...* "a bowling ball," she sobbed moving to wrap her arms around his neck to hold on to him.

I know it's been a lot to take in, my love, but you've been absolutely amazing, he reassured holding on to her.

It's going to keep getting bigger too, she sobbed.

I know, but that's a good thing, my love, he said softly.

I know, she sobbed. *I hate that I hate that I'm going to get bigger.*

I'm sorry, my love, he apologized hurting for her. He knew how much she loved their baby and that she wouldn't change a thing, but he also knew sometimes it was all just too much for her. Her body was going through so many changes. He knew it was hard at times for her to even recognize herself in the mirror. She still looked just like his beautiful mate except with the cutest perfect baby bump stomach and slightly bigger breasts for their baby. You couldn't even tell from behind she was pregnant. Literally the only weight she'd put on had been their baby, but his mate had spent many centuries looking at herself in the mirror without being pregnant. He knew it was a hard concept to reconcile, and he didn't blame her in the least for hurting and being confused.

I'm just glad it's just… just a bowling ball, she sniffled settling down. *I don't think I could handle it if I'd put on a whole lot of weight like a good deal of humans do.*

"Please stop calling your stomach a bowling ball," he told her gently.

"What would you rather I call it? Would you rather beach ball, or basketball?" she sniffled.

"No, my love, I'd rather you stop calling our baby girl a bowling ball or a basketball or… and you are nowhere close to a beach ball," he amended.

"But it's a bowling ball," she whimpered.

"Ruby, please. She is not a bowling ball," he told her gently and was surprised when he felt a strong kick that seemed to punctuate his words. "I know you are struggling but please stop calling her a bowling ball."

"Then what am I supposed to call this bowling ball of a stomach," she asked.

"It would seem she agrees with me," he told her as their daughter kicked her again at another reference to her being a bowling ball.

"That's not nice. I'm the one carrying you, not him," she sniffled at her stomach.

"How about you stick with daughter, or baby, or baby girl, or little girl like you had been? I know I much more preferred those terms," he told her and got a small softer kick in agreement.

She's still a bowling ball, she argued in their head so she couldn't hear.

I will tell her and get her to kick you if you don't cut out the name calling, he told her firmly.

Fine, she sighed exasperated. *You're supposed to be on my side*, she mumbled.

Not about calling our baby a bowling ball, she's our baby, he sighed caressing her stomach.

I'm sorry, Gabriel, she apologized. She hadn't realized she'd been hurting him. It hadn't been her intention.

I know, my love, and I think so does she, but just… he trailed off knowing he didn't need to reinforce asking her to stop. He knew she would now.

I know, I will, she reassured him apologetically.

Thank you.

Gabriel, she whimpered in question.

Please don't start crying again, my love, he told her gently as he squeezed his eyes shut. He hated her tears. They broke his heart. They both needed a break.

I… I think you might have been right, she told him biting at her lip in worry.

About what? he asked knowing she was changing the topic.

About whether or not we should be worried about her hearing us… mate, she whimpered tightening her hold on him. *She clearly seems able to respond to our conversation.*

Yes, but she didn't stop us from being together earlier, he reminded her.

Does that make it better? she asked knowing he had his own doubts.

Ruby, you know we won't be able to keep our hands off each other for the remainder of your pregnancy. I think my greater concern was her being scared and interfering which she didn't.

It doesn't bother you that she can hear us, she asked worried.

My love, us mating is not going anywhere. She's not going to remember this before she's even born, and I suspect there will be decades she's not going to retain. Beyond that… well…

she's going to be raised in a house where her parents love each other, he said.

Gabriel, she asked pulling her buried face from his throat to look up at him wide eyed.

Ruby, we would want our baby to know that she comes from a place of love just as much as she's going to know that she is loved, would we not? he asked.

Well, yeah, but...

Unfortunately, we have very good hearing, my love, and there is no way we can stop mating until she is an adult, that's... that's a ridiculous notion. No matter the size of our houses, she's going to hear us. The only thing we can do is raise her to know it's normal for us, for our species, he told her gently.

You don't know that, she argued.

It's going to be, he assured her. *We need each other and that's not going to change. She will know along with all her other abilities hearing is one of them, and we will teach her just as we know that along with that comes respecting boundaries or privacy of what you overhear. She will learn in time to ignore us, maybe even tune us out. It will be a normal part of life.*

Oh god, we are going to break her, she whimpered burying her face back in his throat.

Ruby, I know you are worried, but it will be normal for her, as will so many other things. We are going to make our own normal for our family.

I don't know, Gabriel, she shook her head.

Ruby, growing up with the animal tribes with your hearing, you can't tell me you never heard plenty of... he trailed off waiting for her response.

Of course, I did, how could I not? she asked.

And did you ever go asking them anything or bringing anything up? he persisted.

I don't know, maybe once or twice when I was really little, I don't remember, but I... I mostly left it alone. I ignored it. I recognized it for what it was, and I ignored it. It wasn't my business, she said shrugging.

And did it destroy and cripple you? he continued.

What? No, they were just... well, you know...

And why should that be any different for our little girl? My love, it will be normal for her as long as we treat it like it's normal. What will mess her up is us lying to her or trying to hide things from her. We will be discrete as we can, just as the animal tribes were in regards to you, but if she has questions of any kind we will answer them as best we can of course tailoring the extent and form of our explanation to her age as appropriate, but my love, she will be fine, he reassured her again.

Gabriel, you are giving me new things to be scared of that hadn't even crossed my mind, she sighed.

The best thing we can do is be honest with her as she grows, my love. You need to stop thinking about this as if we are human. We are not human, and we shouldn't try to be. We will figure out normal for us and we will work this out but lying about and hiding our connection is not the answer. Our bond is our strength and will continue to be as we try to raise this little girl who at some point will likely try like any other child to try getting her way by lying to us about what the other has said.

Ruby couldn't help the laughter that started to bubble up at the thought. *She won't be able to do that.*

No, she won't, he agreed. *And she will learn that lesson very quickly,* he smiled happy to find something to help her feel a little better about the idea of raising their baby. *It's going to be alright, my love.*

I don't know what I'd do without you. I don't know how this makes so much sense and comes so easy to you. At least she has one parent who has an idea of what's going on, she finished softly.

My love, I only know because of you. I know how you wish you were raised, nothing more. We are both going into this blind. Besides, you know a lot more than you give yourself credit for, and I assure you, more than me when it comes to being raised as what we are. You were the one born this way. Just try remembering the good things, and the normal things or what seemed normal. And the bad things... those we will fix for her. I wish I could change things for you growing up, but I can't, however, our little girl has two parents who love her and each other, and she will know that, he reassured her comfortingly.

Good, good, she repeated liking the sound of that. *But she can never know that... that...* she trailed off looking up at him. She understood his logic in being honest with her, but they had agreed she would never know she was an accident.

Of course. Only the two of us will ever know that. I swear to you, Ruby, he vowed caressing her cheek softly in comfort.

Good, she sighed softly relieved. She knew she would never tell her daughter and she could feel the honesty in his words. He'd never tell their daughter any more than she would. *Gabriel, I think... I think I need a nap,* she admitted her eyes drifting closed.

That's alright, my love, he reassured her gently.

But we just got up, she disagreed drowsily.

That's not true, he corrected. *And even if it was, so what? If my beautiful pregnant mate wants to take a nap, she certainly can.*

But you wanted me to lick chocolate syrup off your chest, she mumbled weakly.

I'll have you do that later. Right now, I want you to get some rest. Can you do that for me? he asked kissing the top of her head that was resting on his shoulder.

Ruby nodded her head slightly in answer. Her mate was way better than any 'mother hen'.

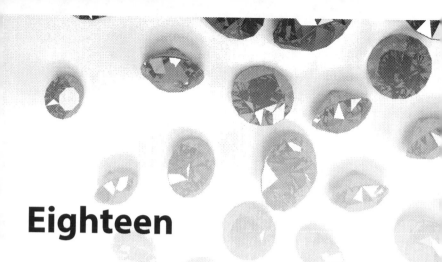

Eighteen

Gabriel, I think I need you to do a c-section, she called grabbing his attention as she caressed her belly.

What's wrong? he asked whirling around to look at her worried. *Ruby,* he questioned pulling her into his arms.

Nothing is wrong. We're fine, she reassured trying to calm him down as she rested her cheek against his chest and held on to his waist. She could feel his acute distress at her request. *We're fine,* she repeated.

You're sure, he asked worried looking down at the top of her head.

Yes, you know I would tell you if something was wrong, not that I'd need to, we both know you'd know something was wrong the second I did. We're perfectly fine, she comforted him softly.

Then I see absolutely no reason to do a c-section. She's fine, and so are you, he hesitated still worried and unsure. His worry when it came to the two of them wasn't easily abated. *My love, we still have a while before it's time for her delivery and I have no reason to think you won't go into labor just like you should at that time. I'm not taking her out early unless something is wrong with either of you.*

I know, I know. That's not what I'm saying. We're fine, Gabriel. Honestly, she repeated knowing he was still on the fence about believing they were alright. *I'm not asking you to deliver her right now. I swear. Nothing is wrong and I don't want her out early any more than you do. I wouldn't risk… I want her to… I want her to grow and develop as much as she's supposed to before she comes out. I don't want to risk something happening to her.*

She could tell he was still struggling. *I didn't mean to scare you. I'm sorry,* she apologized holding on to him. "Baby girl let your daddy know you're alright for me, please," she whispered to their little girl. Trying to encourage her to reach for him mentally. They both talked to her out loud and mentally since they figured out that they could. Granted she obviously couldn't talk out loud and she didn't really use words mentally either, but…

She could feel when their little girl connected with him. She could feel it calming him down, but she also felt him quickly having to control his emotions that she could sense so as to not scare her.

She's fine, he sighed kissing the top of her head and resting his head there.

I know, she agreed. *I wouldn't lie about that, Gabriel.*

I know you wouldn't, my love. It's just…

I know, but she's fine. And so am I, she reassured him knowing he believed her now.

Then why the hell did you ask me for a c-section, he asked her getting upset.

She knew he'd made sure to break the connection to their daughter not wanting her to accidentally feel his agitation. *Because I think I need one,* she mumbled.

I thought we just had this conversation, he asked lifting his head to look down at her confused.

No, we didn't. I'm not asking you to do it today or tomorrow or next month, but I think… I think when it's time to look at… when its closer to time for her to come out… I need a c-section.

No, he denied watching her.

No? That's it, she asked looking up at him hurt.

Yes, that's it. I'm not going to cut into you unless I have no choice, he told her firmly.

Do you really think that I'd ask this of you lightly? I know how much you love me, and how much you hate to see me hurt. Do you really think that I'd suggest this for no reason? she asked hurt that he didn't even want to ask her why. Did he really think she'd ask…?

Gabriel reached up to caress her cheek as he looked down into her face. Her beautiful eyes now brimming with tears. *You really think you need a c-section?* he asked doubting there was any valid reason to arbitrarily perform a c-section on his mate. There was absolutely nothing going on with her pregnancy to support that suggestion.

I… I think it's worth talking about, she nodded weakly.

We can talk about it, but that doesn't mean I will agree, he told her staring down into her face.

I…

Come on, let's go sit down while we talk, he told her gentling his tone. He could feel her hurt which had never been his intention and he didn't want his little love crying. He felt her acceptance to his suggestion and led her over to the couch. Kissing the top of her head his hand slid to the middle of her back while he offered her his other hand to hold on to for balance and support to help her sit down. He knew it was getting harder for her to get up and down from the couch and the bed too for that matter with as far along as she was now, but their little girl still had some more growing to do and they both knew it.

Thank you, Ruby mumbled as he sat down beside her letting go of her hand to caress her belly. She leaned against his side for a moment taking in the comfort of his strength and closeness before she shifted on the couch turning completely towards him resting her hand on his thigh for contact. She leaned against the couch resting her cheek on the back of it as she looked down at his hand resting lovingly on their baby. She had known he wasn't going to move his hand. She didn't want him to, and he knew it.

Gabriel leaned down to kiss her stomach. Sitting back up he rested his arm on the back of the couch and threaded his fingers in her hair brushing his fingertips in soft caresses over her scalp while his other hand remained on her belly. *Why, my love? Why do you think I need to do a c-section?* he asked watching her face. She'd closed her eyes when he'd threaded his hand in her hair. He loved seeing and feeling her peaceful like this, especially given the hormones of the pregnancy and their effect on her, on both of them because of their bond, but he knew this conversation would likely ruin her peaceful moment.

Gabriel, she sighed. She loved saying his name. It was soothing, comforting. *You know what she can do.*

Of course, I do. I've been by your side this entire time, he agreed.

It doesn't worry you, she asked.

Why should it? She's our little girl. Sure, I'm a little surprised, just as you were, to realize that she can do what she can while you're still pregnant. But ultimately, no I'm not surprised or concerned, she's our little girl. It's not like we didn't expect her to have these abilities. Are you worried, my love? he asked gently. He knew she was worried about being a mother, but he hadn't in the least expected this to be a concern for her. Besides, she had seemed to enjoy playing with their daughter showing her how to levitate things.

No, I mean... not exactly. We knew she'd be able to do things like this, she agreed. *It's not so much exactly that she can do them in general. It's...* she trailed off nervously.

It's what? he encouraged gently.

Gabriel, I don't have a problem with delivering her vaginally, in theory. It's not that. I swear, she told adamantly worried he might just think she was afraid to go through labor. *I mean... that was the plan after all,* she sighed.

I know, my love, and now I want to know why you want to change it, he murmured caressing her scalp soothingly.

You know what? It's funny, but the one thing I've never been worried about when it comes to our little girl was that she'd have abilities and raising her with them. I knew she'd be in a home where she felt safe to play with those abilities. I imagined getting to watch her float her toys around the room having fun, even as a baby, and not... not scaring people like I did, not feeling isolated because of it, she told him.

She is, my love, and we will watch her do just that, he reassured her liking the image she conjured.

I knew we'd have to be careful, keeping an eye on her in the early years when we took her out in public, because... well, it will be a while before she understands and knows when she can and can't use her abilities. But that... that just doesn't seem like a big deal for some reason. What? she asked feeling his chuckle.

Nothing, I just find it funny what does and does not scare you about all this. Please continue, my love, he encouraged.

I know there's two of us, so twice as much power or energy for if we need to hold her in check for any reason. Of course, only if we absolutely have to. Though the little incident with the wolf vision might suggest otherwise, but to be fair I think that might just be because of the pregnancy. I mean... me being pregnant with her. I think she might somehow... have access to my... energy or abilities.

Why? he asked curious.

I don't know. I mean I really don't, but then in some ways it does kind of make since. It's my body that's growing her and providing the energy and nutrition she needs to grow. I guess... maybe that also gives her access to my abilities or the energy I use for them in case she deems it necessary, she said.

Why do you say that? he asked.

Well, she was able to hold not one but two of us, and I remember how hard it was to hold you that first day I turned you. She's not even an infant yet, she shouldn't have that kind of power, she told him worried.

You think it's more than just access to your energy too, don't you? he inquired.

We're bonded, Gabriel. I know we've been able to use our abilities through each other. I think... I think she has access to all that energy right now. Which would have made it very easy for her to freeze us in position like she did. She'd have a lot more energy and we'd have a lot less to counteract it with, she explained.

I get the impression you think that will end though, once she's... out, he said softly.

Yeah, I do. I think... I think it's maybe... a defense mechanism.

That doesn't make sense, my love. She's extremely safe right here in you, he told her caressing her belly. *I'm never far from you, and I'd never let anything happen to either of you. And you'd never let anything happen to her,* he said confidently.

I know, she agreed.

You're worried about her having this access, he realized.

No... I mean, yes, but no... well, yes and no, she struggled to think.

You want to try that again, Ruby, he asked shaking his head slightly. Gabriel moved his hand momentarily from her stomach to brush his thumb over her cheek as he leaned down to kiss the top of her head comfortingly, and then returned it to her stomach.

Ruby took a deep breath and slowly let it out. *I'm not worried about it right now while I'm pregnant. I mean sure it had kind of scared the crap out of me that night, but I... I didn't know what was going on and I hadn't expected her to be able to... well, do anything while I was pregnant. Now, that I know she can... well, it's kind of... cute,* she told him.

He couldn't help but smile in return at the soft smile that appeared on her face. He knew she enjoyed playing with her. She was every bit the mother he knew she would be to their daughter. She still had her eyes closed, but he suspected that was part of what was helping her remain calm at the moment.

I'm not worried about it right now, no, but... Gabriel, you've seen for yourself how she can react to my emotions and when she's scared. You know... we both know how scared she felt that night when we both touched her mind for the first time.

Yes, but that was before we'd established the connection we have to her now. My love, she knows who we are, and she knows she's safe with us, he tried to reassure her.

Yes and no. She does, but we've both seen her still react to my emotions, especially when I'm really upset, she contradicted.

Ruby, what is it you're worried about exactly? he asked worried.

I'm… I'm worried about… when I go into labor. Gabriel, she has access to our abilities and… and she reacts to my emotions, she said nervously.

I'm not sure I'm following, he told her gently.

Gabriel, how do you think she'd react to me in pain? she asked him.

What? What? he asked a second time shaking his head.

We've seen what she can do, what do you think she will do when she feels me in pain? she repeated.

Who said anything about you being in pain? he asked narrowing his eyes at her.

Have you figured out how to make contractions painless? she asked finally opening her eyes to look up at him.

No, but… but that's just contractions, he said.

Ruby shook her head in disbelief. *How very male of you. Gabriel, contractions still hurt, and this isn't about my ability to tolerate pain. It's about her feeling them. You make it sound simple, but it's not. It's not one contraction or even an hour of them. We're talking several hours of them, possibly days even. You know this. Contraction on top of contraction. She's going to feel them and not just from me. They're going to be squeezing around her and cutting off her oxygen over and over. Gabriel, on top of her feeling my pain, I very much expect her to be afraid. And if you think I can keep my shit together for days through that, well… well, I have my doubts,* she disagreed.

So, your solution is to have me cut into you. I have news for you, Ruby, a c-section hurts too, especially when it's done without anesthesia, he told her harsher than he intended.

Yes, but I can handle a c-section, she told him.

Can you? And what about her? he asked. *Shit, Ruby, what are we going to do?* he asked pulling her closer to him bringing her head to rest on his shoulder.

I can handle it, and you can help me put her to sleep beforehand like you did before so she can't connect with me. Even then, we both know it wouldn't take that long to get her out, and once she's out she can't... She won't have the same connection to use our energy like she can now, she said.

I can just as easily keep her calm while you are laboring, he told her.

Gabriel, even if you could, which we are talking about keeping her calm continually for days versus a few minutes, how the hell are you going to also keep me calm and also have enough energy to actually deliver her at the end of all of it. Gabriel, I'm sorry, but that is a ridiculous idea, she told him softly.

For all you know there could be some kind of trigger or switch that flips when you go into labor to prevent her from using our energy, he countered.

Gabriel, we don't know that, and I don't want to take that chance. What if you're wrong? What if we go down that road hoping that's the case? She'll start getting scared, which will likely scare me, you'll only be able to keep us calm for so long, and then how are you going to convert to doing a c-section in the middle of all of that? She could prevent you from doing so. Gabriel, please. I don't ask this easily. I wouldn't ask if I thought we had a choice, but I don't want to see anything happen to her in the middle of that chaos and I don't want to put her through that even if she wouldn't likely remember any of it in the long run.

Ruby, I don't want to cut into my mate. You can't ask this of me, he told her shaking his head in denial. *It would be one thing if I was doing it to save her or you or both of you if you were in distress, but... Ruby, you're my mate. I will feel the cut of that scalpel same as you, and I will be the one holding the knife in my hand. I can't. I love you, Ruby,* he sighed closing his eyes as he kissed the top of her head.

I'll… I'll… then I'll do it myself, she told him firmly swallowing hard. She'd do it for their baby.

What? he asked lifting his head and sliding his hand under her chin to lift her head to look at him.

You're right. I shouldn't have asked you. It was cruel of me to do so. I'm sorry, she apologized. *I'll hang a mirror or something for me to see, and I'll… I'll do it. You don't have to worry about being the one to hold the knife. It's alright. I'll be fine and so will our little girl,* she assured him bringing her hand up to caress his jaw. *I'll likely be tired after and… and maybe a little short of blood, so if you could at least keep an eye on her for us for a little while. I'll do it, Gabriel,* she told him gently.

You'll do no such thing, he ordered.

I will if I have to. She has to come out at some point, Gabriel, and I will not risk anything happening to her. Not after… she shook her head trying to clear the memory of the miscarriage. *I won't lose her after getting so far along with her, and I won't put you through that. I'd sooner cut out my own heart than hurt either of you.*

Damn it, Ruby. I don't like being backed into a corner, he told her forcefully.

You don't understand, Gabriel, she said softly closing her eyes. *There is no corner. I'm not trying to manipulate you into anything. I understand your reasons and I accept that, but I… I have to do this, Gabriel. I don't blame you, and you won't lose us, just let me do this.*

Look at me, Ruby, he ordered her to open her eyes and waited until she did. *You know damn well I can't let you do that. Even more than I hate the idea of cutting into you, I loathe the idea of watching you perform a c-section on yourself while I just stand by. One false slip, that's all it would fuckin' take. One small slip,* he paused staring at her. *I'll do it when it's time,* he told her angrily. *But you will swear to me one thing.*

Ruby nodded nervously. She'd never seen him like this, but he was the only one in the world she trusted. She'd swear anything to him.

Swear to me, if you change your mind about trying for another, it will be no time soon, he instructed.

She swallowed hard as she nodded her head vigorously. *I swear, Gabriel. I swear on the life of our baby girl,* she vowed looking up at him.

Good, he told her letting go of her chin. "I need a drink. Several very tall drinks," he told her running his hands over his face agitated.

Ruby nodded caressing her hands over her belly he'd taken his hand off of. She hadn't meant to hurt him, and she knew she deserved no sympathy, but having him remove his hand from her belly hurt more than she could fathom. She couldn't look at him as he stood up from the couch, too ashamed at herself.

"Come on," he told her offering her his hand to help her up.

"I can't drink," she told him not taking his hand not sure he really wanted to be near her at the moment.

"No, but you can keep me company," he informed her sternly.

"You… you sure you want me for company," she asked nervously.

"Ruby, do not try my patience right now. Come," he commanded.

She placed her hand in his struggling to keep it together as she stood up with his assistance. He retained hold of her hand as he left their room headed downstairs for a drink. While he didn't move to wrap his arm around her waist or pick her up as he usually did when it came to the stairs not wanting to risk her getting hurt, she knew he was keeping a close eye on her steps. She found herself using the handrail to help steady herself too considering how anxious she was at the moment.

Once he'd grabbed a glass and a bottle of whiskey, he led her to the couch in the living room. Sitting down next to the arm rest, he poured himself a tall drink while he kept an eye on her as she used the back of the couch for support to sit down next to him. He pulled the couch pillow out from behind him and set it on his lap for her to lay down on her side resting her head in his lap. He intended to get drunk which was not an easy feat given their metabolism, and she would feel every bit of it just as much as he would because of their bond, but without the possible detrimental effects to their baby as if she was actually drinking.

Neither of them said anything there was nothing to say. They both knew he just needed time to cool off and that she was struggling to keep from crying wanting to let him be angry.

He was four drinks in before he slid his hand from resting along the back of the couch to her stomach. "I still love you. You know that," he told her as he poured another glass. It had been a statement, a reminder, but he found he also needed to know that she did in fact know that he loved her.

Ruby nodded her head on the pillow. She knew he was just hurting, but that was also because he did love her. She had been relieved to feel his hand on her stomach, but she couldn't talk. She knew if she tried, she'd start crying. For now, she just needed him to keep drinking, so he could relax and... well, so could she and then she could get some sleep and some distance from her emotions. She knew they'd be fine. How could they not? She loved him and he loved her.

"Go to sleep, Ruby," he told her after swallowing the refill. "We'll be fine and so will our baby," he assured her as he refilled his glass again. "We both just need some rest," he told her lifting the glass to take another swallow. He knew she was starting to feel the effects. He loved her more than he could imagine and that was what was killing him at the moment. They'd get through this he was sure, and he'd be calmer in the morning. He'd make sure his mate and baby that he loved desperately were safe even if that meant doing a c-section he did not want to do. "I love you," he repeated feeling her starting to drift to sleep.

I love you, she managed to mumble as she passed out resting in her mate's care.

Ever After . . .

Ruby moved to sit up. She'd been laying down in bed beside Gabriel with her head resting on his chest while she watched their daughter sleep. She'd handed her to him to hold resting on his chest after she'd finished feeding her so that she could lay down beside him.

Where do you think you're going? Gabriel asked catching her hand.

I'm just going to get something to drink, she told him.

We'll come with you, he said holding their daughter steady against his chest as he started to try and sit up.

No, don't, she stopped him placing a hand on his stomach as she leaned back towards him. *She's asleep. Please, I just got her down, Gabriel. Don't wake her,* she pleaded looking back and forth between him and their daughter. *I'll be right back. I swear,* she promised looking at him.

Hurry or I will come and find you, he told her not wanting to be separated from her.

Ruby had felt Gabriel fall asleep as she'd entered the kitchen to get a glass of water. She couldn't help smiling to herself. Their little girl was only a couple weeks old and she woke up every hour or two to feed, three if they were lucky. They were both tired to say the least. She set the empty glass down on the counter and headed back upstairs to her mate and baby girl.

She stopped in the doorway leaning against the door jamb as she looked at the two of them happily. Her little girl was sound asleep resting on her sleeping mate's bare chest. Her family. If you'd asked her two centuries ago, she'd never in the world thought she'd be here.

Come here. You need rest, Gabriel called waking up having felt her nearby but not lying in bed beside him as she should have been.

One moment, she told him entering the room but going to the bedside table instead of getting in bed with him.

Don't, he told her knowing what she was up to even as she ignored him and pulled out their cell phone anyways.

I want a picture, she told him as she turned on the screen to pull up the camera.

Ruby, don't, he persisted. *What if these pictures wind up in the wrong hands?* he asked her. *This could be dangerous,* he suggested.

Dangerous, she scoffed. She knew he just didn't want her taking a photo of him especially when he was tired and half asleep. *Dangerous was you taking pictures of me when I was very pregnant and hormonal and terrified when it came to our little girl,* she informed him as she focused the camera screen and took a picture of him with their baby.

Oh come on, my love, he pleaded gently. *You looked beautiful carrying our baby girl. I wanted to remember that. Besides, I only took pictures of you when you were happy or smiling or calm and resting. I know you like those pictures too otherwise I wouldn't have taken them, or you would have deleted them which you didn't. I know you were scared, but you love our little girl and as hard as it was those pictures hold good memories that I knew you'd want to keep,* he told her gently. He knew she'd switched to looking at the old photos after taking the picture of him and their baby.

I want to remember this too. You two look so sweet together, she told him looking up at him.

Come here, he repeated motioning with his hand for her to come to him.

Ruby headed over to him as she continued looking at the phone. *Besides, if you really thought it was so dangerous, you wouldn't have taken these pictures of me and her. You know our phone and computers run on our own secure network that I regularly keep updated,* she reminded him as she sat down on the bed and snuggled up next to him as she continued flipping through photos. *I especially like the ones you are in too,* she told him as she paused on one of her favorites that he was in with her. He had a knack for taking pictures. She'd always hated the idea of pictures given their lifespan and the risk for exposure. She'd never had a single photo taken of her before him.

It's easy to take good pictures when you're in them, he reassured her as he took the phone away from her.

Hey, she exclaimed turning to look up at him. *I was looking at that,* she told him.

Trust me. You'll thank me, he reassured her as he floated the phone into the air with his mind. He'd already pulled the camera back up and had switched it to the front facing camera so that he could see the screen. He'd already managed to capture a picture of her looking at him before she realized what he was doing and turned her head to look at the camera at which point he'd stolen another picture of the three of them for her.

Stop that. I'm not dressed. All I have on is your shirt, she chastised him looking up at him again.

Nothing is showing and you look adorable, besides these photos are for us and no one else is ever going to see them, he reassured her. *So, you like our little bowling ball,* he teased softly using the term they'd once had an argument about her using while she was pregnant.

Yeah, she sighed looking at their little girl as she rested her head on his chest. *I love her. Though I think she looks much cuter now than she did while I was carrying her,* she admitted as she reached over to rest her hand on their baby's back. *Gabriel,* she exclaimed hearing the camera go off again. *I thought I told you to stop. You did that on purpose,* she realized shocked as she looked at him. She'd been too distracted by his question and their little girl to realize what he'd been up to.

That one was a good one, he told her indicating for her to look at the phone as he pulled up the photo he'd taken while she was looking at their baby.

I love you, she told him turning around and reaching up to kiss him on the lips in appreciation at which point she heard the camera again. *Gabriel,* she reprimanded him. *Am I going to have to take back your phone privileges?* she asked shaking her head at him.

No, I'm done, he pretended to surrender as he returned the phone to her having gotten the photos he wanted.

Ruby wiped at her eyes and the tears that had formed as she looked at the pictures he'd taken.

Hey, none of that now. I didn't take those to make you start crying, he told her gently as he ran his hand comfortingly over her back. *If you keep crying, I'm just going to delete those right now. Give me back the phone,* he teased lightly.

No, don't. I love them. They're perfect, she told him looking up at him. *You're perfect.*

I'm glad you like them, my love. Now, put the phone down. You need some sleep. We both do, before she wakes up wanting to feed again. I love you, he told her as he turned out the light and pulled the comforter up around her with his mind as he held her to him. *Both of you,* he reiterated as he kissed the top of her head.

I love you two so much, she told him as she reached over to rest her hand on their baby with his as she reluctantly closed her eyes to go to sleep. She always found it so hard to go to sleep, to stop watching her, afraid something would happen. But she knew she'd never let anything happen to her and she knew Gabriel would never let anything happen to either of them. She knew how much he loved the two of them and she couldn't believe she'd gotten so lucky.

The End

Printed in the United States
By Bookmasters